GALVESTON

spans three generations in the life of a rich, romantic city. Three women carry its passionate story forward . . . a story that unfolds in wave after wave of stunning revelations . . . of secrets and sins that link lives together in a fate as violent, tantalizing and consuming as the tides that threaten to engulf the magnificent Texas island.

GALVESTON

Novelist William Goyen was the first reader. What he wrote as he introduced this extraordinary novel to his editors has been echoed by every reader since:

> "When I saw the pages dwindling, I truly regretted knowing that the haunting story was coming to an end . . . I can't forget it."

GALVESTON

"CASTS A SPELL!"
—*Publishers Weekly*

"IMAGINATIVE GUSTO . . . FEVERISH . . . THE MOST SEDUCTIVE KIND OF FIRESIDE READ."
—*Harper's Bookletter*

GALVESTON

Suzanne Morris

*This low-priced Bantam Book
has been completely reset in a type face
designed for easy reading, and was printed
from new plates. It contains the complete
text of the original hard-cover edition.*
NOT ONE WORD HAS BEEN OMITTED.

GALVESTON

*A Bantam Book / published by arrangement with
Doubleday & Company, Inc.*

PRINTING HISTORY

Doubleday edition published March 1976
2nd printing —————————— *August 1976*
3rd printing —————————— *August 1976*
Doubleday Book Club edition published May 1977

Bantam edition / October 1977

ISBN 0-553-10606-6

Published simultaneously in the United States and Canada

Bantam Books are published by Bantam Books, Inc. Its trademark, consisting of the words "Bantam Books" and the portrayal of a bantam, is registered in the United States Patent Office and in other countries. Marca Registrada. Bantam Books, Inc., 666 Fifth Avenue, New York, New York 10019.

PRINTED IN THE UNITED STATES OF AMERICA

for J.C.
and my parents

and for WILLIAM GOYEN,
without whose help the publication of this book
would yet be but a dream

THE AUTHOR WISHES TO EXPRESS SPECIAL
THANKS TO:

MR. LARRY WYGANT, Archivist; Mr. Bob Dale-
hite, former Archivist; and Miss Ruth Kelly, former Assistant Archivist, Rosenberg Public Library,
Galveston, for their ever willing assistance in my
quest for authenticity in the background of this
book;

MRS. CAROL THORNTON of Houston, who served
as typist for much of the manuscript, and whose
long-standing friendship I count among my greatest blessings;

MRS. REGA KRAMER MCCARTY of Tacoma, Washington, my teacher and close friend, whose guidance
and encouragement have helped immeasurably in
all my writing endeavors;

MR. LARRY COOK of Houston, whose help in
photographing me at various Galveston sites was
invaluable in making the task an easy one;

MRS. KAREN GIESEN, for her special assistance;

and MR. FRANK PAGE of Houston, my father
and photographer, whose accompaniment on nu-
merous trips to the island over the years has helped
to enhance my intrigue with Galveston as it is today and as it might have been. . . .

CONTENTS

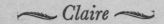

Claire

March 1, 1877—April 4, 1886

PART I

Chapter 1

Nightfall.

The breeze glides gently across the porch and winds around me, then passes on. The only sound I hear is the squeezing wicker of my rocking chair, and I am alone.

Now let me tell you how it was this morning, how inevitable the tragedy which occurred next door and how innocent I remain of causing it, regardless of how well it seems to suit my purposes.

To begin, I've never loved my husband, Charles Becker, not in the way a man expects love from his wife. Yet I've stood by him both in success and failure. Surely this is fair exchange for all the deep desire and affection I might have showered upon him had I adored him as he thought I did, from the start.

In fact I married Charles for every good reason except love. And to be fair, my decision was influenced by my mother, who thought him fine and brilliant, and by my cousin Betsey, who considered him a responsible man. Yet I pride myself on honesty, so it must be said that would his brother Damon have taken me away with him, I'd have gone and never looked back at Charles. Yet Damon Becker presumed to trifle with my affections, mistaking me for a woman of no account, so what better way to show him the error he made than by marrying his brother?

So it happened that we made the match everyone back home in Grady had come to expect and Charles, known for his tall, erect figure, his distinguished looks and Vandyke beard, was said by many to seem a little less solemn, his smile to be a good deal broader across his well-turned face, and his hazel eyes a bit brighter now that he'd finally won the woman he'd loved for years.

It was little more than a year later that he took me far away from Grady and brought me here to Galveston: the city of stairs.

Now, most people who know Galveston will remark on the coolness of its Gulf breeze, the length of its sandy beaches, the state of its port. I shall always think of the blood rising to my head as I climb the stairs, and the sinister sinking feeling which comes over me as I descend them.

I won't argue the steep stairs elevate us from danger of high water; I only wish to point out that high water is scarcely the only danger to be found on Galveston Island. There is danger in the stairs themselves, for instance.

There are ten leading from our outside walk to our front door and twelve at the yellow, white-shuttered Episcopal rectory next door, and I watched from our parlor window as Janet and Rubin Garret carried the last of their household goods up those stairs on the day they moved in, the first day of May in 1877. All I knew of the Garrets then was what I had heard others say—she was from a wealthy Virginia family; he was a man of the cloth, newly established at St. Christopher's Church several blocks away.

What struck me as I watched them move in was that he looked no more like a priest than she did a parson's wife. His frame was husky, shoulders and arms too massive to seem at home behind a pulpit, his complexion tanned, and his hair light as fresh honey: bleached by the sun, I suspected. She was tall—not more than three or four inches shorter than he—but reedlike and wispy, with tendrils of blond hair streaming down her long, narrow, fragile-looking face, and somehow I couldn't imagine her presiding over church receptions and planning fall bazaars.

When all the boxes had been lifted up the stairs, the two of them disappeared through the front door, opening off the side of the verandah. I wanted another look—it was curiosity, nothing more—so I waited at my window hoping they'd come out again.

One minute passed, maybe two, then suddenly she appeared at the window directly across from mine. She gave me a quick, surprised look, said something over her shoulder, and pulled down the shade.

I looked away, embarrassed at being caught prying, but thinking at the same time how strange she'd looked just then, encased in shadows, her eyes wide and sorrowful, the skin stretched taut over the bones of her face. Had I not known better, and were I of a superstitious mind, I might have believed Janet Garret a ghost.

Later that day, when Charles came home he remarked all the shutters were drawn over there, and so they remained for the next four days, as though the Garrets wished to barricade themselves against all intrusion, even the polite overtures of friendship by their neighbors.

Then one evening Rubin Garret came to call, and as we talked I sensed a quiet power in his voice, as though he possessed a great reservoir of emotions kept carefully checked. His eyes were full of fun, mischievous almost, yet had a quality of magnetism that kept my gaze fixed on them constantly.

Shortly he cleared his throat and shifted in the chair. "You must come over and meet my wife, Janet," he said.

"We'd like to, but we noticed the shutters have been drawn and thought she might be ill," Charles said.

Rubin hesitated a moment, then answered, "No, not ill, but she's been in low spirits since we've been here. I think it's hard on her, having to get to know new people, but she agreed that moving here was a good thing. Have you been here long?"

Charles explained we'd come two months earlier, and that he was gradually taking over the practice of an attorney named J. P. McBride, who wanted to retire within the next couple of years. "Galveston offers so much opportunity," he said with a wide sweep of his arm, then his voice dropped, "and of course our little son died just a few months ago . . . Claire and I felt we could forget more easily in a new place."

"I won't ever forget," I said.

"I hope he didn't suffer," said Rubin, turning to me.

"Not that we know of. He just died one day. Three doctors looked at him afterward . . . all three said suffocation; none could tell us why. He was all I—we—"

Rubin looked uncomfortable, and dug a finger inside his tight white clerical collar. "A true test of faith, losing a child," he said. "We don't have any children yet, but I hope someday we will. And perhaps the Lord will bless you with others."

He rose abruptly to leave, yet lingered at the door, clasping my hand in his. "And please, do call on my wife. She'd be delighted to have you," he said. My hand was still enveloped in his, like a pussycat in a warm blanket, as he continued. "She's a person of many interests, you know, paints and even writes a little poetry though she doesn't think it's any good and won't show it to anyone."

"Does she paint portraits?" Charles asked. "I've wanted one of Claire for the wall of my study."

"Oh, I'd think she would find Mrs. Becker an interesting subject. I've always found people with widow's peak so striking . . . almost mysterious, as though they know something no one else does." He looked embarrassed then, as if he felt he'd said too much, and released my hand.

"We might visit sometime at your church," I said.

"Oh, you're Episcopal?"

"No, but we've visited Trinity downtown and liked it . . . we were thinking of changing from Congregational."

He smiled. "Fine church, Trinity . . . bigger than ours, of course, but I like to think St. Christopher's will catch up one day. Well, maybe I'll see you soon."

After he had left, Charles said, "Why did you tell him that? The service at Trinity was foreign to both of us."

"Look at it this way. Rubin Garret's church is close by, so we might as well go there as any place."

He shrugged, then said, "You know, there's something about that man that reminds me of Damon."

My heart quickened as I looked away without replying. His comparison was so logical it plunged through me like a double-edged sword.

Chapter 2

I'd known Damon Becker long before I'd met Charles. Back in Grady I kept a fine palomino stallion from the time I was eighteen until I was twenty-one, when he contracted a disease and had to be destroyed. I loved Sandy, and kept his golden coat so shiny the sun all but glinted off him as we rode the paths of the countryside surrounding the town.

One torrid afternoon when I was about twenty, I was riding Sandy along the edge of an open field that ran parallel with a dense thicket. I gave Sandy his lead and let the wind blow my hair and cool my face. I was soon lost in pleasant thoughts of everything in general and nothing in particular.

I sensed my stallion's temperament was in harmony with mine as he galloped swiftly along, enjoying as I did the freedom, the openness ahead. I wasn't watching as I should have been, had taken the dangerous luxury of closing my eyes for moments at a time as we surged forward, yard after yard . . .

All at once Sandy gave a furious neigh and reared up until his body stood vertical to the ground beneath, throwing me off his back and into a bush. It happened so fast I wasn't at first aware of what had caused his fright. Then I saw—an immense black hound, teeth vicious as a wolverine's.

In an instant Sandy had bolted away across the field, and the dog turned his eye on me and crouched low to plunge. As I lay back, helplessly snarled in the bush, all I could see were his gaping mouth, his red tongue and white teeth: the teeth were branded on my mind as I thrust an arm to my face and closed my eyes, knowing death awaited me. . . .

A powerful gunshot split the air. I opened my eyes to see the animal pitch high above, like a fish thrusting up from the surface of the pond. His body bowed, he gave a pitiful whimpering sound and hit the ground with a dull thud not two feet from me.

My breath came in gulps as I looked across through the glare of the sun to the open field beyond. And there, astride a horse black as midnight, sat a man I had never seen before.

He was some hundred feet away and replaced his rifle before he gave a spur to his horse and came unhurriedly to where I still lay, too frightened to move. He did not get off his horse, but leaned down and offered me a hand. His hair was auburn, his face smooth and young; his eyes were smiling even as he said, almost mockingly, "You look fit enough."

I couldn't take my eyes off his face as I stood, unsteadily, below him. "You saved my life," I stammered. "I'm so grateful . . . I could hardly believe . . . you seemed to have appeared out of nowhere. It happened so fast."

"Your horse is over by the thicket. I'll go and fetch him."

I nodded.

He smiled. "You'll be all right, here?"

I nodded again.

He was back with Sandy in minutes, or seconds, what

was time to me? "Your horse is all right," he said. "No wounds on his ankles that I could see. You'd better get home now. Have you got your wind back?"

"I'll be all right," I said, lifting myself into my own saddle again. "I'll never be able to thank you enough—Mister . . . ?"

"Damon Becker, at your service any time. The dog was mad," he said, looking down at the stilled animal, "that or starved into a frenzy. Look at those ribs.

"Ah well, it's over now, and I must be going."

I sat on Sandy and watched him gallop off, disappointed he had not offered to accompany me back into town—surely any gentleman would have done that much. In a short time he had disappeared around the other side of the thicket. I touched Sandy gently and led him back toward town, but on the way I began to wonder what it was Damon Becker was doing: I pulled in the reins and led Sandy off to the left, so that we could circle around to the other side of the thicket. I felt half foolish, half brazen, but burned with an overpowering curiosity.

We had gone a half circle around the thicket's edge when I saw two horses—one was Damon's stallion—grazing nearby. I got down off Sandy and crept forward a little ways, knowing I was half mad to dare so and would probably be caught. Maybe he'd robbed a bank and was burying the money with his partner in the shadows of the trees, I thought . . . that or some other important secret business. . . .

I stopped about twenty feet from where the horses were grazing. There were noises coming from within the thicket. I listened hard. It was laughter: liquid, giggling throaty sounds, coming from a woman, in concert with low, cooing masculine noises. I could hear, above all, the crackling of fallen leaves.

I stalked back to Sandy and whipped him hard all the way home.

Damon had gone off to sea shortly after that day, though I didn't learn this until a year or so later, when I met Charles.

Charles was an up-and-coming attorney in the town, and my cousin Betsey was his client. One day I noticed a letter signed by him lying open on a table in her house, and the last name struck a chord in my memory.

"Becker," I remarked, spying the letter.

"Yes, seems to be a fine man," said Betsey, then looked at me thoughtfully. "I don't believe he's married. How would you like to meet him?"

"Of course, why not?" I told her, though I didn't mention my curiosity about the man lay only in his last name.

And so Cousin Betsey invited Charles and me to dine one night with her and her young daughter Ruth, and I asked him across the table, "Are you related to a man named Damon Becker?"

"Why yes, I am," he said, surprised. "He's my older brother. Do you know him?"

"I met him once, some time ago. In fact, he saved me from the attack of a mad dog. I don't think I'll ever forget him."

"Well, Damon hasn't been around for—let's see—better than a year and a half now. He went to sea. If you'd known him well, you wouldn't be surprised he chose that sort of life."

"He did seem adventurous, all right," I replied.

Charles asked to see me again after that evening, and soon had won over my ailing mother and Betsey. I didn't dislike Charles. He was kind and good, as attentive to me as a man could be, and handsome in his way. Yet his looks reminded me just enough of his brother to make me wish I could meet up with Damon again, and I'd often ask Charles if he'd had a letter from him saying when he planned to make a visit home.

"He doesn't come to Grady very often," Charles told me. "The town bores him. He was home once after his first voyage, and hardly stayed long enough to get the smell of seawater out of his clothes. Damon and I aren't close, as you can probably tell," he pointed out.

"I did suspect that," I said, thinking that Charles was a Damon with his features all smoothed out, the rough edges of his personality ground into mellow rims, and coated with a layer of diplomacy.

By the time Damon returned again, a full three years since the afternoon I'd met him, Charles had begged for my hand in marriage several times. Yet I'd put him off. I'd grown fond of him as one would of a good and steady friend, but the lack of fire in his eyes, the lack of forcefulness in his nature, left me limp and without desire to spend the rest of my life with him.

There was a party held for Damon when he came home and I begged Charles to take me, "so I can thank him properly for what he did for me so long ago."

"All right," he agreed, "though I'm not crazy about what Damon does at a party and you probably won't be either after you've been there for a while."

"Maybe not," I said, and arranged to have a new dress made.

What surprised me most, when the party night came and we assembled in a hall decorated with green bunting and "Welcome Home" banners, was that Damon was far bigger than I remembered, and far more handsome. He had grown a lush red beard during his time away and acquired a deep tan and blazing cheeks. He stood in one corner, telling sea stories, the crowd surrounding him engaged in awed silence followed by rollicking laughter. His voice carried across to where Charles and I stood, in another corner, Charles speaking legal chitchat with an attorney friend.

I tried to hear the stories coming from behind, while appearing attentive to the conversation taking place in front of me, and finally I urged Charles away and made him take me to meet Damon once again.

My heart thumped a rhythm to the screech of the fiddle sounding out a square dance tune as we walked nearer and nearer to where he stood. "This is Claire Haines," said Charles to his brother. "I understand you two have met before."

"Oh, have we?" said Damon, staring at me for a moment.

"You saved me from a mad dog once, three years back. I never got a chance to say a proper thank-you."

He studied me again, then his eyes lit up with recognition. "Of course, how could I forget?" he said, bowing slightly. "Do you still ride around on that magnificent horse?"

"No, my Sandy took ill and had to be put to death. I haven't had much interest in replacing him."

"Ah, that's too bad," he said, then looked at Charles. "So now I find this pretty little dark-haired woman on the arm of my own brother. . . ." His eyes drifted off.

"Will you be staying long?" I asked him.

"No, Charles here can tell you I hate dust storms and dry weather. I soon get a bad case of parched lips," he ended, looking back at me. I opened my fan in front of my breast and fluttered it slightly.

"Well, we'd better be going," said Charles, who appeared to see the evening at an end.

"Stay around, the party hasn't even begun," said Damon as he looped his arms around the waists of the two women nearest him, young sultry types, neither of whom I recognized as residents of Grady.

"Oh, I'm quite sure of that," said Charles, "but I have clients to see in the morning, and they wouldn't be too happy about paying a lawyer's fee for a fuzzy head. Good night."

Oh, how Charles Becker paled beside his brother.

I couldn't sleep that night, nor for many nights after, thinking of Damon, and—despite Betsey's opinion that I was crazed to dangle a man like Charles Becker from a string around the end of my finger, and my mother's oft-expressed wish that I'd settle down before her death, for she knew she would not get over the disease that confined her to bed—how he excited me in a way Charles never could.

Though I knew I ought to quit seeing Charles out of fairness to him and because his slight physical resemblance served only to rekindle my imagined place in Damon's arms, I couldn't let Charles go because if I did I'd have no way of learning about Damon's infrequent visits . . . might never see him again.

He did come home once more, at a time when my future in Grady loomed hopelessly lonesome, yet I was still unable to bring myself to take the obvious step and marry Charles. It had been about two years since my mother's death and a little longer since I'd seen Damon for the second time. In truth I was strongly considering going away alone for a while. I had a little money—enough to get me by so I could do some thinking—and maybe I could find another place to live, meet new people who didn't know my twenty-sixth birthday would soon be coming and wouldn't care if they did know. Oh, the small-town tongue-trilling of Grady was getting to me as it must have gotten to Damon himself.

Charles told me two weeks in advance of Damon's visit.

"It'll be nice to see him again," I said, trying to conceal my elation at the news, which to my confused mind was like a lantern flashing in the night. "And I suppose they'll be having a soiree in his honor?" I ventured.

"I suppose," said Charles, as though the matter bored him.

"Although his taste in entertainment may differ from yours, it's well to remember he doesn't come home often, and after all, he is your brother."

Charles smiled. "I guess you're right, although I have a suspicion it might just be you've a mind that favors parties."

I merely smiled back in reply.

I didn't bother with a new party dress for Damon's homecoming this time, but instead bought a horse—a brown gelding not nearly so fine as Sandy, though he'd serve my purpose well enough—and took up riding again.

On the night after Damon's arrival the inevitable party was held by his friends, and I sat outside Charles's office awaiting him to finish some business for a client. For an hour and a half I heard the sound of lively music through the open window. The party was going on not far away.

Once Charles opened his door and looked out. "You don't have to wait if you'd rather not, Claire. Go on and I'll join you there," he said.

I almost agreed, then thought of the danger of giving my feelings away too soon, and said, "Take your time, Charles. I'll be fine."

When at last we took the short walk to where the big hall stood, its windows lit up, doors opened wide, and its floor dusty from the strut of frolicking people, Charles said, "Slow down, Claire. What's the hurry?"

"I'm tired of waiting for you, that's what," I told him.

"Well, forgive me for keeping you. Since you didn't get fitted out in a new dress, I figured maybe you weren't any more anxious than I was to go tonight."

"There's no point in going at all if we're going to miss most of it, is there?" I said tartly. Though I wouldn't tell Charles, it was not strictly the waiting that had me on edge. I'd been wondering all that day whether Damon Becker could possibly live up to the man I remembered, or if I'd allowed myself to dream him into someone so awesomely desirable that my seeing him again, in the flesh, could only lead to disappointment. . . .

It wasn't to be. He was if anything more magnificent than before, his face roughened by the salty air, his red beard fuller, his eyes stunning and grown more alert by his experiences with the tricky nature of the oceans he sailed.

"You remember Claire Haines," said Charles, tapping his big shoulder.

He turned around to face us, and at once I knew he didn't remember me at all. "Of course," he said, his eyes searching. "Charles always has had uncanny good luck in finding the town's most beautiful women, eh, Charles?" He took my fingers in his warm, rough hand and lifted them to his lips. His beard tickled them and and sent a shiver from the base of my spine to my cheeks.

I knew I must make him remember. "I've taken up riding again," I said, "though my horse is not nearly as fine as the palomino I once owned."

Something registered in his eyes.

"I find the same paths around the thicket as good as ever, but nowadays I'm more wary of dangers that might lie ahead."

"Is that so?" he said. "Yes, riding is good sport around Grady, especially on long afternoons."

I nodded and looked deep into his eyes. More than words had passed between us.

The next afternoon I rode the horse I hadn't bothered to name and wouldn't keep for long down the paths near the thicket, and soon I spotted Damon across the field. He waved with one black-gloved hand and motioned for me to join him. I went slowly as he had come to me the first time we met. "It's blasted hot today, for this time of year," he said as I drew up. "Would you like to rest in the shade?"

He handed me down from my gelding, the breeze stirring his auburn hair, a mischievous smile across his face. The fleeting thought strayed across my mind that the hands locked around my ribs could just as well crush them with a simple change in mood. He pointed toward a broad-trunked oak and, sitting down beside me, told me he had already had as much as he could countenance of dry land—his ship had pulled in better than a month ago—and would soon be off to sea once again. This confession of his dictated my movements from the moment it rustled the quiet air around us.

I leaned across him to pick up an autumn leaf, one of thousands fallen from the tree. He sensed my design in doing this and lightly fingered my hair. Now, Damon was not a man inclined to go less than all the way in any pursuit, so he took my face between the black-gloved hands and studied it for a moment, then kissed me, lightly at first as the way he had touched my hair, then harder and harder still, and then his arms went around me and I felt along my back the motion of the black gloves being removed.

A thrill of fear rose up inside me but I was powerless to stop the hand that now made its way with ease into my blouse and around my breast, and the force of the body that laid me down upon a nest of newly fallen leaves and arched itself above me. . . .

When it was over I knew I had been won by Damon Becker, and, knowing too, of his fickle nature, asked quickly, "How soon did you mean to leave?"

He was not one for commitments of even the shortest span. "I'll meet you tomorrow again, here," he said, and mounted the horse and rode away. I brushed the autumn leaves from my skirt and buttoned up my blouse. I wanted to shout with joy and cry with relief and cover my face with shame, all at once. But I mounted my horse and rode from the thicket thinking of nothing further away than tomorrow. . . .

We had twelve tomorrows, each at the same place, and I had never felt so fulfilled, so happy or blessed, so sure the future would hold nothing but lovely joyful things and beautiful, faraway places and days and nights of bliss; oh yes, I had begun to hope I was in Damon's eyes different from the other women he'd known.

But then on the thirteenth day he did not come.

I waited an hour or two before riding back to town, thinking maybe something kept him from coming, some simple explanation for his leaving me to wait, and all I found, when I returned home, was Charles's buggy out front and him waiting on my porch to see if I'd like to go on a picnic.

"I had a special basket packed for us at the hotel cafe," he said. "Everything's here we need. All you have to do is board the wagon."

"Where is Damon?" I asked dazedly.

He looked at me in puzzlement. "Why, Damon left town early this morning; you know him, gone off to sea again, I think to Spain, though he promised to write, not that I count on letters from him. Why?"

"Oh, nothing. Picnic, you said? Sure. Why not?"

I waited four days, to see if a message would come to me from Damon, and when none did I made up my mind. I called at Charles's office and right there, amidst the clutter and stuffiness, said, "Let's not wait any longer to get married. I'm willing to go ahead right away, that is, if you still want me."

He came around the desk, his face alive with bewildered happiness, and took me in his arms. "I have to travel for the next couple of weeks on business," he said. "When I get back, we'll call the preacher and set the date."

And so, within six weeks of my first and last taste of the sweetness of satisfied desire, I watched Charles Becker gently slip a wedding band on my finger and spent the night locked in his arms, pretending. The sensation of pleasure that had been mine when I thought of marriage to Charles as a way to get back at Damon Becker was lost that night, and only a dull sense of hopelessness remained at the pit of my stomach and in all the open chambers of my heart.

Within another six weeks I found, for certain, I was expecting a child, yet could not be certain whose child it was to be until I went to see a new doctor in town. Charles insisted I see Dr. Hardy, who had treated both of us for almost everything we'd ever had, but I insisted on having my way. When the new doctor confirmed the pregnancy took place during the days I secretly hoped—the days with Damon Becker—I went to see Helga Reinschmidt. She'd been my mother's housekeeper and companion for the last ten years of her lifetime, and after my mother's death, had taken a job with another family in Grady. I told her she had to come to work for me and why.

Helga had loved my mother and she loved me, but was not one to show outward sympathy or affection under any circumstances. She listened to my story with a concentrated frown, then drew up her tall, gaunt figure and said, "So I'll come. There's hardly a choice. When the baby arrives we'll say it's early, that I know from experience, and in the meantime you should do a lot of walking to keep the baby small, do you hear? I don't care what anyone says, I know what I'm talking about.

"You're a silly girl," she added without so much as the hint of a smile to soften her hawkish face, "but you probably had the one taste of happiness you'll ever get and I'd do anything to save a scandal that might reflect back on your dear dead mother. Now get on. I'll make my settlement with these people and move within the week."

Charles was so happy at the prospect of a baby, he would have agreed to anything I asked (although he'd always disliked Helga Reinschmidt's stony personality), and surely I deserved at least to have my choice of midwives at my side. And when Damon came home, in his time, I thought, I would tell him the whole truth and he would take me away from Grady, from Charles, far away, and it would not matter what anyone thought about it.

We never had a letter from Damon beyond the first one he sent to Charles, saying he was bound for Spain, and within five months after the marriage between Charles and me we'd received word that Damon's ship had been caught by a storm and he was no more.

Now Charles cried and was in need of consoling, but even then I couldn't reach out to him, not when I hurt so much inside. The only thing that kept me going, got me over the loss of Damon, was the certainty I carried his child. I would, I knew, lavish all the love and affection on that child there was within me to give, and I told myself had Damon known the truth in time, he would have rushed back to me without a moment's hesitation. I had his child within me, how lucky, how lucky! I was to hold the only part of him left to the world and carry the knowledge to my grave.

My time came. Helga was there. Charles paced nervously and Betsey ran between the room where I lay and the room where Charles paced nervously, concerned into a frenzy Helga would not do things right, and convinced he should have insisted I stay in the care of the doctor, most preferably, the doctor he wanted me to have.

"A son," said Helga finally. And added, when Charles entered the room, "The lad's a mite early, say a month, month and a half—you can see how small he is. We'll have to take extra care of him to get him strong."

And Charles, teary-eyed, came to my bedside and held

my hand and thanked me and thanked God above, and said, "Can we give him my name, Claire?"

I was a little surprised Charles had not thought of naming the child Damon, in view of his brother's recent death, yet I had no need to argue, had I? I'd received everything in the world I wanted. A healthy child and part of Damon that couldn't be taken away no matter how fickle-minded the man I loved might have been. "If that's what you want," I said, and kissed his forehead.

For four months I knew a happiness that encompassed the world and knew no limits beyond it. My son took the milk from my breast like the sweet nectar of the gods, and grew and thrived in the surroundings of so much love, and I gave no thought to the warnings of Betsey I'd soon have him spoiled deplorably, or the glances by Helga that said I'd best pay a little mind to Charles, who seemed delighted by the son he thought his, yet almost awestruck at my possessiveness of him.

And then one day my baby died in his sleep, his crib not two feet from my side of our bed. There was no help for it. Three doctors said so. Some babies just didn't make it, no one knew why, and Helga, her face pinched with grief, said, "The lad was early, you know, and probably didn't get the start he needed. I've seen it happen before."

I was far too overcome by my own grief to worry about what Charles might be feeling and I remember only one statement he made to me, after the burial was done and we returned from the cemetery. "God help me, I didn't know life could hold such sadness," he said, almost in a whisper. "First Damon and now our son."

You haven't lost a son, I thought, then looked at him quickly to be sure I hadn't said it aloud.

Chapter 3

Charles did not know how close he'd come to losing me in those weeks following my son's death, how many times I'd opened my mouth to say, "Go to Galveston alone, I want no part of it *or* you," then shut it just in time, and smiled instead like a pliant woman willing to be led wherever her husband wanted to take her.

Had he wanted to, he might have seen that nothing tied

me to him except a sense of duty; instead he spent our first few weeks in Galveston trying to please me, believing he could help me overcome my grief as he was overcoming his. The house at 707 Avenue L, he thought, would be perfect for improving my state of mind, and he described it one day, drawing a map. "Here's the island—shaped kind of like a long thumb—the port up on the north side, the beach on the south, and Broadway crossing it from west to east at a slight downward angle. L runs parallel with Broadway, two blocks south. The house is about six blocks from where the avenue veers off to the beach. The Gulf breeze hits it crosswise—perfect for circulation.

"It's a white two-story, with three pointed gables above, french doors in the center and a big, railed verandah. The roof's deep red and the latticework and shutters and doors are dark green. It'll be even more beautiful after you've planted a garden. Oh yes, and there's a small barn out back where we could keep a horse and rig."

I'd nodded disinterestedly, so he'd continued, "And we have a view of the Gulf of Mexico from the top of the roof—you should see it!" Then he paused and added, "Now, if you're afraid it isn't safe, don't worry. The whole area was developed after the storm of '75, and the stilts underneath the houses are better than eight feet tall—higher than the water got at any point on the island."

I'd said all right and he'd bought it.

Getting me acquainted with our new neighbors was another of his gestures designed to bring me happiness, so he was anxious that I overlook the queer ways of Janet Garret once her husband explained them, and urged me, the morning after Rubin's first visit, to call on her.

"I notice the shutters are open," he said.

"All right, I'll give it a try," I told him.

Earlier that morning I'd watched as two men planted six oleander bushes, three on either side of the steps leading up to her porch. The top of each bush brushed the edge of the porch floor. When I went to pay my call about four o'clock, she was out on her front walk, sketching one of the lush pink blossoms that still clung among the leaves.

"Hello, Mrs. Becker, and how are you today?" she asked, without looking around. Thus was I to learn of her eerie sixth sense. It served her well, most of the time.

"Fine, thank you. Mind if I sit here on the stairs?"

"If you like," she said, her attention still fixed on the canvas before her.

I cleared my throat and waited as a subject awaits a word from her king.

Finally she said, "This is my first time to paint an oleander. Do you like flowers?"

"Oh yes, my garden in Grady was the envy of the town. You're lucky to have some healthy bushes . . . everything around here is so barren."

"Barren . . . yes, that would describe everything well, I think," she said, and smacked the brush to her canvas as one would stab a piece of meat with a fork, then smiled at me. "The bushes were a gift from the church," she said. "I understand oleanders grow quite tall."

"Oh, really? I don't know much about them . . . they're peculiar to this climate, I think. How do you like Galveston so far?"

"It's fine. I like the fences particularly."

"You do? I think they're a bit strange—a low brick fence might connect with a white picket, then on to an iron and maybe a cornstalk. But I suppose that's—"

"Strange, or interesting . . . depending upon your point of view."

"Don't you find it odd the houses are so close together? Back home in Grady there was at least a mile between one house and the next. You could go for days without seeing anyone unless you went into town."

"Still, privacy isn't a problem here, if you seek it. The shutters work very effectively." I understood the full meaning of her remark and was tempted to point out that normal people used the shutters only during bad storms and cold weather, but I could already see our relationship was getting off to a bad start and after all I did have to live next door to her.

"May I have a look at your sketch?" I asked.

"There isn't much to see at this point," she said, and she was right—only skeletal shapes.

"It's going to be very good, I'm sure," I said to her back.

"You must have a very keen eye to tell so soon."

"Oh well, I don't know—" I began, but stopped as she turned abruptly and stared hard at me.

"Rubin has suggested I might paint *you* someday. I think he was quite taken by your interesting face. If I could cap-

ture just the right shade of green for those eyes . . . greens
can be so difficult, you know . . . maybe . . ."

I stood uneasily as she inclined her head a bit and continued studying me. Then she said, "But Rubin ought to
know I haven't done any portraits lately."

"I see . . . well, there are lots of things to paint around
Galveston. You could go down to the wharves and see all
the ships docked there, and along the beach, too."

"I do hope to do some sketching of the Gulf," she said,
dabbing at the canvas again. "Pity the island isn't very
large, for we'll have to move again after I've painted everything."

I stared at her. Was she serious?

"Anyway, I'm glad you like the sketch. Perhaps I'll give
it to you for a present. Such a blossom as the oleander is
best preserved on canvas; that way it's as harmless as it is
beautiful."

"What do you mean?"

"The oleanders. Didn't you know they're deadly poisonous?"

"No, I did not. I'll be sure to stay clear of them."

"It doesn't hurt to touch them, only to eat them," she
said, plucking a blossom from the bush. "Look, they have a
sweet, heady fragrance and are softer than a baby's cheek.
Here, put it next to your face."

I drew away; her actions repelled me.

"It's all right if you don't want to," she said sweetly,
brushing the bloom across her own cheek and sitting down
again.

"I must go and fix dinner. Charles is coming home early
tonight so we can see a play at the Tremont." I backed
away toward the gate.

"How nice. Do come again, though. May I call you
Claire?"

"If you like," I said, and hurried home to make some
tea. I always drink tea in times of stress. It is a very lonely
feeling to imagine yourself bereft of friends when far from
home, and I wondered that day for the first of many times
if Janet was peculiar and unstable, or quick-witted and
cruel.

Had Rubin told her of our recent loss of a child? If so,
did she compare the poisonous blossom to a baby's cheek
out of meanness, or thoughtlessness? Could she have imagined what horrible memories would spring to my mind?

"You'd hardly know the baby is not sleeping peacefully," had said Mr. Weimer, the Grady undertaker, "his skin so soft. Some people like to touch one final time. . . ."

The teakettle singing, I lay my head down on the table and wept.

Charles found me there when he came home, and rocked me in his arms. Oh, what a useless source of comfort.

Chapter 4

We spoke of moving after that.

Charles said he wasn't going to have me upset by unkind remarks from Janet Garret or anybody else.

"Back to Grady?" I asked hopefully, thinking of Betsey and Ruth.

"No. Somewhere else on the island," he told me. Then, noting my disappointment, he said, "Living in Grady is professional suicide for me, Claire. You know that."

"Never mind then, I'd sooner stick it out here than move around the block. Besides, we can't be sure Janet meant me harm."

"Yes . . . and remember, from what her husband told us, she apparently has some problems. The poor girl probably deserves a little understanding."

It was deliciously cool that night as we sat on the moonlit verandah, and I was able to escape a reply by leaning my head back and taking in a breath of fresh air. Finally he said, "Of course we have lots of other neighbors we haven't even gotten to know yet."

I nodded, thinking this a pleasant prospect.

It was several weeks later we learned there was to be an oyster roast for the people on Avenue L. "Would you and your man be able to come?" said Agatha Mueller one day. She was small for a German woman, yet sturdy-made with big shoulders and hands. "It's goin' to be down to the beach next Saturday night. All you have to give is a quarter. That'll help buy the oysters and the rest will be taken care of by the ones of us plannin' it."

I told her I guessed we would come.

"And the preacher and his wife next door, 'ya know . . . I stopped at the gate but saw the shutters drawn. Has there been a death in the family or sump'm?"

"No, nothing like that. Sometimes Janet—the wife—prefers them shut. Here's fifty cents. I'm not certain the Garrets will be able to come, but just in case."

"Oh, I do hope so. When we used to live further down toward town, the block parties were always a big event."

"You've lived here in Galveston a long time?"

"Since before the war. Seen the reconstruction days from here, and survived one yellow fever epidemic and a bad hurricane or two."

She looked proud. These were the badges of her station. She was stepping carefully, sideways, down the stairs. "Till Saturday then," she said. "My boy Jeremy and course my man, Jeb, will go down early to dig the trench and start the fire. You and the preacher—all four of you, I mean—come along around seven or half-past."

When Agatha Mueller was gone, I shaded my eyes and gazed up at the yellow house, and thought for the first time what a burden it must be for a clergyman to be married to a woman like Janet.

On the afternoon of the roast, Janet surprised me by asking if she and Rubin could walk down to the beach with us that evening. "If you like," I snapped, with a twinge of satisfaction, and turned away.

Oh, could I have only seen, the coming pattern of our lives was winding around me like thread on a spool! On the way to that cookout which seemed so trivial and incidental, yet held so much portent for all of us, Janet and I walked behind Rubin and Charles, Janet stopping now and then to smell a honeysuckle vine growing along a fence, or pausing to consider the sound of a cricket.

"Lovely evening," she said, inhaling deeply, her face upturned.

I walked silently along, not about to appear the groveling fool I'd been the first day we met. I believe as we drew nearer to the beach, she sensed my feelings and decided to act a little more friendly. She asked about Charles's family and mine, and when I told her all our parents were dead and we had few relatives between us, she shook her head and told me she was lucky both her parents were alive, and that she had one sister living in Virginia. "My folks are getting on in years, but both of them are as spry as ever," she said. "Dad wrote in his last letter that his tobacco crop is good this year, so he's in good spirits. Curing begins pretty soon now. . . ."

"It must have been fun, growing up on a farm."

"Oh, it was," she said. Then her face clouded and she said more softly, "Most of the time. . . . Now, tell me, where did you grow up?"

"In Grady—that's in the northwest part of the state. After my father died, my mother remarried a man who owned a general store, so I spent a lot of time helping out and the rest of the time going to school."

"Oh? Does your stepfather still have the store?"

"No, he died long before my mother. And later she sold—almost gave—the store to my cousin Betsey. That was how I met Charles. He wrote up the purchase contract for Mother, and made everything legal. It was just paper work really, but Betsey wanted it that way."

"Charles seems such a fine man, you're lucky to have him. Of course, I'm fortunate to have Rubin, the most patient man ever . . ."

He'd have to be, to put up with you, I thought, and it was just then we reached the party.

Eight o'clock and growing dark. In my memory of the first oyster roast there is a long bar of fire on the beach, its smoke rising through the iron grate and around the craggy oyster shells. The young boy, Jeremy Mueller, stands by importantly, holding his shovel at one end of the trench. His face is aglow from the fire. He might be Satan, the shovel on which his arm rests a pitchfork, the fire below, his kingdom. Jeb Mueller is at the other end supervising, and calls to his son that he has a batch beginning to pop. The tall, skinny boy runs to the other end and scoops up a bunch of hot shells, heaves them onto a big wooden table behind.

Agatha Mueller is not to be disappointed, for there is a crowd of people milling around. Andrew Jeffcoat, restaurateur, has furnished ears of yellow corn and butter. Helen North has brought tomatoes and cucumbers from her garden. Bonnie Fitzgerald has made a dozen loaves of bread. Someone else has furnished cold watermelon. There is a keg of beer, and everyone is happy.

Everyone is curious about everyone else. Holding forth with a dripping ear of corn, a young-looking man, red-haired and red-bearded, with small hands and feet, introduces himself as Dory Fitzgerald. He eyes the four of us. "I know you. You live near the center of the block. And you're a preacher," he says to Rubin. "Episcopal, is it? I'd have known if you were Catholic. I know all the Catholic priests around. What's your trade?" he asks Charles.

"I'm a lawyer."

"Ya don't say? I think you're the only lawyer on the street. Got a banker, though, have you met Arthur and Helen North? A charmin' couple indeed! And an undertaker. Have you met Tom Driscoll?"

"No," Charles tells him. "We just got here, and haven't had a chance to get acquainted. By the way, what do you do, Mr. Fitzgerald?"

"Oh, I drive a hack, and call me Dory. Everyone does. Don't forget to try the bread. My Bonnie made it. One taste and you'll think ye've died and gone to heaven."

We fill our plates and Charles brings a mound of oysters in their shells on a piece of newspaper. It is difficult negotiating the oyster from its home, and I eat only three in the course of the evening. Rubin and Charles drink generously of the beer. Rubin, who wears no clerical collar tonight, holds his head back and quaffs his from the mug as though he drinks beer often, and I envision how he must look in his priestly robe on Sundays, delicately serving wine. The two impressions are so incongruous that I smile. He looks across at me, sees the smile, lowers his eyes.

After the beer is gone and the food eaten, we all sit on logs around the remains of the roasting fire. It is cool, and Rubin wraps a shawl around Janet's shoulders. Charles leans forward and lights his pipe.

A man sitting near us on the log asks Charles for a light. He is a man whose balding head is just a size too large for his body. "Alex Monroe," he says. "Most people just call me Doc."

"Oh, are you a real doctor?" I ask.

"Yes."

"What a comfort, having a doctor nearby," says Janet. "Where's your office?"

"At my house. This is my wife, Sheilah." A pale face, plain but warm, smiles at us. The wife's face is older than her husband's.

There is talk around the fire of who lives in which house. Several people remark on the handsomeness of ours, and I stifle an urge to tell them the house in Grady was much larger. I ask instead for someone in the group to tell me about yellow fever. It is a subject much on my mind because I have heard it spoken of in tones of icy fear, and, there being no such disease in Grady, I am anxious to learn all I can about avoiding contact with it here.

"My brother died from it back in the epidemic of '67," says Claude Stillman, who works for the Galveston Wharf Company. "I'll never forget how that poor boy suffered . . . he was delirious at the end, and had the black vomit. Lucky none of the rest of the family caught it from him."

My eyes widen and a finger of fear trails up my spine like a blaze through a forest. I am like a child who's begun to hear a ghost story: so afraid I want to close my ears, yet so fascinated I cannot stop listening. . . .

"Hogwash!" says Doc Monroe. "Yellow jack isn't contagious, and anyway, we rarely have cases of it anymore."

"That's right," Jeremy Mueller speaks up, the firelight playing on his young face. "I've studied all about it. That's why our cisterns are filtered nowadays, to keep the yellow fever mosquito from getting into our drinking water and breeding."

Agatha Mueller looks over and pats Jeremy's forearm. "My son's going to be a doctor," she says proudly.

"Is that so?" says Doc Monroe. "Come around sometime, Jeremy. I've got some books you might find helpful, and maybe I can show you some things."

"Thank you, sir."

After that exchange, everyone relaxes and is soothed again into fire gazing and idle chitchat about the general state of affairs in Galveston. It seems the evening will soon have a pleasant finale, until Tom Driscoll shifts a bit and says, "About the only thing we have to worry about now is the Octopus of the Gulf."

The remark has a queer silencing effect on the crowd. The people look uncomfortable, and some whisper to one another. "What is it?" I whisper to Charles. "You mean there's a giant octopus out there?"

"No, no. The term refers to the Galveston Wharf Company. I'll tell you about it some other time. Stillman works for the Wharf Company, and I think Driscoll is just now finding that out."

I look across at Mr. Stillman, who is getting up and preparing to, what? Leave? Assault the cheeky undertaker? But Driscoll speaks quickly. "Nothing personal meant by that. Lots of fine people at the Wharf Company."

"Sure as the world there're at least a few good folks in

the undertakin' profession, too," says Stillman. "However, it is getting a shade late. Come on, Blanche, where'd Carl go off to?"

Soon after, everyone else gets up from his spot on the logs, and the oyster roast is over. Once I know there is to be no skirmish between Driscoll and Stillman, I lose interest in the Wharf Company, and forget to ask Charles what is meant by "Octopus of the Gulf." It seems a question of little importance at the time.

The people of Avenue L walked back home that night in odd groups and pairs, our way lit by lanterns and what faint light was provided by the slice of moon and scattering of stars above. Janet hurried her normal pace to keep up with Doc Monroe and Jeremy Mueller, and Charles walked with the Driscolls, perhaps in an attempt to mediate the differences between Tom and Claude Stillman. Rubin appeared at my elbow just at the edge of the beach, and I couldn't explain the way my heart jumped as I realized he intended to walk home alongside me.

Soon he said wistfully, "Oh, how nice it would be to have a cookout for the church . . . it would be such a help in drawing the parish together." I told him he ought to do it, but he shook his head and said, "No, I don't think Janet . . .", then changed the subject by telling me that before becoming a servant of the Lord he'd been a hard-drinking wrangler involved in a number of brawls and had even spent a night or two sobering up in jail.

"Did you know Janet then?" I asked him.

"Heavens no," he said. "I met her later."

I was anxious, of course, to learn how this new and surprising information about the shady past of Rubin Garret had reconciled itself with Father Garret, man of the cloth, shepherd of foundering souls. I also wondered whether the warm feeling reminiscent of being courted that I'd felt as we spanned the distance between the waves licking peacefully at the shores of the Gulf and the front gate of our yard was shared by him, as I'd suspected when he said, "I can't remember when I've had a more pleasant walk."

It was these curiosities that led me to awaken Charles early the next morning and tell him we'd put off visiting St. Christopher's long enough. Although I was not yet willing to allow anyone to take the place of Damon Becker, it was soon after we'd seated ourselves under the dark, narrowly arched ceiling of St. Christopher's and watched Rubin Garret rest his big arms on either side of the carved wooden pulpit that I thought of how Damon must have looked as he stood on his ship's bow, watching the landscape as he neared the harbor. . . .

Then the truth struck me that part of the former man Rubin Garret remained in the present one, and I realized as rays of color from the stained-glass windows played on his face and shimmered on the folds of his white vestment that this man might somehow bring my second chance for what I'd been cheated of when the sea took Damon from me.

Yet I was not too blind to see that what Damon took lightly Rubin Garret would hold dear, and that I might have to content myself with small flatteries and special looks from him now and then, and stirrings inside should he touch my hand or offer his arm when I descended a flight of stairs.

As though to confirm the truth of my instinctive feelings, out in the morning sunshine after the service, he welcomed Charles and me with an arm on Charles's shoulder and an extra tight squeeze of my extended hand, looking directly at me as he said, "So glad to see you here."

Then he paused before adding, "Poor Janet was out of sorts this morning and couldn't come. I'm anxious to get home and see about her."

Chapter 5

In late September of that year a storm approached stealthily by night and crept upon us as we slept. I was dreaming that my child, locked in a room with Charles, was crying out for me, and whenever I'd try to go in Charles would laugh and slam the door in my face. This nightmare repeated itself until finally I awoke screaming, my clenched fists beating the air, then opened my eyes and realized a shutter come loose, banging against the house, had worked itself into my dream.

The darkness was punctuated by sudden brightenings and the cooling breeze was damp and more persistent.

Charles was not in the bed. I lay back and thought of my Charlie but could not envision his face.

Soon the banging stopped and Charles returned. "Hinge was rusted through, but I tied it back," he said of the shutter. "Sorry it woke you."

"We're in for a bad one, aren't we?"

"I doubt it. The wind's up, and we'll probably have a lot of rain, but the bad storms don't come too often."

"How often is that?"

"Oh, every fifteen, twenty years, maybe. I've pulled the windows down except in here. If it doesn't improve by morning I'll close all the shutters before I go to work."

"You'd leave me here alone?"

"For heaven's sake, Claire, I can always come home if the weather gets too bad. Get some sleep, now. Tomorrow will tell."

I settled down then and tried again to think of Charlie's face, but it wouldn't come and after a while Charles moved closer to me and began to kiss me gently on the neck. I pretended to be asleep and presently he turned away.

In the morning the storm went on teasing us, and sent only a slight, steady rainfall, which is always good for filling a low cistern and soaking a thirsty ground.

"It's only a precaution," Charles said, "but before I leave I'll close the shutters, though probably by tonight we'll be laughing at the whole thing. You never know this time of year, though."

"Just leave one kitchen window unshuttered. That won't hurt, will it, at the back of the house? Then I can see out. I hate the thought of not being able to see out—like being locked alive in a casket."

"All right."

"You'll come home, if it turns mean."

"Yes. I'll be down at the courthouse this morning, and I should be finished there by ten or so. Then I'll go to the office. You stay busy and try not to worry."

He left at eight-thirty, and I sat down with another cup of coffee and tried to concentrate on the newspaper as the rainfall grew steadily more intense. I read three times the story of some foreign monarchy sending its king and queen for a visit to Washington, but it was no use trying to absorb any news that day for I could hear the low rumble of thunder and the singing wind as it grew steadily louder.

I polished all the silverware, and the tea service that had

belonged to my mother, and went again to look out the kitchen window. It was then about half-past ten and growing darker. The rain hammered against the house and ground like the feet of angry Indians during a war dance.

Charles might think it bad enough now to come home, I thought, but more likely he'd make a stop at the office to check on the mail, so I went to the parlor and picked up my sewing basket, realizing just then this should have been washing day and growing irritated the weather could so foul up my routine.

I learned then there is not another feeling quite like that of being closed up in a house during a Galveston storm. All you can do is pray the house won't collapse with you in it, or fill with rising water that will send you backing up the stairs to the second floor, holding up your skirt as it laps at your feet. You may, if you are so minded, go outside and test the water with your finger. If it tastes clean, it is merely the rain; if it tastes salty then you are in far more trouble, for the Gulf has begun to spread itself over the island and it's only a matter of very little time before all is lost. A neighbor—Andrew Jeffcoat, I think—told me that once at a rain-spoiled cookout.

It struck me that day as I sat with my needlework that I would far rather be in Grady during a cyclone than to be in Galveston during a storm. At least in Grady everyone had a storm cellar and when freakish weather threatened, one could go down into safety. Anyone who hadn't the sense to go downstairs deserved whatever harm came to him.

Suddenly I laughed aloud at the thought of a storm cellar in Galveston, and my laugh had that high-pitched quality that isn't like my regular laugh at all. If Helga were here she would have admonished me not to get hysterical, but of course Helga was not here, thanks to Charles's refusal to bring her with us, and I had not the benefit of her level-headedness to calm me.

At eleven I put on the teakettle and stood by until it made the friendly, whistling sound, then poured a cup and sat down at the table to drink. But it was only half gone before a clap of thunder sent the teacup clattering in its saucer and I took it hurriedly to the sink and poured it out. I was trying to keep my head, and I told myself it didn't matter for the cup was half empty anyway.

I looked out the window again and tried to gauge the

darkness. Was it darker than last time I looked, or only my imagination? And where was Charles? Surely he'd had time to get back here by now. Having robbed me of Helga's quiet strength, he might have been generous enough to provide me with his own at this point, and I strained my eyes to see if the rig would appear through the veil of rain.

When it finally did, around noon, pulled by Gypsy as though the trip from the drive into the barn were a steep uphill journey, I heaved my first sigh of relief, for I was glad all at once to see Charles and ashamed that my fears of the morning hadn't included the fear something might have happened to him. I hugged him, wet mackintosh and all, when he got into the kitchen, and scolded him for not staying in the safety of the office instead of making the trip all the way home.

"I never got to the office, because I was late leaving the courthouse," he said. "I was worried about you here alone, so I came straight home. You can't see your hand in front of you, and Gypsy was scared senseless every time a clap of thunder came. Lord, I'm exhausted!" He shed the wet mackintosh, muddying the floor with his boots.

"Go upstairs and change into something comfortable. I'll fix you a hot rum toddy."

"Wonder if Rubin's home today. He might be stuck down at the church."

"He's in Houston for that conference, don't you remember? Took the early train, if he went."

"That's right! I'd forgotten that. I'd better go over and get Janet. She'll be scared out of her wits."

"She isn't the only one," I said, tired of hearing about the delicate state of Janet's mind.

He was gone quite a time, and I took up watch at the kitchen window so I could have the door open when they reached the porch. I'd never before seen such a rain. The wind drove it sideways across the yard, and by now the clothesline was down and the flowers planted along the back fence, I knew, were leveled. I wondered whether everything we were ever to build in life would be destroyed before we'd had a chance to get used to it, and thought about moving the downstairs furniture to the second floor.

She was hanging onto him like a child to its father when they got on the porch. He'd wrapped her in a quilt so that only her face and feet were visible: a mummy with wrappings not yet complete. "We started across under Rubin's big umbrella," Charles said as he carefully peeled the quilt away and sat her down at the kitchen table like a doll, "but the thing turned inside out halfway here. Claire, get her some tea, will you?"

I had already thought of that, and had the kettle boiling. Janet sat silently while I poured all three of us a cup. Her hair had come loose from its coil and stuck out in all directions; her whole body was shivering as I handed her the tea. Only then did I look into her face, and her expression was very queer: her eyes were like those of an animal who has been beaten before and sees the whip.

"Look, dear, you've got to get hold of yourself. This will all be over before long," I told her, and was steadied, to a degree, by my own utterance of the words. She looked up at me trustingly and nodded. "Would you rather go upstairs and lie down, instead of sitting here?"

"Oh no, please don't make me go to sleep. I want to stay awake—I'm afraid—I want to stay awake." There were beads of perspiration on her forehead and along the ridge above her lips.

"All right," Charles said. "We'll drink our tea, and try to think of pleasanter things."

There came, then, a new offering from the storm: a crackling sound that commanded our attention to the window. Charles took a closer view, and reported it was hailing. "I guess before the day's over we'll have some snow and ice. We've had just about everything else." He sat down again and lit his pipe.

Janet was now calmed somewhat. "Listen to that sound," she said, "it's like pearls falling from the broken thread of a lady's necklace and bouncing along a wooden floor."

"Those are very nice words," Charles said. "Rubin told us once you write poetry."

"He shouldn't have said that," she replied testily. "It was just a childhood dream, becoming a poetess . . . most of what I write now goes into the wastebasket."

Janet took a sip of tea and looked at us, her face softening. "Please forgive my rudeness today . . . I suppose I owe you an explanation as to why I'm so undone by a storm."

"Not at all," Charles said, but she continued anyway.

"I want to tell you a story I've never told anyone except Rubin," she began haltingly, and her eyes took on a dimension of emptiness, as though to blot out the story from her mind, even as she unfolded it. Her voice became a mere whisper as she talked. "I was thirteen years old, back on my father's farm. . . .

"One day when the weather was much like it is here now—only not a tenth as bad—I was at home alone. It was harvest time and we had fifteen extra men working for us—my father never owned a slave, even before the war, for he didn't believe in it. One of the men, who had been there only three or four days, kept looking at me. I was just at the in-between stage—beginning to grow up, hoping to be as pretty as my sister Cleo—and very conscious of my looks. I was flattered that this man would notice me, because he was handsome.

"Oh, and I was so trusting of people—men and women—in those days, as any child with a good family and a happy home would be. So that was why I thought nothing of letting him come in that day, when my parents were gone. I'd left only the screen door closed. It had been so hot, and was finally cooling off as it rained. I'd been reading *David Copperfield* for the second time.

"At the door, he asked if my father was home. Foolishly, I told him I was alone, and asked whether I could do anything for him.

"He walked in and let the screen door close softly behind. 'Well now, maybe,' he said. He had this kind of mean leer across his face. Sort of smiling and mean at the same time—I shall never forget it as long as I live. . . .'"

Charles stopped her then, and told her she needn't go on, but she did not seem to hear him, or even to be aware either of us was in the room.

"He was very tall; his presence filled the room. He just ambled across to the chair where I'd been sitting and picked up my book. 'Dickens,' he said. 'Quite a big book for a young girl like you.'

" 'I'm thirteen—almost fourteen,' I told him, just as he wanted me to, I'm sure.

" 'Maybe it's time you had some learnin' that don't come from no books,' he said, then looked back from the book to me and grinned. Suddenly I was deathly afraid, but unable to move from my tracks or speak. It was thundering, hard . . . as though it would wrench the house apart.

"He walked over and took me into his arms. I struggled—oh, God, how I struggled! I kicked and writhed and screamed. Of course, it did no good." She took a deep breath, and clasped one arm around her ribs. "After he finished . . . he left me lying on the floor and bolted from the house. We never saw him again."

Charles's face was pale. "How horrible . . . how horrible," he said.

"Awful," I agreed, and looked down dazedly at my tea.

"But if you'd told your parents, couldn't they have tried to track the scoundrel down?" Charles asked.

"No. I was too embarrassed to tell them, and afraid the scolding I'd get for having let him into the house would just worsen a situation that was already bad enough . . . I tried once or twice to tell Cleo, but couldn't bring myself. For nights after that I had terrible dreams, and I'd wake up screaming. In the dream I would be running from a grinning face, and always just a few yards ahead and out of reach would be my father. I would open my mouth to scream for help, yet not a sound would come forth. That's the point where I would awaken screaming.

"My parents worried over me for a long time, but I never told them the truth about the dream, only that I was running to Daddy for help but couldn't reach him. For a long time afterward, too, I looked for the man everywhere I went, afraid of finding him watching me. Of course, that finally passed and I haven't had the dream about him for years.

"Then one day a couple of months before we came here to Galveston, I was in the dry goods store, digging through fabric remnants. I felt someone watching me, and looked up.

"He looked so much like the man—probably wasn't him at all—but I got out of that store and ran all the way home, leaving our horse and buggy tied up in front. I was in such a state when Rubin got home that . . . anyway, we decided to accept his offer from St. Christopher's."

The kitchen lay in stillness; outside the rain had stopped and the wind died down. While Janet unraveled her story the storm had gone from the island like an unwelcome guest, and the sunlight now poured through the window.

She shouted triumphantly, "It's over!" and ran outside, Charles following. When I saw her next she had stepped off the porch onto the soaked grass, and was twirling around and around, shouting in merriment with her head upturned to the sun.

It was almost as though, that day, Janet Garret had single-handedly banished the storm that threatened all of us, and exorcised at the same time the ghost who had stalked her all the way from Virginia. She seemed to believe her luck had changed for the better, and for a while, anyone might have agreed.

Chapter 6

Rubin visited us a day or two later, alone, and it occurred to me he must often serve as Janet's ambassador, explaining her queer ways or putting into words what she herself would not bother to say. "All the way to Houston I worried that perhaps I shouldn't be going, that she might need me, that the weather might get worse," he explained, his eyes troubled. "And to find that you came to her aid! You don't know how it relieves my mind, how much better I'll feel, knowing I have you as neighbors."

"We were glad to have her with us," said Charles.

"She told me her visit was pleasant in every way," he replied.

Charles and I exchanged a glance. Apparently she hadn't mentioned to him she'd confided her secret to us.

"Well, I must be off now," he said. "I've got to work up a report for the vestry about the Houston conference. Hope I can get enough information together to make it satisfactory. Thank you both again."

After he left Charles said, "Poor Janet. Rubin's visit makes me think of how unfortunate she is. Imagine having something so awful happen to her as a youngster, it will affect her the rest of her life."

"Yes, poor dear," I said, but truly felt she received more sympathy than she deserved. Like me, Janet had been dealt a swift blow by fate once; yet at least she'd been given a second chance in the form of the handsome and charming Rubin Garret, whereas ill fate wouldn't let go of me, not since the day I first knew the strength of Damon Becker's arms around me. As far as I was concerned, Janet Garret ought to have been smart enough to realize how lucky she was, and try to be a better wife to her husband.

Several weeks later, while Janet sat behind shuttered windows next door, Rubin paid us a visit and invited us to have Thanksgiving dinner in their home.

"Are you sure we wouldn't be imposing?" Charles asked, as we were both struck by the oddity of the one-sided invitation.

"Oh no," said Rubin. "Janet wouldn't have it without you. We're having several couples from the church. Since she's not feeling well this afternoon, she asked me to be sure and stop by."

"I guess we could—Claire?"

"Of course. May we help?"

"No, no," said Rubin quickly. "Janet is going to handle everything." He looked proud as he said it, as though it were something of a triumph for her and thus caused him joy. Yet, when the day arrived, her behavior seemed to indicate he may have pushed her into holding the affair against her wishes.

Janet was clearly unequal to the task of cooking for ten people. Clarence Chichester, the church organist, and his wife, Roberta, were there, and the John Nimmonses, he sat on the vestry, and Marquita and Stephen Southby, who sang duets the first Sunday of each month.

After dinner I followed Janet into the kitchen just as Charles was telling of the letter we'd received from Cousin Betsey after the storm, in which she asked if reports were true that Galveston had been all but leveled during the catastrophe, stories having a way of becoming exaggerated by the time they reach the Grady *Star*. Everyone at the table was chuckling at the story for it was so far from reality— the only damage that I heard of occurred on our own block, where a few pieces of loose roofing slate flew in the wind and crashed through a couple of unshuttered windows in unfinished houses—and Janet and I were hardly missed as we withdrew to the kitchen for cutting the mince and pumpkin pies.

Poor Janet was forever disorganized; the kitchen was a total mess of piled-up dirty dishes and pots and pans from the cooking, and cabinet doors open here and there as though she must have been in an awful hurry to finish things before her guests arrived.

While I took a knife to the mince, she looked in drawer after drawer, cupboard after cupboard, for the server, and seemed to be quite unnerved about not being able to find it, and finally she stopped, leaned against the counter, and drew a hand to her forehead.

"Sit down, for goodness sake," I told her. "I'll find the server."

"It's the heat, that's all, so stuffy in here," she said, lowering herself into a chair. "Would you pour me a glass of water, please?"

I poured the water and took it to her. She sat with her face down on the table. I was impatient to keep things going, although it wasn't my party. Her lack of ability to get herself together, particularly at a time like this, grated on my nerves. Perhaps if everyone wouldn't indulge her by feeling sorry for her all the time, she'd straighten up a bit, I thought; Lord, you'd think she was pregnant or something. And then it struck me she might well be.

"Have you come 'round this month?" I asked.

She raised her head and looked up at me, obviously surprised. "I don't keep track; I'm sure I wouldn't know." She took a sip of water and put the glass down on the table. "I know what you're thinking, and I am sure you'll agree that it's best not to speculate too much on a thing like that.

"In other words, I'd much rather we didn't discuss it, if you don't mind."

"Of course," I said, "I didn't mean to pry."

"You needn't worry that I'll have a child before you do."

I sat down across from her. In truth this thought had not crossed my mind. Yet, now that she spoke of it, I knew she was right, and the bitter irony of it was that should she be pregnant, she would be carrying Rubin Garret's child, and while up to this time I had managed to keep my wistful speculations about him in check, this sudden new prospect had a shattering effect on my well-founded resolve.

I felt a flush rise to my cheeks and sat blinking at her for a few moments, unable to speak. Then it dawned on me I had to say something, or she'd think me daft, so I blurted out, "That's a cruel remark, Janet. You seem to forget, I lost a child once, and that child cannot ever be replaced, not if I had ten others." She of course had no idea of the full meaning of that statement, but it sufficed just the same.

She put a hand across. "Oh," she said. "I don't know what made me say such a thing . . . just a feeling I had. You know how it is when you don't feel well, you speak without thinking. Forgive me?"

I nodded.

"Come on, let's finish the pies so we can get out of this room. It makes me nervous."

"It would seem so."

"You can see how inept I am at these things"—she nodded her head in the direction of the dining room—"but Rubin insisted we must—"

"Everyone has bad days," I said, remembering how he'd proffered the invitation as though she'd been in favor of it, and feeling sorry for him as I had many times before, that he must always cover for her inability to handle even the most routine responsibilities.

"This isn't a bad day. It's just a day." Her cheeks were flush. She kept sipping the water and sitting there. I picked up the knife and began to cut again.

"You'd be so much better at a thing like this."

"Not necessarily. Everything is fine out there. You're just tired. You can hear the people laughing . . . everyone's having fun."

The door swung open and Rubin looked in. "How are you ladies doing? Janet, is Claire helping you cut the pie there? Coffee ready?"

"Not quite, dear. We'll be out shortly."

He nodded and withdrew, looking a little ill at ease.

"Poor Rubin," Janet said, and rose to her feet.

Though the conversation that day, especially the part in which Rubin took part, was brief, it jolted me into a new awareness. We all knew the truth was staring at us. Janet was wrong for Rubin and no one was more certain of it than he was, except perhaps Janet herself. I could see it in his eyes for that brief moment. Fate had cheated us all. Were we pieces on a chessboard, a simple maneuver would have changed things around and made the situation right.

I spent the rest of the visit with the Garrets knowing that something had clicked into place between Rubin and me, yet wondering whether anything could ever come of it, or were we both to remain trapped forever?

I was thinking, at the same time, would to God Rubin Garret were anything but an Episcopal priest.

Chapter 7

There is a social sector in Galveston, an upper echelon, if you will, that I scarcely knew existed for the first year or so I lived there, except that the island was dotted here and there—especially along Broadway—with handsome homes far bigger and more expensive than ours, and in these houses lived people with names sometimes appearing in the Galveston *News* and across the more prominent business buildings in town, down around the Strand.

Broadway, then, is the name of the street that will draw one's attention when it appears on the reverse of an envelope which comes in the mail. One thus decorated—and the word "decorated" is appropriate when the flourish of the handwriting is considered—arrived the week before Christmas of our first year in Galveston.

The F. Peterson Marlowes of 3600 Broadway requested our attendance at a New Year's Day reception at two o'clock in the afternoon. While recognizing the reason behind such an event, New Year's Day being the traditional visiting day when all the city people call on one another and make merry according to their individual tastes and customs, I failed to recall ever having heard the name F. Peterson Marlowe. It did, however, have a certain ring of importance when I spoke it aloud, and the invitation was engraved on a heavy card. I propped it on the mantel among the holly so that Charles would see it upon his return from the office that evening.

He arrived early, complaining of swollen feet. Charles is often so plagued, especially after a day in court. He looked over the invitation while sitting in a kitchen chair, his feet immersed in hot salt water. Steam off the water rose up and curled around the card as he held it in his hand.

"Hmm . . . Pete Marlowe."

"Who is he?"

"An attorney. His office is located not far from ours. He's with a firm called Marlowe, Turner, and Parks. It's one of the best in the area."

"Can we go to his party?"

"Oh, I don't know . . . I guess we could if you want to.

But there'll be a lot of people there. Besides, we've got to be at Janet and Rubin's that evening."

"There's nothing to keep us from attending an afternoon reception, is there?"

"No, guess not. I wonder if McBride got an invitation."

"Let's hope so. If he doesn't go, I may never meet him."

"Mac isn't much of a socializer. Sometimes when a man has no family he becomes a little withdrawn. I doubt he'd come, but I hope Pete invited him anyway. I'd feel a little funny if not."

"Why?"

"Oh, nothing. Never mind."

When the weather turns fine for New Year's Day, it gives one the feeling that perhaps the year to come will be fine, too. I cannot remember a more beautiful day in Galveston than that one in 1878 when we first visited the Marlowe home. Charles put the buggy top down so we could better enjoy the breeze, crisp as an autumn leaf, during the drive down Broadway, and all along the way we passed others bound to call at one place or another. The holiday feeling in the air was far better than on Christmas Day the week prior, a day of freezing rain and bitter cold that penetrated to the bone.

Broadway is a wide boulevard which severs the island down the center and severs, too, to some degree, the rich from the not rich. Here the fences are longer, the houses bigger, the roofs higher, the porches closer to the ground. It was this enigma about the porches that troubled me as we arrived at the Marlowe house, a dark red brick Mediterranean-style building which rambles along a lot six times the size of our own.

"Is it safe for the houses to be so low to the ground?"

"Up here it's all right. Broadway is the high spot on the island, besides being a good ways from the shore. Probably it would be your best bet during a storm. By the way, did I tell you how lovely you look today?"

"Thank you, Charles. I feel better than I have in a long time. I'm sure we were right in coming today . . . I just feel it."

"Did I mention Mac is coming? Don't know what possessed him, although I did tell him you were anxious to meet him."

"I've asked you to invite him to our house often enough.

He ought to know without being told . . . look, that man up ahead wearing the light gray derby. Haven't we seen him at St. Christopher's?"

"I don't recognize him."

"Would you look at the people! How many do you suppose are here?"

"No telling. Pete's party is always a big one. There may be as many as seventy-five or so, I don't know."

We were ushered by a servant through a round foyer with murals on the walls and a circular stairway up to the second floor, and then to the right into a large rectangular room with two crystal chandeliers, a parquet floor, and windows all the way around. A small ensemble of stringed instruments made music near the door, but there was so much talk going on and so many people milling about, the efforts of the musicians were hardly noticeable, and I thought as we trailed in among the people that we, too, were going to come and go without notice and this was to be another disappointment after all.

But it was soon that Charles saw one familiar face, then another, and someone called to him from the distance and waved, and the prospects of enjoyment began to change. I was glad I had thought to buy a new dress and hat, because this was a very elegant party.

How best explain the glorious feeling born of being introduced to people whose names one has heard spoken in tones of prominence? Lawyers; bank officers; cotton brokers; merchants; fishing fleet owners; wholesalers; retailers. Charles knew many of them, and those he did not know were quickly introduced to both of us by others. He mixed easily with people; he remembered names; he looked more distinguished than I had ever seen him and I was proud to be introduced as his wife.

Someone tapped his shoulder from behind: Horace Turner, one of the partners, a tall, lean bachelor with deep-set eyes and a moustache almost too perfectly groomed to look real. "So this is Mrs. Becker," he said, bending to kiss my hand and looking up at me. "Where have you been hiding her, Becker?"

"Oh, I can't get her down to the office very much. Some reason, she thinks it's stuffy in there."

"If I had known my husband has such charming colleagues, I would have made it a point to visit more often," I said.

"Ah, the lady is a diplomat . . . always an asset in a wife. I'll be moving on though, not to keep you. Have you seen Pete yet? He's up front, near the refreshment table."

"We're just on our way," said Charles.

But we had not gone far before we saw J. P. McBride, talking with several other men near the edge of the floor. "Come on, now's your chance to meet the elusive Mr. Mac," said Charles, and guided me across the floor.

He looked different from what I'd envisioned, mostly in size. He was scarcely taller than I—five feet three inches at most—and had a thick head of hair, salt and pepper gray, muttonchop sideburns and bright, lively eyes under thatches of unruly brows. He saw us coming.

"Here they are," he said to the gentlemen standing with him. "Mrs. Becker, how glad I am to meet you . . . you ought to hear your husband praising you all the time, and I can see why." His voice was raspy, and hearing it reminded me Charles had once said he had some sort of throat difficulty that was worsening. "Here's Mortimer Black, Joseph Stillwell, Silas Courtier, you remember, Charles, from the Chaffin case not so long ago. . . ."

"I do indeed, so nice to see you all again . . . my wife, Claire. . . ."

The trio soon left to find their wives; I gave a friendly scolding to McBride for not coming to visit us.

"Oh, I'm afraid I don't get out very much anymore," he said. "You know, since my wife passed away a few years ago, I do feel like an extra wheel around people most of the time . . . besides, Charles gets enough of my reminiscing up at the office without me imposing any of it on you."

"Nonsense. We'd be delighted to have you come, any time. Have you family living elsewhere?"

"One daughter, lives with her husband and three children up East. I shall go there when I do finally retire and that will be soon . . . spend the rest of my days playing with my grandchildren and fishing in the pond."

"Sounds wonderful, but I hope it won't be too soon."

"Ah, well . . . I was so glad when Charles agreed to come in with me. I've too good a practice not to pass on . . . guess that's my way of believing in my immortality, ha-ha!"

"D'you know, we haven't even seen Pete and his wife yet," said Charles. "If you'll excuse us, we'd better get up there and speak to them before they tell everyone to go home."

"Of course. I believe I'll just get my coat and hat and be off. I've been here almost an hour. Well, so long you two, take care. . . ."

"Ah, my feet are killing me," Charles said as we turned from Mac. "Let's meet the Marlowes and get out of here."

"I had no idea you knew so many people, dear. When do you have time to meet them?"

"Well, we all work down around the Strand, lunch together sometimes; work on cases with each other occasionally. I wasn't expecting to see so many familiar faces today, either." We arrived at the refreshment table and found the Marlowes.

"My stars, if it isn't Charlie . . . come on over here, boy, so I can meet that sweet gal you're carryin' on your arm." Big man, Pete Marlowe, tall and rotund with an almost totally bald head and no hair on his face either. His wife, Faye, short and stout, with mounds of red hair piled on top of her head and too much strong perfume, put her arms around me like a long-lost sister.

"Honey, I'm so glad to make your acquaintance. Pete was afraid you wouldn't come."

Where, I wondered, did these people come from with southern drawls so strong they seemed obvious even in Galveston?

"Charlie, will you allow me to have a word with your charmin' wife? Mrs. Becker, may I call you Claire? Has your old scoundrel of a husband told you we've been tryin' to git him interested in comin' in with Turner and Parks and the rest of us?"

I was quite astounded, and it must have shown because he added, "I can see he hasn't let on yet. But you conspire with me to win him over to our side, won't 'cha? Your husband is a brilliant man, and we need him over at our place."

His tones were commanding, not to be defied.

"Oh, Charles doesn't talk much business with me. I let him make all the big decisions."

"Now, don't you let Pete bully you, Claire," said Faye. "When he takes a notion to get somethin' he very often perseveres a bit strongly." She eyed her husband warningly. "Folks got to do what makes 'em happy, regardless of what anybody else thinks." She patted my hand.

"Great party," said Charles. "It's taken us almost a half hour just to get up here and meet the hosts . . . we won't keep you, we know you have a lot of guests to see today."

"Get yourselves a plateful," said Faye. "If all the guests don't do their part and eat, I don't know what we'll do with all the leftovers tomorrow."

We nodded and went to the table. A woman out of place, I thought, but perhaps this is what it is to be rich. No need to worry over remarks you make lest they be inappropriate or offensive to others. . . .

Before us lay surely the most elaborate spread of food on the whole of the island that day. The table was a good ten feet in length, brilliantly lit with long tapers in silver sconces and decorated with evergreen and colorful spiced fruit. Oysters were presented in every describable form, from cold ones on half shell to hot fried ones served from a banquet-size chafing dish and simmering ones in some kind of hot sauce with a queer, exotic aroma. Mushrooms stuffed with crabmeat salad; deviled eggs; caviar; olive sandwiches; cold smoked ham and turkey; steaming hot breads and orange butter; pickles; almonds; raisins; trays of crisp celery and cherry tomatoes stuffed with cheese; individual fruit pies; chocolate creams—chilled champagne at one end of the table and coffee served from an exquisite silver urn at the other.

"Don't look so goggle-eyed," said Charles. "All this is paid for by the business, which is the reason people like you and me were invited."

"If my expression appears strange, it may well be from the shock of what Pete Marlowe just told me."

"Oh, I'll explain that later . . . tell you what, when we get out of here, let's take a drive down the beach. We've plenty of time before going to Rubin's."

Whenever we drive along the beach I am always reminded how flat an island Galveston truly is: just a finger of low-lying turf poking up from the Gulf, really, connected to the rest of the world by a spindly wooden railroad bridge.

It was pleasant on the beach that day, and chillier than on the rest of the island as always, a nice change after the stifling atmosphere of the party. The breeze was a gentle thing that cooled my face and made me drowsy. I languished against the leather seat, allowing my mind to drift from one inconsequential thing to another until Charles brought me up short.

"I've been meaning to talk to you about something, Claire, something of importance to both of us."

"You mean Pete Marlowe's offer?"

"No, not that." He paused then, as though unsure how to broach the subject on his mind. "You met Esther and Dexter Osborne at the party—remember them? He's tall; he wore a pince-nez. She has auburn hair, quite a nice figure."

"I do indeed. Her dress was cut so low you could see traces of the talcum powder she'd dusted in her cleavage."

"Yes . . . well, Dex is in commercial properties here, and I've drawn up a few contracts for him. He came by the other day to ask me a question about something or other—remember that Sunday a couple of weeks back, when I spent all day at the office?—anyway, he brought his three youngsters along.

"Lord, what a bundle they were! Climbing all over my desk and looking into the wastebasket; pulling out books from the shelves and generally throwing everything into disorder. Finally Dex looked up and shouted at them and they behaved. Dex is like me—he gets so enthralled in what's being discussed that the building could fall down around him and he'd just brush away the dust and plaster and go on working."

"How horrible. You must have been a nervous wreck by the time they left."

He had pulled the rig to a halt now, toward the rippling Gulf, and looked at me intently. "The fact is, I missed them when they were gone. It made me wish . . . well, to tell you the truth I'm beginning to wonder if you're ever going to get over the loss of our little Charles and think about having another child or two."

His reference to "our" son and his calling him "little Charles" always grated on my nerves, but I did my best to hide it that day as all others. "Sure, what makes you think I don't want to? But you have to understand that a woman never fully gets over the loss of a child, no matter how many more she has. I didn't think I'd have to tell you that, Charles."

"Yes, I can see that, and I think I've been patient. I knew it was rough on you as long as we were in Grady, and I could even see that moving to Galveston wouldn't solve everything all at once, but Claire, we've been here

nearly a year, and . . . well . . . you never seem to want
me. I love you and want you so much."

"Oh, Charles, really."

"No, I mean it. And because I love you I want more
children. Think how much fun it would be, like at Christmastime, giving them toys, and on Sundays going for picnics, going to the beach, taking them to church all dressed
up, and all the joys of seeing them learn and grow, seeing
ourselves in them."

He looked young when he said it, full of wonder as a
small boy. "Well, I can see the prospect doesn't excite you
much."

"Of course it does, but I . . . just give me time, that's
all. You don't realize what it is . . . what I've been through."

He sighed, but said nothing, only kept staring at me as
though trying to figure whether I was speaking frankly.
Had he guessed the truth about Damon and me, known my
Charlie wasn't really his? Or more lately, had he noticed
the attraction between Rubin and me? Surely not that, for I
had taken great care to play it down, always to speak
highly of Janet, to appear more sympathetic to her problems.

Finally Charles said, "I wonder whether I didn't make a
mistake in bringing you here. You really don't like it, do
you?"

I couldn't reply at first. The breeze grew chillier, yet my
face and neck were hot. I pulled out my fan, then realized
to use it would be to give myself away, and put it back.
Finally I said, "There's nothing wrong with Galveston . . .
really, Charles, you do adjust to new places so quickly, I
quite admire you for it."

"All right, but let's not wait too much longer, Claire, I'm
nearly thirty-six, you know."

I looked ahead, knowing that now I'd have to play the
pretending game with Charles again, just as in the first few
months of our marriage, and it was hard to fake enjoyment
at love-making when you had known what real joy in a
man's arms could be. The conversation was getting to me. I
thought of the remarks made by Pete Marlowe and leapt
on the subject as if it were a wagon passing by. "What is
this with Pete? Has he made you a real offer?"

"Several times. The offer gets a little better each time,
and I'll admit it's tempting, especially in terms of money."

"Why don't you do it? When McBride retires, you'll have an easy out, won't you?"

"Yes, but to tell you the truth I'd rather stay where I am and be able to pick my own cases. It isn't the easiest way, because there's no one but myself to keep track of whether or not a client pays his fee; and I can't send some underling across town or across the state to deliver papers for me. All the same, I want to be sought out to handle cases on my own merit. That is, for me, the challenge that keeps it interesting."

I didn't pursue the conversation any further, and we rode in silence back home from the beach. Charles had always made his own choices about his career—it was the one area where he stood fast against any interference from me—so it seemed pointless to carry on the discussion when I didn't really care that day what he did about Pete Marlowe's offer. All I could ponder was the bitter fact that, while other people seemed to have options open to them on all aspects of their lives, I was a person whose wishes carried no more weight than a feather fluttering in the wind.

Chapter 8

The truth of my assessment that day was brought home to me when we arrived at the Garrets later that evening for music and light refreshment (thank heaven Rubin did not insist Janet cook dinner for the small group). A singing quartet visiting St. Christopher's from their home parish in Houston had participated in Rubin's morning service, and he in turn had invited them to come to his home that night to lead a sing-song. Janet seemed in good spirits, had seemed so for a couple of weeks, and worked hard to put a high polish on the piano in their front room. She'd even had the instrument tuned up too, just for the occasion.

I was not feeling well, having eaten something at the Marlowes' which was not setting well with me. I was uncomfortable sitting in the hard-backed chair, listening to the people gathered around the piano go through the heartier and more joyful songs in the Episcopal hymnal, most of which were unfamilar to me. I decided to make myself useful by combining the finger sandwiches now only half covering four silver trays onto one tray. It would make for a neater table and I could wash the other trays and get them put away. I didn't notice, as I rearranged the crusty sandwiches, that Janet and Rubin were not among the guests around the piano. Charles was there, following along in the hymnal, apparently enjoying himself enormously.

I stacked the three empty trays, gathered a few used napkins and a glass or two, and, without a free hand, turned and backed into the swinging kitchen door. As I turned around I saw them together, Rubin enclosing his wife in his big arms and kissing her full on the lips. They looked at me in surprise. I lowered my eyes, left the trays on the kitchen table, and excused myself.

Could there have been a better demonstration that I had been wrong about the way Rubin had been looking at me? It didn't seem so that night, nor many nights following, as I began to realize I was about to get caught again in a web of wanting someone I couldn't have, and for the most obvious of reasons: however ill suited was Janet as the wife of a clergyman (or any man, actually), Rubin Garret loved her.

I knew I must throw my energies elsewhere, and get my mind off Rubin, and in the long run we'd all be far better off. Yet the way of doing this eluded me for a few weeks, until Charles, inadvertently, gave me the answer.

One night in early February, he came home from the office and said, "By the way, I had lunch downtown today with several people, among them Pete Marlowe. He told me to be sure and remember him to you. He thought you were 'right charmin' and a 'real lady'—you know how he goes on. I promised him I'd tell you."

"Why, how nice," I said, and then it hit me. Maybe I couldn't openly persuade Charles to go with Pete Marlowe's firm, but I might be able to do it without his being aware of it, and if so, it would mean we'd move among that elite group of people in Galveston that had so fascinated me at the Marlowe party a month before. These people had teas, receptions, evenings at exclusive restaurants. One read about their busy lives in the newspaper. Charles and I could become a part of their crowd in time, if I worked it right, and we might eventually move to Broadway, far away from Rubin Garret, and if I was to be forever denied the man of my choice, I could at least live a life so busy and full of excitement that it might not matter so much the one basic ingredient of happiness was missing. My mind spun forward to visions of wealth and social importance, entertaining as only I could do it, parties, dances. . . .

"Charles, you know it really would be nice to reciprocate the Marlowes' hospitality."

"What? Oh, how do you mean?" he asked, looking up from his paper.

"Well, maybe have them to dinner sometime."

"Um-hum," he said, focusing back on his newspaper.

"You know a lot of trouble goes into a party like that, and I'll bet you not a fraction of the guests invited ever have the decency to reciprocate. Now that I think of it, it seems almost . . . well . . . ill mannered."

"If you say so, Claire."

"Could we invite them?"

"I guess so, if you want to."

"When?"

"Oh, I don't know, we can talk about it."

"Let's set a date."

He put down his paper and drew on his pipe. "All right, if it means that much to you. Tell me when you want to do it and I'll see if they're free."

I was surprised at the ease with which my wishes were carried through. The Marlowes came one evening in early spring, arriving promptly at seven-thirty, a Darby and Joan if ever there has been and acting as though it were not the first but the hundredth time they'd come to our house for a meal.

Charles explained them eloquently a week or so before, when I was poring over menus and worrying whether the linen or the more formal crochet tablecloth would be appropriate: "Pete was raised on a dirt farm somewhere in North Carolina," he had said, "and Faye was the daughter of a clerk in a small-town bank. Believe me, dear, you don't need to fuss. They're home folks."

After I disregarded the elaborate style of the New Year's Day party and thought of the personable nature of the two Marlowes, I decided he was correct and was put somewhat at ease, and as though to reaffirm this, Faye with her bejeweled chubby fingers took a knife to the hot bread and helped me put the food on the table just as a friend of long standing would do.

The table conversation was launched on our lavish compliments over their recent party and Charles's expressed surprise that McBride had seen fit to come. "Only way I could git him over to the house was to remind him he'd be retirin' soon, lucky rascal, and movin' away from Galveston, and he might never have another opportunity to see a whole bunch of people who were comin'."

"You certainly had a good crowd," I said.

"Reckon we had about sixty all told. Course our party is nowhere near the size of some of the others around on New Year's Day, but then we keep our distance from the more illustrious people on the island," said Faye.

"Like whom?" I asked.

"Mainly the folks connected with the Wharf Company. They're the ones who really own Galveston, and don't let nobody kid ya'," Pete said.

I thought of the neighborhood oyster roast a summer before, and the awkward moment following Driscoll's faux pas over the Wharf Company.

"By the way," he continued, "I've got a client who wants to lease some land along the north side of the channel for puttin' up a warehouse. The petition goes before the council next Monday, but just between us, I don't think it has a chance."

"Why not?" I asked.

"Because goods stored in that warehouse would go directly aboard the sailin' vessel, escapin' the drayage and wharfage charge. The city wouldn't pay it any mind if it was small pickin's, but this one's gonna be a considerable building and they're not gonna like losing all that money. They haven't got sense enough to see they'd make more revenue off taxes on the property if the warehouse was put up than they would from their interest in the wharfage," Pete replied.

Then Charles mentioned hearing a rumor that the already exorbitant wharfage rates were going up again pretty soon, and Pete said, "Could be; the Wharf Company's got nothin' to stop them—a closed corporation holding two thirds of the stock, and no competition!"

"Well, can't the city do something?" I asked.

"Not likely," he said, his face reddening. "It took a court rulin' to get them their measly one third of the stock in the first place, and that much ain't worth a pot of spoiled black-eyed peas.

"I'm tellin' you, it's outrageous that a handful of individual stockholders could have a death grip on the best port on this part of the coast, and, mind you, if they don't quit

paying themselves dividends—seventy grand one year not
so long ago—instead of usin' their profits to expand the
wharf facilities, they're gonna play right into the hands of
Houston."

I'd read newspaper stories now and then of Houston's
efforts at dredging their own channel, but hadn't taken
them seriously. After all, Galveston was situated on a natural harbor; Houston's only connection with the open sea—
fifty miles away—was a few tortuous, moss-hung bayous.
However, Pete was obviously fired up about the subject, so
I didn't argue.

"That's right," Charles was saying, "and while we might
be the largest cotton exporter in the South right now, how
long before we lose our place when our channel continues
to shoal and deepen according to the whims of nature?
Right now it's only eighteen feet deep and ought to be at
least twenty-five, to handle the bigger ships. Our compla-
cency is going to get the best of us one day."

"You bet," said Pete, then leaned back without another
word, surprising me by giving Charles a chance to elaborate.

"Look how many people already hate the Wharf Company," he continued. "Take the cotton farmer, for one. Although Galveston draymen are willing to move his cotton
from railroad car to shipboard for about fifteen cents a
bale, they aren't allowed on the wharves. Only Wharf Company people can put the cotton aboard, and they charge
forty cents a bale. Now, after suffering the high cost of rail
transportation to get the cotton here, the farmer doesn't
look too kindly on having a big wharfage fee slapped on
him."

"But what can be done?" Faye asked.

Pete wiped the crumbs from around his plate and let
them drop from his fingers onto the empty plate, then answered, "The city would buy the other two thirds of the
stock and make the wharves free for public use. This has
been talked about several times before, but mysteriously
dropped. And maybe it's just as well. The city needs revenue.

"On the other hand, maybe we could get a court rulin' to
force the corporation to go public—thereby bustin' the monopoly. That's unlikely, though, because there's politics involved."

"But if what you're saying is true, Galveston is doomed.

All those people up in Houston have to do is figure out a way to dredge a deep channel up one of those bayous. Seems like people here either don't give a hoot, or are afraid to buck the monopoly," Faye replied.

"Well, let's don't spend the whole evening talkin' about the Wharf Company," said Pete. "I do tend to get carried away on the subject. Besides, I didn't want to let the night pass without askin' Charles how soon old Mac is gonna move out."

The moment had come. I looked at Charles, who appeared unruffled. "He says next year, but you know Mac. He may stick around for two, three years. Then again, he may pack up tomorrow afternoon and buy a ticket on the evening train."

"Mac's been around a long time," said Pete. "You know, they say he lost his wife in that yellow fever epidemic back in '67, nearly killed him, losin' her. Never looked twice at another woman after she went."

"He rarely mentions her," said Charles, "but he does keep her picture on his desk. She was a fine-looking woman."

"Gonna be lonesome down there all by yourself, boy, when he's gone. . . ."

Faye reached over and put a hand on Pete's arm.

"All right, Mama. I just want Charlie to know my invitation remains open."

"I'm much obliged," said Charles.

Later, as Faye helped me cut apple pie in the kitchen, she remarked, "You mustn't mind my husband pushin' Charles a bit. I haven't known him to be so taken with another lawyer in all the years I've been married to him."

"I'm sure Charles finds it flattering."

"Don't ever underestimate your husband, honey. He's got charm; he's a very nice-lookin' man; and he is smart. That's a winnin' combination."

When we walked into the parlor I became conscious of a pain in the small of my back. It had bothered me at dinner, I now realized, yet I was too interested in the conversation to notice it. Charles had lit up his pipe; Pete was smoking a cigar, telling Charles about his son Teddy.

"He has one more year left at military academy, then off to college. Boy don't know what he wants to do yet, though, and I'm concerned he might take to a military career."

"Have you tried to interest him in the law?" Charles asked.

"I'm afraid to. If I suggest it he may rule it out on general principle. The boy is a rebel in his own way. Our other kids—we got two married daughters back in Carolina—were easy to raise compared to Teddy. But he's a good boy, and I got my fingers crossed he'll come into the firm one day."

As they were leaving, Faye asked if we'd ever been to the Garten Vercin.

"No, but I've heard of it," I told her. "Some sort of recreation club, isn't it?"

"Yes, they have special functions—dinners and dancing, concerts and so forth. We're members, so one night you must go as our guests and see how you like it. Pete loves the tenpin alley. Do you bowl, Charles?"

"Haven't for a long time, but it sounds like fun."

"Good, we'll git together one night and go over," said Pete. "Maybe git some other fellas together. The place looks best in the summer—the gardens are full of flowers and the trees are filled out. Course there's somethin' goin' on there all the time. And they have the best German sausages ever touched your palate."

"As you can see, my husband pays particular mind to the menu," Faye interrupted, poking at Pete's ample stomach.

"Hush up, Mama," Pete said, then added, "It's a German club, you know, only German folks can be stockholders. Plain folks like us can only be members."

"Sounds like another Wharf Company," Charles said with mock intrigue.

"As a matter of fact, I do believe the man who once owned the land it lies on was an original incorporator of the Wharf Company. The Octopus probably started as innocent as the Garten Verein. Anyway, the Wharf Company is an economic and social evil, and somethin' ought to be done about it."

The remark seemed no more than idle talk that night—as indeed it probably was—like the general talk several years earlier that something ought to be done about the scandalous Grant administration. When Faye and Pete walked down our stairs, I'm sure none of us had any idea we would come any closer to solving the problem of the Octopus than we had come to solving the Grant scandals.

I had a dream that night: I was alone, treading water out in the Galveston harbor on a damp, foggy morning. My legs ached so I could hardly keep them moving, and my body was all but rigid from the cold.

I dared not swim out in any direction in the fog, for I had no idea in which direction safety lay. And so it continued, hour after creeping hour, until I was sure this was it for me and fate had finally slammed the door and swallowed the key.

Finally, the wall of fog began to meander unhurriedly away, blowing in curly wisps across the surface of the water and thinning above to allow in the sun. At last I could see the wharves, and I summoned all the energy left me to swim toward them.

Yet it was a trick, for as I swam nearer and nearer and the gauzy mist continued to lift, I could see the wharves were all but deserted; no ships were berthed in their outstretched arms and only four men were visible, walking along near the landings. These men carried a sign which I could not read until I was near the landings. Then its red-lettered message became clear: UNESCORTED LADIES WILL NOT BE ALLOWED TO CROSS THE WHARVES, IN ACCORDANCE WITH THE POLICY OF YOUR GALVESTON WHARF COMPANY, SERVING YOU BETTER.

I awoke then. The room was bathed in early morning half-light, and Charles lay beside me, his face toward the ceiling, and these things were comforting after the dream; yet something about the dream was real. I raised up from the bed and knew.

My legs ached and my stomach was in knots. There was a dizzying sensation in my head. I wouldn't make it halfway across the floor before the menstrual flooding would begin like a spring which had discovered a new outlet. It would mean two days in bed at least, maybe more, depending. Charles would have to go out and refill the prescription for pain medicine which was given to me when this happened two months before.

When he awoke at half-past eight, I was back in bed, propped on pillows and watching the morning through the window. "I'm afraid I am in for another spell," I told him. "There isn't enough of the brown medicine to last me . . . will you go and get some more?"

"Of course," he said, and grabbed for his trousers hanging across a chair.

"Not now, just sometime today."

"But do you think I can get anymore of it? Didn't the doctor say he wanted to see you if the flooding occurred again?"

"Yes, but there isn't anything he can do for me now. I'll go in sometime next week."

"Have you taken a dose this morning?"

"No, I've been waiting until absolutely necessary. It really is vile."

"Well then, how about some tea?"

I listened to the sound of his footsteps on the stairs, then heard the doorbell. It was Rubin . . . curious time for him to come calling. I wondered whether something had happened to Janet, for even in those days she struck me as a person to whom something untoward might happen.

The easy ebb and flow of the muffled conversation told me not. Presently the door closed and Charles walked to the back of the house and into the kitchen.

One can hear little of what is going on in the rest of the house from the bedroom Charles and I occupy. When we moved here, he favored the larger front bedroom, because it gets greater benefit from the ocean breeze. But I told him if he wanted that bedroom he'd have it alone, for in front of the deep windows is a dais, designed to hold a large bed. The dais reminds me of the bier on which my son's coffin rested for a day and a night, and I have no wish to sleep on anything resembling it.

One can hear sounds in the kitchen from our bedroom, however, because it is directly below. I heard Charles as he rustled among the dishes, and only then remembered the state of disorder I'd left the kitchen in the night before. My back had ached too badly after the Marlowes left for me to consider cleaning it.

Now, I knew, I would think of it constantly until I could get down there to put it in order. Things out of place weigh heavily upon my mind.

When Charles returned with the tea tray I asked him what Rubin wanted.

"He's ordered Janet a wicker swing for the verandah—a surprise—and apparently it came in on a ship this morning. He came over in hopes of persuading you to keep her busy for a couple of hours this afternoon while he goes to pick it up. He wants to have it hung when she sees it. Of course I told him you weren't feeling well."

"Listen. Is that someone at the back door?"

"Hm? Lord, I guess it is. I'll go and see."

This time, Janet. I heard him call her name although, even from above, her small voice was barely audible. They spoke for several minutes, longer than he'd spoken with Rubin.

When Charles came back to the bedroom, he told me that Janet had asked if she could do some sketching in our backyard. "I said sure. Then I remembered something I'd thought about but never followed up on—taking her around the island to show her some good spots for painting, like the wharves, or the railroad depot, maybe Bolivar Port. The lighthouse would make a lovely picture. You know, she doesn't get out much because Rubin spends so much time at the church. So I suggested that if you were doing all right, I'd take her out this afternoon. It'll get her out of the way long enough for Rubin to bring the swing home."

"What did she say?"

"She was worried about you, but I told her I thought you'd be all right and that I'd ask you about it."

"Of course."

"You *are* all right? I can pick up the medicine while we're out."

"Fine. How about taking this tray down? I think I'd better have some of what's left in the bottle now."

"Good. While you're resting, I'll do the dishes and tidy the kitchen. I know how you hate . . . listen, I wanted to tell you how grand everything was last night. The Marlowes were very impressed, I'm sure."

"Does it mean anything to you, that they were impressed?"

"If you're wondering whether I might be taking his offer seriously, I can only answer that, for the moment, no."

"That doesn't mean you'd rule it out in the future?"

"It doesn't mean anything one way or the other. Now, take your elixir and go to sleep."

I slept until the afternoon cast shadows across the bed, and awoke to the sight of Charles sitting across the room, smoking his pipe and reading the *News*. I felt hazy, as though there were a thin veil separating me from everything around. It was the work of the medicine, and another bottle of it now sat on the table beside the bed.

"What time is it?"

"Oh, I didn't know you were awake. It's past four-thirty, at least."

"My heavens! I've slept the day away?"

"You certainly have. I've cleaned up the kitchen—didn't break a dish—and taken Janet for a turn . . . that burned up three hours or more . . . picked up your medicine at Schott's—"

"Did Rubin get the swing hung?"

"It was up when we got back. You should have seen Janet—it's a handsome thing, and she was delighted. Clapped her hands and made over it just like a kid under the Christmas tree.

"Say, you must be famished. I'll go down and fix you a tray."

When he was gone I thought of Janet in her swing. She would look proper sitting there of an evening, rocking to and fro and humming a tune or reciting a poem. Such a frail human being, Janet, her existence somehow more ephemeral than anyone else's.

Chapter 9

Late in the spring of '78 we took instruction and joined the Episcopal Church. Charles had come to love the service at St. Christopher's, and while I'd begun to wonder if it would be wise to put myself into a position of spending more time in the presence of Rubin Garret, I could hardly voice any objection to Charles when I'd been so determined to join shortly after we came to Galveston. One Wednesday evening with six others we were confirmed and took our first Holy Communion in the candlelit chancel of St. Christopher's, from the hand of the Very Reverend Malcolm Palmer, Bishop of the Diocese of Houston-Galveston.

On that same evening, and in conflict with the dignified tea reception which followed the six-thirty ceremony, was held across town at the Union Hall a rollicking stag party in honor of J. P. McBride. Charles hurried away early from the reception to be with his retiring partner for the final making-merry. It was the only farewell party Mac would agree to, and he would come to the office the following morning, pick up a few of his things still left there, and board the afternoon train for Boston. I imagined what care he would have taken as he swept the gilt-framed picture of his late wife from his desk and put it into his satchel. I'd seen the picture on the one occasion I went to Charles's office, a day when Mac was not there. I remarked then to Charles the lady had a sweet, sleepy-eyed look, but did not tell him that I searched the face for a clue to early death. I've always believed one could see that in a face.

Soon after the retirement was done and Charles faced the loneliness of the big, stuffy office, Pete Marlowe like a powerful locomotive began to gather momentum in his thrust to hire Charles. He invited him for rolling tenpins at the Garten one night, and mentioned in advance Horace Turner and Gilbert Parks would be along.

I sat on the edge of the bed while Charles dressed. He was already tired, and without much enthusiasm about going. The fact he did go held significance, then.

He stood in front of the mirror, buttoning his shirt. "I know what's coming tonight, and I'm in no mood for Pete's pressuring."

"Don't kid me, Charles. You must be interested, or else why would you go?"

"Because I don't want to alienate him, either."

"Did he come to Mac's party?"

"Oh yes, big turnout from his firm there." He stood before the mirror, parting and re-parting his just washed hair.

"I wonder why he would be after you? There must be dozens of lawyers in this area who'd jump at the chance to go with his firm."

"True enough . . . I certainly don't know why, except perhaps for my diversified background—practicing all those years in Grady. But there may be something about Pete you don't understand. In his own way, he's as hungry for power as those at the Wharf Company he despises. His firm is one of the largest in the Galveston and Houston area, and he likes to see it grow."

"Before we met Pete, I wasn't aware there were so many holding grudges against the Wharf Company. I thought they were one of our beloved institutions here."

"Hardly. They're not popular anywhere in the state, and if they hurt Galveston, in the long run, it hurts Pete."

"You too, then?"

"To a degree, although I'm pretty sure Galveston will always be able to support its share of hard-working attorneys. But Pete's business handles a lot of big accounts in this city—everything from wholesale grocers and manufacturers to shipping outfits. I think he also has an interest in one cotton brokerage firm, and owns quite a bit of land down on the southern shore. If cotton factors and shippers, and various related businesses, start moving out to Houston, it's going to hurt Pete's business badly."

"What's good for Galveston is good for Pete."

"Right. And I'm late." He pulled on his coat and kissed my forehead. "See me downstairs?"

There is something oddly depressing about following someone down the stairs at night. Our stairway is dimly lit; darkness hovers and shadows follow. "I feel terrible, leaving you like this," he said on the way. "I seem to be spending what free time I have lately doing all sorts of things except being with you."

"It's all right. I've letters to write, sewing to be done. It is nice to be alone sometimes."

"Oh, is it?"

"Sometimes. I didn't say all the time."

He kissed me again at the back door, and I watched him walk through the yard toward the barn and wondered what he would have said if I'd told him, "Yes, Charles, could you not possibly stay at home with me tonight? Tell Pete some other time, and stay home?"

But of course I didn't want that at all.

A sudden rain; a cooling off. Several minutes past nine o'clock, a knock at the front door. Janet, standing alone on the porch, wrapped in a shawl.

"Come in. This fickle weather, one never knows what to expect. Charles is gone. I'll make tea."

"Rubin, too, a meeting I think."

"Oh, but this is Wednesday. I thought he wrote his sermons on Wednesday night."

She followed me into the kitchen. "Something came up," she said, and sat down at the table. I looked at her and opened my mouth to speak, but did not. There in the light, I could see: she'd been crying. I turned toward the stove and started the kettle.

"What a nice surprise, your coming. You so seldom do, when there are just the two of us to visit." Why could I not look at her? I busied myself pulling cups and saucers from the cupboard.

"I saw a notice in the *News* today," she said. "The annual art show is to be held down at Woollam's Lake next month. Do you think I ought to enter?"

I was surprised she deigned to ask me such a question. "Of course, why not? Is there a prize?" I forced myself to turn and face her.

"Only the proceeds, if you sell. I've got several things, as you know, and I thought I might offer to do some quick portraits. I used to be fairly good at that, though I haven't done it for a while.

"Thought I'd give whatever I make to the Church . . . I give so little to it. Of course, I may not sell anything."

"I'm sure you will. Charles says in the two or three times he's taken you on outings, he's been too busy admiring your painting to do the work he brought along."

"Yes, but for him I'd have nothing to sell. I can't paint flowers in the backyard or oleanders in the front forever. You don't mind him taking me around, do you? I'm afraid to go alone and Rubin is always busy at the church. . . ."

"It hasn't been all that many times; I really don't mind."

"I think I have a fairly good rendering of the lighthouse on Bolivar as seen from the end of Galveston Island. It would be great fun, of course, if you could come along with us when we go—"

"You're worried that I'm jealous, and I assure you I'm not. In fact, I appreciate your giving Charles the opportunity of getting out in the sun. He stays cooped up in his office too much."

The kettle was singing. I poured two cups and put some ginger cookies out on a plate. I knew Janet wouldn't eat any, of course, but true hospitality demands these amenities. She sniffled and turned from the table, fished in her pocket for a handkerchief, and blew her nose. "I must be catching cold," she said. "By the way, are you all right?"

"Me?"

"That day you were sick, the first time Charles took me out on a paint jaunt. Rubin and I were worried."

"Oh, that. It was nothing, really. I've had it before and probably will again. I guess—for me—it's part of being a woman."

She giggled then and I looked at her in puzzlement. "Forgive me," she said. "Not that it's funny, but men are so cute about things like that. Charles wouldn't tell us a thing about your illness, so of course I guessed right away it was female problems. Have you seen a doctor?"

"Yes. Twice since the first of the year."

"Has he been able to help you? Is he a specialist?"

"He is a specialist—first one I've ever been to—but not much help beyond prescribing pain medicine for cramps. He cited only one other alternative and I declined to consider that."

"What?"

"An operation to remove my ovaries. Seems that's all the rage nowadays. Even if a woman has no dangerous growths, which I haven't, many doctors are removing one or both ovaries just as a safety precaution. Dr. Hutchisson wasn't highly in favor of it because he isn't convinced it's really the answer. Almost half the women who have such surgery die from it."

"Gad, what a frightening thought—surgery."

"Well, I suppose it can't be too much more difficult than giving birth to a child . . . seems funny to think back on it now, but in Grady there are three doctors, all just plain ordinary medicine men. When you think you might be expecting, you simply go to one of them and find out. If he confirms it, you go home and wait out your time, and a midwife comes over and helps you with the birth, and takes care of you afterward.

"As far out as we lived when I was carrying Charlie, it's a lucky thing we had Helga when my time came round, for, as you might have known, he came a month early, and rather quickly, too."

"Oh yes, your housekeeper . . . I think you mentioned her before. Pity she couldn't come to Galveston with you, that way if you and Charles ever again—"

"Yes," I interrupted, "but Charles didn't care for Helga. He had some foolish idea that she made a mistake during the delivery of the baby that brought on my bleeding spells, because I began having them shortly after Charlie came into the world. Nonsense, of course. She's the best midwife I've ever seen, and a good friend too. I still keep in touch with her, though I don't mention it to Charles."

"Where is she now?"

"In San Antonio, living with her brother."

"I see." She sat still for a few moments, stirring her tea. Then she said, "Claire, can this doctor of yours help other problems in women?"

"I suppose so. Are you having any?"

"Not any pain. Nothing like that." She paused, as if uncertain what to say next, and began to open and close the hand which held the wadded-up handkerchief.

"What is it, Janet? Anything wrong?"

She rose from her chair. "It's children. I don't believe Rubin and I'll ever have any. No, I'm sure we won't."

Determined as I had been lately to get Rubin Garret off my mind, and as well as I had succeeded so far, I would not deny the twinge of satisfaction her statement gave me. Yet I said, "Well, if you think a specialist could help, I'll give you Dr. Hutchisson's address."

"Yes . . . maybe sometime. I'd better go now. Rubin ought to be home soon."

I followed her to the door and out onto the front porch. "It has stopped raining," I said, obliquely, for this was an obvious fact. One says ridiculous things when there is nothing else to say. "Just let me know, if you want to see Dr. Hutchisson. He's one of the best specialists in this area," I added.

"Oh, I don't know . . . I rather doubt he could help at that," she said. "I do thank you for the tea and companionship, though. Good night."

As she slowly retraced her steps between our house and hers, bundled in her shawl, I was struck again by what an odd pair she and Rubin were. Something obviously was wrong between them that neither of them had so far discussed with us, but what? Could it be I was right the first time about Rubin's interest in me, I wondered? Then I shook my head, thinking of the night I caught them by surprise, embracing in the kitchen.

I went back into the house. It was almost ten o'clock, yet I wasn't sleepy, and I had a sudden curiosity as to where Rubin had gone. There was no church meeting that I knew of that night. I turned off the lights in the front room and sat down on the sofa against the window, and looked out into the night. I sat there till nearly midnight, watching the rain start and stop from time to time, and finally the big moon push its way through the clouds. I never saw Rubin come home.

I went up to bed then and lay awake for a while, still puzzling over the Garrets with a kind of detachment. Shortly after the clock struck one, I heard Charles come in, and I turned up the bedside lamp, eager to hear how the evening went for him.

"You still awake?" he said, his voice slurred, his eyes bloodshot and glazed.

"More awake than you appear to be. How was it? Did you win?"

"Won two frames, but I also drank too much beer and ate too much German sausage." He loosened his tie and sat down on the edge of the bed.

"Where's your coat?"

"Coat? Oh, I guess I left it in the buggy. Hell with it. I'll get it tomorrow."

"Sounds like the end of a perfect evening."

"The four of us had a pretty good time, at that. Pete has apparently decided to go easy on me."

"Four went? I thought there were three."

"Oh, yeah. You r'member when we were at Marlowe's party on New Year's, and you thought you saw someone you knew?"

"Yes, just as we walked in. The man in the gray derby."

"That was Lucien Carter. He owns a shipping company based here. Goes to St. Christopher's. That's where you saw him, just as you thought." He yawned, and pulled off one shoe then the other, uttering a grunt for each, then rubbed his feet. "Oh, yeah, I'll never r'member this tomorrow so I'll tell you now. There is to be a dinner dance at the Garten next month. Pete wants you and me to go. He's gonna invite some other people, too. He said to ask Janet and Rubin along, since Carter said how much he likes Rubin. Take care of it, will you?"

"Of course. But what are we supposed to wear?"

He did not answer, instead lay back half-dressed, and after one loud garlic-flavored belch, fell asleep.

I turned down the lamp and lay awake, my detachment toward the Garrets dissolving moment by moment. My thoughts fled to party dress fabric and candlelight, and moonlit gardens, and dancing in circles of splendor with Rubin (how perfect we'd look!), and of poor, mixed-up Janet, who did not belong with him at all.

Early summer: sunset under a blue and pink mackerel sky.

We boarded the rig with an air of importance, Janet and Rubin, Charles and I, and headed for our meeting with Charles's destiny.

On the lantern-lit terrace projecting from the clubhouse

of the Garten Verein, we greeted Pete and Faye, Lucien
and Isobel Carter at Pete's table: the best available table, of
course. Horace Turner hadn't come. A bachelor, he had
realized the awkwardness his presence would bring and was
not known to keep company with women. Gilbert Parks's
wife was ill and he wouldn't leave her alone, so the party
was honed down to eight people.

"Your dress is exquisite," said Isobel Carter, a foreigner
with dark hair pulled back severely, and large, dark eyes.

"Didn't I tell you?" Faye said to me, then looked at Isobel. "Madame LaRoche, from Louisiana. Best seamstress in
Galveston."

"Yes, Faye referred me to her," I explained.

"Poor old thing's got a lame leg and her apartment looks
like a troop of Yankee soldiers just looted it, but she can
work magic with a piece of material."

"Oh yes, her shop's down on Market, isn't it?"

"That's right, and she don't sew for just anybody," said
Faye, patting my arm.

Lucien Carter, a slight man with impeccable moustache
and handsome features, was nursing a gin when we arrived.
He continued to drink steadily throughout the evening in
measured sips, and smoked cigarettes as well, lighting each
from the candle between us and often looking across at me
as he did. I shifted my eyes, smarting from his penetrating
gaze.

It wasn't long before the pleasant dinner conversation
turned to business, and as Lucien was Pete's client, attention centered on him. "What do you think can be done
about the high wharfage at our port? Surely your business
must be hurt by it," Faye said. I wondered then whether
Pete usually briefed her on what to say in front of specific
clients, to shift the focus on them.

"That's true, Mrs. Marlowe, but at present the Wharf
Company might just be the lesser of two evils plaguing the
shipping down here," Lucien answered. He spoke in the fine,
clipped tones of someone reared and educated in the
East.

I asked him what the other would be.

"Commodore Morgan, who's making matters equally
rough for Houston," he said.

"Why would that matter to you?" Janet asked.

"Houston is where I might go, if I'm ever forced from
here by the high wharfages," he said, and went on to ex-

plain that Morgan owned a steamship company based in Louisiana, and until about four years ago had received huge discounts on wharfage at Galveston. Many locals thought no better of him than they did of the Wharf Company.

Then Pete interrupted, "And his freight rates were about ten times as high as those charged by other shippers, such as Lucien here."

"Then one day the Wharf Company cut him off flat," said Lucien. "At the same time, they raised the wharfage rates again."

"And laughed in his face when he put up a fuss," said Charles.

"Yes. He was angry about other things, too. The Board of Health here imposed quarantine against Louisiana ports every year during peak business season, so Morgan's ships had to lay over a month whenever they pulled into the Galveston harbor. Of course there was no real danger of disease . . . the Board concocted the quarantines so Galveston merchants could sell off their old merchandise before accepting the new cargo he brought."

"Quarantined against which disease?" I asked.

"Yellow fever," Charles said.

For a few moments yellow jack seemed almost a joke, rather than a dread disease, until I thought of Anna McBride and wondered whether her body had retched near the end with black vomit. . . .

"So Morgan turned on his heel and took his business to Houston," Lucien continued, "and in exchange for stock in their ship channel building company, he signed a contract to build a twelve-foot-deep, hundred-and-twenty-foot-wide channel from Galveston Bay to Houston. He also bought a couple of railroads leading to the city from inland, so you can imagine he gathered quite a bit of power—from both ends."

"And all because of being snubbed by Galveston," Janet said.

"But then, Morgan became greedy about the waterway he'd dredged out," said Pete. "He collected heavy tolls, and to keep ships from passin' it without payin' the tolls, he connected a big chain across it. It's still there."

It seemed logical to me that as long as Morgan was in control of Houston's port we'd have nothing to worry about, but then Charles was saying, "Don't think Morgan won't eventually strangle on his own chain. I've seen those Houston people turn the most confounded situations to their favor, and they'll do it again.

"We can't become a major seaport by default—it's too risky, especially when there are positive steps we can take. We've got to deepen our own channel and dredge the inner and outer bars. And we've got to get rid of those wharfage fees! Once the bigger ships have emptied their cargo onto barges, that cargo can just as easily go further in to Houston as stop here and pay wharfage."

Something happened then: a glance exchanged between Lucien Carter and Pete Marlowe. I knew instantly they had spoken of Charles outside his presence, and would do so again in the light of what he said tonight. I took a sip of wine. All was going well.

There was an announcement then that dancing would begin within a quarter of an hour. Tables had been cleared around us, and Pete rose from his chair. "We'd better git out of here before they move us along with the table."

We danced to the music of a sixteen-piece orchestra that night and Pete, good man, did insist right after the first waltz that we change partners. No one could have known how I waited that night for the moment to come when Rubin would look across at Charles and say, "You must permit me this next waltz with Claire."

Then, giddy as a schoolgirl, I chattered incessantly about Madame LaRoche while we twirled around the floor, when all he had done was to compliment me on the lovely dress I wore, and to say that red was definitely my color.

Chapter 10

The sea is a constant threat to our existence here. Even during the months when the Gulf is lapping peacefully at the shore, and one need not fear a hurricane is forming somewhere, gathering energy to strike like a coiled snake, the salt air and humidity are busy attacking our homes and buildings so that repairs of one form or another are a continuous source of expense and bother.

At the beginning of our second summer in Galveston, Charles took upon himself the task of painting the exterior of our house on Avenue L. He felt after I'd worked so hard getting the grass to grow and the flowers to bloom that the house was beginning to look shabby. Things had slacked off a bit at the office, and we both agreed he could use the sunshine and exercise.

Midmorning on the Monday he began, the postman brought a letter from Betsey. She was too busy minding the store and caring for Ruth to waste time on unnecessary sentiment, so she wrote letters only when she had something to tell, or to ask.

As a result, when her letters arrived they were generally lengthy, bulging from their envelopes, and because her handwriting was almost indecipherable it sometimes took me a couple of days to satisfy myself I'd read each word correctly.

Today her letter concerned Ruth, and before reading too far I stopped to fix ham sandwiches and lemonade for lunch. I took the tray of food and the letter out to the verandah and called to Charles to come down from the ladder and eat.

Charles was fond of Betsey and Ruth, and always glad to hear their news, so I read aloud as we ate. " 'Do you think they might be able to use one slightly shopworn store owner down there? It's so hot up here my clothes are sticking to me like gauze to a bleeding sore.

" 'Well, it looks as though Ruth has found her love at last. He lives here but will be going back to college at Southwestern in September. She spends all her time with him, and he's certainly an attentive suitor. They've gone on hayrides together, a round of dances, and [next word unreadable], and summer cookouts. He takes her to church in his own rig every Sunday morning.' "

"How old would she be by now? Seventeen, eighteen?" Charles asked.

"Nearly eighteen. Betsey was married at seventeen, come to think of it. I hope Ruth makes a better choice than she did, when she settles down."

"Sounds like she might be about ready to do just that."

"I don't know. If he's going off to college in the fall, sometimes romance fades during extended absences. We'll see . . . listen to what else she says:

" 'I was out at the cemetery last Saturday, to check on Charlie's grave, and all looks well. I left some yellow mums and will put some flowers again when his birthday comes around.' "

I stopped reading and put the letter down. Part of me had lost him all over again when I read her words. I hadn't forgotten his second birthday would have been coming up within days, but somehow it was upsetting to see it on paper. Charles closed a rough, paint-streaked hand over mine. "Doesn't it help, knowing what good care Betsey takes of our son's grave?"

"Some, but not much," I said, smarting at his reference.

He pulled his hand away and took a bite of sandwich, and I stared across at him, wanting at that moment to tell him everything just so he'd stop crediting himself with my son. Had we gone on sitting there, I might have told it all and changed the course of the rest of our lives, yet it was then that Dory Fitzgerald walked hurriedly along the fence and Charles looked out at him and said, "G'day, Dory, where are you off to?"

"Haven't you heard, now? The Mueller boy, Jeremy, has gotten himself lost from his buddies in the surf yonder, and a search party is bein' organized."

"Oh, God! I'm right behind you. I'll go and get Rubin Garret."

"Shall I go down too?" I asked.

"No, you'll only be in the way." He hurried down the porch steps and across the yard, jumped the fence, and took the Garret front steps three at a time. He knocked and waited, knocked again and waited, and I glanced up at the shutters to see if they were closed. They were open, however.

People from up and down the block had now begun to appear, the men hurrying down Avenue L toward the beach. There was much excited chatter going on and children pleading with their mothers to be allowed to go along with older brothers and fathers on the search.

Presently Janet came walking around from the far side of her yard. She was wearing a faded calico dress, an old floppy sun hat, and work gloves, and held a bunch of flowers in one hand and a pair of shears in the other. "Here I am, Charles. What's all the commotion?"

"One of the neighbor boys is lost in the sea. Is Rubin home? I want him to go down to the beach with us."

"Oh no! Charles, he isn't here right now. He's gone to visit Mrs. Sampler in the hospital. You go and I'll send him along as soon as he gets here."

He nodded and hurried off, an almost comical figure as

he disappeared down the block in his baggy work pants and faded shirt, with blotches of green paint dancing on the background of his old blue trousers.

Janet stood looking after him for a moment, then put the shears and the flowers down on the ground and walked over to the fence. "How awful. Who was it?"

"Jeremy Mueller."

"Oh yes, that nice young man studying medicine with Doc Monroe. How horrible."

"I wanted to go down but Charles said no. Want to join me in some lemonade?"

"I guess so. I suppose all we can do at this point is wait. Rubin ought to be back pretty soon. He was going to work at home today."

A fly had discovered the uneaten food on the table and was buzzing purposefully around it like a vulture who's discovered a dead body in the lonely desert. I took the tray away and went into the house to pour some lemonade for the two of us. When I got back on the porch she was seated, and had taken her hat and gloves off and put them next to her chair. There were threads of wet hair around her face and a spot of dirt on her nose, and she was wiping her forehead with a lace handkerchief. "Even cutting flowers and doing a little weeding in the garden is exhausting in this weather," she said. "I wish I could have as much success with my garden as you do with yours."

"If this kind of summer means a bad storm in the fall, as it did last year, I'm afraid both our efforts at growing things will be thwarted again."

"Oh, how I dread the thought of another one. . . ."

"Really? I didn't think it was so bad."

"You mean all that wind, that driving rain, didn't scare you?"

"Oh, I was a little frightened at the time, but later my fears seemed silly. After all, look how high the houses are built up. We're safe enough."

"Yes . . . yet even on this fine, sunny day, poor Jeremy Mueller's life may be in danger. It seems strangely cruel, doesn't it."

"They might find him safe yet," I told her, thinking that if she'd ever lost a child of her own, she wouldn't be so quick to give up hope.

She looked out across the porch toward the beach, as though she could conjure up a vision of what was going on

down there. "Yes," she said with brightness. "Maybe
they've found him, revived him . . . oh, I do hope so.
Perhaps he'll appear somewhere on the beach even, wondering at all the fuss." Then she looked back round at me
and said: "You know, Claire, I have a strong suspicion
they won't find him alive."

I opened my mouth to reply but she interrupted, a
shadow creeping across her face. "I wonder if he ever
thought what it would be like to grow up, marry, have children . . . to get old . . . oh, Claire, do you know that
when I think about getting old and watching Rubin grow
old I can't get a picture of it? It's like a fading face, do you
know what I mean? Like something that isn't going to happen."

I could have told her something about fading faces, but
instead leaned across the table and said softly, "Janet,
sometimes you really worry me . . . how maudlin you
get!"

"Oh, you sound like Rubin," she said, and shifted in her
chair. "Why is it so gruesome to . . . to believe you won't
live a long life? Doesn't the Church preach that life after
death is so much better? Well, doesn't it?"

Just then Rubin appeared at the edge of the yard, hurrying toward us. "Good day, ladies. I hear the Mueller boy is
missing."

Janet rushed down the stairs and into his arms. She
spoke to him rapidly and pointed toward the beach. He
gave her his coat and hat, and took off running down Avenue L.

She walked back up to the porch, and gathered her
things. "Think I'll be going home now," she said. "Thanks
for the lemonade."

I watched her svelte movements as she walked back
home, a queer sense of doom overtaking me. I leaned over
the verandah railing and looked around. No one was to be
seen except Tom Driscoll, the undertaker, who'd walked
out under the cupola at the edge of his verandah and
peered out around the street. Seeing me, he lowered his
eyes and walked back into his house.

Much later on that Monday, when evening had fallen
and the houses on the street glowed with light, the search
party returned. I was sitting on the verandah when I heard
them coming up the street, a slow shuffling of feet without

spirit which told me even before they came within sight that Jeremy Mueller was doomed.

Charles dropped off from the group at our gate and came into the yard. "No luck then?" I asked him.

"None." He walked up the stairs and sat down on the edge of the porch, resting his head on his knees. "Chances are slim by now, and it's too dark to look further."

"Where's Rubin?"

"He stayed down there with the Muellers. They won't leave, they say, until he is found . . . Agatha seems to be in a state of shock."

"You look done in. Come on and have a bath and some supper."

"I'm not hungry. I just wish something else could be done to find the boy. Imagine what it would be like never to find him, never to know, to be able to say, 'Well, he is gone. He drowned in the sea, and we found him and buried him in the earth. We know, because we saw him.' "

"Charles, you're talking nonsense. Come on."

He didn't seem to hear me, just kept sitting there. I sat down beside him. "Was he swimming with a big group of boys? Where were they?"

"Not far from the end of L, really. There were three of them, and it seems the other boys just looked around and he was gone. We went as far down as the end of the island, where the old brush jetties used to be, in case he was sucked under down there. But we found nothing. Likely he went into a sucker hole."

"What's that?"

"Something like a whirlpool, a hole anywhere from, say, ten to twenty feet deep—with an undertow that'll suck you down before you know what hit you. The water in that area where they were swimming isn't more than five feet deep at most. They weren't very far out."

"Do you think they'll ever find him?"

"Tide changes, he ought to turn up. Tomorrow, day after. . . ."

On Wednesday the Gulf offered up the body of Jeremy Mueller and laid it gently on the shore, within a few yards of the point where he and his friends had waded carefree into the water on Monday for a swim. Doc Monroe took his flatbed wagon down and brought the body back up Avenue L.

Like the other neighbors, we watched from the porch as the wagon made its way up the street, Jeb Mueller seated beside the doctor and Agatha in the back of the wagon, above her son's head. The body was covered with a faded bedspread. This we could not see until the wagon was past, and my eyes traveled up from it to the face of Agatha. There was neither pain nor sorrow in the face; only utter disbelief.

Tom Driscoll offered his services as undertaker, and the funeral ceremony was held in the Muellers' living room on a fine, sunny afternoon. A curious custom, that: the people most awfully affected by the death of a loved one are expected to open their home to stage the most grotesque part of the letting go.

Having no particular religious affiliation, the Muellers asked Rubin to officiate. He'd been with Jeb and Agatha almost constantly since their son had been swallowed up by the Gulf, and had opened his wide arms and offered his prayers for them.

Charles attended the funeral ceremony and followed the throng of people out to the City Cemetery. It seemed the Muellers had quite a number of friends from around the neighborhood, and the Ludtke Iron Foundry, where Jeb worked, closed for a half day so that his friends could be present.

My fear of funerals had long been professed, so there was no explaining necessary when I stayed home and cooked a cake and a pot of chicken and dumplings that afternoon. Later in the evening, Charles helped me carry the food down to the Muellers', six houses away, and everyone but a handful of relatives was gone by then. An ancient woman, wizened and snowy-haired, sat in a corner of the living room in a rocking chair, her knobby hands closed around a dog-eared Bible. The other two Mueller children, both young girls, sat together at the foot of the stairs, quietly playing jackstones.

Jeb and Agatha sat huddled together on the sofa, and we first took our offering of food to the kitchen, placing it among the other foods hardly touched, then went to pay our respects to them.

Agatha took my hand and searched my face with her swollen eyes, then said, "You didn't come to services. Tom had him fixed so pretty, right over there in front of the window."

"I, too, have lost a son."

She nodded in apparent understanding, then added, "He was goin' to be a doctor, you know."

"Won't you sit down, stay for a spell?" said Jeb.

"No, we'd best be getting home," said Charles.

"I can't thank you enough, for what you did. Agatha and me, we didn't know what fine neighbors we had till this thing happened. . . ."

" 'Twas an awful high price to pay," said Agatha, and buried her head on his chest.

He put one long arm around her shoulders and said, "Oh, Mama, don't go to cryin' again," but the tears were welled up in his own eyes, too, and I thought just then of the hopeless tears spent by Charles when the son he thought of as his own had been taken away from him.

Walking home we both stared silently ahead. Thankfully, Charles did not mention the parallel of the two tragedies, ours and the Muellers', as I feared he might. In the early morning of the following day, he donned his old clothes again and went back to painting. Except for the hollow feeling in my stomach and the general quiet around the street, you might have thought nothing had happened to interrupt the hazy peacefulness of the summer routine.

Chapter 11

Rubin Garret had a way of drawing people to his parish. Of a Sunday morning, when the people filed from the dark church into the sunshine, he would remember to ask after Mrs. McIntyre's aching bones, to question John Treadway about his brother's health, to inquire of Maude Patterson whether her boy Timothy's broken leg was healing properly, and to remember a host of other personal things about his parishioners that showed he cared. I would often think to myself as I watched him that he went about his duties with double the normal amount of zeal, to make up for Janet's lack of participation in the activities of the church.

By early 1879, when he'd been at St. Christopher's two years, the number of families listed as members had increased from fifty to close to one hundred and fifty, and plans were in the making for a new church school building on the far end of the three-lot tract making up the church property.

The white stone church itself was situated at the other end of the tract, and a cloistered walkway led from out its side across the grounds to a small building which had served since the beginning of the church as office and church school. Parish meetings, receptions, and other activities were held in a converted rent house on property adjacent.

The new church school building, then, would replace the rent house as parish hall, the small office and Sunday school building presently standing, and thereby encompass all church activities other than services under one ample and handsome roof. Charles and Rubin were discussing this pleasant fact one Sunday while sitting around our dinner table, and I came upon an idea which was not intended to put me in a position closer to Rubin, at least not consciously, although it was true that the more time passed, the more we were thrown together by circumstances purely beyond our control, the more I watched his expressions of exasperation from time to time when Janet failed him by not being up to attending some church function or another, the harder it was for me to look into his eyes without believing there was a glimmer of wistfulness there. And Charles, despite all of Pete Marlowe's overtures and my subtle persuasive remarks designed to make him realize his career would no doubt blossom in partnership with Pete's firm, still showed no signs of budging from the little stuffy office he'd occupied since we came to Galveston, and moving us into a new social circle which would have helped me keep my mind off Rubin.

"It's a pity to build a new structure on the grounds of St. Christopher's," I said.

Everyone looked across at me.

"I only mean the grounds are so utterly bleak, both summer and winter, why bother trying to improve the looks of the property with a new building? The building may be functional, but believe me, the appearance will not be enhanced to passersby and potential members of the parish."

"You're right," said Janet. "Just a long expanse of grass that has never grown properly and that one huge, ugly palm right in the center of the yard. And those poor, forlorn-looking shrubberies along the cloisters—what are they called?"

"Croton, and they'd look all right if they were taken care of by someone who knew what they were about."

"Claire's an expert on flowers. We would do well to put her in charge of improving the grounds," Janet said then, as though she knew of my design.

"Wait a minute," said Rubin. "What about Peabody, the sexton? It's his job to look after the grounds. I wouldn't want to hurt his feelings by——"

"Oh, Rubin, you needn't do that at all. You could form a committee—with Claire at the head—and Mr. Peabody could work right along with the group."

"You know, that's a splendid idea. You could begin next spring."

"But what about the construction going on?" Charles asked. "Won't it be a pretty big mess around there for several months?"

"We could leave the part at the far end till last, concentrate on the other end and the cloisters in the beginning," I said. "I've envisioned many different patterns, as a matter of fact, and of course it would have to be a perpetual thing, go on from year to year."

"Why, my dear, you sound as though you've been planning a gardening committee for sometime," said Charles.

"Not at all. However, you will admit I have a talent for organizing things and making them grow. One could hardly glance at the church property without noticing it's crying out for attention."

"You're so right," said Janet. "It would make a good drawing card for the church. You know, Trinity is rather limited as to how it can be improved on, being right in the middle of town."

"You ladies speak of God's house as though it were a dry goods store," said Rubin, and Charles began to laugh.

"This is serious, and I'll thank you not to laugh, Charles," I said. "Rubin is misinterpreting our idea, that's all. There are always going to be churches and there are always going to be people to go to them, so what's wrong with a little worry over catching people's eye? If you don't get the people into the church, you'll hardly have an opportunity of preaching God's word to them. Isn't that so, Rubin?"

"Of course, Claire, and don't believe for a moment I take your concern lightly. It's just that I'd never really thought of the big old palm as being ugly, and never thought how much nicer the property might look with some special talent used on it. I can see we've been wasting you."

"You'll never know how much."

"Very good, then. Tell you what. I'll approach the vestry about it at the next meeting. If they're attuned to the idea, I'll mention it from the pulpit and ask for volunteers to help you."

The vestry officially named my committee the St. Christopher's Garden Guild (although most often it was referred to as "the garden committee," and as time went on and my name remained synonymous with its accomplishments, it would be called simply, "Claire's garden"), and gave the full responsibility for planning and carrying out the project to me. The vestry allocated thirty-five dollars for expenses, and suggested people might donate cuttings and shrubs, and Rubin promised to bring up the proposition from the pulpit one Sunday shortly after the new year began. "I want you to plan it out," he told me privately. "If I just suggest to the congregation we need flowers and shrubs, no telling what they'll come up with, and we could hardly refuse someone like Mrs. Travesty, for instance, if she were to offer a bunch of things totally out of line with what you're trying to accomplish. You know how she is. She'd probably leave the church and never come back again. And others might be hurt if they donated plants and never found them blooming in the garden.

"So give me a list of what you want, and the thirty-five dollars can go for the things you aren't able to get donated."

"A birdbath."

"How's that?"

"For the courtyard, behind the cloisters. I've already picked it out. It's going to have sweet peas around it—I'll donate them myself if need be—and bougainvillaea climbing up the walls either side."

"Sounds good."

"Oh, Rubin, you have no idea how much it means to me for you to be proud of it. I'm going to work very hard."

"What we want of course is for all the congregation to be pleased," he said, and shifted his eyes from mine.

"Of course."

And so they were, from the start. Rubin can be very winning, and after the service, when he'd mentioned the list of things needed and asked for volunteer workers, a total of fifteen women enthusiastically offered help. Some weeks later with a crew made up of five of them a day, and the helping hand of Mr. Peabody, I started my garden to grow, and the course of all our lives to change.

Chapter 12

Janet announced, shortly after digging began, that she was bound for a trip home to Virginia. "I want to see my parents," she told us one night. "They're getting old, and somehow I've had the feeling lately I ought to pay them a visit."

"When are you planning to leave?" I asked.

"Early in April. I'll stay a week or two, no more."

"Well then, Rubin, you must count on having your evening meals with us. We'll try to fill in for Janet so she won't worry about your growing thin and unhealthy while she's away."

"I do appreciate that," he said, and laughed. "I can't impose myself on you every night, however."

"Very well then, we'll leave it an open invitation," Charles said. "We always have plenty, so come over any night you've got nothing else planned."

"Or any day," I said. "For lunch."

"I'd better not stay away too long," said Janet, raising an eyebrow. "You might spoil my husband so he won't want to have me for a wife anymore."

It surely would not take much doing, I thought.

There came a sudden rain shower one day shortly after.

I had dismissed the other ladies working in the garden, and stayed long after to finish one plot in the far left corner of the courtyard. There were rocks in the soil, and pieces of wood and chunks of cement which had been covered over and left when the church building was put up.

Rubin was working at his desk, which had been moved temporarily into the rent house when his little office building was razed to make room for the new structure. I hadn't known he was still around, but apparently he'd seen me from the window, for when the rain began he hurried toward me with a big umbrella and hustled me inside the rent house for the duration of the shower. He put a protective arm around my shoulders and held me surely closer than necessary to shield us both with the umbrella, and the sound of my heart thumping inside my breast was louder in my ears than our steps across the soaking grass.

After we were safe inside, Rubin poured us both cups of coffee, and said, "Lucky for me making good coffee isn't a qualification for entering the priesthood." He handed me mine. I wanted to make some witty reply to his remark, but could think of none.

"What made you become a priest?" I asked instead, for it was a question I had long puzzled over. He sat down behind his desk, lit up his pipe, and looked thoughtful for a moment.

"*Made* me?" he said finally. "Well, if you mean, was I the recipient of a holy visitation, or did a bolt of heavenly lightning strike me in my bed one night, I guess I'd have to say that nothing 'made' me become a priest, that is, nothing so dramatic."

"People sometimes say a life of religion is a 'calling.' Was it so for you?"

"Only in the sense that I'd journeyed so far away from God—as you well know—that when he did get my attention, he got it good and made excellent use of it . . . at least, I hope he feels he did." He was smiling now, looking across indulgently into my face.

"You think it a childish question."

"Certainly not."

"Has Charles told you much about his brother Damon?"

"Not really. Why?"

"Because you remind me—and Charles, too—so much of Damon, and it would have been thoroughly unlike him to have given up his freedom and become harnessed by a life of subjugation."

"My dear Claire, we are all subjugate to the Lord. We are only truly free when we accept him as our savior."

"Yes, yes, I know. But something drastic must have happened to change you from being Damon's kind of man—a few saloon brawls and a night or two in jail wouldn't have been enough."

"I don't know that I was really as like him as you think. Perhaps I was worse—or more liberal, let us say—than Damon, so once I finally saw the error of my ways it was a rather startling realization."

"You would have liked Damon. Sometimes I can scarcely believe that, some time or other, you two didn't meet, exchange stories, drink together. . . ."

"I did plenty of that, let me assure you. But as far as I know I never met up with Charles's brother. You seem to have known him well."

"Briefly."

"And thought well of him."

"Yes."

"How lucky a man Charles is, then."

"What do you mean?"

"To have won your affections over his brother."

I looked away, toward the window where he had doubtless watched me digging in the ground only minutes earlier. "You think then, that I am something of a prize?"

"I certainly do. You're very lovely, accomplished, surely an asset to any man."

"You flatter me?"

"Not at all. I speak the truth, as I am bound to do. Sometimes I almost wish—" he began, but stopped. From the corner of his eye he could see what I now saw from the window. Charles had drawn up in the rig; the rain splintered off its brougham top.

Rubin looked back at me, then crossed to the window and waved a hand. "It's Charles," he said softly, "come to our rescue."

Now, Janet Garret wasn't a bad hand with flowers, though she did tire easily while working out in the hot sun. She went down to the church with me once or twice right at first, but we'd hardly begun work on the garden when time for her trip approached. On the day before her train left, in fact, she took time out from packing to bring sandwiches and iced tea for all of us at noon. It was a kind gesture, but so like her to do it at a bad time, and I surmised when I saw her coming with basket and jug that I'd have to spend my evening helping her finish packing so she would be ready for the morning train. It was, of course, important she did not fail to make the train. Could I be blamed for wanting to see how things would develop, knowing how much Rubin had left unsaid that rainy day in the church office, when Charles had interrupted us? Since then I had felt myself pulled along as though by a forceful current, toward what end I'd scarcely the nerve to imagine.

"By the way, you have a letter at our house . . . meant to bring it but left it on the table by the front door," she told me as we unloaded the picnic basket. "It came today and got stuck in our box instead of yours."

"Did you notice who it was from?"

"Someone in Grady, I think. The handwriting was difficult to read, and of course as soon as I realized it wasn't for Rubin or me, I didn't take further notice."

"Must be Cousin Betsey. It's about time for a letter from her, and with her handwriting it's a thousand wonders the letter made it to Galveston at all, much less to one house down from us on Avenue L."

The church grounds were alight with activity that day, the workmen hauling wood all over the place and hammering nails, and Mr. Peabody helping two of my girls to plant some new shrubbery along the cloisters. I was anxious that Janet's picnic not turn into a long affair, for there was much work still to do, so I hurried everyone through lunch, the letter skipping my mind until that evening at home.

I'd guessed correctly: it was from Betsey. "Dear Claire," it began, "This letter will be short because we've been so busy at the store, I don't really have time to write. But I've been so concerned about my poor daughter and I want you to help me out if you can.

"Remember the boy I told you of, the one Ruth was so fond of last summer? Well, when he went off to school in the fall, he lost interest in her. She was so looking forward to his visit this spring, for at Christmastime you'd have thought all was the same as usual between them and I expected him to ask for her hand in marriage. But he wrote a few days ago that he's to marry someone else. Just like that!

"Anyway, Ruth, poor dear, is just at the depths. She would be furious if she knew I were writing to you, but could you and Charles just happen to invite her down for a spell this summer? By that time I can find someone to help out in the store in her absence, and knowing the trip is coming up might help take her mind off *him*. I know there are bound to be more eligible young men her age down there than there are here . . ."

It occurred to me as I read Betsey's letter that Ruth's presence might be a hindrance for she might guess about my designs on Rubin, yet I couldn't refuse Betsey anything, no matter what she asked. I gave it a good deal of thought that evening before Charles came home, and by the time I showed the letter to him I'd decided that as I was willing to take the chance of Charles or Janet finding out my feelings for Rubin when they were both ever present, surely I could afford the more remote chance of being found out by Ruth. Besides, I wanted to see her, if for no other reason than that she came from Betsey and was therefore special to me, and even if she did accept my invitation to come, she wouldn't arrive for at least a couple of months. Much could happen in two or three months' time.

Charles was at first indifferent about the idea of Ruth's visit, because he couldn't think of any eligible young men that we knew.

"Well, there's the young people's group at church," I said. "They do things in the summer—go on picnics and hayrides, and whatever. Then Teddy Marlowe—he seemed a nice young man when we met him New Year's Day. Won't he be here for a while this summer?"

"I suppose he will. And Driscoll down the street has a young son, too, come to think of it. Nice boy . . . works for a dry goods store downtown."

"Ruth won't be interested in him, when she learns what his father does."

"Oh, silly. Everyone doesn't scorn undertakers the way you do. Driscoll doesn't go round envisioning his neighbors dressed out in shrouds, and he assures me he washes his hands of the embalming fluid at least once a week."

"Oh, stop it!"

"Seriously now, I don't think Josh Driscoll is planning to follow in his father's footsteps. Anyway, he might not be interested in Ruth either. She might be fat and ugly for all we know. It's going on three years since we saw her last. Kids change a lot in three years."

"I never thought of that. The poor little thing was at the gawky stage, wasn't she—all arms and legs—but she'd be eighteen by now, a young woman. I'd be willing to bet she's a pretty little thing. We already know she did have at least one ardent suitor for a while."

The third day of April was dark and gloomy, stalked by heavy showers that began before Janet's train departed at eight o'clock. I rose early to prepare a box lunch for her to take along—food at train stops is something almost ungodly, and one is generally given no longer than twenty minutes to consume whatever part of it might chance to be edible.

Rubin took Janet alone to the train, and I feared she'd miss it after all, because they were no more than halfway down the block when I saw Rubin's horse double back, and bring the rig up to the front of their house again. She'd forgotten something she had promised to carry to her mother. I worried until I was certain enough time had lapsed for her to have been back home if she missed her connection, then I went to work cleaning house and cooking all of Rubin's favorite things. He'd promised to have dinner with us that evening.

By six-thirty I had the table set and had put on fresh clothes and combed my hair, and noticed the rain had finally ended and the sky was beginning to clear. It was Charles I expected to see when I looked out the front window then, for he was half an hour late getting home. Yet it was Rubin coming down the block and up the walk, and for a moment a fairy tale flashed through my mind: he was coming not just for dinner, but coming home to see me and would stay not for an hour or two, but for the whole night through.

I stepped out on the porch to greet him, and the cool air gave me a funny, light-headed feeling after the stuffiness of the house. "Come in, Charles isn't home yet. You can keep me company while I finish dinner."

He nodded, followed me in and through the hall to the kitchen. He'd probably followed in my footsteps hundreds of times since we had lived next door to each other, yet today I felt as though he must be gazing at my movements and was tempted to look behind.

He sat down in a kitchen chair. "I smell cherry cobbler," he said. "You know, I just can't countenance cherry cobbler."

I turned around and stared at him in astonishment, not catching the most obvious of jokes. Then I saw his smile, and realized how ridiculous I must have looked. "I know it, that's why you force down three platefuls whenever I make it. It's a little warm in here, but I've coffee made if you care for some."

"Sounds good," he said, and I turned back to the stove and lifted the lid on the pot. It was a silly thing to do. I knew the coffee was ready. I went to the cupboard and pulled down two cups and saucers, wondering whether he really was following me with his eyes or if I only imagined it. "Won't be a moment," I said, and wondered why I had said it for it was obviously true.

When I placed a cup of coffee in front of him and one across the table for me, the cups clattered just enough to give my nervousness away. "I've—I've hurried too much today. It's gotten me nervous."

"Well, sit down, for goodness sake. You look a little flush." He crossed one black-trousered leg over the other, drummed his fingers on the table. It was surely the quietest evening I have ever known . . . no sounds coming from outside, no children calling to each other, no dogs barking, no mothers scolding. We opened our mouths to speak at the same time. "You first," he said.

"I was just going to say we're doing fine on the garden."

"Ah, yes. And what are all those tubs about? I almost walked into one under the cloisters today."

"Oh, I completely forgot. Those are oleander cuttings. They have to root in tubs of water for ten days, you see, before being put into sand . . . we can move them out of the way if they're a bother."

"No, no. Now I know why they're there I'll be more careful where I step. What's that on your hand?"

I picked it up and looked at it. "Oh, just a hazard of gardening I guess. Must have cut it." I put the hand down again on the table, as though it were something unconnected to me, and he stretched his own hand across and covered it.

"You've no idea how much we appreciate your efforts," he said, and took his hand away.

"If it gives you pleasure, that means a lot to me. Rubin?"

"Yes."

"Remember that day, in the church office when we talked, then Charles—"

"Yes, yes."

"What were you going to say to me, Rubin? Tell me now."

He looked away, but I could see enough of his face to recognize his expression of resignation, and it made me catch my breath, wondering if I'd spoken too soon, or if I was wrong altogether and had spoken out of turn completely, and I wished profoundly I could recall the words. I opened my mouth to tell him "never mind," but it was too late.

He rose from the table and walked across to the kitchen counter, and stood there against it, his arms outspread and resting against its edge. "It's best, I think, that we get this out in the open now, Claire, before it goes any further and someone is hurt. I was about to tell you—that day—sometimes I wished I'd have met you first, before Janet."

My heart danced at the sound of the words. I blushed and looked down at the table, like a schoolgirl who's just been kissed by her first beau.

"I admire everything you are—your strength, your ability to organize things. How many times I've wished to call on you to stand beside me, be my hostess at church functions when Janet could not or would not. As much as I love her, as much as I am saddened by her confusion and her inability to handle routine matters, I have found since we came to Galveston that the patience I expected of myself on her behalf is just not there.

"And I think perhaps it is because I see you so much and I'm too human not to compare your gifts with her inabilities, and it makes it so hard to keep things in perspective and to remember my obligations.

"I—it's hard sometimes, Claire—people at the church don't really understand about Janet and I feel as though I'm walking a tightrope sometimes, trying to please my parishioners, to make excuses for her, and then I grow angry inside and, afterward, I go home to her and look at her and my guilt at having betrayed her in my thoughts makes me almost sick . . . can you understand?"

"Yes, I think so."

"And that isn't all."

"Yes?"

"Claire, you must have guessed, must have sensed, that I've found you attractive in other ways, too."

"Oh, Rubin—" I began, and looked at him. If I had taken a breath, I would have cried.

"No," he said, raising one of his hands. "No, don't. Let me finish. Claire, Charles is one of the finest men I've ever known, finer than me, believe that, and I regard him as the best friend I have ever had. Do you see where all this leaves me?"

I nodded because I couldn't speak.

"It means that nothing can come from this and if it isn't stopped I shall have to go away, find another position in another town, perhaps it's what I ought to do right now."

"No, Rubin, no, please."

He came across and put a hand on my cheek. "You see, nothing has happened and nothing must. You do see, don't you?"

"Yes, yes."

"And I do love my wife, love her with all my heart as you must love Charles."

I said nothing; I couldn't lie to Rubin Garret.

"And someday she will be strong and over her . . . problems. You see, just getting this off my chest has brought back some of my old optimism. It will be so much better for me and for you that we were wise enough to stop something that could only bring hate and bitterness in the end.

"And now you know the answer to a question you put to me that day in the office. Perhaps some priests do have a calling, and maybe that's why I have so many trials, for I don't have that special 'calling.' You see, I'm only a man, and at times not a very admirable one."

"And I'm only a woman, Rubin," I said. "And I want you and have felt all the things you've felt, but if that's the way it must be—the way you say—then it shall be so, and I won't interfere."

He stood straight and sighed, then smiled down at me with tenderness in his eyes and relief flooding his face.

"And we'll get over this," he added, "and turn out stronger and better human beings for overcoming temptation."

That night at dinner Rubin's mood was more animated than I had ever seen it, and he and Charles ate a whole cherry cobbler between them, and later had several glasses of Charles's favorite madeira, while I sat by, scarcely able to believe what had taken place between us and wondering whether I would be able to do as Rubin said we must. Yet I was determined to try, if only for his sake, because I knew that I loved him then in a way I had not loved even Damon Becker. His truth and honesty in front of me had won me for good and all.

Chapter 13

I was not certain, even in those days, that there would not be a time for Rubin and me, that some turn of events would not eventually occur, a sort of reward for our good behavior, our putting others before ourselves, and this thought helped me through the weeks following until, long after, my feelings for him mellowed, even withered a bit for lack of nourishment on his part, the memory of his words ennobled by his strictness in keeping to his bargain.

There was, from the first, my fierce determination to keep his image of me on the high plane where he'd kept it before the words passed between us, and I managed this by keeping frantically busy: that was the most effective way I knew of dealing with my own passions, for I am not one by nature to suppress true feelings, though much of my life up to that time had been thus spent.

When planting was done with in late April, I gave high tea for the ladies on the gardening committee, and made it a point to tell Rubin I was in hopes of Janet returning to Galveston in time to attend. Of course she failed to make it back in time, for both the tea and for the April art show, which she had resolved again to enter after having backed out the year before. Her mother took ill during her stay so she delayed coming home until the second week of June.

In the interim we invited Rubin three times to take meals with us, but he came only once, and when he did I cooked Charles's favorite dishes rather than his, and I noticed he took care not to look directly into my eyes whenever we exchanged conversation across the table.

In May I attended two Chamber of Commerce dinner meetings with Charles. He'd been on the Chamber since January, but until mid-April had taken no great part in its activities. Then he was appointed to the Committee for Industrial Expansion, and right away was asked by the committee chairman to prepare a short speech upon the importance of diversifying the manufacturing industries in the city.

I sat next to Faye Marlowe during the speech, and was impressed with his ability to present it. Afterward the members, themselves impressed, stood and gave Charles an ovation and Andrew Swearingen, the president, said, "Ladies and gentlemen, I doubt if every one of you have met Charles Becker's charming wife, Claire. Will she please stand so that we might all know her tonight?"

Pete Marlowe hastened to pull out my chair and whispered, "Smile purty, now," and I rose to be applauded, knowing that, with or without Charles's joining Pete's firm, we were becoming "known" as a couple around Galveston.

Early in the same month, Ruth wrote she would arrive the second day of June, and after reading the letter I walked into the despised front bedroom, the one with the dais, and considered ways of making it more attractive for a young woman. I bought a milk glass hurricane lamp with hand-painted roses on it, a new pink chintz bedspread, and a small hooked rug. I made a new cushion for the rocking chair and polished the brass headboard on the bed, and was thankful when all was done, because the room now had a welcome look.

Is it not true that each of us should have one person in the world on whom we may lavish all our love, who will ever be deserving of our devotion and never disappoint us or become disloyal, no matter what? For me, it is Cousin Ruth, almost from the day of her arrival as special as my own child in terms of affection.

She was, I believe, a surprise for all of us.

Though she stepped from the train an unpolished pearl—plainly clad in schoolgirl clothes and wide-brimmed hat, ribbon trailing behind—she had a quality of freshness, a wide-eyed enthusiasm for everything around her that would have endeared her to anyone, and seemed especially appealing to Charles.

As to beauty, she held possibilities I knew I could bring to life throughout the summer. Her light blond hair was long and straight, with a fringe of straight bangs across her forehead. Her cheeks were high, her nose small and upturned, her large eyes brown and coy.

Even as she assailed Charles with a round of questions during the ride home from the train station, I thought of the ways her good features might be enhanced, so that I could send her home to Betsey at summer's end as an accomplished young lady.

"What are those ships over there carrying? Where do they come from? Where is your office, Cousin Charles?

What's that big, tall building over there? What a lovely house—who lives in it? That's the tallest tree I've ever seen—some sort of palm, isn't it? Are the oleanders really poisonous? I've read they are. Where is the beach from here? I just adore the water. The only place for swimming at home is the old pond south of town . . . but of course you knew that, didn't you? Can we go to the beach?"

Ruth talked fast and staccato, but Charles seemed unruffled by her manner. He answered each question patiently, though she stayed one or two ahead of him all the time. "You bet we'll go to the beach," he said, "and to Woollam's Lake for picnics. And we'll have to take you to the Garten Verein, won't we, Claire? I'm sure Pete can get us in there. Maybe we'll even take out a membership of our own. . . ."

Of course we had to explain about the Garten Verein, then about Pete, and this proved convenient because we soon passed in front of his house. "Oh, I don't think there's anything as elaborate as that in Grady," she said. "It's like something out of a picture book—all the houses are."

"Pete's a close friend of ours," Charles told her. "He has a fine boy who wants to meet you."

"Oh? Is he very handsome?"

"I don't know. Claire, is Teddy handsome?"

"My goodness, I never gave it much thought. No, I don't think you could consider Teddy handsome, but he is at least nice-looking, and about your age."

"Oh."

"Don't you like young men your age?"

"They're all right, though I kind of prefer men a little older. Maybe it's peculiar to Grady, but most of the young men I meet seem so childish. Of course if I'd gone to the public school instead of the Pedagoguery, I'd have had more of a chance to meet boys. But Mother says the Ped's a better school."

I had had my term in the Pedagoguery at her age. It is a finishing school for young women, and the only one of its kind anywhere in that part of the state. A woman named Helen Tannery from England, who came to Grady with her husband ten years before the war, had started it, and in the beginning people had laughed at her, almost booed her out of town at the foolhardiness of such an idea, for people in Grady don't take kindly to frivolousness. Yet she

stayed—probably out of spite as much as anything—and
the school soon thrived, drawing girls from wealthy families miles away, even across the state line. Of course Ruth
was far from wealthy, and so were Betsey and I when we
attended. It is the room and board which makes the Pedagoguery School expensive. Day students need not have
much money to go there.

"Is Helen Tannery still running it?" I asked her.

"Yes, although she's getting so old she has an assistant
doing most of the work. Did you know her husband died
last year? Um-hum, consumption, I think. Anyway, she has
a hard time keeping good teachers. Nobody wants to come
out to Grady. Everybody just wants to leave, and when I
see Galveston I can understand why you two picked such a
place.

"I've a feeling it is going to be a terrific summer."

"I don't know," said Charles, teasingly. "The mosquitoes
are pretty bad in the summertime, and I have to keep a
rowboat and oars at the house because when it rains hard I
have to take a boat to work. Horse doesn't know how to
swim."

She stared at him for a moment, stunned at this new
information. Then, realizing she was being fooled, burst
into gales of laughter. Ruth's laughter is pleasant: like the
sound of a fingertip as it is pulled across the strings of a
well-tuned harp.

"By the way, have you got a piano?" she asked.

"No," said Charles, "but Janet and Rubin Garret—our
neighbors—have one that I'm sure they'd let you play if
you want. Janet's out of town now, but as soon as she gets
back you might ask her. She's a very talented woman, you
know, paints and writes poetry . . ."

"Does she play piano?"

"Not much, I don't think. But she'll probably be thrilled
to learn that you play. Did you bring music?"

"Yes, unfortunately I haven't the ear for playing without
it. But I brought only a few pieces. I was afraid of filling
too much baggage, and one whole grip is full of presents
Mother sent for the two of you."

In the evening I helped Ruth unpack the sparse amount
of clothing she'd brought along. The clothes simply would
not do for meeting the Marlowes and attending the Garten

Verein functions. "Tell you what," I suggested, "tomorrow we'll go shopping. There's a great place downtown called the Emporium, where I buy fabric. Then there is Madame LaRoche, whom you must meet—a dressmaker. We'll pick out some material and have some outfits made for you by her—she is the best in Galveston."

"Oh, I hadn't thought much about clothes," she said, sitting down on the floor. "In Grady there isn't much emphasis on that kind of thing, though we did study fashion a little at the Ped. But I didn't bring a lot of money. Is Madame very expensive?"

"Don't worry. I want to do something for you after your mother sent all these presents to us. I wish she hadn't sent all these things . . . makes me feel beholden."

"Not really. You did her quite a favor, inviting me. Oh—don't look like that. She never fooled me for a moment. I know she asked you to do it."

"Well, she loves you, that's all, and anyway, I'm so glad she did. We've gotten so involved in things down here . . . I might never have thought, never have known what I missed by not having you. And it'll be good for you to get away after—"

"After being jilted," she said, and leaned against the bureau, picking up an embroidered handkerchief and toying with its design. "Want to know what got me the most about him? I trusted him. I really trusted him. That's hard to do, when your own father deserted you so long ago you can't remember what he looked like.

"Are all men so untrustworthy? No, of course they aren't . . . look at Cousin Charles. He must be very fine. You're lucky, Claire."

"I am, in a way, but Charles isn't the only trustworthy man around. Someday you'll find one. Take my advice, dear: never marry for anything except love. You'll save yourself a great deal of heartache in the long run."

She looked at me for a long time then, probably wondering where in my own experience I had learned such information, and, afraid I would give something away in my face, I prodded her again about her own lost lover.

"Cornel Talbeaux is his name—French heritage. He's been all over the world."

"What was he doing in Grady?"

"His father bought six hundred acres outside of town for

ranching and horse breeding. We—Cornel and I—met one
day when he came into the store for supplies.

"I should have known . . . in Grady I was perhaps
among the best of the lot of girls, as far as looks anyway,
although that's not saying much, and I'm terribly bow-
legged—of course he had no way of knowing that!—but I
wouldn't kid myself about the choice he'd have had once
he went away to school."

"How old is he?"

"In his late twenties. He didn't start college until they
came over here from France. He's going to be a surgeon.
You ought to see his hands: beautiful, almost delicate. And
very steady . . ." She held her own small hands out in
front of her and studied them.

"You're young yet. Don't think you have to find someone else right away. People make mistakes when they
marry too young."

"I know. Look at Mother. Lately I've decided maybe I'm
better off Cornel dropped me when he did. I mean, suppose
after we were married he found someone else and left me?
That would have been far more terrible, I know."

I stood up. "Right you are. Now, while I can't promise
you a string of beaux on Galveston Island, I can at least try
to show you a good time. Let's find Charles and go sit out
on the verandah. I'll make something cold to drink."

"Let me help you," she said. "After that marvelous dinner, and I didn't turn a hand. At home I do most of the
cooking, and I must say I could use a few lessons from
you."

"No, you hunt up Charles—I expect you'll have to pry
him from his study—and go on out. I'll expect you to help
me some while you're here, but tonight is your first with
us, after all. And of course I'll be glad to give you some
pointers on cooking. Until we got rid of Helga, I didn't
know how myself. But I learned quickly."

"Oh, Claire, you have no idea how glad I am I came . . .
I did need to get away, and after just being here today I
can tell I'll find a cure for everything."

"It's our pleasure having you. It's good for me, too, having you just now."

"I'm so glad. I'll get Charles. See you outside."

"A person could get killed on these things," she said,

standing at the edge of the porch and looking down the stairs. "How treacherous they look. . . ."

"You get accustomed to them after a while," said Charles.

"I suppose so," she said doubtfully, and sat down.

It was then, I believe, that Rubin stopped by briefly to welcome Ruth, and to say Janet would return within a couple of weeks. He stayed but a moment, pleading he was late getting started on next Sunday's sermon, and when he was out of sight Ruth asked, "What color is his hair?"

"Light, blondish," I told her.

"That's funny. In the moonlight it looks silver."

"Hardly," said Charles. "Rubin and Janet are younger than Claire and I . . . speaking of silver, I notice I'm getting a few strands of it in my hair, right above the temples. Have you noticed that, Claire? Guess it comes inevitably when a man gets close to forty."

"We're not over the hill yet," I said. "Rubin's but a year younger than I am, you know."

There was a shuffle down the block then, and presently young Josh Driscoll appeared at the edge of the fence and walked to the gate. "Evenin', Mr. and Mrs. Becker," he said, tipping his straw hat. Seeing him there, tall and impeccable, yet pathetically plain-looking, I was sorry we'd made a point of telling him Ruth was coming. She surely wouldn't be interested in him.

"Come on up and meet Ruth Miller, Josh," said Charles. "This is Claire's cousin from Grady I've been telling you about."

The boy was clearly demoralized in Ruth's presence. She must have made a winning picture, sitting there crosswise, her legs stretched out in front of her and her well-developed bosom outlined against the moonlight.

He removed his hat again and held it in front of him, and nodded at Ruth as though incapable of speech. Josh Driscoll has round, bulging eyes like his father and freckles from his mother's side. Tonight the eyes were all the more noticeable under the moonlight, and I had this terrible urge to push them back into his head.

Ruth was demure. "I'm very pleased to make your acquaintance, Mr. Driscoll," she said, twirling a few wisps of her long hair around her finger. "Goodness, if Cousin Charles had told me how nice the young men were down here I'd have come long before now. You live in the neighborhood?"

"Yes, no, yes . . . that is, at the end of the block up yonder," he said, cocking his head to the right and twirling his hat around in his hands. "May I call again, sometime?"

"Why, of course, any time, Mr. Driscoll."

"Please call me Josh. That's my name—that is, my name is Josiah but hardly anybody calls me that except my grandmother and Mr. Klein down at the dry goods store. But of course—"

I could bear no more. "Do call again, Josh," I interrupted. "Give our best regards to your mother and father, will you?"

"Yes'm," he said, grateful, I am sure, for the reprieve. He wished us all good evening and backed down the walk. Then, narrowly escaping a collision with the gate, he stopped, put his hat back on, jumped over the gate instead of opening it, looked surprised at himself, and took off at a pace somewhere between a rolling gait and a fast dash.

Ruth was holding her hand across her mouth to keep from laughing aloud, "Poor dear," she said softly. "He must not meet many girls."

"What did you tell him about Ruth to make him act so silly?" I asked Charles.

"Absolutely nothing except she was about eighteen and coming for a visit. Better that way, not to say anything at all." He drew on his pipe. "Besides, I didn't know what to expect myself."

I leaned back again and thought of Janet's pending arrival. How tiresome it would be, having to explain her foolish moods to Ruth, and poor Rubin, having to pretend he was glad she was back, for he would be pretending on that account, I was certain.

Chapter 14

Dark treetops against a lavender sky: sundown at Woollam's Lake. Couples rowing in small boats on the glassy water; others leaning against the big trees, talking, and some hiding in the shadows, spooning.

I sat with feet tucked under me near the place of our

picnic, watching Charles and Ruth among the boaters on
the lake, sorry a little that I dislike the water so. Charles
sat in one end of the small craft, turning the oars; Ruth
languished at the other, her face hidden by the huge sun
hat we'd bought her the previous week, and which she
seemed today reluctant to cast aside.

The first week of her visit had been a good one for us
all. I'd taken her fabric shopping at the Emporium the day
after she arrived, then up the street to Madame LaRoche's
for tailoring. As the shapeless schoolgirl clothes were shed,
Madame had remarked: "Even in my youth my hips were
not so firm and well-shaped. Clothes will hang well on
Miss Miller."

Embarrassed at Madame's candor, Ruth suggested we
hurry because it was almost time for us to meet Charles at
the Imperial Room.

We had been to Goggan's to buy more music, and spent
one rainy afternoon making chocolate pie because Ruth declared mine was the best she'd ever eaten and wanted to
know how I accomplished it. One evening we'd all three
gone to the Tremont Opera House to see Joseph Jefferson
in *Under the Gaslight,* for which Charles had gotten seats
in the parquet circle. The afternoon before the one at
Woollam's Lake we had gone to the beach, and she and
Charles had waded at the water's edge, Ruth wearing her
new bathing outfit she'd ordered from a catalogue and
brought from home. I had sat back in the buggy, sewing,
and pointed out they looked like the pelicans who hang
around the islands all the time, picking their way along the
water's edge—especially Charles, who had his pants legs
rolled up to the knees.

We left Woollam's Lake around six o'clock—a lot of
people were out that evening, many of them awaiting the
availability of a boat to rent, so Charles and Ruth stayed
out only a short time. When we arrived at the house Janet
and Rubin were coming from the opposite direction, and I
could see right away Janet and my Ruth were to be
kindred spirits. Looking back on it now, I marvel that I
hadn't guessed it would be so between them earlier, for
Ruth was young and easily influenced, and Janet, almost
bereft of friends, must have been hungry for someone who
would admire her creative talents and learn from her.

After the initial introduction and Ruth's inquiry about
the piano, Janet said, "Please do come over tomorrow. I'll

just need tonight to unpack and tomorrow we'll lift the piano lid and dust the keys, have the thing tuned if need be.

"Do you like poetry? Oh, how grand! And I'll be glad to teach you all I know about sketching if you want to learn . . . I have some books . . ."

I smarted a little, knowing I couldn't interfere without seeming selfish and domineering, and knowing too that Ruth's first week here—the one just past—would be the only one in which I would occupy all her attention.

And of course I was correct. From the time of Ruth's arrival, the normally withdrawn Janet was like a butterfly fresh from its cocoon, and I don't remember a single occasion all summer long when her shutters were drawn without cause. When Ruth wasn't at her house learning to sketch or practicing piano, or out with some gentleman caller or another (she was courted by several young men from the church, and went out once with Josh Driscoll to a party, before becoming acquainted with Teddy Marlowe), Janet was over at our house.

I would sew and listen to them discuss a poem or a book, seldom joining in. Both admired Longfellow and Whittier, and Hawthorne and the novels of Collins. Wordsworth was often subjected to their analytical discussion and both loved talking about Robert Browning's work and its symbolism.

Once they talked at length about the expatriation of the writer Henry James and the painter James McNeill Whistler. Ruth wondered why anyone would have to leave America in order to better himself in the arts, and Janet told her, "Oh, but in Europe they are so far ahead of us in the realm of culture. I do believe, I just know, if I could have had a chance to study over there I could have been . . . well, I just wish I'd been lucky enough to, that's all. . . . Oh well, did you know Henry James's new novel *Daisy Miller* is coming out soon? I've ordered a copy all the way from England, and you may read it when it arrives."

Once drawn in by Janet, Ruth became less interested in new clothes and hairdos and it took a great amount of effort to prod her into going to Madame's for fittings, even though I pointed out Madame was highly selective in her patrons, and wouldn't countenance people who failed to show for appointments. Ruth crinkled her nose and consented to go, adding, "All right. It isn't that I don't appreciate your doing this for me, Cousin Claire . . . it's just that, well, if she wouldn't stare at me so. Gives me goose bumps." This was but a convenient excuse, of course. Madame thought of nothing but the garments she fitted to women. She saw each as a work of art, and rightly so.

"I wish you could be a little more cooperative," I told Ruth one day. "I'm only trying to help you, after all. It's scarcely a week before the evening we've planned with the Marlowes at the Garten, and once you've met Teddy, I'm sure there'll be no end to the parties you'll be attending, the other people you will meet. If you want this to be a good summer, you've got to put some effort into it."

"All right, but I'm just a simple country girl, really. I'm having fun enough learning to paint and to play new pieces on the piano—did I tell you I've almost mastered the 'Minuet in G'?—and Janet's such a love, to put up with me all the time."

"I expect she won't have to so much once you've met a few people your own age. And believe me, dear, when we're through dressing you up, you will dazzle them all."

"Maybe so . . ."

I believe Ruth must have pined away after her Frenchman throughout the summer, for I would hear her crying softly in her room from time to time, for no apparent reason, and while I thought at first she'd probably overcome her sorrow as the summer wore on, she seemed to become more prone to sudden tears as the days went by, rather than happier and more self-assured.

Certainly Josh Driscoll failed to hold her interest, as I suspected he would. She returned from their only evening together with a look of relief across her face. "He is nice," she said to Charles and me as we were having a late cup of tea in the kitchen, "altogether *too* nice. Too patronizing, too proper—not that I don't believe in propriety, you understand. But it's as though he wears it like a shield. Then of course I have no luck talking with him—he's too nervous for one thing, and for another, we have nothing in common.

"I am sorry, though. I don't mean to be critical. I know you're both trying hard to entertain me and I appreciate it so much. The truth is, I'm having a marvelous time even if I haven't found any interesting men here . . . it's just I'm no good at pretending when I—"

"Don't worry," said Charles. "You needn't see Josh

Driscoll again for our sakes. When is it we go to the Garten, Claire? Wednesday? Good. Perhaps you'll like Teddy. But don't feel you must. Dishonesty wouldn't suit you."

He was right, of course, yet I couldn't take the importance of the coming dinner party as lightly as he, for I had more at stake in the situation than he did. So I did a good deal of worrying over the days which followed, while trying not to seem obvious to either Ruth or Charles. Yet on Wednesday afternoon I began another menstrual flood, and it was apparent that whatever happened between Teddy and Ruth, I'd be no witness to it.

"We'll cancel if you can't go," she said. "We can do it another time."

"Nonsense. After I pulled teeth getting you fitted into that yellow organdie, and we spent all that time curling your hair this morning? You'll simply be accompanied by Charles alone, that's all. He and the Marlowes are great friends, and I'm sure there won't be any awkwardness about the odd number. Pretty soon you'll find them talking about some business or other, and it will leave you free to get acquainted with Teddy. I'd only be in the way, probably."

She looked disappointed. "All right, but we'll be home early. It just won't be any fun without you." She kissed my cheek and started out of the room. "Anyway, I'll probably have a headache from all these pins in my hair. Honestly, it feels nine pounds heavier since we curled it."

"The discomfort of being beautiful is part of a woman's lot in life, I'm afraid. But it's getting late. You've got to hurry and get dressed, and I want to see you before you leave."

"All right. Did you take your medicine?"

"No. I won't take it until you and Charles leave. It makes me too groggy, and I want to see how you look."

"Okay, but I don't know whether I'm ready for that dress or not. Not that it isn't pretty, and any girl would be delighted to have it. But when I think of how I looked just a few weeks ago when I got off the train . . . well, Mother probably wouldn't recognize me if she saw me in it."

After she was gone I indulged in a small triumphant smile.

There was a nice afternoon breeze sifting through the open window, and soon I dozed.

When Ruth returned to the bedroom to awaken me, it took several minutes to realize she actually stood across from me, like a picture from a storybook, in a dress that was without doubt another triumph for Madame, fitted tightly around the waist and designed to enhance the bust line. She'd studded her cascade curls with tiny yellow rosebuds picked that morning from my garden, and pinched her cheeks to heighten their color, the way I taught her to do.

She will never know how proud I was at that moment, for all the superlatives I uttered, and I commanded her to turn round four or five times so I could feast my eyes on every line of the dress. Finally I leaned back against the pillows and asked where Charles was.

"He's bathing, I think," she said. "I wanted to be ready early, so I could show off my new dress to Janet and Rubin."

"So it's not so bad after all, looking like a princess."

"I do, don't I?" she said, her eyes glowing. "I don't think I realized how grand it would look once we put everything together. Thank you, Claire," she said, and put her arms around me. "Thank you, thank you!"

"Um, you smell good. What's that scent?"

"French Bouquet, the real perfume. Cornel gave it to me along with the dusting powder and I've never worn it before. I never even wore it for him. Isn't that funny?"

"Get your mind off that bounder, and have fun tonight. Believe me, there are plenty of men who would have given their eyeteeth to have had what he gave up so easily."

"It's too bad really," she said thoughtfully. "Could he have seen me tonight, he might . . . oh well, you're right. It's all over and I'm going to have fun in Galveston."

Ruth always washed her hair on Monday, and often when she was finished we'd sit together in the backyard, the sunshine drying her long tresses as she pulled a hairbrush through them.

On the first Monday following the evening at the Garten Verein, then, we discussed Teddy Marlowe. It seemed an age since we'd had any time alone, for I had been in bed from Wednesday through Saturday, too dopey from the medicine to care about talking to anyone, and Sunday Teddy had called to take Ruth to church, then spent the afternoon and evening with her.

"Well now, tell me, what do you think of the Marlowe boy?" I said. She was sitting on a quilt spread on the ground in front of my chair, and had all her blond hair brushed forward, hiding her face.

"Oh, he's all right . . . more fun by a long shot than Josh Driscoll or that other boy I went with one night from St. Christopher's—what was his name, Steven Winnebank, or Winneberg, or something?"

"Teddy certainly seems taken with you. His father told Charles he'd mentioned your name quite regularly over the past few days."

"Is that so?" She lowered her head still further, then raised it up straight, pulling all the hair to the back. "To tell you the truth, Cousin Claire, Teddy can dance circles around his father, but Mr. Marlowe is much more interesting to talk to. And I do get such a kick from watching him get all fired up over something . . . then Mrs. Marlowe touches his arm or gives him a dirty look—to quieten him down—then she gets started on something and talks twice as loud as he did. They really are a pair."

"Teddy, though . . . he seems a bright boy, doesn't he?"

"Oh yes—ooh! There's a tangle—you know, I think he knows more about the war than anyone I've ever met. He'll probably grow up to be a general in the army or something."

"His father fears he may favor a military career, but, you know, Pete really hopes to get Teddy into his law firm one day."

"That reminds me, I'm going to begin helping Cousin Charles in his office a couple of days a week, typing."

"Oh? He doesn't own a typewriter, does he?"

"No, but he thinks he can get a Remington from someone going out of business down from his office. I learned to use one last year at the Ped, and I even won a prize for being the best typist in the class."

"But haven't you enough to do?"

"I guess so, but I was fascinated to hear him and Mr. Marlowe discuss their work. Then I was astounded to learn poor Charles writes everything out in longhand, himself. Think how much I could help him—then he'd be free to get away from the office more and go on picnics and things."

"I don't know, I don't hold much with going down there myself."

"I know. He said you'd only been there once. But more and more girls are becoming interested in office work. One girl in my typing class is working in a bookshop this summer, typing orders and even doing book reviews for the *Star.*"

"My, my, book reviews in the *Star?* Times have changed! When do you go to work?"

"Tomorrow, if Charles can get the machine. Types in upper and lower case, he says. That's the kind of machine I learned on—nothing but the newest and best for Mrs. Tannery, you know."

"Have you and Teddy made any plans for this week?"

"We're going to a young people's dance at the Garten Friday night. He wants me to meet some of his friends that are home for the summer."

"Marvelous! But you'll need another party dress, won't you?"

"Janet's offered to make me one out of some light green crepe de chine she never got round to using."

"But I'm sure Madame would—"

"Nothing doing, Claire. You've spent far too much money on me already. Besides, this is short notice and I know Madame wouldn't be able to get it done on time. Now, don't look disappointed . . . if I let you indulge me all summer, I'll be too spoiled to go back home to Grady and dust merchandise again."

"But are you sure Janet can do a professional job?"

"We're choosing a simple design—not elaborate like the yellow organdie—this isn't to be that formal a party."

"Very well, then. You know, I saw a gorgeous mint green fan at the Emporium not long ago—hand-painted ivory with lavender flowers . . . we could put lavender flowers in your hair this time—I can see it now. I must get Janet to show me the dress design. Maybe I can help."

"Oh, Cousin Claire, really, I wish you wouldn't make over everything so much. I can't ever repay you for what you've already done."

"Forgive me, dear, but I never had anyone to make over or dress up, and I never realized until you came just how much I'd missed."

She put a hand out and touched my knee. "I'm sorry, Cousin Claire, really I am. I didn't realize you felt that way . . . but then don't be silly. You're not possibly old enough to even give a thought to being my mother." She sat back down and began stroking her hair again.

"But your mother is not that much older than I, dear."

"I know that, but she *looks* so much older."

"That's because she's worked so much harder. She's had a harder lot."

"That's true, all right. You know, there was a time when I worried awfully about her. But I finally decided she thrives on that store. I mean it. She's down there from seven sharp every morning, till after nine o'clock at night. She knows everyone in town, and will go to any length to fill special orders for people. Everybody loves her."

"Oh, how I long to see her! We've simply got to make plans to go back before long."

"I know. I tried to get her to come with me this summer, but no one could wedge her away from that store."

"Maybe this fall, or after Christmas perhaps, we could go. Of course I may not be able to go anywhere. There's a strong possibility I may have to have an operation if things continue to go as they have."

"Oh no! Doesn't the medicine help? Or can't they do something else for you?"

"The medicine kills the pain and makes me sleep, and that's all. I think the bottle I've just opened must be stronger than the last. It certainly seems to have more of an effect."

"Do you go through this every month? Oh, if I had to I would simply die!"

"No. That's the curious thing. It will go on for four or five months straight, then suddenly go back to normal. A year or so later, it will start all over again."

"Oh, I do hope you're not confined to bed anymore for a long time—forever, of course, if possible. But I miss you when you have to stay cooped up and you don't get to go places with us."

"Don't worry about me. I'm so thankful for having Charles to fill in for me. And I guess, Janet too . . ."

"You don't mind my spending time with her, do you? We seem to have so much in common. And I don't think I've ever met anyone who seems so alone. A preacher's wife! You'd think she would spend all her time planning bazaars and going to meetings . . . yet she does none of these things. She seems a person apart from everything around her, somehow, as though she doesn't really belong. Does that make any sense?"

"It does indeed. I've felt it many times myself."

"Sometimes the look she gets in her eyes . . . a kind of faraway, receding look . . . gives me the shivers."

"Yes," I said, amazed at Ruth's ability to put into words what I had so often felt but could not describe.

Chapter 15

Much of Ruth's summer lies hazy within my memory, like a dream once poignant yet now faded, so that it dances several feet distant when one tries to catch it up, and laughs at one's inability to reach it.

I do know I spent much time in bed from June to September, the first bleeding siege denying me the party at the Garten, then another two or three weeks later, lasting four or five days, then still another and another, and on and on. It seems to me now that I was always uncomfortably hot; always had limp hair dangling around my shoulders; always had the smell of medicine on my breath and the taste in my mouth.

Charles got his Remington, and Ruth spent the rest of the summer working two—sometimes three—days a week with him, both of them returning tired at the end of the day, yet still devoting much of the dinner conversation to cases Charles was working on, Ruth obviously as interested in their outcomes as he.

The longer her work with him continued, the more it pleased me, for the experience, I realized, might prove invaluable to her someday, and Betsey, being practical, would appreciate this aspect of her visit perhaps more than any other.

And of course she had less free time for piano playing and art lessons with Janet, especially since she soon began seeing more of Teddy Marlowe. It was a bit strange to witness at first, for she had seemed almost passive about him in the beginning. But then, within a couple of weeks after their first evening together, she appeared almost to embark on a concentrated effort to go with him whenever and wherever he wished, rarely turning down an invitation from him. Finally, unable to contain my satisfaction any longer, I wrote to Betsey:

"Ruth has become quite the belle of the ball around Galveston. She and Teddy Marlowe, son of a prominent attorney here and a good friend of ours, are keeping more and more in each other's company, attending gala parties at least once a week and outings with friends at the beach and lake when time permits. Believe me, if summer's end saw a commitment between them, you would laugh at your worries over her being jilted by the Frenchman in Grady. Teddy Marlowe is the top choice among the eligible bachelors here, and will no doubt one day be as prominent in the legal profession as his father . . . and of course will inherit his father's wealth. . . ."

I knew as I sealed the envelope I'd exaggerated a little about Teddy's future as an attorney, when he was still reported to be considering a military career. Still, I saw no harm in looking at the bright side of it, and mailed the letter without changing a word. Shortly after though, I was to learn it wouldn't have mattered what I had said in the letter, and I wished I'd never put it in the post office box.

One night toward the end of summer I passed by Ruth's bedroom door and heard her crying. I knocked, yet she didn't answer. Finally I tried the door, and found it unlocked. "Ruth, dear, forgive me for barging in, but what's the matter?" She lay diagonally across the bed, her face hidden.

"Nothing. It's all right."

"It isn't all right, if you're upset," I told her, and sat on the edge of the bed. She looked so pretty then, with her long hair hanging down the back of her dark green robe. I wanted to help her, was afraid I'd done something to upset her.

"It's just that everything is in such a mess," she said, still refusing to look at me. "I should never have come."

"It's Teddy Marlowe, isn't it? You've been seeing him for our benefit, and now he's done something to upset you."

She pulled up and turned over to look at me, her face pinched and wet. "He wants to marry me," she said. "Wants me to wait for him till he finishes school."

"Do you want to?"

"Want to? No, I couldn't possibly, now . . ."

"What do you mean? What happened?"

"I mean . . . now that I know I don't love him, of course." She rose from the bed and walked to the bureau; picked up her hairbrush and drew it through her hair. "I've overstayed my visit," she said. "I know Mother needs me back home—I've been gone three months, you know. I think it's time for me to go."

"What about Teddy? Did you make any commitment to him?"

"No. I told him I would think about it. I didn't know what to tell him really."

"Well, I can tell you something, if you're worried that your failing to marry him will put our friendship with Pete in jeopardy, don't give it a thought. Pete's crazy about you and would love to see you married to Teddy, I'm sure, but he's also a smart and practical man. Only unhappiness can come from anything less than a love match. Besides, a summer is too short a time for deciding one's fate."

She looked at me for a long time then, and an expression of relief came over her face. "That's so true," she said finally, and gently touched a hand to my face as though it were me needing comfort. "Claire, I'm sorry. Please forgive me, please."

"Don't be foolish," I said, and knew I must have somehow betrayed my own hopes about Teddy Marlowe to her. "What is there to forgive? People your age tend to make too large a matter of such things. Believe me, I know. I was your age once, don't forget.

"And as far as overstaying your visit is concerned, you're welcome to stay here as long as you like. Of course I know you worry about your mother. Maybe you could go back now, and come again next spring—next Christmas even. You might even bring Betsey along if you can pry her away from the store."

"No, I doubt I shall ever be back. . . ."

She was gone from us less than a week after that conversation, carrying with her several times over the sparse belongings she'd brought along at the beginning of the summer, and wearing an air of reserve becoming to a mature young woman that defied any of us to believe she was the same person who'd been but a schoolgirl, full of wonder and endless questions but a few months before.

Although I was the only one to weep openly as she

waved good-by from the flashing train window, she was missed by all of us. Janet disappeared behind shuttered windows for two days; Rubin retreated to his work at the church office; Charles spent several evenings alone on the porch, smoking his pipe and not asking for company.

I tidied the room which from that summer on I would think of as hers. She'd left little out of order—only a thin film of French Bouquet dusting powder settled on the dresser; an empty cream jar and some tissues in the waste-paper basket; and an aura of emptiness about the room that wasn't there before she came.

The rest of the year sped by. Charles began traveling quite a bit around November, making a zigzag between Austin and San Antonio because of some legal case or another which he wouldn't discuss.

Then on New Year's Day at the Marlowe party, a formal announcement was made: Charles Becker would be joining the law firm of Marlowe, Turner, and Parks. I did not know, nor would he ever say, what prompted his decision to go with Pete. Nor did I press him to explain. I have always felt he did it for me.

PART II

Chapter 1

The sunbaked beaches are, some say, a fortunate drawing card for Galveston. In the past few years, some businessmen have undertaken to capitalize on the long and deep expanse of mocha sand by constructing halls for staging events that would draw to the seashore not only the bathers, but even those people who do not like the water.

Thus did the Galveston Pavilion—site of vaudeville shows, three-act plays, skating derbies, circus performances, and musical concerts—bring Charles and me, Janet and Rubin, and Serena down to the seaside with regularity during the years between 1881 and 1883, and none of us attached any particular significance to the fact we were going to watch Monsieur La Faira play a piano concert on the stage in the big building one Sunday afternoon in August 1883.

It was so hot in the Pavilion that day, by the time Monsieur La Faira sat down to play his first selection I was wiping perspiration from my forehead and wishing Janet had not been so insistent we should all spend our afternoon in this way.

Of course, there was the added irritation of Janet and Rubin's adopted child, who'd grown cranky soon after we took our seats on the third row from the stage. Serena—whose name was something Janet thought up as a combination of Rubin's mother's name, Sara, and her own mother's name, Irene—had come to them from God alone knows where, through some Church agency, shortly after she came into the world in May of 1880. Nothing was known about the parentage of Serena beyond the fact her real mother had been in what we call, "embarrassing circumstances." All other pertinent information was held in strictest confidence by the agency.

Her coming had taken Charles and me by surprise, for neither of us knew the Garrets were considering such a move. I had no reason to hold anything against the little girl, yet I could not help remembering my own predicament years before, and wondered what would have happened to me if Charles Becker had not been around to marry. One thing was certain, however: I would not have given up Damon Becker's child for anything or anyone, no matter how embarrassing the circumstances, and could not imagine any mother carrying a child for nine long months then just giving it over to someone else she didn't even know.

As to the Garrets' decision to take the child, that was their business, although it seemed to me they were taking an awful chance—what if the little girl grew up into a person of low morals, with inherent traits that all the love and caring she received from Janet and Rubin could not squelch? I couldn't resist pointing this out to Charles, and for some reason, he seemed irritated by the remark.

"That's rubbish, Claire. What counts is the love and training the child gets growing up. And anyway, what makes you think Serena's parents were necessarily 'no good' individuals? Sometimes people—good people—make mistakes, you know. Sometimes they let their hearts overrule their minds."

He almost glared at me when he said it, and for a moment I suspected he'd known all along that Charlie was Damon's child, but then as soon as the thought crossed my mind I realized its foolishness. Like as not he was just in one of his bad moods. He'd gotten so he had more and more of them over the past few years, the years he'd been with Pete Marlowe's firm, and as I was quite contented with his being in partnership with Pete, I always tried to smooth over his moments of irritation or frustration.

"You needn't get your back up," I said. "I know how close a friend you are to Rubin, and anything he and Janet do is always fine and dandy with you. I wasn't meaning anything personal toward them. I was just theorizing."

His face softened. "She is a sweet little angel—Serena—isn't she?"

"Indeed she is," I said, and I meant it honestly for she was a winning child most of the time, except, for instance, the day of Monsieur La Faira's ill-fated concert, when she squirmed in Janet's lap and rubbed her eyes, and pushed her lower lip out, making herself extremely unattractive. Her curly hair was the color of corn silk, though it grew a little darker by the day, and also straighter, and she had wide brown eyes set in a cherub face. One might have mistaken her for Janet's own child, if not for the fact that her features were more sharply hewn and clearly defined.

To both Janet and Rubin she appeared the fulfillment of long-held dreams, and though she was less than overjoyed in my presence usually, she had taken to calling Charles her Unca Sharrie, which he seemed not to mind at all.

The Pavilion was filled to capacity that day, and Charles remarked in a whisper, "The place must be making money hand over fist for the Colonel." Colonel Sinclair owns the Galveston City Railway Company and also the big Beach Hotel down the sand a few hundred yards. He had envisioned the Pavilion, as Charles earlier explained, as a means to make money for the streetcar system, for anyone on the island could catch the streetcar at any of its stops and be brought directly to the Pavilion entrance. Of course we lived only a matter of blocks from the building, and always walked.

The Pavilion was the first structure in the state to have been equipped with electric lights, and because of this, it was a source of great pride to all who lived in the town. Otherwise it was truly an architectural nightmare, painted brown and shaped like a big mushroom, with turrets, battlements, towers, and ornate carvings choking it from all angles.

Monsieur La Faira appeared unimpressed by the supposed magnificence of the setting arranged for him (four potted palms and four large candle sconces), as he stretched his long fingers over the keyboard, and a hush came over the audience.

"I just can't believe we got such good seats," Janet whispered excitedly. "He's come all the way from Chicago, you know. They say he is quite talented and well known in the Midwest."

"I can't help thinking how Ruth would have enjoyed him," I said. "I see here on the program he intends to play the 'Minuet in G' . . . really brings back memories."

Janet nodded, whispered something to Serena, and turned her attention to the stage.

True to her word that summer of 1879, Ruth had never returned for another visit, nor had Charles and I managed to get away to Grady in all these years, yet her name was often mentioned in conversation and we did have letters from her occasionally. She'd married a young man who shared a second-hand furniture business with his father in Grady. His name, she had written, "is Edward Byron, just like the English poet, and he's been here all the time, though we noticed each other just a few months ago (didn't know Grady was that big!)."

That letter came in the spring of '81, and within the year following, she and Edward had married and Betsey had taken ill and died. Both events we learned of after the fact, and had it not been for my great affection for Ruth, I would have been unforgivingly angry with her for reporting by letter that my own beloved cousin had passed away. Yet Betsey was ill only a few weeks before she died, as though she thought it impractical to waste any more time than that on preparing for death, and had requested upon her death-bed that Charles and I not be told until after she was gone. Once I learned this, I knew I had no right for being angry with Ruth. It would have been like Betsey to want to save me from the agony of watching her being put forever into the ground, and just like Ruth to carry out her wish.

Still, I wept for days at the thought of such unfairness, for Betsey, like me, had been whipped by fate. In her adult lifetime she had never done anything but work hard, then was struck down before she lived long enough to enjoy the fruits of her efforts.

I've often consoled myself that at least she had seen Ruth grow into womanhood, had seen the metamorphosis brought on by her stay here with us, and had watched her joined together in marriage with a young man she apparently loved. Yet losing her was for me almost as heart-breaking as losing Charlie, like the wrenching away of a limb of one's body. I shall never get over her death entirely. Ruth places flowers regularly on her grave and on Charlie's up on the hill in the Grady Memorial Cemetery. Ruth is the light of my life.

There was a burst of applause in the Pavilion hall now, and Janet leaned toward me and said, "You look in another world, Claire. Did you realize he was playing the 'Minuet in G'? You know, I've always kind of wished Ruth might have gone into music professionally. I really believe she could have made it. Do you suppose she still plays? She never mentions it in her letters."

"I don't know. Even though they sold Betsey's store after her death, I'm sure Ruth stays busy helping Edward in the furniture store."

Rubin, seated on the other side of Janet, now held out his arms to Serena and took her on his lap. He whispered something in her ear which obviously delighted her, and she clapped her hands and hugged his neck. He looked well that day, as always. In the years I had known him, he seemed to have become more youthful, while Charles continued to amass more and more gray streaks in his hair, and I waged a continuous battle to keep the gray in mine from showing.

Charles was tapping my shoulder. "What time is that Chamber banquet tonight?"

"Eight o'clock, why?"

"Nothing. But I do want to run over my speech a couple of times before we go down."

"Lord, Charles, you've worn out the paper it's written on, going over it. I'm sure you'll be splendid tonight."

He'd been chairman of the Industrial Expansion Committee for a couple of years, and his speech tonight would deal with three manufacturers he'd been courting lately, all of Houston, whom he had persuaded to open plants here. One was a lace-making business; one a candy factory; and one a textile mill. The speech symbolized something of a triumph for him and his committee, although he would not admit to it. "I'm just doing my job like the other committee members," he'd told me. "It's a tough one though, because the Octopus of the Gulf has a way of hurting our image as a city."

As the afternoon wore on I became increasingly uncomfortable in the hard-back chair. There was the telltale pain in the small of my back—a sure sign I was in for a bleeding spell soon. I'd been through more and more of them over the past few years. Dr. Hutchisson had given me little hope of ever conceiving another child, and told me also that eventually I'd have no choice but to submit to the surgery I dreaded.

This fact did not seem to bother Charles a lot; perhaps, I thought, because he'd long since passed the stage of wanting a family. And though I was saddened that I probably would never again know the joy of giving birth to a child, I

supposed it was just as well. If I could not have a child of
the man I loved with all the urgency and passion I'd loved
Damon Becker, then to have one under other circumstances might have put limits on the amount of love I could
give to the child, and it would have been cruel to have it
grow up a poor substitute for the child I loved who was
dead. For this reason I was thankful Charles did not suggest we might adopt a child just as Rubin and Janet had,
although in truth I felt I'd probably be a better mother
than Janet Garret. Ah well, I'd long since quit making myself miserable over the seemingly tenuous relationship between Janet and Rubin. It looked as though they were
bound to live with each other forever, especially in view of
their decision to bring a child into their lives.

Serena, lulled by the soft concert music, had fallen asleep
in her father's arms. Janet, entranced by the music, sat on
the edge of her chair. Occasionally the whimpering of an
impatient infant somewhere in the audience could be
heard, and one could sense a general stirring around the
hall of people who grew weary of the performance. Monsieur La Faira, I thought, would not be finding this an easy
audience to play to. He would probably not come again if
invited, and would probably not be invited by the astute
management of the Pavilion anyway.

As though in reply to my thoughts, the Pavilion manager
walked out on the stage—Monsieur La Faira was then exe-
cuting one of Chopin's mazurkas—and for the length of
time it took him to cross to the piano and whisper something into the maestro's ear, I thought with astonishment
he was asking our guest pianist to leave.

Then he turned toward the audience and said, "Ladies
and gentlemen, a small flame has been discovered in one of
the towers, and while it is now fully under control, we must
take every possible precaution for safety. Therefore, will
the audience please exit from the building by the two exits
on either side of the stage. I repeat, we are in no danger.
Do not panic. Leave calmly. Your money for today's performance will be refunded."

Everyone began talking at once, yet there was no sense
of panic among the audience that I could see. Janet came
closest no doubt: her face turned ashen, and she looked
pleadingly to Rubin as though he might say a prayer that
would save her from the horrible fate of burning alive.

"Come along," said Charles. "The door to the right of the stage is our closest."

To save distance, we and others trooped across the stage which had been built especially for Monsieur La Faira, and there the piano sat open, its ivory keys exposed like teeth in an open mouth, for Monsieur La Faira hadn't hesitated long enough to close the lid before hurrying out the door. Two of the potted palms were overturned, dirt spilling across the floor, yet the sconces, whose flames the manager had doused before he left the stage following his announcement, both stood intact. Someone tripped over the leg of the empty piano bench just as we walked up, and I heard the sound brought forth by someone's hand touching hard on a random group of piano keys: an awful, grotesque chord which pounded through me. And still we went like soldiers, filing four or five at a time through the open exit doors.

The tower from which the fire billowed out was located at the opposite end of the building, off the front lobby, and as we walked out into the sunshine we could see the blaze and smoke coming forth through the window and knew the manager had lied to us for our own sakes. The blaze was clearly out of hand. Not until the building was empty of people did the first fire alarm sound.

Only a few minutes had passed—five, maybe seven or eight. The crowd stood out and away from the wooden building and watched as the fire consumed it. Down the beach, not far distant, more people stood on the wide promenades surrounding the big Beach Hotel and gaped at the growing spectacle. They, like those of us who'd just escaped the building, now looked upon what was happening as a new form of entertainment. Rubin raised Serena upon his shoulders in order that she might see.

People talked and talked, exclaimed and gesticulated, pointing out the route of the flames as they swept across the side of the building and up on the roof. A man standing near us spat out, "That damn manager ought to be strung up for lyin' about how bad the fire was!"

Charles turned on him angrily and shouted back, "You fool! If he'd told us the truth we would have panicked and all of us been killed while we ran around like idiots!" The man calmed down then, and I was thrilled by Charles's authoritative manner . . . so unlike him.

By the time the first fire wagon made its way up to the

building, the fire had complete control of its prey: the Galveston Pavilion now looked like a giant mushroom afire. The best the poor firemen could do was to keep control of the burning cinders which flew from it and might well have caused several other fires along the dry sand. The building itself was gone within the space of twenty-five minutes, start to finish.

As we walked back home Charles said, "I hope everyone realizes that the manager saved us from a paralyzing wave of panic. I can't believe it's possible for a building to go up in flames so fast that even the fire wagons can't reach the scene in time. This is utterly outrageous. Something must be done."

"I never considered the danger of taking a child into a place like that," said Rubin. "How horrible, how horrible."

Serena stroked her father's face and crooned, "Daddy, don't be sad . . . don't hold me so tight, okay?"

Charles was still shaking his head in dismay and I said, "The weather has been so dry, dear. The building was like a tinderbox—we've hardly had any rain this summer. It probably couldn't be helped."

"Couldn't be helped?" he repeated. "By God, it has to be helped! Something must be done about our system of fire prevention here and our water supply. I can't believe that I—of all people—could have been so ignorant of the necessity of—"

"Charles," Janet broke in gently, "I'm afraid Serena may be getting f-r-i-g-h-t-e-n-e-d by the tone of your voice. Could we discuss it later?"

He stopped walking and turned toward the child, his face stricken. "Oh, Serena, Serena, come let me hold you in my arms."

"Let me ride on your back, Unca Sharrie," she said, and happily made the transfer from Rubin's arms to Charles's shoulders.

We walked the rest of the way in silence, except for Serena's constant yammering in Charles's ear. Janet walked beside Rubin, and I walked alone behind Charles and the child. When we drew up to their house at last I noticed the oleander bushes which flank the front of their porch were losing their blooms. "It will soon be the end of summer," I said. "You can always tell. The oleander blossoms stay around to the end, and yours have been particularly good this year—better than those around the church."

"Those are the tallest bushes I've ever seen," said Charles. "They'll soon reach the top of the porch."

"They hide the porch," I said. "Can't even see Janet's swing from the street anymore."

"Yes, I like it that way. . . ." she said.

We had no more than arrived in our own house than Charles left again. "I'll be home in time to get dressed for the banquet," he said. "I've got some business to tend to."

"Where are you going?"

"No time to explain. See you later," he said, and I watched him walk to the barn to get Gypsy. I was nervous after the ordeal, although I hadn't realized it until he left. Watching the raging spectacle of flames had given me an almost detached feeling; yet now, at home alone, it was strangely more real. When I closed my eyes I could see the fire. My clothes smelled of smoke; I changed and walked next door.

Janet was feeding Serena her supper in the kitchen, and Rubin was talking quietly to the both of them. "Hi, Caire," she told me between bites.

"Hi, darling. You weren't afraid of the fire, were you?"

"Yes, but Daddy says everything is gonna be okay."

"Come on, Serena, eat your vegetables," Janet said impatiently. I could see the afternoon had taken its toll on her.

"You must forgive Charles being so upset," I told them. "You see, he lost his parents in a fire when he and Damon were just a little older than Serena. He was raised by an aunt. So he can see the magnitude of all this more easily than the rest of us."

"Apologies aren't necessary, Claire," Rubin said. "Charles is a man of action, and he was justly alarmed. Such a man can save a community sometimes, much as Christ saved the world."

"Poor Charles," said Janet. "There are families who seem to be stalked by fire. I knew one in Virginia. . . ."

Chapter 2

The Pavilion fire marked a turning point in our lives. Surely as it leveled the big building to the ground, it also ignited Charles's spirit in a way I had not before witnessed.

Before that, each thing Charles became involved in was resultant in some way, directly or indirectly, of the driving force of Pete Marlowe. Although Charles did work very hard in his own right for the Industrial Expansion Committee, I have always felt his being appointed to its membership was Pete's doing.

Then, sometime later, Charles's involvement in the Galveston Deep Water Committee was only a veil covering work actually carried on by Pete. The Deep Water Committee was instigated by a number of important citizens— most notably one or two stockholders in the Wharf Company—for finding ways to raise money for harbor improvements and dredging the swiftly shoaling inner and outer bars. Since Pete had come out both publicly and privately time and again against the Wharf Company, his presence on the committee would hardly have been welcomed.

Charles, on the other hand, had no known enemies among the elite members of Galveston business society. So while Pete quietly contributed money, Charles went to meetings and worked on devising plans for getting the necessary work done. He muttered privately though that while the Deep Water Committee might help Galveston to an extent, the only way to assure its place as a port of the future would be to destroy the monopoly held by the Wharf Company.

Once he told me, "Of course our doing this work on harbor improvements is helping Houston too—don't think her people have missed the point that when Galveston money is spent to deepen the channel, she benefits too. Any ship that can pass over the bars to Galveston will be just that much closer to Houston's port. Only when we put an end to our exorbitant wharfage fees are we going to remove the impetus for Houston's own effort at getting deep water."

In between the committee meetings of one kind or another several nights a week, we landed our share of social invitations. I hobnobbed with the wealthy and prominent, content to flirt with the curled edges of city society. I knew I wasn't an actual participant, only an invited guest by virtue of knowing Pete and Faye. I amassed a closetful of creations by Madame LaRoche, and would go along to the social functions on the arm of a man as often as not introduced as Marlowe's partner, and smile and be charming

the evening long, then go home and not even remember
names because they didn't seem important at the time.

Then the fire. "What's the point of all this?" Charles
asked me that night after he returned. "I spend my time
trying to get new business blood flowing through the veins
of this town, and rack my brain along with several others,
trying to figure out how to finance the harbor improvements. And all the time we sit here unprotected from the
whims of nature. The fire brought it all home to me. Fire
destroyed my parents. It could have destroyed Serena.
Could have killed you and me, Janet and Rubin, and
everyone else in the Pavilion today.

"Don't you see? If a fire started on this island when the
wind was blowing right, the whole town would go within a
matter of hours."

And that was it. What happened afterward for months
to come was a result of Charles's own motivations, regardless of how it appeared.

Shortly thereafter a movement was under way to change
over the city's fledgling group of volunteer fire companies
into one citywide system of paid employees. I know there
were others involved in it, and that Charles probably met
with several of them that evening after the Pavilion fire.
But for most of them it probably *was* just another civic
committee. For Charles Becker it was a labor of love, and
made all the rest of his work for Galveston matter more
than ever.

March winds can be scathingly cold on the island, and
on one particularly windy night in 1884, Pete Marlowe
came over unannounced and brought with him Lucien
Carter. The two stood on the front verandah with woolen
scarves wrapped around their necks, overcoats on, and red
noses. Pete's appearance at my front door came as no great
surprise; Lucien Carter's, on the other hand, caught me off
guard. We didn't see very much of him.

"Come in, come in," I said. "We've a fire in the parlor.
Go and warm yourselves. I'll get Charles."

He appeared surprised when I interrupted his work in
the study, and looked at his watch. "Was I supposed to
meet with Pete tonight?"

"I don't know, but he and Lucien are wrapped up like
eskimos, and Lucien's carrying his brief case. Maybe it's
something about business. I'll make some hot chocolate."

"Later," said Pete, who'd come down the hall to the study door. "I want both of you to sit in on this conversation. Besides, I don't seem to be able to git an appointment with Charlie at his office these days," he said, laughing, and we all trooped back into the parlor, where Lucien now stood before the fire, warming his well-manicured hands.

There was a sense of imminency in the air as we sat down to listen.

"You know, Mr. Fuller took the town by quite a landslide in yesterday's mayoral election," said Lucien. "Not that it came as any surprise. He's been mayor before, some years ago, and was popular then."

"It's pretty common knowledge our illustrious Wharf Company was pullin' for his election this go-round," said Pete.

I looked at Charles. He nodded in agreement, pulling out his pipe and lighting it calmly. The statement seemed academic. What could anyone do about an election already over with?

"To get to the point," said Lucien, "as long as the Wharf Company has the city officials on its side, there is little can be done to bust up the monopoly, and the monopoly, as we've all agreed before, is going to bring us to ruin. Either that, or the people like me are going to move somewhere else."

Charles leaned back in his chair and crossed one leg over the other. "I'm in total agreement with you as far as that goes; but what have you in mind?" Lucien's last statement had given it away, but Charles always takes one point at a time.

"By startin' now," Pete said, "we might have a chance two years from now when the next election rolls around, to beat Fuller with our own man. It will take some money, of course, and also an effort at educatin' people of the city to the importance of a new face in city government."

"I'd back such a campaign as far as I was able," said Charles, and drew on his pipe.

"We don't want you to back the campaign, son," Pete said. "We want you to *be* the campaign. We want you to run for mayor."

I sat with shoulders tensed, waiting.

"I told you I'd back a campaign for new faces around the city in any way I could, but don't believe for a moment I think I'd have a ghost of a chance. And anyway, why me?

Why not you, Pete? You've been here far longer; have a good deal more influence than I."

"Drat it, I'm too old to run for public office. Few years ago, maybe I might have, but not now. Mother wouldn't hear of it. You're the one; the perfect candidate: clean background, free of scandal. Your work around Galveston is reachin' the eyes and ears of everyone. You're young—at least by my standards—yet old enough to know the ropes and still have the energy to fight the battles, for there will be battles, even after you've been elected. Don't think you can't make it. Stranger things have happened in my experience. The Wharf Company don't have everybody paid off. There are twenty-four thousand people in this city, and a fair percentage of them can vote." He was huffing and puffing now, his face growing red. He had his thumbs looped in the armholes of his waistcoat.

"You don't have to answer tonight," said Lucien. "We need to begin this thing early, but we do have a little time. I've a list of supporters here in my brief case, but I'll just hold it for now if you like, till you've made up your mind."

"A little time we have, yes," said Pete, rubbing his hands together. "Time enough for Fuller to warm up the mayor's seat down at city hall. But that's about all. Don't say no because you think it will be a losin' battle, Charlie. Remember, a hundred years ago a small band of young upstarts successfully revolted against the Crown of England."

"That's true," said Charles, "though it strikes me they might not have been so successful if England had had the Galveston Wharf Company on her side."

After they were gone Charles stood gazing into the fire. I had managed to remain calm during their visit, yet now they were gone I could no longer contain myself. I went to him and put my arms around his waist, and pleaded with him to answer "yes."

"Poor Claire," he said softly, the firelight playing on his cheek. "I haven't made you very happy, have I? Forcing you up and away from the home you loved, bringing you all the way down here, where you knew no one."

"It's all right. I've been happy, honest I have. Besides, that was ages ago."

"Would it really mean so much to you, my running for mayor?"

"Oh, if you only knew how much. It's what you've been aiming for since you came here. And after you've done it there will be other, greater things for you. The doors will continue to open in front of you. I can see it!"

"And what if I should lose?"

"You won't lose. I just know it. It's time something changed for the better . . . maybe this will be it."

"What do you mean by that?"

"Oh, nothing. Only that we've been pivoting around in a circle for all these years, never getting anywhere. Suddenly it's all worthwhile, all the waiting . . ."

He looked at me for a long moment then, and said, "You'd have to consider the strong possibility that I may not win—may not even score."

"I'd take the chance . . . haven't I always taken a chance with you?"

"Yes, but you don't take disappointment lightly. I haven't lived with you for all these years without learning that."

"I've had my share of disappointments, but I just have a feeling this time I wouldn't be getting my hopes up for nothing. I don't know—maybe it's because Pete is involved in it, and he's so strong a man—so well known, I—"

"If you think I'd do it at Pete's bidding, you can just get the thought out of your head. Running for mayor isn't something one does as a pawn. . . . If I decide to do it, it will be for my own reasons. He'll have nothing to do with it beyond coming up with the idea in the first place, and giving me his support."

"Does that mean you'll do it?"

"No. It means I'll consider it, and in the light of your wishes maybe even more seriously than I otherwise would have." He gazed into the fire and then looked again at me.

"You know, this town has a lot of advantages—its people, its beauty, the new fire department, the Deep Water Committee—it would be nice to feel one had had a big part in making Galveston into a great metropolis, like New York or Boston. And I really believe that it's all within our grasp if we handle it right, if we make everything come together as a unit.

"Still, it's a lot to give, running for public office . . . I began as a lawyer, and a damned good one if I do say so myself, but lately it seems any number of things get in the way and it's hard to decide which is more important."

"There are a good many fine lawyers; there are fewer fine mayors, and probably none as fine as you would be."

"Yes, but there would be a certain risk involved," he

said, turning again to face the fire. I left him there, and went up to bed. I had some of my own thinking to do.

It seemed to me as I lay there, too excited to sleep, that things had truly worked out for the best, just as Rubin said they would so long ago, when he forced me to come to terms with my foolish infatuation for him. There was, I knew, no end to what Charles could do now, for Pete Marlowe was a smart man and knew how to pick a winner. There was no doubt in my mind that night that, should Charles decide to run for mayor—for whatever reason—he would win. I saw it all like a vision before my eyes. And after mayor, there would be other, greater honors, more important posts, Congressman, Senator, President!

How fortunate I'd stuck it out all these years, kept my head level on my shoulders, stayed with Charles out of duty when I couldn't do it out of love. Maybe I'd never again know the love that haunted my dreams so often, never have another child as the product of that love. But in turn I'd have what surely many women must long for all their lives: wealth, position, prestige. Oh, I had been so wrong about fate playing ugly tricks on me. Fate was saving me for something else, that was all . . . perhaps not what I instinctively desired as all humans do, but something on a higher plane. Yes, perhaps even Rubin could see my talents had great meaning as all God-given talents do, and was noble enough (or loved me enough?) to want to see them put to the best possible use.

It must have been hours before I finally fell asleep, and my dreams were full of magnificent halls with great chandeliers, of beautiful gowns that put to shame even the creations by Madame LaRoche. Never had I had such a sleep, or awakened more refreshed. . . .

The following week was a long one—probably the longest I have ever spent—in which Charles sat hour upon evening hour inside his study, saying little to me.

I felt so helpless, knowing he might decide not to do it, and knowing I could do nothing to change his mind. I could scarcely eat or sleep, and would often find myself studying him across the dinner table, trying to guess what was going on in his mind. His face would go through the most curious expressions: he would knit his brow for a moment, then relax his face and even nod or shake his head slightly. Sometimes when I'd speak to him his eyes would be very wide and vacant, and when I had finished whatever

I was saying, he wouldn't reply, and I'd realize he hadn't heard a word.

It was too early in the year, and the weather too bleak, for me to occupy myself with the garden either at home or at St. Christopher's. So I polished silver, rubbed furniture, embroidered pillow cases, read magazines, waiting, waiting, for the moment when Charles would burst through the door and say he would do it. Yet when he did tell me of his decision we were in the middle of roast beef and potatoes, and his statement lacked drama or even the enthusiasm I had assumed would be forthcoming.

"I've decided to do it," he said simply. "Not, perhaps, for the reasons some may think. Certainly my main platform will be the Wharf Company question, but my own thrust will be quite different."

I was too elated to ask him what he meant, and he took a sip of tea before continuing. "I've worked on the fire department for the past few months, and I'm convinced the difficulties with it are as complex as those with the wharves. We haven't got sufficient water supply here to meet the demand and we must go to the mainland to supplement it. It's radical, and highly expensive, I know, but there it is."

I started to interrupt—I could not contain my joy any longer—but he went right on as if he didn't notice.

"I think people just might be able to see the importance of this problem . . . perhaps even more than they can the evils of the Wharf Company. After all, fire is a matter of life or death for everyone. Of course, I assume Fuller will take full credit for any success the newly organized fire department will have over the next two years. But from what I've been able to learn, he and others feel we can solve the water supply problem by digging artesian wells here. And that's preposterous!

"I may just be able to pull off the election if I can convince the people of the need to go elsewhere for water. Oh well . . . it's two years away. Perhaps nothing will come of it after all. What do you think?"

"Think? You've never made me so happy. I'll do anything to help you get elected—hang posters, talk to people—anything within my power. Oh, I can't eat another bite. Let's go and tell Rubin and Janet—I've just got to tell somebody!"

"Claire, please. I keep getting the feeling you have no

idea how serious this is. It isn't as though I were competing in a spelling bee. If we show our cards too soon, it will only give my opponents an advantage over me. I don't want you telling anyone just yet. I've told Pete and Lucien, and that's it."

"But isn't Lucien going to talk to his business friends to try and raise money for the campaign?"

"Not yet. Just now I'm going to begin studying the platform, do some preliminary research. The candidacy will be announced probably in the summer of '85. Right now Lucien will begin a little indoctrination work, that's all."

"But it's a long time till next summer."

"I know. A lot can happen between now and then."

"Can I write to Ruth?"

"All right, all right. And you can go tell Rubin and Janet if you're bursting to talk about it. But remember, that is as far as it goes."

By the time fall first blew its chilly breath across the island in 1884, our social life had wound down considerably because Charles was using more and more time to study the questions which would arise during the campaign of '86. I was constantly amazed that so much work must be put forth to run for the office of mayor. Charles brought home engineers' surveys on various ports around the country; books on artesian wells and water depletion; statistics on the trade done by Galveston harbor and also by the Houston harbor; drawings of possible water supply plans. Before long, his already crowded study was bulging with papers and reports on aspects of city life I had never dreamed existed.

As the project of running for public office began to look more and more like the preparation for writing a history book, my enthusiasm began to wane, and the length of time which must pass before the exciting part could begin seemed to grow longer rather than shorter.

And yet those were peaceful days nonetheless. When I looked upon the well-kept garden and grounds at St. Christopher's and saw before me the result of the many hours of work put into making them a credit to the church, it gave me a true feeling of belonging in the community. The process of leaving one place and beginning anew in another was difficult to be sure, but by staying and involving oneself in things to be done, the transition would eventually be complete. I seldom thought of Grady as home any more. With Betsey gone and Ruth married, there was little left to go back to. And Ruth, busy herself, I was sure, never invited us for a visit.

Home was here among the tall palms and the oleanders with their splash of bright color rustling in the same ocean breeze that stroked your face as you walked along the street or sat at night on the big verandah.

Near the end of summer, a communicant from St. Christopher's donated six good crepe myrtles to be planted around the church school building. I gathered four or five of my committee girls, and we went to work planting them. This task took us several days, and after it was done I continued to come alone for several days more, piddling here and there, pulling up weeds, trimming a hedge or two, scrubbing the birdbath in the courtyard, content to busy my hands in surroundings I'd come to love. I hardly noticed the comings and goings of others during this time, allowing my thoughts to dwell on pleasant things here and there . . . to speculate on how Ruth might be doing up in Grady, and whether or not to invest in some new lavender silk I'd seen lately at the Emporium, and what to cook for the Marlowes when they came to dinner the next week . . . then I looked up, toward the church office, and happened to see a very odd thing.

Rubin Garret stood at the window, looking out at me, and when he noticed I'd seen him he didn't wave, but instead drew the curtains closed. Well, maybe he hadn't seen me after all, I thought; perhaps the sunlight was causing a glare on his desk and he closed the curtains to shut it out. I bent down again and pushed my hands into the dark, fecund soil, my heart beating just a shade faster than before.

Now, I knew better than to let my mind dwell on this obviously innocent occurrence. There was nothing between Rubin Garret and me any more than there had been long before, when I'd let my wishful thinking get the best of me. I kept working until I was too tired to work any more, and walked back home. Rubin always kept his horse and rig in the shed behind the church, so I didn't know whether or not he was still around when I left.

Yet the sight of him standing there at the window, just before he drew the curtains, stayed with me into the evening and occupied my thoughts after all the lights were out and I lay in bed. Small forgotten incidents began to sift back into my memory, unusual shows of attentiveness from time to time such as the night we held a dinner party at our house not so long before, with Rubin and Janet and several other couples from the vestry of St. Christopher's attending. He had followed me into the kitchen to get the beverages ready, and said, "Now, let's see, it was tea for Norman and Alice, right? Here, let me pour it . . . and a glass of milk for Henry . . . fruit juice for Stella McKenzie, wasn't it?" And when we were through he insisted upon taking the tray from my hands and carrying it into the dining room. The little event seemed meaningless at the time, except that it was unlike Rubin to be helpful at kitchen chores; he was more often mingling with the guests, telling stories to get everyone laughing, or discussing parish business in his own diplomatic way that always won him his point.

Then there was a day, several weeks earlier, when he came out to the church garden at noontime—it was a terrifically hot and humid day—and offered to go down to a little cafe by the shore that made box lunches to order and bring back one for each of the garden workers. I knew him to be especially busy that day, working on a talk he had to make at a diocesan meeting in Houston over the weekend, and was surprised first by his offer to get lunch, and even more surprised that he seemed to be enjoying eating along with us, lingering so long that even our own work got behind, and pausing before he went back to his own work to say just to me, "You'll never know how grateful I've been for your dedication to St. Christopher's. You're every bit as responsible for its place of importance in this community as I am."

"Oh bosh, get on with you," I'd said, embarrassed at his unusual candor.

Then there had been the afternoon just the week before, when he'd stopped by my porch as I sipped lemonade alone, writing a letter to Helga Reinschmidt about Charles's bid for mayor of Galveston. "Having a bit of refreshment in this heat, eh?" he'd said.

"You want to join me in a glass?"

"No, no, I haven't time," he answered, but came up on the porch and sat down anyway, on the top step, looking away from me. "Charles tells me how much his running for mayor has occupied his time lately—all the studying and so on."

"Yes, it seems endless."

"Well, if there's anything I can do to help you out, I mean, if you need help moving furniture or rearranging pictures or something like that, you know where I am."

"That's kind of you, Rubin."

"Well, good day, then," he'd said, and left, and I had sat there for a while looking after him. How queer he was, I'd thought. One never knew just what to expect from him. Yet every bit of his behavior could have been looked upon as neighborliness. I closed my eyes and went to sleep. Later I awoke with a start. It was not Rubin's actions of late that were so odd to witness. It was Janet's changed way of looking at me, her expression a little wary from time to time, almost as if she suspected something between us.

Next day I came back to the garden again and went about my work as usual, and nothing seemed to have changed; yet I had a curious sensation of being watched and several times looked up and around, shading my eyes from the sun. Nothing. I worked on into the afternoon, becoming more and more involved in what I was about, when all at once I became aware someone was standing behind me, and I looked up with a start. It was Rubin.

"It's getting late," he said.

"Oh, is it? I've lost track of the time."

"Can I give you a ride home?"

"Well, it's nice of you but I can walk . . . that is, unless you happen to be leaving now anyway."

He nodded. How strange his manner seemed. "The rig's out back, in the shed. I could bring it round—"

"All right."

"That is, unless you'd want to walk back with me."

"Well, all right." I stood up, uncomfortable under his gaze, and conscious of the cloak which had covered my feelings for him for such a long time slowly easing away, as a heavy blanket is pulled from off the top of a bed.

We walked side by side across the wide lawn (surely the lawn had never been so wide as it was that day), and entered the shed, the thin layer of hay crunching beneath our feet.

His new rig, a gift from the church he'd made so prosperous, stood awesomely big inside the shed, the horse hitched up and hanging his head low as though he knew what was about to take place and did not want to see.

Rubin held out a steadying hand as I climbed aboard, and my skirt hem caught on a rough edge of wood. "Wait a moment," he said in a voice unusually soft. "Perhaps I can dislodge it without tearing it." Gently he freed the fabric as I watched, then walked around and boarded the rig on his side.

He made no movement toward hustling the horse to ride from the shed. He seemed to have something to say, yet feared to say it, and my own throat might have had a fist in it for all I was able to speak.

"Claire?" he said finally. We both looked straight ahead, out into the afternoon sunshine.

"Yes, Rubin."

"I've been . . . been watching you out there."

"Yes, I know, Rubin."

"I love having you here, watching you do your work."

"I'm glad that it gives you pleasure."

"You told me that once before, long ago."

"Did I?"

"I've seen you bending over the flower beds for hours on end, working them with your hands . . . I've seen you straighten up and rest your hands on your hips, and lean back for a moment to rest. I've watched you wipe the sweat from your brow and look around at what you've done, and I've felt the pride you must have known . . . I've almost believed I shared it with you. And I've often thought how empty this place would be without you . . . if I didn't see you in the morning when I come, know you were here during the day, live impatiently through the winter, waiting for the spring because it would always bring you again, I'd feel a part of me was missing.

"God, forgive me my human frailties . . . I need you, Claire."

I could have told him I'd been waiting for him all along, but instead I took his hand and put it to my face and kissed it, then moved it to my breast. And then his big powerful arms were around me, almost crushing me, and he was kissing me with a hunger that seemed to have been waiting for years to find release. I was hardly aware of our descent from the rig and of being laid down against a bed of hay soft as autumn leaves; and as Rubin entered into me, every part of me so long dead was made alive, every nerve responding with joy and rhythm so long suppressed that at

the end I was left without strength, exhausted and spent
and dazedly happy. He clutched me tightly for a prolonged
moment, then raised himself up.

His eyes were full of dismay.

He helped me to my feet and into the rig, then went
around to the other side and pulled himself in beside me.
"Oh, my God," he said.

I reached for his hand. "Rubin, I love you," I said. He
pulled it away before I touched it and took in hand the
reins, and just then, in the wink of an eye, came the pleasant voice of Mr. Peabody the sexton, and we both looked
out to see his husky frame in the shed opening, blotting out
the sunlight.

"Aft'noon, Father Garret, Miz Becker," he said. "Someone left a hoe out to the garden there. I'll just leave it here
in the shed so's it won't get rained on and rust out."

"Yes," said Rubin. "I was just taking Mrs. Becker home.
Thank you."

"Anythin' else I can do for you today, sir?"

"No, nothing. Give my best to Mrs. Peabody. Good
day."

"G'day, sir," he said, and walked out of the shed.

Rubin let out a breath, and without looking at me again
said, "Do you think he saw?"

"No, of course not. Rubin—"

"No, Claire, not now, please," he said, and guided the
horse out into the daylight. Later, on the way home, he
said, "You know, we've put so much work into the church.
Nothing must ever come to light that would ruin what
we've accomplished."

He was speaking in riddles. What did he mean? Didn't
he know what I'd give if only he'd ask it? Charles, the
church, the mayor's race—all of it be damned if he wanted
me?

It is a very short way from the church to where we live
on Avenue L. Before I could gather my thoughts to speak
we were home. Serena was out in the yard. Her face dirty,
her clothes soiled, and her hair flying, she ran across the
yard and waved and called to us. Rubin waved back, then
turned to me silently for a moment. What his expression
held I can only guess for I kept staring straight ahead.

I allowed him to help me from the rig, walked through

our gate and up to the house. When I got inside I bathed my face and fixed tea, and wondered as I sat there sipping it, was this to be a beginning or another dead end?

Chapter 3

Three months, four, and nothing more happened. Rubin kept away from me most of the time, and when he was near, kept his eyes averted. I was going out of my mind with frustration, as a person for many years imprisoned in an institution, then by some error let out just long enough to get a taste of freedom, before being recaptured again when the error was discovered, and thrown back into a dark, windowless cell.

And all through this I had to pretend there had been no change in my lively interest in Charles's political career. I was possessed of a sharp, uncomfortable feeling all the time, like rubbing my tongue over my teeth after eating a peach.

Early into the new year we received a letter from Ruth. "We're expecting a child around the end of August," she wrote. "Naturally, Edward is overjoyed and expects nothing short of a boy. I'm feeling fine; of course we have no sophisticated specialist up here as you have in Galveston, but Doctor Lanahan assures me I am fit and not aiming for any problems he knows of. Will keep you posted. . . ."

"Does it hurt anymore?" Charles asked me after reading it.

"You mean, do I still miss Ruth?"

"No, I mean, do you still think of our little son?"

"Charlie!" I blurted out, his reference especially maddening in view of my current state of mind. "I mean, no, not too often," I added quickly. "One gets over those things after such a long time, I guess."

"Yes, it has been that . . . a long time."

Not long enough, I thought, that it did not still give me a desolate feeling when I tried but was unable to conjure up his little face in my memory. "How I wish we'd had a picture made of him. It would be something to keep," I said.

"I thought of that, too, but it doesn't seem so important now. I'm only sorry we never had more children . . . guess it's too late now."

"Yes, I suppose it is." In truth I didn't think it was impossible I might conceive again. My spells had subsided just lately and Dr. Hutchisson had never said there was dead certainty I might not conceive another child before the inevitable surgery. Of course I had never told this to Charles, and never would.

"Well, life goes on. We find other consolations."

"Indeed."

"It won't be long, you know, before announcing."

"Yes. Where are you going to do it?"

"At Pete's. We're making a list of people to invite. The public announcement will come fairly quick after, but this will be for known supporters. I'm going to present my platform, of course."

"You've worked so hard on it. It must be good."

"I hope so. Claire, are you all right?"

"Of course. What makes you ask?"

"Nothing you could name. It's just that you seem to be walking around in a daze half the time these past few months, and I've noticed you're losing weight."

"Am I? Well, I'm not sick. Nothing wrong with me. When is your speech going to be ready? I expect you to read it to me first, you know."

"Not for a while, but I had counted on sounding you out."

Just then, Rubin knocked at the back door. He was holding Serena's hand. "We've just received word that Janet's father is ill. I've got to get her to the station for the five o'clock train. We're so rushed. Could you keep Serena?"

"Of course, come in, sweetie . . . Claire, did you hear?"

"Yes. I'm sorry. Poor Janet. Let us know if we can do anything. Does she need help packing?"

"No, I'm helping her get organized. I think we'll make it all right. I've no idea how serious her father is; the telegram didn't say. Came from Cleo, her sister."

He turned and hurried down the porch. "Godspeed," said Charles. Serena had already found her place in his arms. "Unca Sharrie, is Mama sick?"

"No, dear, your mother is just fine. It's her father. She has to go and be with him for a while. Now, if we can talk Claire into pulling out those toys she keeps around here, I'll bet you and I can have a lot of fun tonight." She hugged his neck, and he kissed her loudly on the cheek. Having the child with him was always a momentous occasion for Charles, and I knew he'd forfeit all work to be done in the study this evening to play with her.

As the situation turned out, Serena spent a great deal of time at our house in the next few weeks. Janet's father rallied for a while after his first spell, but within a matter of days took a turn for the worse.

Rubin came one afternoon for Serena while she was napping upstairs. Certainly he must have known he would have to face me, sooner or later, alone. He'd apparently come to terms with this that day because he had always brought Serena in the morning when he knew Charles would still be at home, and had always waited till evening after Charles's rig made its way down the drive to come and fetch her.

We began with a game of cat and mouse.

"Come in and sit down," I told him. "I've made coffee and an extra large batch of chicken and dumplings so you and Serena can eat with us tonight. Or you can take a pot home if you'd rather. You look tired."

He lowered himself into a chair. "Yes, I am."

I poured two cups of coffee and touched my free hand to my forehead as I leaned over to pour.

"Are you all right?"

"Yes, though I do have a headache. Don't worry. It'll go away."

"Let me take Serena and we'll leave you alone. I've imposed on you so much these past few weeks. . . ."

"Nonsense. Keep your seat. I took some medicine I keep for pain a few minutes ago. My only problem is I haven't had any coffee or tea all day. I need to sit down with a cup and relax."

We sat across from each other in silence, stirring our coffee as though we were dolls and had been wound up to do so.

"Any word from Janet?" I said, finally.

"Not for a few days. It kind of worries me, not hearing. Oh well, I'm sure she'd let me know if anything happened . . . by the way, I guess it won't be long before the campaign is launched. Charles says he's been boning up on artesian wells and harbor improvements and . . ."

"Yes. If he's successful, it's going to make a difference in our lives."

"How do you mean?"

"I don't know. I've never been married to a mayor before."

"One thing is sure . . . you two will be quite a prestigious couple and in demand all the time for social functions and civic affairs."

The medicine had begun to take effect. I felt light-headed, giddy. Probably if I had taken the medicine and gone to bed I would have been asleep by now; drinking the coffee, though, was having an odd countereffect.

"Yes. We might even move away from here, up to Broadway."

"Oh, no, Charles would never do that."

"Why not, Rubin? Because of your deep friendship with each other, huh?"

"Please, Claire, you don't understand. I've been through the tortures of hell since that day when we, when . . ." His voice trailed off. He rose from the table and went to stand against the counter, looking out the window.

"When we what, Rubin? When we made love to each other? Why can't you say it out loud? I'm not ashamed of it. Why should you be ashamed of so honest an emotion as love and desire for another human being? Don't you see, it's the only thing in life that really counts?"

"No, Claire, it's not that simple—oh, how I wish it were! So much has happened. So many lies have been spoken, so many secrets, so many things have gone wrong." He was speaking softly, gazing out the window as though something out there had him mesmerized.

"Listen, Rubin," I said impatiently, "we could go away now, or any time you say. Damn the mayor's race; damn anything and anybody that keeps us from being together. It seems I've spent my life living a travesty. I've never loved Charles, except perhaps in the way you love Janet—not with passion or urgency or any of the things that make life worth living. I loved his brother Damon that way, but I couldn't have him and I married Charles instead, and I knew then it was wrong and unfair, but I've lived with him, tried to be a good wife, to help him in his career. . . ."

"Claire . . ."

"But damn it, Rubin, when is *my* turn going to come, and when is yours?" Tears welled up in my eyes. "We could leave it all; Janet and Charles would survive, people *do* survive what they have to, and we could go anywhere you say. And, Rubin, I could give you a child of your own,

I know I could, and you just don't know the happiness you
would feel in that moment when you held him in your
arms, your *own* child, not somebody else's.

"Rubin, I've waited so long for you to do what you did
that day in the shed. I've spent years waiting for our time
to come. . . . Rubin, I can give you happiness you'd never
dreamed existed if you'll only have the courage to do what
you really want to do."

I bowed my head over the table and let the tears roll
down my cheeks and make plip-plops on the table cover,
even then marveling at the bold words that had rushed
from my lips.

Was Rubin unmoved? I couldn't tell. He stood at the
open window as though his feet were riveted to the floor.
Finally he turned from the window and came back to the
table to sit. I looked up at him. There was nothing I wished
to hide.

All the color was gone from his face. "Claire, let me tell
you something that will explain . . . please, I feel I owe it
to you. But you must promise me you won't tell anyone
else about it, not Charles, not anyone."

I nodded.

He looked across at me imploring as a child who begs
forgiveness for breaking a dish, then he began. "Janet and
I," he said, then paused.

"Go on, go on," I commanded.

"We don't—can't—have never . . . lived as man and
wife."

The meaning of his statement did not immediately filter
through the cobwebs of my mind. I looked at him aston-
ished, trying to interpret. "How can that be?"

"We just don't."

"But you couldn't lie next to each other night after night,
year after year . . . how absurd. I don't believe you."

"We don't . . . lie next. My room is separate from hers."

"No, I've let you talk in circles to me before, but this is
too much. How perfectly—is this your way of explaining, a
lie? Please don't. You are a man—how impossible—"

"I am a servant of God!" he said, his voice raised.
"More is expected. What could I do? I love her, and I've
never given up hope that one day she'd get over that horrible event in her childhood that makes her repelled by me
. . . by all men. Don't you see how much wrong I've already done, betraying her trust when she has no defense

against it? What I've done to her is far worse than it would be if she were, well . . . normal.

"If I could ever lay my hands on that scoundrel who forced himself on a thirteen-year-old child—did you know my poor dear Janet had been raped, Claire? Violated against her will when she was too young even to understand what was happening to her?"

"Rubin?" I stretched a hand across to touch his face. His eyes were filled; he would cry in front of me, I knew, and I couldn't stand it. He took my hand away and gently laid it on the table. "So you can see, I could never leave her. It would be a sin far worse than those I've already committed. I can hardly live with myself now. I'd sooner be dead than to commit any more wrongs against her . . . or anyone."

"Oh, Rubin, please, please—"

"No, I must go. Claire, please forgive me as Christ has taught us all to forgive." He rose from the table and went to the back door. "I'll come for Serena later," he said quietly, and walked out, closing the door behind him.

I sat at the table long after, my clammy hands outstretched, unable to comprehend what had just taken place. At first, the only part of it that penetrated my mind was the fact of Rubin's celibacy with his wife. I didn't know whether I ought to be pleased or repulsed, and couldn't get my thoughts together.

Then little bits and pieces of memory returned like the trickle of water into a cup. Janet's telling me of Rubin's patience and understanding that evening we walked to our first oyster roast; and later, when she became so angry at my insinuation she might be expecting—gad, no wonder!—and still later, when she came over one night and asked if my doctor could help women who had "other" problems; Janet as a young girl being held down and raped.

I lay my head down on the table and wept. It was a curious thing to do, because I did not know for whom I was weeping.

It was soon after that day that Rubin came to tell Charles and me the wire had been received about Janet's father's death. When I asked him if he'd be going to Virginia, he glanced at me quickly, then looked down before answering. "No, Janet will be coming home soon. Cleo will stay and help for a while."

After he was gone Charles remarked, "Rubin seems to be taking this pretty hard—did you notice how washed-out he looked?"

"Isn't it so," I agreed, though I knew the state of Rubin's appearance had nothing to do with the telegram he held in his hand. I felt so sorry for the man, yet at the same time so utterly frustrated that he would not accept the kind of help that only I could give him. My confused mental state after our day in the shed was nothing to compare with my dispirited feelings following our bizarre conversation at the kitchen table. I lost all appetite and had trouble keeping the simplest thoughts straight. I couldn't remember where I'd left my sewing basket from time to time and lost my handbag while out shopping one day. I misplaced magazines and mail and once found I'd packed a sterling silver teaspoon between layers of clean bed linens.

In early May I took fabric to Madame LaRoche. Charles's announcement at the Marlowe home in June was to be a formal affair with a buffet dinner and reception, and, for the first time I could remember, he'd expressed the wish that I should have something new to wear. I picked candlelight silk with seed pearls and soft blue lace. When Madame took my measurements—she always took new ones no matter how little time had lapsed since the previous time she had made a frock for a customer—she said, "Ah, Mrs. Becker, what has happened to you? Your waist has decreased an inch and a half, and your hips have lost some of their roundness. It's good I took new measurements today . . . you probably bought too much material."

A look in the cloudy full-length mirror confirmed her estimation. Even my cheeks had grown hollow. A horrible irony struck me then: after awaiting Charles's announcement for months on end, and planning my own appearance at the gathering, I would look my worst instead of my best.

Still, it was Charles himself who truly brought me to my senses. I could hear him pacing up and down in his study when I returned from Madame's that day, and I knocked softly to show him I was home.

"Claire, is that you? Come in here, will you? I want you to listen to something in my speech. It seems a bit awkward."

I walked in and sat down obediently in front of him. As he said nothing for a few moments, only stared at me, I finally asked him why he didn't get on with it.

"Claire, what in heaven's name is the matter with you?" he asked. "I make my decision to run for mayor of Galveston, in no small measure because it's what you want, and almost from the moment I tell you, you begin to change from an enthusiastic helpmate to a slow, lethargic mute. Have you changed your mind? Because if you have, I'll be damned if I'll go through with it. It's going to be difficult enough, without worrying about you. Now, tell me the truth. Are you ill?"

"No."

"Well, if not, what in God's name is bothering you?"

"Nothing. Of course I haven't changed my mind. I want this almost more than anything in the world. It's just— I haven't had much appetite lately. The heat, I guess, and then so much time worrying over Serena this spring with Janet gone, one thing and another, and then I haven't had much help with the garden and I've been working awfully hard."

"All right. But I want to see some pink in your cheeks this time next month or, I swear to you, I won't go through with this business. I'll call it off before it really begins."

"No, please. I'll eat, I promise. You'll be proud of me by the time the day comes. Now, read me that part of your speech."

His lecture had a rallying effect on me, and helped put matters into perspective again. Could I not have Rubin, I would be foolish to jeopardize what blessings had been given me. If I couldn't force my heart into the mayoral campaign, I could at least throw my energies toward it, and I did. I overate at meals until I was sick at the sight of food. I took long afternoon naps when time permitted; I stayed away from the garden and away from Rubin (the latter of which was no difficult task to accomplish). I lunched with Faye and Isobel at the Imperial. I shopped for new hats. I restyled my hair into an upsweep with curls. I bought more fabric; had more outfits put into the making. By the night of the announcement I felt better twenty times over, and when Charles watched me model the candlelight silk he smiled contentedly and said, "Well, even if we go down in defeat, we'll do it in style."

The magnitude of the situation had left my awareness over the past few months, not only because of what had occurred between Rubin and me, but also because over the many months since Charles decided to run, the mayor's campaign had been reduced to a speech on paper and endless nights of his pacing the floor with it.

That night of the announcing, though, it all became real again. Handsome rigs, one after another, were pulled up along the front of the Marlowe property and down the block when we arrived.

"I thought only a few were to be here tonight," I told Charles.

"Oh, about fifty, I guess, counting wives."

"I don't know how you can be so calm."

"There's nothing to be worried about tonight—this is a gathering of friends. I feel prepared, and I'm determined to enjoy this before they throw me to the lions a few weeks from now."

"Charles, you do want it too, don't you? You're not doing this just for me?"

"No, I'll admit the idea has grown on me a bit. But I'm still not kidding myself. We have only a small chance of beating Fuller. Did you know he's decided to run again?"

"No, I hadn't heard, but I'm not surprised."

"Not that it really matters. If it wasn't him, it would be someone else of the almighty men's choice—some other puppet to do their bidding."

Just as we approached the wide porch a male voice came from behind. "If this isn't a winning couple, I've never seen one."

We looked around to see Lucien Carter, immaculate as ever. Isobel was at his side, a stunning figure in a deep green taffeta gown with sparkling emeralds encircling her throat and plunging down her soft breast. We bid them a cheery hello and walked in together.

I never expected the sight which greeted us when we got up to the entrance of the Marlowes'. The buffet itself was set up in the large dining room so that people could walk around the table and fill their plates, then proceed into the ballroom. There, at one end, were small round tables and chairs set with candles and silverware. Further back, to the rear of the room, chairs were set up classroom style with an aisle down the center. At the tail end was a podium that rivaled one I'd seen before in a daguerreotype of some presidential inauguration long ago. It was a massive platform, hung with blue bunting with a slender speaker's stand in the center and five chairs behind.

"What'cha think?" Pete inquired.

"I don't know what to say. It's so grand. Forgive me, I'm quite overwhelmed at all of this suddenly. I had no idea it would be anything like this."

"Your husband is a very important man, young lady. The trappings for his platform speech had to be in keepin' with the occasion."

Many passed before us in a reception line soon after we arrived. Of these, one man in particular remains in my memory. Porter Jackson, prosperous nursery owner, suggested we have a telephone installed for the campaign. "We've just gotten one at the store," he said proudly, "and you've no idea what a fabulous contraption it is." Galveston had been the site of the first telephone installation in Texas several years back, but there were relatively few phones on the island as yet. I smiled and said, "Why, certainly—what a wonderful idea," but thought to myself a telephone was a bunch of tomfoolery.

I was a little surprised at the appearance of some of the guests, having had no idea their wealth was sufficient enough for them to pledge dollars to Charles's campaign, but then Charles has always said not all wealthy people put on show.

After we'd greeted everyone, Pete announced from the podium in his folksy manner, "Ladies and gents, we're gonna eat by and by, but before I git your stomachs full and git you all comfortable and sleepy, I want to progress on to the business at hand. So if everybody will have a seat up here in front, we'll start."

The chairs behind the podium were for Lucien and Isobel, Faye and Pete and me. As we made our way to the front, I felt my first misgivings about the whole thing. I hadn't realized what an awesome task we had before us. All these people were here because they expected something great from Charles. They expected him to save their city for them, or else they would have never gone out on a limb in his behalf. I felt so small, inadequate. I looked at Charles as he took my hand and lifted me up to the platform. He looked confident; distinguished. I wondered whether I would ever learn to appreciate him fully.

His figure was tall and fine as he stood up in front of us, and I kept telling myself over and over, "This is it. We're finally here. It is only the beginning." Yet my body tensed at the deep, resonant sound of his voice and I clenched a fist around my closed fan. He outlined the situations he believed so threatening to the progress of our city, and followed with his plans for solving each of them. He spoke about all the issues he'd spent months researching—from his intent to solve the water supply crisis by piping in water from the mainland, to his proposal to break the stranglehold of the wharf monopoly once and for all. I realized his convictions had never been so earnestly and cogently expressed, his plans never so feasible, as his voice carried smoothly out among the audience, where every eye and ear remained on him from the beginning of his speech to his closing comments.

For one or two moments after he uttered his thank-you, a silence hung in the air and my heart seemed to swell until I could feel it in my throat. Then all at once the room was alive with applause. As Charles nodded and drew back from the podium, the applause evolved into a standing ovation that seemed to go on and on. Just when I'd begun to relax a little and open my fan Charles turned around and grabbed my hand, pulling me up beside him as the clapping and shouting continued.

I knew suddenly how thrilling the role of the candidate could be, and how easy to believe in one's victory. Pete was up there beside us then, holding high his arms and shouting at the top of his lungs, "VICTORY FOR BECKER IN '86, VICTORY FOR BECKER." I looked at Charles's perspiring face. It was suffused with a delight and wonder I had never before seen there.

Chapter 4

From that night on the campaign was a force that caught us up and drove us through each day, and depleted us of all energy and ability to think clearly by the time we went to bed at night. It was not long before the *News* described Charles's campaign as "the most vigorous mayoral campaign ever to take place in this city." The *News* sided with Charles from the start, and staff reporters came out often to interview him on the progress of the campaign.

There was nothing complicated about the race. Charles spoke before people in parks, before club meetings, in front of special interest groups—anywhere he was invited. I went a few times to witness his campaign speeches, but often did not attend. I would be at home waiting for him to arrive, with a bucket of hot salty water ready to soak his tired, swollen feet, and a good hearty dinner—enough for Charles and anyone who came in with him.

Often Pete came, talking incessantly, making suggestions, commenting on his reception of the evening. Charles would be nodding, looking to me for encouragement. "I tell you, Claire," Pete must have said a hundred times that summer and fall, "we're gonna give that Fuller a run for his money, you bet'cha life. Must have been three hundred people at the park tonight, cheerin' and carryin' on like you never seen. Don't you believe we haven't got those scoundrels at the Wharf Company shakin' in their boots—"

Still, the fact Fuller would be hard to beat couldn't be denied. He'd pleased a lot of people in Galveston during his career. He praised the existing wharf facilities, and it was easy enough to say to the people that Houston would never have a prayer of coming up to our standards as a port. "A major port fifty miles from the Gulf of Mexico? Preposterous!" That was what he said one night at some dinner where he spoke, after first reminding those attending that Charles's election would most assuredly mean an increase in city taxes. His words about the port were recorded next day in the *News* as part of the context of a scathing editorial which also noted Fuller would be saying that when the port of Galveston consisted of nothing but boarded-up wharves and empty docks.

Once Pete followed up on Porter Jackson's suggestion—the night of Charles's speech—that we have a telephone installed at our house. He had one in his, and he wanted to stay in constant contact with Charles throughout the campaign. I listened intently to Charles's reaction. "I won't have my home turned into a campaign headquarters," he said. "It's bad enough the office is in a state of disruption all the time."

"All right, boy, whatever you say."

Even without the phone, however, our home would never be quite the hideaway of solace it had been before the campaign began. There had been handbills printed up, and as they were so shorthanded down at Charles's office I was chosen to solicit the help of neighborhood boys to place them at as many locations throughout the city as possible. The copy on the handbills was thought up by Isobel

Carter, and she made the original for duplicating. They were about fifteen by twenty inches in size, with a large picture of Charles in the center. At the top they read, "Save Galveston," then below the picture, "Vote for Charles Becker on March sixth."

Rubin went with Charles to his first campaign speech toward the end of June, and from that time on was as engrossed in the campaign as any of us. He attended as many rallies as he could, and his name appeared one day in the *News* as being a Charles Becker supporter. How could any of us have known of the consequences that benign piece of news would bring?

Throughout the summer Janet kept to herself, just why I had no time to ponder. Since she'd returned from Virginia in early May I hadn't had a decent conversation with her, save the night Charles and I both went over to her house briefly to offer our condolences about her father. She appeared saddened, yet resigned to his death, and I felt this was probably because she was with him during his illness and could see that he was suffering.

I do remember walking by her house once or twice and seeing the shutters drawn, and I would recall then how many years the thought of her lying in Rubin's arms had tormented me before the day, which now seemed years ago instead of months, when I'd learned the truth about Janet and Rubin. Since then I'd often thought how queer, how very, very queer they were, and my attraction for Rubin had steadily dulled. At times it seemed almost laughable to remember how much he once reminded me of Damon.

Then one day everything went into reverse. There was to be a small surprise gathering to celebrate Faye's birthday in a couple of days. ("Nothin' too elaborate," Pete had told me. "Lord knows we got enough to do without havin' birthday parties. Just the same, she's put up with campaign talk till it runs out her ears, and I feel I owe her this.") And as Charles had the rig down at the office that day I'd walked to Schott's Drug Store to buy Faye a bottle of Essence of Sweet Orchids perfume. It was her scent—the one she used so generously—and I had heard her remark one day she was almost at the bottom of a bottle. It wasn't much of a birthday gift, but what could one give a person who already had everything? While there, I noticed a display of Huyler's Bon-Bons, and in a fit of nostalgia over the fact Teddy Marlowe had often gifted Ruth with the candies the summer she visited so long ago, I bought a box for Faye.

I was walking back when I saw Janet at the edge of her front verandah. How pale and wan she looked as she clutched the banister and made her way slowly, carefully down the twelve stairs . . . almost as if she were ill, I thought. Then, perhaps because I'd been reminiscing about Ruth just moments earlier, something she'd said once struck me again. "Receding," she had called Janet, a person with a "faraway" look. I caught my breath as the obvious reason for her withdrawal over the past few months dawned on me. Janet was dying.

I continued to gaze at her until she'd reached the front walk and looked up. "Oh, hello," she called, "I was just on my way to see you, didn't know you were gone."

"Are you all right?" I asked quickly.

"Yes, I think so . . . for now," she said, walking toward me, the edge of her lips curved into a tentative smile.

I invited her in for tea then, and as she followed me through my gate and up the front stairs, each step seemed to bring forward another clue looming at the back of my memory—simple instincts felt not only by Ruth and by me, but voiced by Janet herself. She couldn't feature growing old, she'd remarked once, long ago. And the photograph of Anna McBride I'd seen so many years ago in Charles's old office: a woman from whose face I tried to discern the subtle shadow of early death. Now the resemblance between that face and the face of Janet Garret glared at me, and Ruth's word repeated itself again and again: receding, receding . . . yes! Receding into darkness and oblivion . . .

Had Rubin felt it too, and reasoned that if Janet were to be taken from him early, surely he could grant her the kindness of standing by her for as long as she lived?

We were inside the house now, and I could hear her skirt rustling behind me as I swung open the kitchen door. It was almost too much . . . realizing in one instant the tragic predicament of Janet Garret, then, with scarcely a chance to come to grips with the certain knowledge, to be placed in the uncomfortable situation of entertaining her at my kitchen table.

I put the kettle on as she eased down into a chair. She pulled out a hanky and wiped her forehead. "It's still awfully hot, isn't it?" she said. "I know this year I'll be especially thankful for the cooler months ahead."

"If you'd rather drink something cold, I can get—"

"No, no. Odd, isn't it, but hot tea has a steadying effect on me, even in the heat."

"Yes, for me, too," I said, and wondered then if she knew the full truth of the seriousness of her condition. Perhaps a doctor would withhold that sort of information as long as possible.

It was a while before I spoke again, and she was silent as I groped for something to say. "We've been so caught up in the campaign, I've hardly seen you lately," I said finally, trying to keep from staring at the grayish pools underneath her eyes.

"I haven't been feeling very well," she said.

Just then the teakettle began to sing, startling me so I almost leaped up from my chair. "Ready!" I said, too abruptly, and rose to fill the cups. Making conversation was easier with my back to her, so I continued, "Have you seen a doctor?"

"Oh yes," she said, then paused. "You see, Rubin and I are expecting a child."

I pivoted around and stared at her, unable to speak. She was quite mad, I thought at first, and not to be taken seriously. How best to talk to someone who is mad? I studied her eyes. What was their expression? Defiance, yes, decidedly. Was it possible I'd been the object of a cruel joke? Was Rubin even now sitting over there laughing, waiting for Janet to return and give him my reaction to her story? I measured my words ever so carefully when finally I spoke. "My dear, how nice. When?"

"February, March. Doctor says first babies sometimes tarry. I've felt so wretched. But, except for a little dizziness, I am getting a little better now; after the first four months, I suppose one becomes accustomed."

"How wonderful, a baby brother or sister for Serena."

"Yes. She is most delighted, I assure you. I want to share the experience with her, want her to love the baby when it comes. It's a very hard thing for some children to get used to a new arrival—all depends upon how the child is prepared, don't you think?"

"Yes."

"Well, I must get back. I promised Serena a trip down to the beach this afternoon."

I saw her out, watched her go down the porch steps and across the yard, knowing she had undone me and that someday I would get her back. Best now to shove it from my mind; concentrate on the election.

I walked back into the kitchen and passed by the current *News* Charles had left on the counter. I envisioned a new headline on the front page: "Priest and Wife Conspire to Drive Friend Insane." How hysterical. I began to laugh, and I laughed and laughed until tears ran down my face.

Chapter 5

It was the strategy of the "Charles Becker for Mayor" campaign that voters should be made aware of the candidate and his platform quite early, then later allowed to watch current events in the city while savoring the image put forth by him. Therefore, after better than two months of heavy speaking engagements, the thrust toward victory would be laid aside to cool—while the Galveston weather did the same. Then with the opening of the new year— election year—campaigning would again become vigorous and hold with the pattern until election day.

As the month of September rolled around I was thankful to see the change in schedule coming, for the pace of the summer had begun catching up with Charles. He looked drawn and tired, and confessed to missing acutely the time he was accustomed to spending at practicing law. "Confound it, Claire," he told me one day, "Pete keeps delegating legal cases that would normally come to me out to others because my time has been consumed with this thing. I told him yesterday if I didn't begin handling my share of the cases, I would likely forget what I know about the law. Then if we lose the election, I'd be in fine straits."

"You've said it yourself, one must work a good deal harder when approaching the voters with a totally new concept in city government. Besides, you're not going to lose."

"Don't count on victory. It looks good, but it also looks highly favorable for Fuller. He's done his share of campaigning, I can assure you, and our spies report his turnouts are every bit as good as ours, sometimes better."

"What do you mean, spies?" I asked him.

"People we send to watch his speeches and gather what he's talking about so we'll know how to counteract."

"I see. And does Fuller send people to watch you?"

"Of course, Claire. Don't be naïve. Politics is cutthroat at any level."

"Do you think Fuller would have launched his campaign so early if it hadn't been for you?"

"I doubt it. The other two contenders—Smith and Doaks—don't pose any threat. It's essentially between us."

"That's life, isn't it?" I said. "Political race, war, whatever, it always comes down to one-to-one in the end, doesn't it?"

"My, you're philosophical today. What's that thing you're knitting?"

"A blanket for Ruth's baby James. The boy's been in the world almost two weeks, and I've known he was coming for months. I've never had time till now to make anything to send to him."

"Ah, yes, and I've hardly had time to think of him at all. You know, Pete told me something the other day that really surprised me. His boy Teddy—you know, Teddy will be coming into the firm before long—wrote letters to Ruth for a couple of years after she went home that summer. I never knew that, did you?"

"She never mentioned anything about it to me. I shouldn't wonder, though. Teddy was quite taken with Ruth, but for some reason she just didn't cotton to him in like fashion. I would have been happy for them to have gotten together . . . in fact, at the time it seemed incredibly important . . . but one person's attraction for another—or lack of it—is one of the world's great wonders."

"Yes. That's quite true."

Just then I heard a knocking at the back door. At first I thought someone was playing tricks, for when I opened the door no one was there. Then Rubin walked up from the side of the back porch. "I was just admiring your yard, Claire, and thinking how I regret seeing the time of year come that will kill the grass and flowers. The church grounds look so pretty still . . . Charles home?"

He had not looked directly at me while speaking, though of course this came as no surprise. I felt it likely his reference to the beauty of our yard was but an excuse for having something to look at while he spoke to me. I had said nothing to him since learning from Janet they were expecting a baby. Any remark I might have made would have sounded foolish, and he would have seen straight through it.

"Yes, in the parlor. Come in."

He followed me through the hall and into the parlor, and I had an urge to stop walking and turn around suddenly, to see if he was watching me.

"Rubin, my good man, come in. My first afternoon off," said Charles. "I'm relaxing and being waited upon. Sit down."

Now, in the dim afternoon light of the parlor I could see something was troubling Rubin.

"Everything going all right? Onward to victory, and so forth?" He made a fist with his right hand, a hearty gesture that would have suited him on other days, yet today looked unnatural.

"The lull before the storm," said Charles. "I've got till the first of the year to recuperate from the summer."

"Actually, it's the campaign that I wanted to speak to you about," he began. "You remember that item in the *News* not so long ago, mentioning my name as having been in attendance at your speech in Oleander Park?"

Charles nodded.

"Well . . . it appears I've caught the notice of Bishop Palmer. Although he's in Houston, he follows the Galveston *News* as faithfully as he did when he lived here on the island. Anyway, to make a long story short, he came to see me this morning. You might say he was adamant about the situation—my appearing at a political rally. I've had my hands slapped verbally. First time since I entered the priesthood."

Charles leaned forward in his chair. "You mean he was angry just because you went to hear my speech?"

"Priests are expected to be nonpartisan souls."

"But did you explain you were only among the audience? I mean, it's not as though you were up on the stand with me, or had spoken publicly in my favor, from the pulpit of St. Christopher's. What could possibly be wrong with—?"

"A great deal, apparently, although after hearing him out I'm still not sure exactly what. Bishop Palmer is very conservative. Perhaps anyone else would not have seen the situation in the same light as he."

"But that's outrageous! I thought priests were supposed to be free citizens."

Rubin put up a hand. "Now, don't take the man too seriously. It's only that I'd planned on lending your campaign a good deal of support come the first of the year, and I wanted to explain that I would be able to take no further part in it . . . on express orders from the bishop."

"Can't you protest?" I said. "Can't you go to someone higher up than him? Is he so almighty?"

"No, I wouldn't have him do that," Charles said. "I've already been the cause of some expense on Rubin's behalf, and I won't be anymore. It isn't worth it."

"Of course, there is nothing to keep me from going to the polls in March to cast my vote. It's only that I wanted to do something more for my best friend, that's all."

There was an awkward moment following the remark, in which I could see Charles was deeply touched. Rubin seldom labeled anything; that was why it took Charles so by surprise. "You've already done more for me than any best friend could ever be expected to," he told him.

Rubin looked away. "Well, I must be going. We're getting rid of some things to make room for the baby, and I promised Janet I'd haul off a wagonload today."

"How is Janet?" Charles asked.

"She has her good and bad days, I'm afraid. The doctor told us she's in delicate health. He's seeing her more frequently than usual. You know, she has never been a strong person. But so far, everything is fine."

He rose from his chair, and I put my knitting aside. "No, don't bother seeing me out," he said.

When he was gone Charles said, "Poor Rubin. All he has done for me and now I am to be the cause of trouble for him."

"Really, I can't see why this bishop's attitude should be so much of a problem. Surely nothing further can come from it."

"No," said Charles. "No, I should hope not, though you never know."

It was an easygoing, lackadaisical fall season during which, except for a few brief meetings between Pete and Charles with Lucien attending from time to time, there seemed almost no sign a campaign was in progress. Charles got busy again with his work of drawing contracts and handling lawsuits, appearing in court and reading briefs and the *Southern Law Review*. The rest from the hectic pace was doing him good—I could see the healthy color returning to his cheeks.

My own appearance, regrettably, was not in keeping with his. I'd begun to lose weight again, and no wonder, for my stomach was like a spinning windmill most of the time. I tried to keep my mind off Janet and Rubin, but with the ease-up in the campaign schedule and with Charles busy working, it was impossible. Every time I saw Janet it seemed her body under the loosely draped clothing she'd taken to wearing had changed a little more. She was a long time in showing that child, because she was so tall, and thin as the leaf on a willow tree.

I'd made up my mind to something that fall: if Charles did succeed in becoming mayor of Galveston, I would do everything in my power to persuade him to move from this house and into a bigger and finer one on Broadway. It had to be Broadway, for he would believe my motivation for moving there was strictly one of gaining prestige. Actually, I didn't care about moving there. I only knew that if we did not move, things between Rubin and me were bound to surface again one day and everybody would wind up being hurt.

The breeze cooled off the island in early October, but real winter didn't set in until well into November. One Friday night there was a particularly strong gale blowing from the northeast. The wind was all we knew about when we went to bed that night. By Saturday morning, though, the greater part of Galveston's most heavily populated business-residential district had been laid to ruin.

We had been up late, playing whist with Janet and Rubin because Janet was confined to the house by this time and wanted company. We left their house at midnight, both of us bone tired and me with an aching head from the sheer tension of being with them for such a long time. I hadn't wanted to go but Charles insisted, so what could I say?

We had left one window up about halfway in the bedroom because we both like to sleep under mounds of cover and feel the coolness of the wind across our faces. Shortly after falling asleep we opened our eyes simultaneously. The fire alarm was loud and shrill enough to bring the devil up from hell. The stiff breeze had blown the curtains aside, and one panel had swept up and caught on the rod.

We ran to the window. "Damn it, you can't see a thing from this room. I'm going down," said Charles. He grabbed his robe and I grabbed mine. I had no idea what time it was, but from the color of the small patch of sky visible from our bedroom window, I assumed it was nearing dawn. We hurried down the stairs, and I glanced at the clock. The time was one thirty-five. How ridiculous, I thought, the clock must have stopped in the night. Yet as we stepped outside I realized I was mistaken.

It was my first impression the fire was much closer than it actually turned out to be. The sky was an amber haze and even from the yard I could see the tips of the roaring flames. Charles ran to the stable, the tail of his robe flying like a flag behind him, and brought open the doors. I could hear Gypsy inside, whinnying and shuffling in fear of the unremitting sound of the bell.

In a few moments Charles came out with his stepladder. "We can't do anything until we find out where it's coming from. My God, it looks like it's consuming the whole island," he said.

He put the ladder against the house and instructed me to stay down, but of course I was one step behind him as he reached the rooftop. The strong gale plastered my hair to my head and I had to squint to see anything. The flames were east of us, quite a distance away.

"I've got to get down there," Charles cried. "It's the Strand, looks like, about Sixteenth or Seventeenth."

By now Rubin had come out and was standing below. "I'll go with you," he told Charles. "Claire, will you stay with Janet? She's frightened and I fear for her in her delicate condition."

It was a voice of desperation and there was no time to think of disobeying it. As I walked across to their yard Charles and Rubin hurried out front on foot. There was no question of taking the rig. Gypsy would probably have taken off running in the opposite direction and ended up drowning them all in the Gulf.

Serena was standing out on the porch in her gown, barefooted. The child was scared to death, probably from all the commotion as much as the sight of the flames themselves. She was shouting through tears to Rubin, begging him to take her with him. I whisked her up and tried to comfort her as best I could. "Come on in, dear, we've got to stay with your mommy. Daddy will be back soon."

"Oh, Claire, are we going to burn up?"

"No, child, the fire is quite far away and the men from

the fire department are putting it out right now. Can't you hear the alarm?"

I only wished I could feel as confident as I tried to sound. After all, the fire department's efficiency was one thing. The water supply—still the unsolved "crisis" as Charles termed it in his speech—was quite another. From the size of the fire I doubted every cistern combined on the island plus what other water supply existed would be adequate to control the flames.

I carried Serena inside and up the stairs, and went into Janet's room. She was sitting up in bed, looking wide-eyed as the first time I had ever seen her. "Have they gone down there?"

"Yes, though I don't know what help they'll be able to give."

"Come here, Serena," she said gently. "Naughty girl. You shouldn't run outside like that. Get into bed with Mommy." Serena went to her mother's arms and Janet rocked her gently until her weeping stopped.

"I'll make tea," I said. "Best way to calm one's nerves and while away the time."

"Yes, but, please, don't he long. I feel safer with you near."

Janet's kitchen was in its usual state of disorder, with dirty dishes lined up haphazardly along the counter and piled in the sink. I searched the cupboards until I found two clean cups and saucers, then pulled out a glass and found some juice for Serena. I knew I should have gone up while the kettle was coming to a boil, but I sat down instead by the table, and, noticing that crumbs from the last meal eaten there were still upon it, got up to find a cloth and wipe it.

It seemed that a long time passed before the teakettle began to whistle, and in the interim the fire alarm bell ceased its wild clanging. When it stopped the house seemed oddly at peace, as it would be in early morning when the sun is just beginning to rise and one sits at the table for the first cup of coffee of the day. I fixed a tray and took it up.

"Oh, God, do you think they'll put it out before it covers the island?" Janet asked.

"How would I know? Charles says it is down near the Strand. That would be a distance from here, so probably it will never come near to us."

"Those poor people who live down there. How awful!" She was speaking softly because she had finally managed to croon Serena into sleeping and didn't want to wake her. "Sometimes I wonder how many things can happen in Galveston . . . sometimes the island itself seems almost doomed."

That was an odd remark. It seemed to me that since we had lived here not so many terrible things had happened. There had been no outbreak of yellow fever, no influenza epidemic, no great hurricanes. But I supposed the first storm she experienced, mild as it was, still weighed on her mind, and then of course, the Pavilion fire two years before. "Try to keep calm," I told her in my most dutiful fashion. "Remember, you've got the child inside you to worry about. You could bring on early labor."

"Yes, yes," she said. "Claire, you were so kind to come. I suppose I'd better lie back and try to relax." She took a sip of tea, put the cup on the table beside the bed, and lay back on the pillows. She could be so childlike in her trusting. . . .

I left the room and went outdoors a couple of times to see if there were any changes in the sky, but as far as I could tell the fire still raged as it had when we had first awakened. The wind was down. Women and children were gathered in the streets, watching. Their men I assumed to be down at the fire, helping. I waved at Agatha Mueller and Florence Middleton, but did not go out and get involved in the conversation, which I knew to be chiefly speculation. I went back upstairs and sat down in the rocker in Janet's room, and that is where I stayed for the balance of the night and into the morning.

I awoke to the sunlight streaming through the window, my back and shoulders aching as though I had plowed a field. Serena and Janet lay bundled together, sleeping, and looking at them I wondered whether Janet's love for her adopted child would wane a bit after she experienced the thrill of giving birth to her own baby.

The bedroom clock showed eight-thirty. I walked outside to see if anyone was around who had been at the fire, or, indeed, whether it was over. It was chilly, even inside the house, and I found a shawl lying over a living room chair and wore it outside.

The sky was still hazy but there were no more flames. How long it had been since the last of it was extinguished we would not know until Charles and Rubin came home, or until I spotted someone else who had been there. But the street was clear of people. I looked down the block and saw no one. By all appearances one might have thought the fire had been a terrible dream. Yet up through the trees, the smoke hung, a truth-teller.

I went back inside Janet's house, and, eager to pass the time, went to washing the dishes and straightening the kitchen. I made coffee and looked around to see if there was anything suitable to fix for breakfast.

It must have been nine-thirty before I heard Rubin and Charles outside, and I ran out on the porch to greet them. They looked like walking death, and were as dirty as two chimney sweeps.

"Janet and Serena are still asleep. Come on in, I've got breakfast ready," I told them. "If you've any energy left, please spend it to tell me the news."

"Is Janet all right?" Rubin asked.

"Of course. I told you, she's asleep."

They washed up and sat down at the table. "There isn't much to tell yet," Charles said. "To look upon it you would think the whole town has been leveled, but I imagine the damages won't cover more than twenty blocks or so."

"Do they know what started it?" I asked.

"Not yet. I don't think anyone stopped long enough to investigate. So many people lost their homes. We helped to move some of them out, saving as much as we could, and the city park has become one huge storage area."

"Yes, looks like a Gypsy camp out there," said Rubin. "But at least I don't think there were many people hurt. No deaths, I don't think, though who would know at this point?"

"Oh, Claire, you should have seen the sight up close. The flames were the biggest I've ever seen and all the wild-fowl—geese, ducks, sea gulls—were circling back and forth above like vultures over a dead man."

"Course it would have never spread so far except for the wind," said Rubin. "The wind carried sparks and pieces of burning wood over the housetops so that it was virtually impossible to extinguish what was already afire and catch up with the progress of the blaze at the same time."

"What about the fire department? Was it effective?"

"As much as could be expected," said Charles, "though God knows they're going to be verbally massacred because the fire reached such great proportions. The water supply's at fault, not the firemen. But there were enough people around the city who were against changing over from the volunteer system so that the new paid department is bound to become the scapegoat. That's the way people are, I guess."

"What about your office, Charles?"

"No damage there that I know of. But then I didn't cover the whole area. I heard somebody say the new public school building went down. . . ."

"Yes, and the Exchange Hotel. They say that the fire spread to the rear of the courthouse, but the building was saved."

"And there were some homes destroyed on Broadway further down from where Pete lives."

"There's no way of getting a full account of it now," said Rubin. "Last night it was sheer mayhem, nobody stopped long enough to ask questions."

"When was the thing finally put out?" I asked him.

"Must have been six-thirty or seven."

"Lord, better than five hours of burning," I said, only then realizing the degree of seriousness of the fire.

It was several days after that we began to learn the full details. The fire's source was thought to be in a furnace inside the Vulcan Foundry which had been left burning Friday night. Apparently the winds, which reached a velocity of thirty miles per hour during the night, stirred up the flames and sent sparks flying out the vent. Of course, from there the fire went wild. Probably because of the fact it started early in the morning when no one was awake, the fire alarm was not sounded immediately. By the time the badly understaffed fire department arrived, they had a king-size holocaust on their hands.

The fire covered not twenty but forty blocks of Galveston, and it left twenty-five hundred people homeless. The whole city was immobilized by it, and five days later there was a meeting called at noon in the Cotton Exchange Building, for considering how best to help those who suffered and rebuild what was destroyed.

Charles and Pete, Lucien and also Rubin were in the audience. Charles told me upon his return that the meeting had been presided over not by Mayor Fuller, but by George P. Stanley, one of the principal stockholders in the

Wharf Company. Mayor Fuller and other members of the Wharf Company sat up at the head table. I could see by Charles's expression that afternoon he was disturbed by the meeting.

"They've assessed actual damages in dollars at something over a million, but I don't know . . . somehow that seems a little low because it must be too early to tell. Anyway, they've set up several subcommittees to handle the work involved in getting necessities to the families who were put out of their homes.

"Then there's the task of doling out the money that's been pledged. That's where the trouble comes in. It seems that offers for help came from cities all across the country—Dallas, Memphis, St. Louis, Boston, New Orleans, to name a few. And do you know what Fuller did with most of them? He flat turned them down. I remember one particular letter from some group in Boston was read aloud. Fuller had replied, 'Thanks—but our affluent can take of our poor.' Those exact words, I'll never forget them.

"When I heard that, I was livid. Doubtless Fuller expected a great round of applause for his illustration of faith in Galveston's ability to solve her own problems. But I thought it was unforgivably crude and stupid, and I stood up and told him so."

"You did?"

"I told him I had no idea that Galveston—or any other city—was so self-sufficient it could exist through any circumstances without benefit of outside help, but I thought before he so cavalierly and, I might add, curtly, turned down offers from people who only wanted to help us, he might well have checked with a few of those people who lost everything they owned in the fire. They might just have felt differently."

"Then what happened?"

"Oh, there was some applause, I guess . . . and I was sorry I had said anything because it looked like I was playing to the gallery, when I really wasn't."

"Did the mayor answer your statement?"

"He said in his most well-oiled tones, 'My appreciation for your thoughts, of course, Mr. Becker, but might I remind you, you are not mayor yet.' "

We weren't sure how Charles's outburst would affect the campaign, but then, once again we had the *News* on our

side. An editorial entitled "Facts and False Pride" came
out shortly after the meeting, calling the mayor's action a
bad blunder and reminding the members of the relief committee that every hour was bringing more proof that the
seriousness of the calamity had at first been underesti-
mated, and we could most assuredly use all the help we
could get. The exchange between Mayor Fuller and
Charles was not mentioned, a fact for which Charles was
thankful. He felt the fact he had made his feelings known
and that the *News* agreed with him was more than sufficient.

By Christmastime the city still labored under a cloud of
sadness and hopelessness brought on by the fire. To drive
downtown was a miserable experience; seeing acres and
acres of charred ruins reminded me of accounts I had read
of the burning of Atlanta during the war. No one doubted
eventually that part of the city would be built again; still, it
gave one a helpless feeling to know that in one swift, dead-
ening stroke, the lives of hundreds could be affected. I only
drove down to see it once. I couldn't bear to look at it
again. Madame LaRoche's place had been burned to the
ground, and she had left the city for good, saving only the
clothes on her back and a box of family treasures, a few
jewels which had been handed down to her from ancestors
in Louisiana. Faye told me of her leaving, but did not
know where she had gone, and we have never found out.

We kidded ourselves it was the fire to be blamed for the
slim showing of people at the Christmas Eve service at St.
Christopher's. This service traditionally filled the church to
capacity. Every family came—even those whose attendance
at other times of the year was sporadic at best.

This year, however, was an exception, and I still imagine
part of the reason was that some St. Christopher's families
had suffered by the fire. But there were not enough such
families to have made the great difference that Christmas
Eve, and we might not have known the main reason for the
sparse attendance except that one of the vestrymen, Marvin
Goethe, told Charles that over the past few months, around
fifty families had notified Rubin they were transferring
their membership from St. Christopher's elsewhere. Many
of these worked for, or were somehow connected with, the
Galveston Wharf Company.

Rubin would have never said. He is that kind of man.
Charles was aghast at the news, and both of us knew well

what was happening at St. Christopher's. Christmas Day he spent some time talking privately with Rubin, and I fully expected him to walk out of their talk ready to give up running for mayor, but he did not. Not then.

Chapter 6

It was a time for unusual events: a time of manipulation by things beyond our control. Charles's first campaign speech for the new year's thrust was slated for January eleventh. Sometime during the early morning hours of January tenth, snow began to fall.

"If I hadn't seen it myself I would have never believed it," he said, looking out the window on the morning of the tenth. The ground was already covered with a white carpet of snow; the fences looked as though they'd been sprinkled with sugar, and children were outside playing, throwing snowballs and building their snowmen. "If this keeps up, I guess I'll have to cancel the rally tomorrow night."

The snow was a beautiful sight to behold, more beautiful in Galveston—with the houses close together and the snow along the fences forming a sparkling chain, linking all of us together as a unit—than in Grady, where snow comes a sight more often, and only adds to the bleakness of the sparsely populated landscape out from town.

"Look, there's Janet," I said. She'd come out on the lawn with Serena, both of them bundled up from head to toe, enjoying the experience of snow together.

"Lord, she stays cooped up so much lately, I guess I hadn't realized how big she was getting," said Charles.

"Her time is near."

"You know, I've a good mind to go out there too. Look at Serena—she's having so much fun. I could help her with that snowman."

"Go on if you want. Maybe you can persuade Janet to act as though she has some common sense and get back indoors. In her condition, really . . ."

The snow continued for three days, and while I did not get out and Charles only went as far as the yard, we read in the newspaper that snowfall had been measured at some points on the island at twelve to fourteen inches deep. Water in Galveston Bay was frozen, and huge tentacles of ice

hung from the sides of oyster boats and schooners docked
there.

Galveston has no facility for snow; nor do her people
have the means of conducting normal business during a
snowfall. There are no sleds, of course, though a few people
pulled in small boats and used them for gliding up and
down the streets. As a result, the town's serious business
took a holiday, just as it had following the fire, only this
time the whole atmosphere was one of pleasure seeking. "It
might just be the lift all of us needed since the fire," said
Charles. "Sort of a release for all the pent-up frustrations."

At any rate, it seemed good medicine for Charles and
Rubin. They built two snowmen for Serena, and wound up
having several free-for-all snowball fights along with neighbors from up and down the street. I stayed inside by the
parlor fire most of the time. I couldn't seem to stay warm,
and had the feeling in my stomach a good bleeding spell
was about to come. I prayed not; I hadn't been through
one in such a long time, and if I were to go through another one, I wished most earnestly it would wait until after
the election in March.

Charles's first campaign speech for the year was resched-
uled for the eighteenth of January, and he had to wear
heavy coat, boots, gloves, and woolen neck scarf. "I am not
sure whether I'm going to the Union Club tonight, or up to
the mountains in North Dakota," he said, half jokingly and
half in irritation. Charles hates to bundle up.

The snow had been slow in melting because the sky had
failed to clear, and now the streets were filled with a soup
of dirty mud and slush. There was a sparse turnout that
night, but it was more than made up for during the
speeches which followed in the next couple of weeks. "It's
hard to get a second wind, though," Charles said one night.
"I almost wish the election had been done with at the end
of the summer."

"It's just the cold. By election time the weather might be
prettier, and all of us will feel a lot better if it is."

"That reminds me, have you heard from Janet or
Rubin?"

"Not in the past couple of days. I saw Rubin once, and
he told me he's sticking close by. Janet hasn't been out of
the house since that morning she played in the snow with
Serena."

"Is Serena going to stay with us for a few days after the baby comes?"

"No. I believe Mrs. McCambridge from the church is coming. Her husband is on a boat right now, and she has time on her hands. She'll watch after Janet and Serena, and cook for the family."

"Oh, I was hoping Serena would stay here."

"You'll have enough on your hands without worrying about a child."

"She wouldn't be any worry."

One afternoon in mid-February a man whom I had never seen came to our door. He was slightly built, carrying a satchel, and wearing a big coat and a black derby. He inquired in the politest tones whether Charles was home.

"Not yet, though I do expect him any minute. Is there something I can do for you?"

"My name is Marcus Keyroy, and I'd like to see Mr. Becker if I may. It concerns some private business."

"Do come in. Warm yourself by the fire, Mr. Keyroy. Will you have some coffee? Let me take your overcoat?"

"No thank you. I won't be staying long," he said. He stood in front of the fire, warming his hands and looking above the mantel at a landscape Janet had painted for us one Christmas.

"Nice painting," he remarked finally. "Galveston in summertime. Warms one to his very soul on a day like this."

I agreed with him—this was one of my favorites of the paintings Janet had done for us—and before I could tell him she had painted it, I heard Charles enter the back door. "Oh, there he is now. I'll just fetch him and tell him you're here."

"Many thanks, Mrs. Becker. You're very kind."

Yet Charles didn't recall the man's name. "Oh well, I've met so many people the past few months, I'll probably remember when I see him," he said.

He went into the parlor while I hung up his coat, and then I heard the two of them walk into Charles's study and close the door. They were closeted in there for such a long time that eventually I ate my supper alone and left Charles's plate on top of the stove. Finally, I heard the doors open and waited to see if Charles would invite the man to stay and eat. But then I heard the front door open and shut, and Charles's footsteps back into the parlor.

I kept thinking he'd come into the kitchen, but he did not, so finally I walked into the parlor to get him. "Supper's ready—" I began, then stopped. He was sitting down in a chair facing the window, holding a glass of madeira.

"Charles, you shouldn't drink that on an empty stomach. Come eat. Your dinner's been ready an hour."

"I'll be along. Just let me sit here alone for a while."

It had grown dark in the room, but when I started to light a lamp he stopped me.

"Had a rough day?"

"The roughest."

"Who was that man? What did he want?"

He looked up as though puzzled by the question. "Oh, just someone with campaign business. Was Pete coming by tonight?"

"Later on, I think."

"Good. I need to talk with him."

"If you don't hurry up and eat, you won't have time before he gets here."

"Put it away. I'm not hungry."

Charles and Pete were in the study for over an hour that night, and I will confess to having passed in front of the doors several times with a keen ear. Oddly, I could hear nothing but the soft rhythm of Charles's voice. Usually Pete did most of the talking, his words barreling through the door as though meant for everyone in the household. But tonight Pete was listening. After their conversation, he left without telling me good-by, and this departure from the usual was what alerted me something odd was going on.

Charles returned to his study and shut the doors. He'd said scarcely two words to me since coming in that evening, and by now I was overcome with curiosity as to what was bothering him.

I knocked on the door softly.

"Come in," he said, as though he expected me.

I opened the door slightly and looked in. He was seated behind his desk, looking pensively into an open drawer where he kept a small handgun. The desk was so scattered with papers, the shelves and tables around him piled so high with books and folders, he looked like a newspaper editor who's just realized he missed a deadline.

"Darling, what's the matter? Are you ill?"

"In a way," he replied, and slowly shoved the drawer in.

"Look at me, Charles. What's happened? Something at

the office? Something to do with that man who came by?"

"Sit down. I want to talk to you." When he lifted his head and looked across at me, his face was pale. "Claire, I don't know how to tell you this except to put it plainly, though I wish there were some other way.

"I'm not going to run for mayor."

"Not going to run? But why? At this stage, when you're almost a cinch to win—even the *News* predicts—"

"The price is too high. I can't do it, that's all."

"Price too high?" I repeated. My head was spinning. He might just as well have taken the pistol from the drawer and shot a hole through my hand.

"I don't expect you to understand; just believe there are many reasons. I know you're disappointed, and I'm sorry for that . . . more than you could know."

"Disappointed? You don't know the meaning of the word! You simply can't back out now. Pete won't stand for it. *I* won't stand for it."

"Pete's been good enough to see my position. I was expecting at least that much from you."

"But you talked an hour to Pete and you must have told him why. You expect me to accept a decree, with no explanation." My words drifted across to him as wind across a desert. I took another tack: "And what about your high-minded ideas for making Galveston into a great metropolis? I thought you were such a dedicated man. What about that?"

I'd hit home finally. He made no reply, but looked down at the clutter of engineers' reports on water supply and speech notes. "Claire, please sit down and keep your voice down. We must talk this out calmly."

"Is it Rubin and the church?"

"That's part of it; part of what made me see what I'm in for."

"But people will forget this election. They'll come back to St. Christopher's in time. Not everybody in this town works for the Wharf Company or has to cater to it for one reason or another. Surely its power can't be that far-reaching."

"Oh, it is far-reaching all right, believe me. But whether or not that was the case, I've realized something about myself: I don't want to run for public office, don't want to go into public service. I've allowed myself to be manipulated by people generous enough to have confidence in my abil-

ity, and I've been convinced that I'm capable of it—even
that I want to do it. It was a terrific mistake. Better to
learn now than to go on with this thing."

"But what's Pete going to do? The election isn't a month
off."

"We're going to ask Lucien to run in my place, although,
just between us, I doubt he will. But if so, I'm going to try
to throw my supporters his way."

"But what will people think? That doesn't make any
sense to me. I'm sorry, but it just doesn't make any sense."

"We'll make a statement as to my health. We'll say that
my physician has urged me to drop out of the campaign."

"Are you really ill, Charles? Have you been seeing a
doctor without my knowing? You do look pale. Go on, tell
me if that's the truth."

"No, it isn't. But it is no one's business. Believe me,
dear, it's best that it end like this. The whole thing is making me sick. It's such a filthy game and I hate it. I hate it,
and won't go through with it."

I knew then he was bent on this course, that no amount
of pleading would change his mind. I began to think of all
the plans I'd secretly harbored over the months: grand
plans that would take us so much further than Galveston
politics. Now I would scarcely be able to face anyone in
town.

"Will you stay on with Pete?"

"No, we've discussed that. After a few weeks I'll go back
into private practice, where I should have stayed in the first
place, because going with him was my first mistake, or, at
least, one of them."

"All very neat and tidy, isn't it?"

"Darling, I know how you must feel. I'll try and make it
up to you. We'll travel—anywhere you want to go. We'll
move from here if you want—maybe it would even be better in the long run—not to Grady, of course, but anywhere
else you'd like. Maybe to Houston—"

"I don't want to travel. I don't want to move. I don't
want to look at you anymore. For the first time in our
marriage, I could see some promise you might really *be*
somebody, might go somewhere, and now this.

"I've known you to be many things, but never a blunder-
ing fool. To give up just when victory is at hand because
some nonsense about self-revelation comes over you, even
when you know how much this race means to me . . .

When I think of the years I've wasted, staying with you, bound by a sense of duty. Oh, I should never have come here to Galveston. Would to God I'd have had the good sense to leave you after Charlie died!"

"But I thought you liked it here. I thought coming here helped you to get over the loss of our son."

"By God, he was Damon Becker's son, not yours!" I shouted, then caught my breath and brought my hand to my lips.

I shall never forget the icy stare he returned to me. Then in a moment he looked past me and said with a hollow voice, "The door. Someone's at the door."

"Charles, I—"

"The door, Claire. Just get the door, please."

I walked out of the study, down the hall, and to the front door as though in a dream. I couldn't think or reason, couldn't believe what had just taken place. I opened the door. It was Rubin. It bothered me he would be coming to the front door, and I kept trying to form the words to ask him why he didn't come to the back. I must have stared at him wide-eyed. He'd been speaking to me and I hadn't heard him.

"Claire, don't stand there like a blinkard. What's the matter with you?" He was literally shaking me by the shoulders. "I'm trying to tell you it's Janet. The baby is coming. I've got to go and fetch the doctor. Can you go over? Tell Charles to go after Mrs. McCambridge."

He let go of me, hurried down the front steps, and boarded his rig pulled up out front.

Chapter 7

It was deadly cold that night, and although I've already managed to forget part of the sequence of events which took place in Janet's dimly lit room, there are some things I shall never forget: the way she looked as she lay in the bed, writhing in pain and gripping the brass rungs above her head, limp hair hanging in cords around her shoulders, her swollen body moving in spasms, and her oft-suppressed cries as the contractions took hold.

She looked at me in her pathetic, helpless way, but I could scarcely bear to be in the room, much less speak to her soothingly. She was in the second stage when I arrived, but I couldn't get my thoughts together as to what was to be done for her, and could only pace back and forth in front of the window, praying that soon the doctor and Mrs. McCambridge would show up.

The feeling I had in the pit of my stomach when I saw Rubin's rig pulling up but no sign of Charles and the midwife was like the slow turning of a dull knife. Mrs. McCambridge lived only blocks away. She and Charles should have returned long before Rubin. Then I recall Janet screaming, "Oh, God, hurry, the baby is coming now!" I turned from the window and pulled up the sheet which covered her. The bed was soaked. The dome-shaped head had begun to push itself from between her outstretched legs. The stench will always stay with me. Why did it smell so?

Doctor Arnold burst into the room. He is a huge man, bigger than Rubin. He stalked across to her bed, and apparently seeing I was going to be of no help, ordered me to wait outside, and sent Rubin down to get hot water. "And bring more light into this room! My God, you can hardly see your hand in front of you!"

I walked out into the hall and watched down the stairs for the appearance of Charles and the midwife.

It wasn't long before Janet's travail was over. The sound of a slap and a cry of indignation from the infant came shortly after I'd left the room. Another moment, two, an eternity. Then Doctor Arnold was shouting for me to get back in there. "I don't know where that confounded midwife is," he said. "You'll have to take care of the child. I've got to see to the mother." He'd grabbed a white cloth off the dresser, and roughly wrapped the infant in it and thrust it toward me. "Take him into the bathroom and clean him up. I've got some ointment here in my bag." He put his hand on the bottle and pulled it out. "Surely you know how to wash the baby."

I took him then and held him close to my breast, and a curious thing occurred. For just that space of time it took to care for the infant that night, I was back in Grady washing Charlie, and his face came fully back into view. I rubbed him with the ointment, then wiped him off, washed his eyes with water, his body with soap, cleaning all the tiny creases of him and then rubbing him with starch powder and wrapping him in a clean towel. It was a soothing

thing to do, a labor of love. I sat down in a rocker with him and rocked the rest of the night away, studying his face and calling him Charlie.

By the next day Mrs. McCambridge had arrived, explaining a little testily, "My own son was lyin' ill in the bed. I couldn't leave him, could I?" I walked out of the Garret household into the bright morning, feeling as though I'd been pent up there for days and days, instead of a matter of hours.

Charles was seated on the steps of our verandah, smoking his pipe, his face solemn. I knew the words which must pass between us, and I felt there was little use in putting them off, regardless of the fact my body ached with exhaustion. I sat down beside him.

"Worn out?" he asked.

"A little. But you can go ahead and say all the things you want to. I guess I deserve them."

"I knew, Claire, knew from the start about you and Damon."

I sat erect and stared at him.

"I saw him the morning after that big party was thrown in honor of his last visit home. Of course you know he always stayed at the hotel when he came home, and never with me.

"Anyway, we met as I was walking to my office, and he walked alongside me for a short distance. I think he was still a little drunk from the party, to be truthful. 'Ah, what a night,' he said. 'The folks in Grady really know how to welcome one of their own.' Then he asked me what your name was . . . called you a 'comely little maid.' When I told him he asked if I hadn't been keeping company with you for quite a while.

"I told him I had, and then he wanted to know why I'd never married you, said it looked like I was going to be a bachelor forever. I told him I guessed the same might be said of him.

" 'Ah, you know me well enough,' he said. 'I'm not the marrying kind. Seawater and women don't mix.' I thought he'd let it go at that, but he pressed me some more, wanting to know why you and I had piddled around so. I told him you hadn't accepted my offers of marriage. 'And after all this time, you're not figuring she ever will,' he said. I told him that was possible. He wanted to know then if I had any ties with you, and in all honesty I had to say I didn't.

"That was all there was to the conversation. He went his way, and I went mine. I had business north of town for the next few days, and when I got back I didn't see him. Then on the morning he left, he came by my quarters early to say good-by. I remember it struck me as peculiar. He'd left town after his visits before without saying good-by unless it happened to be convenient. For some reason he made a point of doing it that time, and I've always wondered if he had a kind of premonition it was to be his last visit home.

"I'll never forget the last thing he told me, going down the walk, carrying all his belongings on his back. He said, 'You'd better get your hands on that little filly while you're still young enough to keep up with her.' Then he winked his eye, gave a roaring laugh, and went off.

"If I hadn't realized what had happened by that time, I would have known by the stricken look on your face and your mention of him when I saw you later that day and took you on a picnic. It was pretty evident."

"Yet still you married me."

"I knew Damon had a way with women, how he trifled with their feelings, how winning he could be. And I loved you a great deal."

"And you didn't guess about the baby?"

"The possibility crossed my mind, I assure you, especially when I began to put two and two together about your stubbornness in seeing that new doctor, and in hiring Helga. But I couldn't be sure. Then when the baby arrived at eight months, I suspected again, even though Helga declared it to be early. She made such a point of it that I was even more suspicious. In fact, I was just about convinced it was Damon's child."

"Is that why you were so anxious to see if I'd agree to name him after you?"

"Yes."

"How have you lived with me all these years, knowing—?"

"The baby's death in the crib changed my mind. I thought maybe its coming into the world early kept it from being strong enough to survive. It certainly was logical, and I wanted so much to believe it was really mine and that you loved me. I guess I convinced myself all my old suspicions were groundless."

"I see." I looked out across Avenue L at the peaceful

houses and the trees and bushes, just beginning to turn on their spring colors. The day looked so full of promise, almost as though it wanted no part of my desolation inside. "Are you going to leave me?"

He was silent a moment, took a puff on his pipe, then said, "No, Claire, I'm not."

I went inside then, and up to bed, while Charles sat smoking his pipe on the porch. I was aware again of how tired I was. My body ached and felt sticky as I lay down upon the sheets and fell asleep. And then the dream began.

Charlie was in his crib, surrounded by a ring of fire, and I was trying to get to him, but my feet moved as though I were walking through molasses. I reached for him, my body bent almost double toward him, and then I realized something was holding me back. It was Charles, pulling me from him, laughing and kissing my neck. I awoke sometime later, lying in a pool of blood.

Almost nightly from that day I have dreamed the dream again, in one form or another. Once my baby was on a raft out in the sea and I was swimming to him, my legs held back by lead anchors that would, when I looked behind me, become Charles's hands around my ankles.

Once he was lost down in a bucket at the bottom of a well, and I was turning the handle, trying to pull him up. I turned with all my strength, then when I had him almost to the top, Charles cut the rope and the boy Charlie disappeared again down into the bottom of the well.

My days became a labyrinth of images and fantasies, when often I did not know whether I was awake or dreaming again. And one day Doctor Hutchisson came at Charles's urgent call, and after looking at me, told Charles, "Surgery, as soon as the bleeding spells let up again, and her strength returns," then looked at my pleading eyes and said, "No, I'm sorry, no more children. It's out of the question. . . ."

I bled three times in that few weeks, each time in greater amounts and longer than the time before. And I kept taking the vile pain medicine, kept taking it . . .

Chapter 8

Black evening shadows now play on the houses and street, and next door Janet Garret's very private porch is dark as a tomb. Somewhere in the distance a lone dog gives a deep and mournful howl. Down the block in an upstairs window, someone lights a lamp.

Now let me tell you how it was this morning.

There was early rain, just enough to set the grass to glistening and the trees aweep. This was to be christening day for the child Donnie Garret. I awoke without the bleeding, yet the effects of the medicine still lingered far through the day.

Charles awoke before me and put the coffee on. We do not talk together very much lately, but practice at being polite, like actors in a play. We haven't discussed the mayor's race since the night Janet gave birth to Donnie, and I still believe Charles is keeping from me his true reasons for backing out. Yet I would not press him, for it is important that we keep up the front, leave our image of contentment intact, if for no other reason than if we did not, we should be laughed out of town as two frauds. Someday, I will find out the truth. One has only to await the proper moment.

Charles has reoccupied his old office, the one in which Ruth typed papers for him that summer long ago. He rarely mentions Pete Marlowe, and once, a week or two ago, when I passed him and Faye on the street, Pete tipped his hat politely but did not bother to speak, and the air was dry in the absence of the friendly southern drawl. Faye pretended not to have seen me at all.

Lucien Carter, I hear, is moving his business to Houston. He refused to run for mayor in Charles's place, and the incumbent, winning by a landslide vote over the other contenders, has been reinstated for another term in city hall.

We are back, then, to the kind of day-to-day existence we lived when first we moved to Avenue L, or at least we were, until this morning.

I was dizzy as I dressed, and knew I should not have taken that extra dose of the pain medicine last night before going to bed. Three cups of morning coffee had helped almost none in removing the haze brought on by it, and my ability to reason quickly was affected. One must understand this before I tell about Janet.

Rubin took Serena to Sunday school at nine o'clock, and Charles went along to serve as usher for early service. At half-past ten I left the house to fetch Janet along with the boy. Charles had left Gypsy hooked to the rig out front, and I was given responsibility for getting the new mother and son to the church by eleven. By then the sun shone brilliantly and felt good against my face, but did not clear the fog curled around my mind.

Ten steps down and twelve up.

On Janet's steps my foot caught in a sliver of wood dislodged from the rest and curled up, no doubt from having been wet and dry, and wet and dry, so many times. I looked at the piece of wood, and thought how easy it would be for someone to trip on it and fall down the stairs.

I rang the bell and Janet, with unusual promptness, appeared. "Come in, I'll just be a moment," she said. After the sunshine outside, the house was dark. The Garret house has always been dark. Janet was cheerful this morning, wearing a white muslin dress trimmed in lace, a gift from Rubin especially for today's occasion. She wore white kid shoes and a white tulle veil as well. I had never seen her look better: more full of promise.

Janet stopped in front of the hall mirror to adjust her hair beneath the veil. "Listen to Donnie cooing there in the crib," she said. "I think he wants his Aunt Claire to hold him."

I walked to the crib and picked up the child, the first time since the night he was born. His face no longer reminded me of the face of my son Charlie. He was changing already, would look like her and Rubin. Janet was still at the mirror, fussing with a defiant wisp of hair.

"When did it happen?" I asked her.

"What?" she said, turning round to face me.

"When you got home from Virginia? Is that when? It counts up right, you see . . . what happened in Virginia that made you come home and take Rubin into your bed, or had he always slept there?"

"Claire, what's the matter with you today? You're not talking sense. Here, don't hold Donnie so tightly. I think I'd better take him. We can walk to the church and you can go back to bed. You don't look well."

She started toward the front door. "He never loved you,"

I said, and followed her. "You know, of course, he's always pretended so as not to hurt you."

She was then just at the door, and turned around to face me. "I don't know what you're talking about—how absurd."

"Not so much . . . you know that I would have been more suited to him than you. Don't you know he must have felt the same? I think you did, even before you went to Virginia. You could see it, couldn't you? So you invited him into your bed finally. That's what happened, isn't it? When you got back, you decided you'd better start acting like a wife?"

"Claire, you're acting insane, you—"

She was backing through the door now, and I was moving toward her, only awaiting her answer, that was all.

"Is that the way it happened?" I asked again, this time louder than before because I had to know the truth at least about one thing I had counted on. She was shaking her head and backing up. She had the boy clasped firmly in her arms. I walked dumbly toward her and she kept backing away; she looked frightened as an animal who sees the barrel of a gun.

I think she realized she'd reached the precipice just before she fell, for she shot me a look of horrified surprise, then was tumbling, tumbling down the twelve stairs. She knocked her head against the post at the bottom, then lay there in a heap. Donnie had flown from her arms and lay several feet distant in the yard. I looked at the child, then at her. Blood was pouring from her head and spoiling one shoulder and sleeve of the white muslin dress.

I looked across the street, and up and down the block, trying to assess the situation before me, to penetrate the fog. No one was within sight, and I knew I was well hidden by her giant oleanders along the porch. I stepped back through the door, waited a moment, then came out again, shouting. I must not have it looking as though I had anything to do with her fall. After all, I never laid a finger on her, or the child.

People began to appear. Something must be done. I shouted for someone to get Doc Monroe. I ran from the porch and boarded the rig, and whipped Gypsy into a furious gallop all the way to the church. And later, as Rubin and Charles came back with me I told them how it had happened. That Janet was in a rush, running late, and I'd gone upstairs to get a handkerchief for her. She'd apparently started down the stairs and tripped on a loose sliver of wood. Poor, poor dear. We must be hopeful she will be all right. I took Rubin's hand in mine to comfort him.

Doc Monroe took Janet in his flatbed wagon to the infirmary. Charles rode up front with him and I rode beside Rubin in the back. He wept and cradled her head in his arms. Once he looked at me and said, "She told me early this morning perhaps we ought not to try and do the christening today. She had a feeling about it, she said . . ."

"Yes, Janet is very intuitive, and of course earlier it rained."

I looked down the length of her long, thin body to her feet. The white pointed-toe shoes poked out from the dress, shifting from right to left now and then as the wagon bumped along.

This evening they have said the child is dead, and Janet probably will not last the night. Poor dear . . . she should have been more careful of the stairs.

...water supply coins by piping of water
...the...ing, in his proposal to break the stranglehold of a...which supposedly once and for all. I noticed his
conviction...had never been so earnestly and modestly expressed,...ever so feasible, as his voice carried
smoothly...among the audience, where every eye, and
retained...from the beginning of his speech to his

～ *Serena* ～

June 1, 1899—September 8, 1899

Chapter 1

Six o'clock, still dark.

I wish the dawn would hurry. Maybe when the jacinth-colored sky rolls up outside my bedroom window, I can borrow some of its calm. So much can happen in the final six hours, and until Roman and I are safely on the train speeding for New York, I won't be able to fight off the fear which grinds at me like a wheel rolling against the sand. No matter how thoroughly planned, there is risk in running away, and we may have enemies here . . .

Only yesterday I told Roman, "I wish we could leave today; I don't know how I can make it through another day."

And he said, "Don't be a little idiot, darling. It's all fixed. King's given the go ahead for you to travel with the band. Our tickets are for tomorrow's train; I've rented a rig to carry us to the station—the one with the biggest brougham top I could find, so you'll be well hidden from view. How could anything go wrong?

"The only danger is in your having a sudden attack of Sunday school morals, and backing out."

He was teasing again, as he does when he wants to dispel my worries. I laughed a little and nodded, and let him take me the way I love to be taken, for I'm as hungry for him as he is for me. And this, more than all his raillery, made me forget my fears for a while. But that was yesterday, and he was there, and this is today and I am alone, and the fears creep back again like little gnomes who make sport of poking at me with tiny pitchforks . . . oh, Roman, I am trying to be as brave as you, yet when happiness is this close, it's difficult not to imagine something will snatch it away.

How silent is a street in morning, before the houses awaken.

I can look out across Avenue L and see a light here and there, in upstairs windows mostly: husbands rising to go to work, wives padding around sleepily in house robes, the smells of coffee making and breakfast cooking soon to rise in the air. It is a day like any other for everyone on the block except me, and although in a few minutes I, too, will softly make my way down the stairs and put the coffee on for Dad, I will only be going through the motions of routine, trying not to betray myself by serving oatmeal with shaky hand or answering morning-time questions too quickly. "How did you sleep, Nan? Going to the beach today? Paper come yet?"

Six hours, six hours.

I suppose I may never see this house or this street with its arbor of oaks, or even Galveston again. The band contract wasn't renewed for next summer at the Seaside Pavilion, so wherever they are playing, it probably won't be around here. Hearing the verdict about the contract had at first elated me, for it seemed to work so well with my hopes and plans. Yet now I can't help being a little disappointed. Surely by next summer I would have been able to gather the courage to own up to everything. Of course I owe no explanation to anyone except Dad, perhaps, and Mother, who wouldn't understand anyway. James already knows the whole story of this summer, and even if I owed him an explanation, it would be unnecessary. He is but fourteen years old, yet understands better than anyone else.

And what difference does it make about Dad? You might even say that what I'm doing today is justified by what he did to me this summer, as in the Old Testament, "an eye for an eye." He destroyed the one thing which gave my otherwise dull life some joy, and anyway, even if he hadn't put a stop to my ballet lessons so abruptly, surely I've spent the past seven years fulfilling any obligation I might be owing him as a daughter. In a way, Galveston has been an island prison for me, and although I shall miss the quiet mornings of bathing in the sea, of having the run of Marybeth Fischer's place as though I were the rich girl and the big house, the private beach, and long pier and bathhouse were mine, I won't have any regrets about leaving. All my poor pleasures before Roman Cruz came along seem more meager than ever when I think what I'll be gaining in exchange. I won't mind if I must carry my belongings in a traveling bag for the rest of my life, as long as I'm traveling with him.

I do pity James, and feel a little guilty over leaving him

next door, with only a meddlesome guardian four times his age and a stone-faced housekeeper to look after him. But then he could have done worse than to have his cousin Claire Becker as guardian. She does have money enough to provide well for him, and the sense to see to his education, and no doubt Roman is right when he says she's just a harmless old tabby. If she has pried into my affairs, probably she's meant no harm. My dislike and mistrust of her all these years is perhaps unfair. Still, I've never been able to help feeling as I do about her. . . .

There it is, sitting next to me on the bed: my whole nineteen years of life enclosed in a carpetbag. One change of clothing, a nightdress, hairbrush, and toothbrush; my dancing shoes (I won't take my practice outfit because Roman says it's not like those they wear in New York), my one-year diary with less than four months of space to be written on, two souvenir programs, and the picture of my mother and father. These things aren't much, but they are the essential things belonging to me, and all I will take because Roman insists we travel light.

"By the way," he said the other day, "I hope you aren't one of those tiresome women who carry six trunks and eighteen hatboxes whenever you go on a trip. I won't have the patience or the time to look after them all the way to New York."

"I've never been on a trip before, and I don't own enough to fill one trunk," I told him. "One carpetbag will carry all I need, and it probably won't even be full."

"Good girl," he said. "I knew you were sensible from the first time we met."

Roman would never stop teasing me if he saw the diary, but I must keep it because it tells so much about us that I was never able to share with anyone else, the beautiful parts of the summer that I'll read of again someday, when we're two old people spending our final days, sitting together on a porch somewhere.

Not being sentimental, he'd probably laugh out loud at me for having saved these two programs, yet much of my happiness is written into them. First is the one from the evening performance of Professor King's Traveling Band at the Seaside Pavilion on June 17, 1899, in which the name Roman Cruz stands out bolder than all the rest.

So intriguing was his name, so commanding had he looked as he stood and raised his trumpet, I probably would have kept the program even if he had not come to hold me in his power just as surely as he did his audience that night.

The other program, from the Emma Abbott Opera Company's production of *The Rose of Castile,* is special to me because it is a souvenir of the first time I ever saw ballet. Claire and Charles Becker took me to the Tremont Opera House on December 31, 1890, and Miss Margueretta Sterling danced a ballet solo between Act II and Act III of the opera. I've only to glance at the program to remember how I sat in my balcony seat spellbound by the beauty of the fragile soloist as she performed. I was unable to believe anyone could create such magic on the points of her toes, could be so perfectly wound into the rhythm of the music from *Swan Lake,* at one with its haunting majesty. And at the end of her solo, the audience had stood from their chairs and yelled, "Bravo! Bravo! Bravo!" above their wild applause, and she had come forth for curtain calls time and again, and someone had brought a huge basket of flowers and placed it in front of her on the stage. Even the curtain calls taken by Emma Abbott herself, at the end of the opera, outnumbered those of Miss Sterling by only two.

On the way home that evening, Charles noticed my starry eyes and asked if I wanted to be an opera singer when I grew up. I told him no, but that I'd love to be able to dance like Miss Sterling.

He paused a moment, then said, "I have a new client, a Madame D'Arcy. She has a ballet studio right here in Galveston. How would you like to take lessons from her, Serena?"

"Oh, more than anything in the world," I answered, then added, "but do you think Daddy will let me?"

"We'll see," he said. "I'll discuss it with him. I have a feeling if he knows you really want to, he'll be persuaded."

And thus, soon after, had begun my ballet lessons, which, even this summer, had taken on still more importance than ever before. How many times, over the years, have I looked at this program, and relived that marvelous and fateful night, never knowing it would lead me to such happiness, would open doors that had yet to appear?

Then there is the photo of Mother and Father taken on their wedding day. Roman would probably say it would be easier to leave the picture here. After all, a clean sweep, cutting all cords with the past, would be more apt to allow one to forget sooner. Yet I don't really want to forget it all. I keep thinking if I can only get away from here and gaze on this picture long enough, I can blot out the past thirteen years since Mother's accident and remember only the good times that went before . . . the days we spent on the beach together building sand castles, the times she read to me of faraway places and exotic people, or of simple things like animals or limericks; the nights I fell asleep in her arms, the one time we played in the snow together, when she was so near the birth of Donnie and we saw Claire watching us through her parlor window. Claire is always watching someone . . .

If not for Mother's accident so long ago, things would have been different for me. I might not be leaving at all, might not have fallen in love with a stranger and felt I needed him at any cost, and under any conditions he might name.

I was about six when it happened, and can remember little about it except that she and my infant brother Donnie fell together from the front stairs of our house and he was killed. She then lived in a hospital somewhere for months and months, and when she came home one morning she didn't recognize me . . . didn't for a long time.

Claire, standing by with me as Dad carried Mother in her peach-colored robe from the rig into the house, said, "So it's true about the brain damage. She doesn't remember a thing."

And I asked Claire, observing the skeletal image with transparent skin and limp hair, if my mother was going to get well.

"Your mother is as well as she ever will be," Claire had said. And I cried because I couldn't connect the warm, vibrant person my mother had been with the wan creature whose robe trailed slowly up the stairs from which she'd tumbled months before, and my father cried too because he'd lost his wife as surely as though she, with Donnie, had died at the bottom of the stairs.

He still cries sometimes, even now.

Claire's blunt assessment of my mother's condition was correct. She never changed from that day on, and even now sits alone in her room, day after day, rarely uttering a sound. I've tried to get her to paint pictures again, as she did in the old days, for she does have use of her hands and can see. However, she uses only one pastime to occupy herself: writing poetry.

Her poetry is nonsensical, often bizarre, yet I've kept it all in a box in my dresser. I did hope for a while her poems would somehow convey her feelings, and from time to time I've thought she was trying to tell me something through them, yet I suppose they are but the meaningless ramblings of a sick person.

I won't take them with me today, for they are reminders of what I'm trying to forget. I couldn't consider giving them to Claire, although she knows of Mother's penchant for writing them and has often asked me to let her read them. There is a small chance my suspicions are true, and the poems refer to something once done against Claire, and, knowing her, if she should read them and guess . . . .

Claire has been an almost constant presence at our house all these years, bringing oleanders for Mother's room and cooking food for her, which she never eats. It's been hard keeping anything from Claire, especially over the past three years, since Charles's death.

He went quite suddenly, one night while sleeping, and Claire rushed over to our house in her robe early next morning, screaming and begging my father to come home with her. I felt sorry for her then, because she and Charles had been married many years, and he was one of the finest human beings there ever has been. And to waken one morning and find you are lying next to a dead person . . . well, that would be more horrible than anything I can imagine.

I couldn't comprehend then that the man I'd loved as a favorite uncle could be dead. I shed no tears for him then. This summer, I've felt the loss of him far worse, and realized his great value to all of us, and wished I had cried for him as my father did, as we watched them bury him in the ground. . . .

There is the problem now of who will care for Mother after today. Since I was twelve, most of my afternoons have been spent with her, and Mrs. McCambridge, who nursed her after Donnie was born, has stayed with her mornings, at first so I could attend school and later, after I finished, so my mornings could remain free because they are all I've had. Mrs. McCambridge didn't hold with the idea of my dancing lessons with Madame D'Arcy when they began eight years ago, or perhaps she just resented having to stay extra hours with Mother twice a week so I could attend them. But for the past three years I've had morning classes, so that I'm home by noon, and this has put an end to her head shaking at the frivolity of young people. The only irony now is that Dad must have felt the lessons somewhat frivolous too. He seemed puzzled at my minding so when I had to give them up.

I wonder if Marybeth Fischer will go on with her lessons when she comes home this fall, if she comes to stay. Madame D'Arcy's studio is where I met her, and I surely wouldn't have known her at all except we were both dancers, for our backgrounds are opposite. Marybeth is rich. Her family travels to Europe each summer, and her father has allowed me the use of the pier and bathhouse on their property at the end of the island, while they're away. In exchange, I've been expected to keep an eye open for any mischief done to the house, and report any trouble to the police. However, no one has a key to the grounds except me, and the gardener who comes very early on Tuesdays and Thursdays, and anyway, someone breaking in would be unlikely. You hear little of burglaries or plain wickedness for its own sake in Galveston.

I've tried to teach Marybeth to swim, but she is a heap of clumsy arms and legs in the water, and claims to be too unco-ordinated for swimming just as she is for dancing ballet. She dances only because her mother insists, while I would dance if I were dying of some terrible disease and could barely gather the energy to pull on my dancing shoes.

This matter of co-ordination isn't the only difference between Marybeth and me. She's as tall as I am, but pale of complexion, with dark wavy hair and dark eyes. She's more full of adventure than I, or at least than I was before this summer, and it was she who dared me to swim in the nude. "After all, there's no one around our place to watch you in the summer. Try it, and tell me how it feels," she once said.

It did feel wonderful: the warm water spilling over me was like being wrapped and unwrapped, again and again, in a piece of silk. When I told her this, and suggested she try it too, she said she would sometime, but only on a moonlit night when she could sneak away from the house unnoticed. "The adventure of it is just not great enough to be worth getting caught," she told me. "I'd rather save up for something really big, like the time I made Don Singleton hide me in the back of his rig and drive up and down Post Office Street, so I could get a look at a real prostitute marketing her goods."

I do wish I could have shared more of this summer with Marybeth. My letters have mentioned Roman, but not our plans to run away. I can't help believing she'd be proud of me for what I'm about to do.

Will I ever see her again? Probably not, for I can't write to her once I've gone. She'd never tell anyone where I am, but if one of the servants at her house, or her father or mother, were to discover a letter from me, they might rush over to tell Dad and ruin everything. I'll tell him eventually that I'm well and happy, but I'll do it in my own time and won't have anyone interfering.

. . . if I can just get away safely today.

Anyway, Marybeth's last letter from Europe said she'd met some young man from a family who were also traveling abroad, and she sounded more serious about him than usual. He's probably of royal descent or something, and she'll marry him and move off somewhere far away and terribly romantic. Lucky, lucky Marybeth. Things always turn out right for her. . . .

I do hope she'll make a good match in marriage. When I think what I narrowly missed in the way of lifetime contracts I shudder, and know she was right when she insisted I shouldn't marry Nick Weaver.

I couldn't see her point at the time, of course. Nick is a fine, upstanding young man who plays organ at St. Christopher's, and at the time he began to court me more than a year ago, I had no prospects of anything better in the way of a husband. I felt it was simply my destiny to marry him, just as it had been my lot in life to care for Mother and go to dull church parties, and sew needlepoint on Sunday afternoons. Not having known love, I wasn't concerned over going into marriage without it.

"What'll you have if you marry Nick Weaver?" she asked one day.

"I'll admit we won't be wealthy, but you seem to forget, I've never been wealthy so it wouldn't be anything to have to get used to. Besides, he's steady, and has good morals, and Dad says he'll always have a position at St. Christopher's."

"That isn't what I mean," she said, frowning. "Serena,

tell me something, dear. Please don't be offended by my asking—you know, I always speak my mind and you've been good enough to put up with me all these years. Have you ever been to bed with a man?"

I stared at her in disbelief.

"All right, I can see you haven't. Take my word for it, it wouldn't be any fun doing it with Nick, and you'd have to face many nights of it if you married him."

"But it isn't for a woman to enjoy—"

"Fiddlesticks! Gad, you poor little innocent thing. And don't look so shocked. Things are not always so proper as they appear. Just because I went to private school, and dance at Madame D'Arcy's, doesn't mean I haven't had any experience beyond that."

"Have you ever—?"

"Twice. Different men, of course, in Europe. I just wanted a taste. Of course they're far more open over there, not like here, where everyone is so starchy and aboveboard.

"You understand, I only tell you this as a friend, so you won't go getting yourself hitched to Mister Propriety. Don't look like you disapprove. You'd do well to appreciate the benefit of my experience."

"That may be all right for you, Marybeth, but what chance would I have? I've never even been to Europe, have no hopes of getting much further away from here than Houston."

"You give up too easily. The world's a big place with lots of interesting things in it. Take it from me. If we could only talk your father into letting you go to Europe with us one year, I could show you some real excitement."

"Yes, but you know he won't let your father pay my way, and we could hardly afford it ourselves. Besides, who'd take care of Mother?"

"All right," she said with a shrug. "Just do me a favor and don't sell yourself short by marrying Nick Weaver."

"I'll have to do what's best. There's a lot to consider."

"Nonsense. The only thing to consider when it comes to marriage is how *you* feel."

I have often wished Marybeth could have met Roman. They'd have never gotten along, of course, would have probably scrapped like two animals, but I've a feeling they would have had a certain respect for each other.

Yet even that harmless thought comes wrapped in a new

sinister one. What if I have been for Roman simply an adventure, taken no more seriously than Marybeth takes hers? What if he never intended taking me with him today, and will sneak away on an earlier train along with his band cronies, smiling with satisfaction as he watches Galveston disappear from his train window?

And one of his buddies will slap his shoulder playfully, and say, "Escaped again, eh? You better watch out, pal, one day some gal's going to get you yet."

Somewhere in the distance a lonely train whistle blows, and a nervous thrill runs all through me. How absurd to think that of Roman. . . .

I'm just nervous.

He wouldn't do that to me.

He loves me.

Please, God . . .

Chapter 2

I shall miss James Byron more than anyone; I know it's terrible, for my loyalties seem always to lie in the wrong places. But there it is, and at least I can be honest about one thing.

James has been here since June, when his father and mother, Ruth and Edward Byron, were killed in a carriage accident on a hill outside Grady, where they lived, and Claire Becker, being his closest relative of means, was given the responsibility of mothering him. I have felt an attachment to him from the start, perhaps because his mother once spent a summer here, and Dad tells me Mother was very fond of her; in fact, that everyone was. A portrait of her face, captured in shimmering oils, hung in our dining room until a short time ago. The painting is initialed by Mother, dated summer 1879. She is portrayed as a small girl, delicate as a lacewing, with laughing eyes and soft, flowing hair.

James has her eyes. Seeing him the first time, I remembered the picture. I caught him staring at me from behind a bush in Claire's yard as I walked down on my way to Madame's the morning after he arrived in Galveston.

"You there, come out."

A rustle. A moment passing, then he issued forth like

someone who's just been nabbed for making a hand print on the butter. He is small for his age, dark-headed with a fringe of hair in front almost meeting his eyebrows. A small pair of spectacles rest on his nose.

"I'm sorry, ma'am," he said, blinking at the sun. "I only wanted to see who was coming when I heard the door close. I didn't mean to be discourteous."

"Discourteous? Oh, it's all right. I think I know who you are—James Byron. My name is Serena."

He stared at me as though I'd pulled a rabbit from a hat.

"Your cousin Claire told us you were coming yesterday."

"Oh, I see. Then you know . . . everything?"

"About your coming? I'm afraid so, and I am dreadfully sorry. . . . But I'm glad we're going to be neighbors, and I hope you'll like Galveston. Have you ever been swimming at the beach?"

"No, ma'am. Only in the pond back home."

We stood either side of the fence for a few moments, each of us reluctant to say anything else. "Look, I've got to go or I'll be late for dancing class. Tell you what, though, if it's all right with Claire you can go to the beach with me tomorrow morning—not today, because if I've time to go today, I'll go straight from the studio. But tomorrow I'll leave at nine o'clock, unless, of course, it rains."

"Oh, yes, ma'am. I'll be waiting here."

"Good. See you then."

"Is that your dog there, the German shepherd in the backyard?"

"Yes. Don't be afraid of him, though. He's gentle. He just looks a little vicious because he's big. His name's Porky."

"May I play with him sometime?"

"Certainly. Tomorrow we'll take him to the beach. He always goes with me."

"All right, but I don't have a proper bathing suit. Can I wear my knickers? We always did, at home in the pond."

"Of course. Now I've got to go. Madame frowns on tardiness," I said, and started off. He traced down the fence to the end.

"You won't forget tomorrow, will you?"

"Of course not."

As I turned my back and kept walking, I realized he

could be a real pest. However, there was something so lost about him. Even then I felt guilty walking away from him. He was such a long way from home and no doubt in need of a good friend.

I tried to slough off this feeling of responsibility toward him, which caught at me so unsuspectingly. He was only a kid who'd moved in next door, after all. He would be there today, tomorrow, and the day after. Why should I worry about him? He wasn't even related to me.

Yet I kept thinking of his face. All through ballet class I compared it with that of his mother in the picture. More than any other of Mother's paintings—her seascapes, flowers, birds—the painting of Ruth Miller Byron had always held a certain magnetism for me, and when she died I felt almost a sense of personal loss.

After they received the wire about the dual death in Grady, Claire and Helga had taken the next train out. Helga Reinschmidt has been with Claire since shortly after Charles passed away three years ago. I can't imagine why anyone would want such a woman as Helga around, but then I've never pretended to understand Claire anyway.

While she packed for the trip, Helga was dispatched to our house to explain their leaving and say they might be two or three weeks before coming back. Yet they returned within eight or nine days, and Claire came to tell us of the funeral and the boy, James. She talked in short, staccato sentences, as she always does when upset or nervous.

"Lord knows, I hate funerals," she said. "But after all, I am the closest living relative except for the boy and the old man, Edward's father. Thank goodness some friend had already made the arrangements by the time we got there. So I was spared that.

"The boy will be here soon. I couldn't persuade him to come with us after the funeral. He begged to stay with his grandfather. Poor lad, I couldn't blame him. Like as not if his grandfather were younger—he's ninety and in bad health—James would live with him. He's never even seen me before. Probably thinks Galveston is the jumping-off point. I did, when Charles brought me here, you know."

She huffed and puffed, leaned back in her chair.

"I'm going to give him Ruth's room, but I've been storing some of Charles's things in there that were sent from his office after he died, for lack of another place to put them. Lands, you never saw the like of books and boxes in your life. And his office is already piled high with the same kind of things—you know, he never got rid of all that stuff he collected when he ran for mayor back in '86. And of course the attic's been full for years." She sighed. "I'll just have to get in there and get busy. I've never really gone through the boxes properly—seem to be full of duplicate papers and so forth. How I dread the task now."

"Perhaps I could help," said Dad.

"Oh, no, no bother. I'll probably throw away most of the stuff."

"It's quite a responsibility, having a youngster thrust on you suddenly," said Dad. "But I know you'll welcome him because he was Ruth's boy."

"Yes. But there's an awful twist to it. I'm finally going to have a son to take little Charlie's place, but not until I'm too old to be a proper mother to him and, worse still, I'm getting him at the expense of the person I loved most in the world. Ah well, it's nothing new I guess. . . ."

"Will you be going back to Grady for him?" said Dad.

"No. He told us quite emphatically that if he decided to come, which of course he really has no choice about, though I didn't point it out, he is capable of coming alone on the train. He's a sharp youngster, keen on books, and says his dad taught him reading was one of the best things a person could do."

"That's unusual," I said.

"You're going to find James quite an unusual boy."

He was fifteen minutes early for our first appointment to go to the beach, standing the other side of the fence, gripping the wooden pales with both hands. "We are going, aren't we?" he said. "I mean, you haven't changed your mind or anything?"

"Of course not. I've even made chocolate cookies in honor of the occasion."

"Here, let me take Porky's leash."

"I don't know . . . he may not be easy to handle. . . ."

"It's all right. We became friends through the fence while you were at dancing class yesterday. Come on, fella."

Porky was in a running mood that day, and kept darting around the shrubs and trees along the way, jerking James behind as though he were nothing more than a rag wrapped around his tail. I was afraid he'd take a sudden leap and pull James off his feet, but the boy obviously took pride in being able to keep up with him, so I didn't mention it.

"I hope my clothes will be suitable," he said.

"Of course they will. Anyway, it doesn't matter. There won't be anyone around where we're going."

"But I thought there were always lots of people on the beach."

"Porky, calm down! What? Oh, we aren't going to the public beach, unless you just want to. I've a friend who lets me use her place when she's away, and she left for Europe two weeks ago."

"You go by yourself?"

"Porky's along for protection, if anything should go wrong. He wouldn't hurt anyone unfriendly, but he has an uncanny instinct for recognizing troublemakers."

"That's good. I'll have to tell Cousin Claire. I think she and Mrs. Reinschmidt are afraid of him."

"Well, I don't know about Mrs. Reinschmidt, but Claire has always had a fear of dogs. She was against Charles giving Porky to me for my fourteenth birthday, made a big stink about it."

"She is a bit strange."

"What do you mean?"

"I don't know, exactly. When she met me at the train the other day, she was all hugs and kisses. I told her I didn't like her making over me as though I were a kid or something. But now I'm here, living with her, she doesn't act the same."

"She probably decided to respect your wishes, that's all. Before you came, she told me what a bright boy you were, how grown-up you seemed."

"Maybe that's it, but she came into my room night before last, or maybe it was Mrs. Reinschmidt. Of course I didn't open my eyes because I was supposed to be asleep. But I could sense the light over me. Someone had brought a lamp, or a candle, and stood over me for a long time.

"Of course it could have been a dream, but I don't think so . . ."

"Maybe you screamed in the night from a nightmare, and they came to see about you."

"Yes, theoretically it could have happened. It doesn't matter, though. I'm only going to be here till the end of summer, then I'll go back home to live with Grandfather."

"James, who taught you so many big words? Someday you'll say one I don't know, and I'll feel like an idiot."

"My dad. He taught me almost everything I know—more than they teach you in school. He was the smartest man in Grady. We read Greek mythology together, and I've a whole set of Dickens. We also played parlor games. My dad believed they took great skill to play properly, and one should never let an opponent win just out of kindness. When I beat him, it was fair and square. Do you know backgammon or chess?"

"I've only played backgammon a few times."

"That's too bad. I'll have a time finding a chess partner around here, I guess."

"You must have loved your father very much."

"I loved my mother, too!" he said indignantly, and his face clouded up. He looked straight ahead then, and walked on in silence. Porky slowed down to an even gait, sensing authority in James's voice. I had no idea what to say next, or whether to speak at all.

"She was beautiful, you know," he said finally, as though to himself.

"I know. My mother painted her portrait. Would you like to come see it?"

"See it? Oh, I don't know . . . uh, maybe sometime. In a couple of days, maybe."

"Any time. It's hanging in our dining room."

"Mother read books and things too, and played the piano. Her fingers were small and dainty, but she could stretch them better than an octave on the keys. She and my father had a lot in common. They met in the library.

"She was going to give me a brother or sister at one time, but had a miscarriage. So now, except for Grandfather, I have no one."

"It's too bad about your mother losing her baby. When did it happen?"

"Three years ago. She told me she was sorry, and cried a lot after it was over and stayed in bed. I brought her flowers everyday from the garden and read to her, and she told me I was like a golden nugget among a cluster of rocks. She always said I was her undeserved treasure, especially after she lost the baby."

"Well, you must make friends here in Galveston, just as I've had to do. I have no brothers or sisters either, or even

any cousins around here, but Marybeth Fischer—we're
going to her place now—is almost like a sister."

"We'll be friends, you and I," he said. "If you'll take me
along wherever you go, I won't be any trouble, I promise."

"No, I don't think I would ever regard you as trouble."

"You know, I wasn't going to tell you this so soon . . .
but you remind me of my mother somehow. You're pretty
like her. Of course, you're not *as* pretty as she was, you
understand, but like her just the same."

"You flatter me."

"What does that mean?"

"Aha, caught you on one. Flatter means . . . well . . .
to make someone feel very special inside."

Each time I've passed the public beaches on my way to
Marybeth's, I've been grateful all over again for the privilege of swimming off her private beach. Like cattle jammed
together inside a fence, the people play in the water, there
being scarcely enough room to move one's arms up and
down or sideways. For lack of space, no one can swim, and
if anyone ventures outside the ropes, a lifeguard stationed
high above blows a whistle, and orders the adventurer back
inside the bounds. Bathing in such confinement would be
no better for me than staying at home, sitting in Mother's
room all day.

The public beaches were particularly crowded that day,
all the kids being fresh out of school, and James looked on
intently, then remarked, "The people look like ants in an
ant colony. It was never that crowded in the pond at
home."

"Nor is it where we're going."

"What's that building up ahead?"

"The Seaside Pavilion. They have band concerts and
three-act plays there, tightwire walking and so forth."

"We didn't have anything like that in Grady. Only traveling shows."

"We'll have to go in the next night or two, then. There's
a group playing from New York. They come here every
summer."

"It's certainly an odd building, with all those flags and
things poking out."

"Yes. It's patterned after the old Galveston Pavilion that
burned down when I was younger. In fact, Mother and
Father and Claire and Charles and I were in the building

when it caught fire. I don't remember of course, for I was only three. But Charles used to talk about it. He said the Galveston Pavilion had two towers just like this one, but it was round instead of rectangular. Claire still calls it the great mushroom."

The Seaside Pavilion was deserted that day, and it seems odd now to look back on our casual conversation about it, knowing what an important part of my life it became. Even the band members, who often played ball on the beach nearby during their free time, weren't there that day. I supposed them to be rehearsing for the evening performance, a lot of young men from so far away they might as well have been from another country, and I wondered idly as we went along how they were able to draw so many people to their shows year after year. People in Galveston still regard Yankees as rather low-down individuals, though the war has been over almost half a century. Of course, they're not openly ostracized, yet occasionally you hear a slur or two against a person who isn't otherwise well thought of, and if he's also from the North, well . . . it seems to make him all the worse, somehow.

The sunlight shone like a beacon against the Gulf that day, giving off glitters of light on the water's surface like silver beads on a lady's evening gown. The tide was a little low, not the best for playing in the surf, but it would do for my friend and me, and the still cool June breeze would keep James from tiring too easily. A newcomer has to grow accustomed to the climate here. . . .

"Is that where we're going, up there at the big fence?"

"Yes. You can see the pier from here. When you jump off the end, you're in five feet of water."

"Five feet? That's as deep as I am tall."

"Yes, of course, I never thought. We needn't go all the way to the end. There are stairs along the sides midway down. See the little building at the pier's end, with the pointed roof? That's the bathhouse where we'll change clothes. Now, just here, you can get a view of the house. It's really grand."

"Gee, must have fifty rooms."

"Well, maybe half that. The Fischers are from Massachusetts originally, and the house is patterned after one they owned on Cape Cod. Mr. Fischer owns a big fishing fleet here."

"He must be very rich."

"He is. Now, if I can just find my key in this bag. Hold still, Porky. We'll be there in a minute."

"Does Porky go in the water?"

"Sometimes. But he likes to sun on the pier, too, on his back with all four legs in the air. I never stay in the water long because I freckle too easily."

"Yes. Your freckles were something I noticed because Mother didn't have any. But then she didn't get out in the sun much, either. She was too busy helping my father with the store, you see, then she had the house cleaning and cooking."

"Your father owned a store?"

"Yes, second-hand furniture; though he did handle new things from time to time. I helped after school, dusting the furniture for sale and cleaning the mirrors. Do you know how to tell if a mirror is any good? You tap the glass with a closed pocket knife. The sound will tell if the mirror is cheap and thin or good quarter-inch plate. My dad always demonstrated that for customers.

"He never really wanted a store, though. He'd rather have been a teacher. He just did it because my grandfather wanted him to, so it was an obligation."

It occurred to me then there must be many people in the world who inherit what they do from others, spending their lifetimes hacking away at some piece of stone they'd just as soon not fool with. It seemed to be precisely my own lot in life.

And here we were at Marybeth Fischer's, the most independent person I'd ever known. She almost seemed to be breathing down my neck, telling me I ought to consider the wisdom of the little dark-haired half-man who now walked across the lawn with me, gaping openly at the beauty of the house.

His awe reminded me of my own reaction the first time I'd walked with Marybeth across the tree-shaded lawns and gazed at all the pointed gables and graduated levels of the white wooden house. She'd never made any pretense of being rich, and until I went home with her one day after ballet class, I'd never dreamed she was related to *the* Fischers of Galveston, whose names appeared in the paper now and then. She walked into the house ahead of me, throwing her clothes bag down on a mahogany table, almost upsetting a large pot of fresh flowers there, then directed me to a parlor and slumped down into a sofa and ordered a servant to bring ice cream.

That was long ago, and by now I walked across the grounds of her place almost with an air of propriety, had even been guilty a time or two of pretending to myself I really lived here, and might suddenly decide one day to order a servant to pack my bags, and send some employee in my charge to arrange a trip to the Orient. "We'll close up the house," I would say, "and get Marybeth's friend to watch after it while we're gone. . . ."

We'd changed our clothes now and were sitting midway down the pier, dangling our feet in the water. "Serena, I hope you won't get angry with me if I tell you something I did last night," James began. "I meant no harm. If I had, I wouldn't be telling you, would I?"

"That's logical enough."

"The windows in the room where I'm staying are across from one of your upstairs windows. Last night, when everybody was in bed and all the lights were out, I looked there and saw someone's silhouette in the window shade. I didn't mean to pry. I was just looking out into the night and thinking. The odd thing was, all I could see was a head near the bottom of the shade, like a little person standing there. You did say you had no sisters or brothers?"

"Yes. What you probably saw was my mother's shadow. She was in her wheelchair until late last night, when I helped her to bed."

"I see. She's an invalid then?"

"Didn't Claire mention anything about her condition?"

"Only that she's sick. I thought she had a bad headache or something. Isn't she ever going to get well?"

"I'm afraid not."

"May I visit her sometime?"

"I suppose you could, but she doesn't talk, though some days I think she understands what people say better than others."

"What happened to her?"

"She fell down our front stairs thirteen years ago. She was holding . . . well, never mind. She just tripped and fell."

"Oh, the stairs. They're awfully high around here, aren't they?"

"You must mind them, especially after it rains. It had rained the morning Mother fell."

"It's almost as though you lost your mother, as I did mine, isn't it?"

"Yes," I told him, and thought that in many ways, it was far worse.

"If you want to go off the deep end of the pier, I'm not afraid. I can swim."

"No, there's no sense taking chances. Listen, James, there is nothing wrong in being afraid. It's a good idea sometimes, good common sense, as my father would say. Anyway, if we're going to be friends, let's not pretend with each other. You don't have to prove anything to me, and I won't to you."

"All right then. Will you jump first?"

James took to the water from that day, but we didn't stay in long, and when I reminded him of my tendency to freckle he readily agreed to get under the shade of the bathhouse. As I fluffed my wet hair, spraying water on Porky, who was in his favorite sunning position, I asked him, "Well, what do you think of my playground, the sea?"

"I like it a lot, though the sand feels funny under my feet, like suction cups full of grit. The bottom of the Grady pond is smooth and muddy. You have to hang your feet off the edge and wash the mud off before you can go home."

"You'll find you have to wash the salt off once you've been in this water. It gives you an awful feeling if you don't. That's why there's a shower in the bathhouse here."

"Let me look at you. Yes, I think you got a new freckle or two this morning. It's a terrible thing, isn't it? I mean, freckles just appear, nothing you can do will stop them."

"I dab my face with lemon juice and water at night. I read in the *Ladies' Home Journal* that it helps a little, and it does. But I love the water so much that I'd put up with worse than freckles if I had to."

"You're lucky to be able to come down here by yourself all the time. Does your father let you do everything you want?"

"Just about, I guess. Of course, I help him do a lot of things, too."

"How? Does he have a store?"

"No, he's a preacher. I attend teas and receptions, dinners and things, and fill in for Mother. I cook his breakfast in the morning and dinner at night, and stay with Mother afternoons and most evenings."

"Does your father have a big church?"

"Not so big as it used to be a few years ago. There are only about fifty or sixty families going there now. There were more a few years ago, but they went elsewhere. You know, people are free to worship anywhere they choose. Who can tell what makes people leave one church and go to another? It's a highly personal thing. Anyway, that's what Dad says."

"I hope I meet your father soon. I'm surrounded by . . . well, uh . . ."

"Women? I guess you are, at that."

"Not that it's so bad, but Mrs. Reinschmidt is very stern and not much fun to be around. Claire isn't quite so stern, but she's always telling me not to blink or something, or correcting me, and it gets on my nerves. Mother and Father treated me more like a grown-up, you know. They used to let me stay up late nights when they went to parties. When they'd come home, they'd tell me all about it and my father would talk like he had a wad of chewing tobacco in his mouth. It was so funny, I'd laugh and laugh.

"He never was really a chewer, of course. My mother wouldn't have allowed it. It was only the punch that made him talk so funny. He never was a drinking man either, except when they went to parties."

"I'm surprised they'd let you see—"

"Doesn't your father drink? No, I guess not, if he's a preacher."

"He does, some."

It was odd he should have asked that question. My father drinks quite a lot, actually, though I don't think anyone knows except me and maybe Claire. I just hope he can cope after I'm gone. Maybe then, he'll be forced to pull himself together again. Roman says I mustn't worry, that no one can live another's life for him, but I will always worry whether he can make out okay with Mother the way she is. I sometimes believe his spirit, as well as his heart, wound up in pieces at the bottom of those stairs when Mother and Donnie fell.

Chapter 3

Mornings at the beach with James were among the most pleasant I've spent. He went with me almost every day for the next couple of weeks, and his face and arms were soon tanned, giving him a far healthier look than the one he'd arrived with. Each day he seemed more content with Galveston, mentioning less and less often the prospect of going back to live with his grandfather, and eventually he spoke more easily of his parents, as though a good deal of the hurt he'd suffered with their deaths was either dispelled or suppressed. I could never perceive which.

One day on the way to Marybeth's, he said, "It bothers me, not having seen them. I never saw them after the accident. And when the funeral was held, Claire wouldn't allow me to go. I didn't tell her, but I wanted to go because I thought if I could only see them, I could know for sure they were gone."

It was a perceptive remark, but then not so surprising, coming from him. I thought for a minute, then said, "James, I'm sure Claire was right about that. You probably couldn't realize, but it would have been much harder to have seen. Now you can remember just how they were before the accident, the way they'd want to be remembered."

"But when my friend Jeremy Post lost his father, he went right up to the coffin and kissed him. His mother wanted him to. I never even kissed my parents good-by that morning they went off in the carriage together. I was too busy with my butterfly collection . . .

"That night, after it was all over and people were running in and out of the house, traipsing all over my mother's good parlor rug with their muddy feet and cluttering our kitchen with their food, I went to my room alone and destroyed the collection. I broke all the frames and tore the wings off the specimens my dad and I had collected together."

"But why—?"

"I just had to do something. But I'm all right now. I can sleep again. Thinking of them used to keep me awake nights, but it doesn't anymore. Grandfather said time will heal the wounds for both of us, and he was right. He's always right."

"He sounds like a fine man."

"He is finer than any man, except my father."

"I'm certain he is."

"My father and I did so many things together. Like, we used to read in the Greek mythology book and compare the gods and goddesses with people we knew. Last night, I looked in it to find the goddess most like you."

"Did you find her?"

"Yes. Aphrodite. Some call her Venus, but I prefer Aphrodite . . . it suits her better."

"Venus? Well, from what I've heard of her, I'm sure you've paid me a compliment. Why do you think I'm like her?"

"First of all, she loved the sea. She is said to have been of the white foam of the sea. She was very beautiful and pure. Also, she was graceful, and always smiled."

"My goodness. What became of her?"

"It was tragic, really. There was an ugly god named Hephaestus, who took her for his wife. They were very unhappy."

"How sad," I said, and immediately thought of Nick.

"Of course, that doesn't necessarily hold true for you. Things are different here. You can marry whom you want. The fellow I watched you leave with last night, is he the person you've chosen to marry?"

"You watched? My, you're nosy."

"Cousin Claire and Mrs. Reinschmidt and I were sitting on the verandah after supper last night, when he came to call for you. Mrs. Reinschmidt was snapping beans—she's always busy with something—and Cousin Claire was talking about her operation and how sick she was after it—"

"But that was years ago . . ."

"You'd never know it by listening to her. Of course she never has said just what kind of operation it was, only that she'd never been the same after it."

"I see. What were you going to say about Nick?"

"Well, I was sitting on the top step last night, so I got a good view of him. Claire says he's your intended."

"Well, he isn't. He is just a friend. We've talked of marriage, but I'm not ready for that."

"Why not? Claire said you're nineteen and that isn't much younger than my mother when she got married."

"I know, and believe me, you're not the first to point out I'm almost an old maid. Still, I have responsibilities. I'll think about marriage later."

"He wasn't very handsome, the man you left with last night. Perhaps he's Hephaestus and you can now know for sure you shouldn't marry him."

I stifled a smile, but didn't let on I'd been thinking along the same lines. "I don't know as I'd go that far, James. He isn't by any means ugly, and even if he were, goodness and consideration, thoughtfulness, are more important than looks."

"I guess so. But my father was handsome. He was the handsomest—"

"Handsomest man in Grady, and your mother the prettiest woman."

"Yes."

The conversation was becoming deplorable. "Look, James, perhaps you shouldn't boast so much. Someone might take it wrong."

"But I didn't mean . . . please, I'm sorry if it sounded bad."

"Well, it did. After all, we did pledge honesty to each other. It's all right, though. I guess everyone brags sometimes."

"Your being my best friend is something to brag about. I wish I had somebody to boast to about that."

He was impossible to scold. I smiled at him and we opened the Fischer gate.

It was on a Saturday night we went to the Seaside Pavilion to see Professor King's Band, and it was on that night my life really began. It had rained all day, and we feared we wouldn't be able to go. Yet by late afternoon no sign was left of the shower except a million tiny mirrors reflecting on the grass, and the sky turned lavender and pink as the night spread itself over the day.

James appeared at my front door at seven o'clock, wearing his best cotton suit and a new pair of shoes. Nick had asked earlier in the week if he could join us, but I'd told him no. I didn't know why, really, except that I simply didn't feel like having him. I think Nick has always been jealous of James, and felt I was foolish for preferring his company. Yet it wasn't so silly when I thought of Nick as no more than a friend—regardless of what Claire and a lot of others seemed to think—and James was more fun to be around, even if he was still a little shy of fourteen. Nick could only talk about one thing: studying liturgical music, and being the greatest organist in Galveston, or even in the world. He wasn't truly interested in the music students he taught three days a week, except in the fact they provided extra income for him to flaunt whenever he told me of all he had to offer as a husband.

Nick always looked down on popular music, which is what we'd be hearing from the Professor's band, so it gave me no small pleasure to tell him he wouldn't be interested in the entertainment we were going to see.

On the other hand, James spoke of little else for two days ahead of the show. We walked to the Pavilion instead of taking a streetcar as most people do. I enjoyed walking in semi-darkness, and thought it a good way of rounding off an evening which otherwise would probably be more fun for James than for me.

"Cousin Claire knows all about this place," James said on the walk down. "Did you know Charles used to own part of the property it's built on?"

"No, I didn't."

"Yes. She sold it after he died, for a profit."

"How nice."

"She's good friends with the Pavilion owner's wife. Imagine her, knowing someone that important."

"Imagine . . ."

There were no more than a hundred people attending that night, I supposed because the earlier rain had caused many to change their plans and stay home playing whist or casino in the parlor. After buying our tickets, James asked, "Can we sit on the front row?"

"Yes, but we must hurry."

I care nothing for front row seats. They make me feel as though I'm on stage with the performers, and it's impossible to get a good view of the whole show. But it seemed to mean so much to James, and of course he was my main reason for coming. The show was a half hour late beginning, and I shudder now to think I was about to suggest we leave and come some other night, when the white-haired, bearded professor appeared on the stage and all but the footlights in the hall were cut.

"LADIES AND GEN-TLE-MEN, THIS IS PROFESSOR KING, WELCOMING YOU TO THE THREE-HUNDRED-EIGHTY-NINTH

PERFORMANCE OF THE KINGPIN PLAYERS, FEATURING BRASS, STRINGS, DRUMS, CYMBALS, AND AS A SPECIAL FEATURE, MISTER ROMAN CRUZ, THE VERY TALENTED MUSICIAN FROM SAINT LOUIS. AND HERE THEY ARE . . ."

A dozen or so young men, dressed dandily in red and white striped blazers, white pants and straw hats with red bands, bounded out onto the stage, bringing forth loud applause. James's eyes widened. Apparently the traveling shows of his hometown were not quite so glittering as this.

After the musicians were seated, Professor King said, "AND WE'LL START OFF WITH A TUNE FAMILIAR TO EVERY-ONE—A GUSSIE L. DAVIS SONG, "IN THE BAGGAGE COACH AHEAD," AND IF YOU PLEASE, THE BAND WILL PLAY ONE CHORUS, THEN WE ASK YOU TO JOIN IN AND SING THE WORDS WITH US. AND ONE-AND-TWO-AND-THREE-AND-FOUR . . ."

After the Davis melody, the band went into "If They Write That I'm Forgiven, I'll Go Home," and "The Fatal Wedding." They were far better than I'd expected, although people who'd listened to them for the past two summers had reported they were good. Many of their songs had to do with the railroad in one way or another, and most of them were light and lilting, designed to please an audience wanting music for fun. Nick would've been dismayed by their selections, but even he would have had to admit the group played well together.

I waited anxiously for the special feature, for I'd been playing a game all along, trying to guess which one of the young men on stage went by the intriguing name of Roman Cruz. Finally, near the end, the Professor turned and introduced him, and a spotlight was fixed on this man as he removed his hat and lifted a brass trumpet, and began a slow, haunting rendition of "My Old Kentucky Home," giving the song a dignity it had never before possessed. He was a stunning figure, with wavy hair the color of raven's wings and dark, almost oriental eyes. He not only played his instrument: he possessed it. I couldn't take my eyes off him.

James whispered in my ear, "It's Apollo, the musician god, Serena, look at him!"

"Yes, yes," I said. I was in no mood for Greek mythology. On and on he played, the only salient presence in the room, the band's accompaniment soft as a hum behind him. And when he brought the simple folk tune to a close with an arpeggio of notes reaching a full two octaves above its classic finale, a burst of applause vibrated throughout the hall. He nodded confidently, knowing he'd pleased his audience well and would always do so.

I applauded until my hands stung, and when everyone else was silent, I found, much to my embarrassment, I was standing. No one else in the hall was standing, only me. Before I could collect myself sufficiently to sit down again, I saw the trombone player next to Roman Cruz punch him and nod in my direction. I dropped to my seat and bowed my head, while all the people around me snickered.

"James, what can I do? Why didn't you pull me down? I must have looked a fool—"

"Serena, he's looking at you. He's looking at you! He's the best one in the band, and he saw you. Smile at him."

"Oh, I couldn't. When will this be over?"

"The program says one more number. I'll watch and see if he keeps looking. Imagine, Aphrodite has been noticed by Apollo. What a match!"

"Oh, James, this is no time for games. I shall never lift my head again. I just hope there's no one here tonight that I know."

"It's all right. You're the prettiest girl in the room. You shouldn't be ashamed of anything. It's the people here who are lucky, cause they got to see you."

". . . James, you are a treasure, just as your mother said . . ."

As we walked to Marybeth's the following Monday, I said, "Would you trust me with your Greek book for a day or so?"

"Sure. I wish you'd keep it and read it all. See how you can draw parallels between the gods and goddesses and people you know. It was the most interesting game Dad and I ever played, I think. Better even than chess."

"There's no hurry, of course. I'm just a bit curious, that's all."

"About Apollo?"

"Oh, don't remind me of that."

"He watched you until we left, you know."

"You told me. Probably wanted to a good look at an imbecile."

"Nah, he wouldn't do that. He looked at you because you're so pretty."

"James, I'm not really so pretty . . . let's don't talk of it anymore."

"There they are, playing ball on the beach," he said as we passed the Pavilion.

I walked faster. 'If you care to join them, go ahead. I'm sure they'd like to have you."

"No, they wouldn't. I know better than to try to join in with older fellows. They regard the youngest boy as a squirt, and he becomes the butt of all the jokes. I learned that a long time ago. Look, even the Professor is out there today. You know, he reminds me a lot of your father."

"Oh? I can't see much resemblance except maybe in the build."

"It's the hair I noticed."

"My father's hair is light, not white."

"I know. Still, he reminds me—"

"By the way, did I see you playing with the Baker kids down the street yesterday?"

"Yes. Claire insisted I play ball with them. But I'm no good at baseball, and I didn't like them very much either."

"Why not?"

"Because they don't like me. Joe Baker—the oldest— accused me of being a Yankee. Not to my face, of course. I overheard him say it to one of the others. Isn't that stupid? I mean, just because I live further north than he does, it doesn't make me a Yankee."

"What did you do?"

"Pretended not to hear. Joe Baker's bigger than me, and a year older besides."

"You're good at judging things."

"I have to be. When a guy is little and wears spectacles, and isn't handsome, he must be able to figure things out in advance, so he won't be made a fool of."

"James, don't downgrade yourself. You've only got to grow a little older and you'll be far better-looking, and know much more, than all those Baker kids and their pals put together."

"That isn't saying much. Joe picks his nose all the time, and the oldest girl, Delta, chews gum with her mouth open. They're a bore, the whole group. Probably not one of them ever checked out a book from the library."

I was chuckling over his description of the Baker ring, though he was perfectly serious. I gave him the key, and he reached up and unlocked the Fischer gate.

We had been there, probably, forty-five minutes.

I was dangling my feet from the pier, since this was not a day that I could swim. James was playing in the water, enjoying the whitecaps of the swollen tide; Porky was beside me on his back. I heard a voice at the fence and looked around. It was Roman Cruz.

His shoulders were colored by the sun, muscles rounded under the black knit of his swimsuit. "Hey there," he called, "is this private property, or can anybody come in?"

My heart pumped as though I'd already run the length of grass between the pier and the fence, and I hesitated at first, aware of the silly bathing outfit I was wearing, the navy one I'd sewn for myself and had made too small.

I should have said, "Yes, this is private. Please go away," but even at that early moment I bowed to the command of the man across the fence. I waved to him and walked over, uneasy every step because I could feel his gaze on me, and the bathing suit seemed to be shrinking in both directions the further I walked.

At the fence I tried to sound as casual as though Roman Cruz were a delivery boy, bringing something ordered from the house. "Hullo, was there something you wanted here?"

"I was looking for you. I watched you pass by, down the beach a little while ago. I shouldn't think you'd be surprised, after you gave me a standing ovation night before last."

"You must be mistaken. I stayed home and embroidered a pillowcase night before last."

Then James, poor dear, noticed who it was and shouted from the bay: "Hey, it's the guy from the band. He remembered you," and I wanted to be swallowed up by the ground.

"That your kid brother?"

"Next-door neighbor."

"He was the boy with you, then?"

"Well, perhaps it was another night I worked on the pillowcase. . . . Look, I just enjoyed your music. I didn't intend to make a spectacle of myself."

"It's okay. I'm not above flattery, my dear. Now, are you going to open this gate or do I have to climb the fence?"

I unlocked the gate, thankful no one was around. What would people think if they could see me admitting a total stranger into the Fischer grounds?

"This is quite a place. Yours?"

"No. It belongs to a friend who's away for the summer."

"I see. I didn't think it was yours."

"Why not?"

"You don't strike me as the snobby little-rich-girl type."

"Well, you guessed that right. My father's a parson, in charge of a very small church."

My words sounded almost choked, yet he continued to toss questions at me as though I were a companion of long standing who'd just returned from a trip.

"That's quite a bathing outfit you're wearing. It isn't even wet. You just like looking at the water, do you?"

"No. I—uh—was just getting a little sun on the pier."

He laughed softly, and it struck me he knew exactly why I was staying out of the water that day. "Did you know your nose turns red when you're nervous?"

"I'm not nervous; why should I be?" I said, yet reached a finger to my nose, then forced it down.

"It's strange, you know, a lovely girl like you chasing around with a small fry like that one in the water."

"James is quite grown up for his years, and more fun to be around than anyone else I know right now."

"Is that so? Well, I suppose it could be, here in Galveston. Not much excitement going on as a rule, I expect."

"Have you been with the band a long time?"

"Three years. I was here last summer, and the one before. Why didn't I see you?"

"I don't know. I just never got around to going to the Pavilion. I thought James might enjoy it. He was the one who wanted to sit on the front row, so we did—just for him, of course."

"I'm glad of that, or else I might never have met you."

We were approaching the pier now and James, showing more instinct for good manners than he had a few minutes earlier, stayed in the water, his body turned away from us. Porky sniffed at Roman once or twice, but was instantly endeared to him when he put out a hand and roughed his coat a little. "That's a good boy, stranger, keep your place and I'll sit on the other side of your mistress."

He then sat down beside me on the towel, as though he'd done it hundreds of times and this was an accepted thing going on. He was so cheeky that I didn't know how to handle him. I simply couldn't appear high-minded, though. Something told me that would be a mistake.

I yanked on my swimsuit at the top. The sailor collar had always plunged an inch or two too low. He lay back on the towel and raised his head on one elbow, shading his eyes. "You've a great body," he said. "Swimming all the exercise you get?"

"No. I dance ballet at Madame D'Arcy's studio here."

"I see. I should have guessed. I can tell, even under the suit, your legs are good."

What was he doing? I'd never before let anyone talk to me in such a way. Yet he was like a scientist in his observations, analyzing some new biological specimen in the confines of a laboratory. His manner was calmly detached as he mentally stripped everything from me and looked straight through.

"Your parson father would be awfully sore at you for taking up with the likes of me."

"Who said I'd taken up with anyone? You simply asked to come in, that's all. I don't own this place. Who am I to decide whether anyone should or shouldn't come in?"

"Oh, you rationalize beautifully, better than some of the more experienced ladies I've met. I'll bet you have a fiancé hidden away somewhere—at least a steady beau. Someone your family highly approves of and is looking for you to marry. You'll get hitched in a candlelight ceremony and wear your mother's wedding gown, and she'll cry tears of happiness and wave her handkerchief, and hope for a dozen grandchildren."

His badinage can be unbearable at times. "Oh, stop it," I said. "You couldn't possibly know anything about me."

"I can look at you and see. Now, tell me. What's the fellow's name? You've at least got to grant me some knowledge of my competitor for your affections."

"Look, I know you're just playing with me. You think you're very sharp, don't you? Think you know all about the girls in Galveston, that we're not very worldly or sophisticated. Well, the truth is I do have a steady beau, but I'm not engaged and have no intention of marrying anytime soon. Besides, even if I did, I wouldn't wear my mother's dress because she stands a full head taller than I—if she stood, which she doesn't because she's been a bedridden invalid for years."

"Oh, I'm sorry for that . . . truly I am," he said gently. Roman Cruz is like that: just when he gets you to the point of slapping him, his manner does an about-face, and he melts you next with contrition and understanding.

"But you don't really love this young man, do you? What is he, a shopkeeper, shipbuilder, something?"

"Church organist, if you must know. And I haven't decided if I love him."

"How long has he been courting you?"

"Over a year."

"You've decided, then."

"What of you? You're very good at asking questions. What's your family like, anyway, or do you have a family?"

"A mother, back in St. Louis, and in New York one sister who's a ballet dancer, like you. She dances with a ballet corps."

I'd been all set to ask whether he had a sweetheart, or even a wife, for he looked old enough to have either. But now I leapt at his last statement. "How exciting! If I could only ever get a chance to—" I began, but never finished because my words were shot through by a single piercing scream.

Chapter 4

It was James, surrounded by a school of Portuguese man-of-war.

Porky leaped to his feet, barking ferociously, and I gaped in horror, unable to move or speak. Roman jumped into the water and spattered toward James, freeing him from his now frightened predators. James was wild-eyed, screaming all the while at the top of his lungs as Roman pulled him back toward the shore.

"It's all right," he shouted to me, "I don't think he got it too badly. Here—what's your name?—let's get him onto the beach and pack some sand on his leg." I nodded, smarting from my stupidity in failing to warn James of the danger of man-of-war. They look like filmy crystal balls above the water, their long tentacles full of poison, hidden underneath the surface. People often call them accidents of nature.

"My name is Serena," I answered finally, once we'd gotten James calmed down a bit.

"We'll have to get him home now. He'll need some first aid."

"I thought they were colored balls," said James. "I was going to pick one up—I—"

"It's all right, don't try to talk," said Roman. "Here, up you go. Serena, get the gate and lead the way. We'll have to hurry. He can develop a fever from this."

Being referred to as, "what's your name," had not been flattering, especially after having talked with Roman Cruz so intimately for the space of a few minutes, yet of course this fact never dawned upon me until later, after we'd gotten James safely back home. We had looked for a trolley, but as luck would have it we missed the most recent car by several hundred yards, so we half walked, half ran the length of the beach and up Avenue L, where we found Helga Reinschmidt standing on Claire's porch, looking toward the street.

"It's James, he's had a man-of-war sting," I shouted. "Where's Claire?"

"I wouldn't know. She took off an hour ago and hasn't come back. Lunch is waiting."

"Where can we put him?" Roman asked.

"Up to the front room," she said, opening the door as we came up the stairs. "I'll get ammonia from the bathroom."

Her calmness irritated me. "I'll show you to his room," I told Roman. "Here it is, to the right . . ."

When we lay James upon the bed Roman said, "It's lucky we were so near . . . he probably would've gotten stung a lot worse trying to free himself. I got a sting once, and it's no fun."

"It's all my fault. I should have watched him more carefully. He isn't from around here and he wouldn't know that he had to be cautious about this kind of thing."

"Aw, Serena, it's okay. I'm all right, honest," James spoke up weakly.

"You lie still while we get this wound treated," I told him.

Helga was soon there with ammonia and bicarbonate of soda. She's very astute at dressing wounds, yet her unsmiling face shows no sympathy. I've often thought if one could strip away her skin, one would find solid rock underneath.

When she was done, she looked at James and said, "Now, you rest for an hour or two. And mind you, no swimmin' in the sea for a day or so unless Mrs. Becker says." She looked across at me then, and I felt my face redden under the sternness of her gaze.

"It wasn't her fault," said James. "Please don't make such a bother about it. I don't want to be any trouble, please."

"All right. Let's go," said Helga. "We'll leave the boy alone for a bit."

"Maybe he'd like some ice water or something else cold," I said.

"Yes, that'd be swell," said James.

"I can get it—"

"No. You two go on about your business. When Mrs. Becker is away, James is in my charge. I'll tend to him."

"Yes, come, let's get out of here," said Roman.

He held a hand under my elbow as we trailed Helga's black skirt down the stairs, and I was surprised at his chivalry. It was more suited to Nick's personality, this gesture of protectiveness, yet I had always despised Nick's constant showing of patronization because it seemed to reflect possessiveness. I believe I sensed even then that Roman Cruz would never try to possess anyone, and in so doing would possess anyone he chose.

Out on the verandah my voice was too anxious. "You could stay if you've time. I could make lemonade. I live just there, the yellow house."

"All right, but I have rehearsals within the hour."

"We'll sit on the steps, so we won't disturb Mother."

"And also in plain view of the neighborhood," he said, and looked at me from out the corner of his eye. "I do believe I perceive a note of fear in the fair damsel's manner. Not to worry, though. I always leave what virtue there is intact."

As I went to the kitchen to fill the pitcher, I was sure I ought to have nothing more to do with anyone like Roman, yet, by the time I walked back out on the porch, I was already thinking of the first of my diary entries about him.

"You were born here, lived here all your life?" he asked as I handed him the lemonade.

"I was born right upstairs."

"Is that so?"

I was trying to decide where to sit. In the wicker swing across the porch? In the chair by the door? He was seated on the top step, and somehow it seemed too forward to sit down beside him. After I'd hesitated for a few moments he said, "Don't worry, Serena. Sit here beside me. I don't bite people as a rule, unless they say the wrong thing."

I made no reply. When one is so transparent there is little hope of pretending. I sat down then, closer to him than he may have expected, just to show I wasn't afraid of him at all. Yet it was hard suddenly to carry on further conversation as easily as we had on the pier just a few minutes earlier. I wanted so much to find out about him, yet I could think of nothing to say, and even he wasn't as full of questions as before.

"Where do you go from here?" I asked.

"Oh, so you're ready to get rid of me so soon?"

"No. I mean at the end of the summer."

"Back to New York; that's our base."

"But you will be here the whole summer?"

"Yes. We leave early September."

"But you'll return next year?"

"Next year? Oh, that depends on whether the contract is renewed. Our turnouts haven't been anything to brag about so far this summer, but we'll see." He swatted at a fly that had begun buzzing around our faces, but missed the mark. The fly swung back, buzzing more loudly.

"I hope you'll be back."

"Why?"

"I . . . now that I've seen you perform, I want to come again and again. Sorry I missed you the past two summers. You all are very good."

"Ah, but what would you need with Professor King's band when you'll be hearing organ music all the time? No doubt your fiancé is very highbrow."

He swatted at the pesky fly again, missed again. Why wouldn't the thing leave us alone?

"He isn't my fiancé."

"Oh yes, that's right. It doesn't matter, though, for he soon will be, and I'll be gone off to a new town. Eventually, you'll forget even my name in the face of diapers and baby bottles."

"No, I won't. It's a very interesting name. . . ."

"Look. I'm not the sort you should get tangled up with. Probably I ought to get up right now and go back to the Pavilion, and forget about you too. God knows, I've no use for a girl like you. No offense intended, you understand." He was standing now, facing me on the stairs. I wasn't sure whether he was bored with me, or anxious to be free of the maddening fly.

"No offense? How else can you expect me to take it?"

"You're too nice for me—anyone would tell you— you've led a clean, protected life up to now. You'd be better off to keep going in the same direction."

"Why must you behave as though my background were a whip to beat me with? You make me almost ashamed to be a plain, ordinary—"

"No, I didn't mean that. Look, Serena, you're lucky to live on a shady street in a small town, with good people who love you—"

"And you? You must have been loved too, at least at one time. What about your father, is he alive? Is he with your mother in St. Louis? And I've been dying to know about your sister. Imagine, a professional ballet dancer—your family must be overflowing with talent—"

He leaned against the newel-post and looked into my eyes for a moment, as though I'd probed some secret, unlocked something deep inside him that longed to escape but could not. "Talent? Yes, indeed," he said finally. "My father was a talented man of sorts—a riverboat gambler, I understand, though I couldn't say for sure, of course. He left my mother when I was four and I've never seen him since."

"Oh, I see. I'm sorry." I looked away, regretting my nosiness.

"My sister is a great source of pride to my mother, just as you guessed."

I wanted to ask, "But what of you?" but did not, my own inquisitive tongue having tied itself into a knot.

"Well, I've got to get back. Thanks for the lemonade."

"Thank you, for rescuing James."

He walked to the front gate, opened it, then looked back around. "We don't practice early in the morning, only begin around eleven or so. I'm always on the beach early."

I nodded, not sure what he expected me to say. As he started down the fence, walking away from me forever as far as I knew, I suddenly thought there might be a chance. Throwing all semblance of propriety to the winds, I ran down the stairs and called to him from the gate. "I have to dance in the morning. But Wednesday I'll be back at the Fischer place, like today."

I still have no idea whether he heard me, because he

didn't slow down or turn around. He just kept walking with his usual confident gait, off in the direction of the water.

Alone again, yet more so than before, I went back up to the verandah to drink my untouched lemonade. It was fast growing warm from the heat of the day, and as I turned toward Roman's empty glass, I saw the fly again, stepping gingerly around its rim. "Damn fly," I said, swatting at him, then looked up quickly, covering my mouth with my hands, fearing someone might have heard me utter the oath.

I sat there for a long time, comparing Roman Cruz with Nick Weaver.

I had used Nick from the beginning, and wouldn't deny it. He wore the stamp of approval of everyone at St. Christopher's, including my father, so why shouldn't I let him take me to church affairs or anywhere else I wanted to go? He was willing enough to court me without demanding a commitment.

We'd gone out together a full three months before he asked to kiss me, and even then I almost had to prod him into it. We sat out on the porch one night after attending a lecture at the church on the importance of young people accepting Christ, and he kept pacing up and down by the railing, as though there were something important he must say. I remembered, then, his hands had been more than usually clammy that evening, a sure sign he was nervous. Finally he heaved a sigh, leaned against the rail, and said, "I guess you don't like me very much."

Nick Weaver is tall, taller even than Roman, and thinner, with light hair and freckles. He always smells of lavender pomade, and that night his perspiration had heightened the fragrance so that it came in gentle wafts over me as I sat below him on the steps.

"What do you mean? I see you often, don't I?"

"Yes. But I'll admit I haven't very many interesting things to talk about. I've spent most of my life concentrating on my music, and I've had little time left for girls."

"Well, I can certainly understand. Maybe you'd like to see less of me, to save more time for music?"

"Oh, no," he said quickly. "That wasn't what I meant. I always knew when the right girl would come along, then I'd make time."

"Oh?"

"Yes. Serena, I'm three years older than you, you know."

"Yes. Do you think that's too much of a gap?"

"No, no. It's just right," he said, failing to realize he was being teased. "I've a good future in liturgical music, if you can understand that. I might someday even get a position at Trinity. You know, I'm good friends with the choirmaster there. Should he ever decide to leave, he'd be certain to recommend me to replace him."

"Oh, I didn't know you were thinking of leaving St. Christopher's. Dad will be so disappointed."

"No, no. I'm only projecting the future. Trinity pays quite a lot more money for its staff, being a much larger church than St. Christopher's, and when one knows he may someday have a family to look after, he thinks of things like that."

Poor Nick. He always thought his ambitions so lofty. I didn't try and cut him down when it came to his organ playing, however, for this was the one subject about which he was touchy.

"I can understand your reasoning, Nick."

"Well, Serena . . . it's just that . . . well, I've never even—uh—kissed you properly."

He'd been looking down at me as he talked, but now turned his face away and gazed out over the yard. I was in a playful mood that night, and behaved shamelessly. "Do you want to kiss me now?"

"Now? Yes, if you . . . yes."

"Then, why don't you?"

I closed my eyes and puckered my lips, stifling a smile. He sat down beside me, then leaned over and pecked my cheek. I felt we might just as well get the whole business over with as soon as possible, so I kept my eyes closed.

He soon took the hint, and began kissing me on the mouth, more and more forcefully, until he'd pushed me down flat on the porch and was kissing me all over the face, panting like a puppy dog. "Serena, Serena, I love you, I love you. Please say you'll marry me!"

"Nick, for goodness sake, control yourself. What if someone should walk by?"

"Oh, I never thought." He looked carefully up and down the street, then turned around to face our house, to be sure Dad had not heard anything. I sat up straight and smoothed my hair in back.

"It's all right. I don't think anyone saw," he said seriously. "It's just that I've held it in for so long. . . ."

"Nick, I'm sorry, but I can't promise to marry you."

"Why not? I know there's no one else. Why can't you say yes?"

It angered me he should take me so for granted, and I had my first suspicion he discussed me quite openly with my father.

"I'm just not ready to marry, that's all."

"But you're eighteen, going on nineteen. Almost every girl is married by the time she's—"

"I realize that. Still, I'm not ready. You wouldn't want me to lie, would you?"

"Of course not. I know what it is. You can't see much future, marrying a church organist. But remember, I also teach music on the side, have more students this year than ever. I could always take even more pupils. You wouldn't need to worry about me providing well for you. Not that we'd be rich, but we'd get along as well as anyone else, I can assure you."

"Don't be absurd. I just don't want to be pressed right now."

"Does that mean you might change your mind someday?"

"How can I know? Let's not discuss it any more tonight. I'm tired and want to go in. I've got to say good night to Mother."

"Very well, but you haven't said no, so I won't give up. Serena, I do hate to say it, but you could do worse than me, you know. When can I see you again?"

"I don't know. I'll be in church Sunday, if I don't see you before."

"Oh, no. Let me come Friday night. We'll have some oysters at Henry and Joe's place, or even go to the Pickwick if you want."

"I don't know—"

"Please."

"All right."

After he'd disappeared down the street, I went inside and yielded to an overpowering urge to scrub my face with soap and water, and that night while lying in bed, I began to think seriously about Marybeth's warnings of being married to a man I did not love and could hardly bear to be touched by.

Yet the importance of her statement still escaped me then, and continued to until I thought of it again, sitting on the steps which had been occupied minutes earlier by Roman Cruz.

I knew, come Wednesday morning, I would be walking down that part of the beach where the band members have their morning ball games, praying as hard as I have ever prayed for anything that Roman Cruz would follow me to the gate of the Fischer place because he could no more forget me than I could him.

Chapter 5

Mrs. McCambridge and I learned long ago how to join our arms and make a chair for Mother, so that we can carry her down the stairs and put her into a spare wheelchair that stays, when not in use, on the back porch. There is a special ramp at the edge of the porch, and we wheel her chair down into the yard sometimes, and sit with her. Her body is always rigid as we carry her, and still rigid as we lower her into the chair and roll her down the ramp. She relaxes only once we have her chair stopped and its wheels locked, down in the yard.

On that Tuesday afternoon, just before she left for the day, Mrs. McCambridge said, "Let's take your mother down to sit for a while, and when Father Garret gets home he can carry her back."

"Yes, well, I was going to wash my hair. . . ."

"Looks t'me like ye might have stayed home and done that this mornin'. After all, Mrs. Garret's stuck in that room day after day. Seems she deserves—"

"All right, all right. Have you time to wait, though? It would only take a few minutes and could be drying while—"

"No, I haven't. I'm late now, and got my own family to look after."

Mrs. McCambridge is a stout woman, with dark wiry hair and large features. Her breasts are so broad and heavy as to look more like an extension of her formidable stomach, and that day her arms were folded indignantly under them.

She often implied I spent less time than I should with

Mother, and usually it angered me. But that day I was already feeling a bit wicked about hoping to see Roman on Wednesday, so I nodded like an obedient child, and brought paper and pen for Mother and me so that I could write to Marybeth—I was long overdue answering her last letter—and Mother could write her poetry, should she be in the mood.

No one can assess Mother's moods, really, of course, for her eyes hold nothing except, occasionally, a tear, which spills out and trickles down her cheek, or a flash of what could be fear. I don't believe Dad has ever given up trying to reach her, and it's sad to watch him sit in a chair opposite her bed at times, holding her hands, looking into those eyes as though, should he search long enough, he will penetrate the barriers lodged there by the accident.

She seemed eager to write that Tuesday afternoon and, always relieved when she's pleasantly occupied, I sat down below her chair to write my letter. What to write Marybeth . . . I was always tardy answering her letters, for they were so interesting and full of unusual things. She'd gotten a glimpse of a foreign prince on the Riviera, or been to the Ascot races in London, her pick of the horses winning, or she'd been to a party somewhere in Paris where champagne flowed from the mouth of a huge fish made of glass.

Marybeth had done everything, it seemed, and I sat year after year in Galveston, my only piece of news being that I'd finished a pillowcase I was embroidering, or made a new outfit to wear to church.

As I began to write that day, I thought I'd have paragraph after paragraph of exciting news—after all, I'd met and spent a morning with Roman Cruz. Surely there was much I could say that would please her, and convince her I wasn't the prude she always accused me of being.

Yet what could I say to show her how Roman really was? Taken piece by piece, none of what had happened so far was glamorous. He was a member of a traveling band from New York, had traveled for three years and been all over the place . . . exactly where, I had no idea. His sister was in a ballet corps, and on and on . . . I knew it was impossible, then, to capture Roman Cruz on paper.

I wrote on anyway . . . "I've met an interesting man from New York. He's a musician and handsome enough, I suppose. I may be seeing more of him this summer, but haven't yet decided whether I like him enough. . . ."

I read it over, pen poised in the air. The words looked like me trying to imitate Marybeth, which they were, and in disgust I pulled up the sheet of paper and wadded it into a ball. It was then that James appeared at the fence. "Good afternoon. Your leg's all right, then? I'm so relieved."

Porky had been stationed at Mother's feet, but upon seeing James had rushed to the fence, tail wagging. I looked up at Mother. She'd noticed him and was staring. I did, as I have many times, attempt a one-sided introduction, for James hadn't yet been into our house to meet her. He'd seen her staring, and was spellbound by her vacant gaze.

"James, please meet my mother, Mrs. Garret. Mother, this is James Byron, who lives next door with Claire. His mother was Ruth Miller, you know, that nice girl who visited Claire one summer a long time ago."

At first she seemed unable to comprehend, but then, surprisingly, tore off the paper she'd been writing on, and held it out. "You want to give it to James? All right, Mother. I'll take it over to him.

"I think she likes you," I told James softly. "Perhaps she even understands who you are. Will you let me look at what she's written, later?"

"Of course. I was going to bring the Mythology this afternoon anyway, after I walk Porky."

"Good. I'll get his leash. Come over later, after Mother is back in her room. I don't know if she'd mind our looking at the poem together, but just in case, I wouldn't want to hurt her feelings."

"I understand," he said, and slipped the piece of paper into his shirt pocket.

He and Porky soon disappeared down the block, and Mother and I sat together for another hour before Dad came home. She seemed to have written all she wanted that day, and wouldn't pick up the pen again. Instead, she stared toward Claire's house for a long time. I watched for a while, trying to figure what she might be thinking. Yet it was a fruitless effort, as usual, and I gave up and wrote a short letter to Marybeth in which I wound up mentioning James and his man-of-war sting, yet leaving Roman Cruz out of the story.

At sundown, James came over again and we sat on the verandah together, poring over the poem.

> *Come in; you look so tired.*
> *The dark is hiding here with me,*
> *Running from the truth of light.*
> *He will wait here until the lying stops.*
>
> *Do come in; I assure you we've room for*
> *another guest.*

"It's very strange," he said. "I've read it several times, but can't figure out its meaning. But then, I'm not very good at poetry, anyway. What do you think?"

"I wish I knew. All her poems make me think she has something to hide, but heaven only knows what. Probably something mixed up in her mind, something she did once that took on greater magnitude than it was worth, after the accident. I doubt she ever knowingly killed a bug, though. Anyway, I'm saving all her poems. Would you let me have this one?"

"Sure. And here's the Greek. The part about Apollo begins on page 321."

"What makes you think I'm interested in Apollo?"

"I don't know. It's just that guy Roman is so perfect for him. See if you don't agree."

"All right. You'd better go now. I have to cook dinner, and Helga will be calling you for yours."

"Before I go, could I look at the picture of my mother you have?"

"Sure. Come on in."

"Is your father home?"

"No, he's been here and gone again," I said.

Dad had carried Mother up the stairs and fed her her dinner, visited a few minutes, then come down again.

"Who brought the cake?" he'd asked.

"Same as usual, Claire."

"It looked good, but she wouldn't touch it."

"She never eats anything Claire brings."

"Perhaps she doesn't care for it."

"Looks more as though she doesn't care for Claire," I said.

"Ah, Nan, there's no reason she shouldn't, is there?" he asked.

"How should I know?"

It was an oft repeated conversation between us. Dad knew as well as I did that Mother's eyes often held fear when Claire was around, but he attributed it to the fact she was with Mother just before the accident, and felt Mother might somehow connect her fall with Claire, although Claire was not at fault. She'd gone upstairs that morning to fetch something Mother had forgotten, and by the time she returned, Mother and Donnie were at the bottom of the stairs. Of course it has occurred to me over the years that Claire might have actually had something to do with Mother's fall, but she would have had no reason to want Mother hurt then, as far as I know, and anyway, the way she carried on after it happened, the way she cried at Donnie's funeral, she must have been as heartbroken as anyone else, or at least she seemed to be. . . .

Dad was gone soon after the conversation that Tuesday evening, staying only long enough for two shots of whisky, and to kiss me on the cheek and say, "Don't wait up. I'll probably be late."

As James and I viewed the portrait together in silence, I thought perhaps he'd reached some milestone in forgetting, if he could bear to look at his mother's picture.

"It's a little fuzzy, isn't it?" he asked finally.

"That's just the style, I guess, kind of dreamy, elusive, you might say."

"I suppose. She didn't look exactly like that, though."

"I know, I know. She was much prettier . . ."

"No, I only meant, she just looked different, although this portrait does favor her a lot, of course. It's very nice."

"An artist's rendering isn't supposed to be like a photograph. It's more an impression of what the artist sees in her subject. Perhaps Mother looked deeply into her personality and painted what she saw."

"Maybe. Well, I'd better get home. Helga's fixing chicken tonight."

On the way to the door he turned and said, "You know, I think I like your house better than Claire's. It's friendlier."

"That's nice of you to say, but I'm sure Claire's house is friendly, too."

"No, it isn't. I could never be at home there. Helga's always cleaning and straightening everything. And besides, Cousin Claire keeps part of it locked up."

"Oh? Which part?"

"I think it must have been Cousin Charles's study. I looked through the keyhole one day when she was gone, and there's a desk and lots of papers in there. You know, she is gone a lot, and never says where."

"James, I think you're fond of intrigue, and you let your imagination run away with you."

He turned to go. "Oh, by the way, I didn't know your father was hard of hearing."

"What makes you think he is?"

"Well . . . on the way to the grocer's today when I went to get baking powder for Helga, I saw him walking ahead of me—two or three houses further up Avenue L. I called out to him several times but he never turned around and I finally realized he hadn't heard me."

"Well, he isn't hard of hearing. Perhaps it was the direction of the wind or something. Or maybe you only thought it was him."

"Maybe so, though I was pretty sure. Anyway, I only mentioned it because my father was deaf in one ear. Of course, no one ever guessed. He could hear perfectly from the other."

"That's too bad."

"A childhood accident caused it, he always said. Something about a rifle being fired too near him. But, as I said, you'd have never guessed if he didn't want you to know. Well, good night."

That evening after dinner, I took the mythology book and turned directly to page 321. There was a sculpture of Apollo depicted at the beginning of his section: a god of muscular body, broad chest, slender hips. His face was beardless, his long hair pulled back and knotted at the nape of his neck.

He was apparently an amorous god, for there followed a long section about his many loves, and my eyes scanned this section for mention of Aphrodite. Her name wasn't linked with his, though, and, closing the book, I wondered why it should disappoint me so. Greek gods and goddesses! What had they to do with ordinary people in Galveston, in 1899? Still, it bothered me, for James had infected me with his drawing of parallels between the mythological characters and real people, and I decided to look up Aphrodite to see whether she ever found anyone she could truly love.

I fell asleep later, the book resting on my pillow, and

awoke the next morning to a glare of sunlight streaming through the window by my bed. I looked at the time: eight o'clock. Why hadn't Dad awakened me? I looked out across the hall. The door to the little room where he sleeps was closed.

I dressed quickly and went to the kitchen to see if he was up. Then I realized what had happened the night before. There was an Old Saratoga bottle on the table, and an empty glass beside it.

I picked up the bottle. There wasn't more than a spoonful of whisky left. He would still be sleeping, then. I poured the whisky into the sink, put the bottle into the garbage, and washed the glass, just as I always did, for it made it easier to pretend in front of him I'd never discovered it.

Often I wished he wouldn't be so careless. If it weren't for me looking after him, someone would soon find out about his drinking and everything might be ruined for him in the church. What if Claire should come, bringing home-made rolls for breakfast, or biscuits or something? I never could feel certain whether Claire tattled everything she knew to her co-workers on the gardening committee, but there was always the slight chance she might, even though I would have thought it a better guess she would have protected my father and his foolishness to her dying breath.

As I cleaned the table and started breakfast, I remembered the first time I'd discovered my father's drinking habit. He always kept a decanter of port on a tray in the parlor, but before that time, as far as I knew, he never drank anything else. Then one day when I was twelve years old, still too short to reach the top cabinet in the kitchen, I brought a stool around to stand on so that I could reach the cinnamon kept above the sink. When I opened the cabinet and poked my hand inside, I felt the cool smoothness of the whisky bottle. His keeping whisky didn't alarm me; his habit of hiding it did. I was so frightened, I ran up to my room and cried. I'd seen a drunkard once, stumbling around down on Market Street and brandishing an empty whisky bottle that he soon dropped on the sidewalk, splattering glass and whisky all over the place. Charles was with me that day, and a large piece of the glass had narrowly missed striking his leg. Charles had taken my hand, and we'd crossed to the other side of the street.

I was convinced, then, that my father was like the drunkard. Of course he wasn't, and by now I know he drinks mostly in private and doesn't become obnoxious in front of others. I only hoped on that morning, early this summer, that his condition wouldn't somehow keep me from going to the beach. I made a pot of oatmeal, and when Mrs. McCambridge appeared at the front door, I grabbed my bag and left the house, not breathing properly until I reached the front gate.

Stupidly, I'd forgotten about James. He was waiting at the fence in his knickers and old shirt, wanting to know if he should get Porky, and obviously puzzled I'd forgotten him myself.

"Oh, Porky . . . yes, I guess you'd better," I told him, wondering whether I would ever have a chance at being alone on the beach again. "Are you sure it's safe for you to go into the water with that leg?"

"Yes'm. Claire said so. She's gonna buy me a bathing suit today."

"That's nice. Come on, then."

When we were on our way, Porky pulling James along, poking his nose in one place then another, I tried to broach the subject. "Listen, as we pass by the band boys on the beach today, don't look over, all right? Don't look interested in whether they're there or not."

"Oh, are we interested?"

"Of course not. I just don't want to leave the wrong impression."

"Serena, if Roman comes to the Fischer place today, I'll stay in the water. Don't worry. I won't let any fish bite me. Now I know what a man-of-war looks like, I can keep clear."

"Yes, but their tentacles are sometimes very long, so they can be a good distance from you and still sting, remember."

"I know. Last night I read all about them in one of Claire's books. You've bathed around here long enough, and never gotten stung. Certainly it's not going to happen to me again. The law of averages is against it, as my dad would have said."

"It's all right if you want to come out of the water. If Roman Cruz should come over, we'll only be talking anyway. I only pay attention to him because he's from far away, and he's interesting."

"Yes, well, all I want to do is thank him and tell him Claire wants him to come to dinner tomorrow night."

I stopped short. "What?"

"She wants to repay him for what he did for me. She said if we saw him today, to ask him over, and you too, of course. She'll invite your father and you can ask Nick to come, too."

"How nice. Well, I doubt Roman will have time to come to dinner. He'll probably have a show that night. Besides, we'll probably never see him again."

It seemed odd at first, Claire wanting to have a dinner party. She hadn't even been around when we got home with James that day he was stung. Why bother with a party now? Then I remembered what a flair she once had for entertaining. While Charles was alive, she was always inviting people over, often including Dad. She loves making show, especially when she is the star.

As we passed near the Pavilion I looked straight ahead, as did James, yet I could see from the corner of my eye a group of people at the surf's edge. "They're there," James whispered. "Did'ya see them?"

"Oh, are they? It doesn't matter. Come, let me find my gate key. Look, the surf's up today."

James clearly viewed his role as co-conspirator, even when I'd tried to be as offhanded as possible about Roman. He had a sixth sense that helped him to see far more than what lay on the surface. Someday, after shedding his callow youth, he will be a bundle for a young maid to handle.

I spread a towel on the pier and James jumped into the water. He loved the sea now that he was used to it, and while most children his age would have been wary after the sting received only two days earlier, he was content to ride the waves as though nothing had happened to him.

Porky, too, had taken to the surf today, and was splashing around happily with his new-found friend. I couldn't deny I'd cheated Porky lately. He still went to the beach with me, and I'd never failed to feed him or to take care of him properly. But then I hadn't been a companion for him, over the past year or so. I never seemed to find the time to play with him as I had when he was a puppy. Either I didn't want him mussing my dress, or I had to wash my hair, or had somewhere to go that he couldn't conveniently go with me. So, except when I went to the beach, he'd often stayed in his pen, staring between the fence pales as though he wouldn't mind running away should he have the chance. This was another reason I was grateful for James's arrival here in Galveston. He was such a perfect friend for the big dog, and was obviously as attached to him as though Porky really belonged to him . . . as perhaps in some ways he did. James often bathed him, fed him, took him for walks when I was at dancing class, or otherwise busy, rough-housed in the yard with him, and lately was teaching him to retrieve, although this project wasn't proving too successful, probably because Porky was a little too old for training. . . .

Lost in my thoughts as I lay there under the queer relaxing power of the sun, I'd almost forgotten about Roman Cruz. Then there was a voice from behind.

"Unlock this confounded thing, will you? What does a man have to go through to get to you?"

My heart speeding to a gallop, I ran up the pier, across the lawn, and opened the gate. "I'm sorry. I had no idea you'd be coming round today."

"I didn't either," he said, and walked with me back down the length of the pier. I was feeling smug already for the way I'd addressed him—so casual, unassuming.

"Hey, young fellow out there, how's that leg?" he called to James.

"It's fit, sir, thanks to you."

I was afraid James would pick this moment to come bounding up on the pier and invite Roman for dinner, yet he stayed in the water. I wished profoundly there were some way I could stave him off, keep him from mentioning the party at all. I'd had misgivings before, and now, in the presence of Roman, I sensed more strongly than ever he would despise the idea.

"You didn't come to the show last night," he said, almost scoldingly.

"I didn't know I was expected."

"Well, you were. You were supposed to fix up your hair, put on your best dress, and be out in the audience mooning at me as I played. But you didn't show up."

I laughed. "I'm sorry if I hurt your feelings. I can't find time to go to the Pavilion every night."

"You're not like most of the girls around here," he said. "You don't react the same. I like that."

"Oh, do you? Well, don't ever feel you can take me for granted."

"What makes you think I'd be guilty of such a thing?"

"I know your kind. You're—"

"What am I? What do you know of me?" he demanded, and I thought for a moment he must be angry at my flippancy.

"Nothing, nothing. I mean, you're used to having your way with girls, that's all."

"You're right, I am at that."

"I meant no—"

"I like you, Serena, like you a damn lot. If that kid weren't out in the bay over there, I'd try to hold your hand. Of course I don't usually operate that subtly, but for you I would." He was teasing now, and I could feel the red going to my face.

"You'd like that, would you?"

"Maybe."

"You wore a different suit today."

"Yes."

"I like the other one better."

"It doesn't fit right."

"I know. That's why I like it."

I leaned back a little and shaded my eyes. "You're very fresh."

"I know it. You really ought to tell me to leave right now."

It was at that moment James, with his unique sense of timing, came up from the water and told Roman about the dinner. Hanging onto a stair rung, he began a long sermon about Roman's gallantry and trustworthiness that surely was made up of Claire's ideas, rather than his own.

Roman rolled his eyes and laughed. "She tell you to say all that?"

"You'll come, won't you?"

"You needn't feel obligated if you don't want to," I said quickly.

"What night—Thursday?"

"Yes, tomorrow."

"I think I will. We're off tomorrow night—as a matter of fact, it's odd she happened to pick that night. We just found out last night the show has been canceled because they have to work on the wiring or something—otherwise I'd have had to work. And it isn't often I get invited up to someone's house on this side of Galveston. Tell your cousin or whoever she is that I'll be there. What time?"

"Seven. She'll be glad," James said with delight, and

jumped back into the water, sending a shower over both of us.

"Really, you needn't bother," I said. "I've a feeling you couldn't care less about something like that. It wouldn't hurt my feelings if you didn't come."

"Nonsense. How else am I going to get to see you? We can't go on meeting at the beach forever, with a boy and a dog as witnesses. Who knows, maybe your father will even like me, though I doubt it."

"My dad isn't as prim as you might think. He sometimes—" I continued, but stopped. There was no use going into Dad's drinking, just to make him seem more daring. When a man's drinking is a barometer of his sorrow, it's unfair to use it to impress someone else.

"I've got early rehearsals today," Roman said finally. "See you tomorrow night."

"You remember where the house is?"

"Certainly. A man could find his way around this island blindfolded, doing back flips. I'll be there."

Yet I half believed he wouldn't as he disappeared on the other side of the Fischer gate that morning, and would worry about it from that moment until the day and night and day after had passed, and it was time to walk over to Claire's.

Chapter 6

Thursday, June twenty-second, is printed indelibly on my mind: a unit in time with a beginning and end, wedged inside a summer otherwise made up of loose ends, unanswered questions, nameless fears.

Mother awakes that morning looking well rested, and I take this as a good omen. The day is hung over with a cloudless sky Mrs. McCambridge would call "purely blue." Helga Reinschmidt has four clotheslines hung with linens and clothes, billowing out in the breeze. I can see them from the kitchen window as I make the coffee before going to Madame's.

I will not be at my best while dancing today. During exercises at the bar, I will be thinking hard about the evening ahead, and will turn the wrong way and wind up backward to the class, looking directly into the face of

Michelle O'Grady, who is not much of a dancer but always at least technically correct in her movements. Madame will first give me a look of consternation (I can see her reflection in the big wall mirror behind), and in a moment will say, "Serena—come, come, where is your mind, girl?"

I will try to concentrate better on my work, but it will be of little use. I will keep wondering at Claire's desire to throw a dinner party, for I have decided her love of show simply is not sufficient to cause her to go to this sort of trouble. James reports she has spent hours poring over menus, and has had Helga busy polishing all the silverware and the silver coffee service, which is her pride and joy. If for love of show, why not spend it on some of her friends, rather than on us?

At Claire's request, Nick will be there, for Dad would have thought odd my reluctance to invite him, and I am being cautious about betraying anything of my attraction to Roman. Altogether there will be six of us. Mrs. McCambridge will spend the evening with Mother.

As I arrive home after dancing class, I see James standing in our yard, below Mother's window. I open my mouth to call to him, then see a piece of paper flutter down from the window like a bird with broken wings.

James retrieves it, reads it, then looks up. "But what does it mean?" he demands of Mother. She, of course, doesn't answer him, and I know the frustration he feels. I've a thousand unanswered questions for every year since Mother fell down the stairs.

"Come here, James," I tell him. "May I have a look at it? What is it, a poem?"

He hands it to me.

> We're going to Abaddon, our bad sins for to pay.
> We're going to Abaddon, ne'er to see the light of day.

"What's that word, 'Abaddon'?" James asks.

"I thought you'd know; I don't."

"I brought my dictionary from home. I'll go and fetch it."

"All right," I tell him, but I know by the context the word can mean but one thing, and I wonder again what Mother is trying to hide. There must be something in her past she's kept secret, but what? There is a chance Dad might be able to tell me, but he always dismisses her poetry as insignificant, and I don't try hard to persuade him to discuss it, for I can see it grieves him to see her scribbling. Her handwriting is almost bizarre—large, and grotesquely uneven. I have seen samples of it in her younger days. It was round and neatly formed, with circles over the *i*'s, instead of dots.

In the afternoon I wash my hair and take the curling iron to it. Tonight I will wear it pulled back and tied with a blue bow to match my shirtwaist dress. There is a shameful number of freckles across my nose, but it is too late to worry about them now.

Fifty-eight minutes past six o'clock. I have bathed and dressed. I feel flush and nervous, and watch anxiously from the window to see if he will come. When he does amble nonchalantly past the string of fences down our block, humming a tune, I am so relieved I practically shout down to him. It crushes me that he walks on past without looking toward our house, but then, he isn't my escort after all; a few moments from now Nick will pull up in a rented rig and we will walk to Claire's together. The realization of this makes me almost angry at Nick, and when he arrives, bringing a bouquet of daisies, I must concentrate hard to avoid being pesky and short with him.

By seven-thirty, we are all seated around Claire's big candlelit dining table with the hand-crocheted cloth. She has taken care to seat Nick and me side by side, Roman and James together, opposite us. She herself is at one end and Dad is at the other, in Charles's place.

Roman has seemed completely at ease throughout the awkward introductions and trite opening remarks by Dad and Claire about the band. Nick is nervous. He begs permission to smoke, then lights one cigarette after another until the first course of cold shrimp is brought by Helga, clad in her white starched apron and cap. Later, after raisin pie and coffee, he goes back to smoking again and Claire, the perfect hostess, unobtrusively asks Helga to open a window. Helga obeys, but only after giving Nick a look of disapproval that would close a wildflower in bloom. Nick pretends not to notice.

The talk has been frivolous during the meal, consisting mostly of compliments toward Claire's lovely presentation of dinner and Helga's talents in the kitchen. Claire is dressed in wine taffeta with white lace collar, and has put extra rouge on her cheeks, giving her face a phony, made-up look, as I see it from above the candlelight.

As Helga picks up the last empty pie plate, Dad pats his mouth delicately, pushes back his chair, pulls out his pipe. "Well, James," he says, "you look none the worse for being stung by a man-of-war, eh?"

"No, sir. It didn't bother me long, sir."

"Of course, the purpose of our gathering tonight is to thank Mr. Cruz." Claire smiles sweetly across at Roman.

"It was kind of you," he replies. "I was only glad to have been around when it happened."

"Anyone would have done as much," says Nick.

"Of course," Roman agrees.

James gazes down at his place; he has hardly touched his food. Dad breaks the silence. "Claire, I guess you and your committee will be down at the church all summer, putting the perfect touches on the garden, and weeding out all those unwanted dandelions." Dad always mentions the church garden when there is nothing else to fill a painful conversation gap.

"Yes. Too much sunshine this year, though," Claire answers. "It's better when we've a balance between that and rain."

There follows another awkward silence. The air is pregnant with unspoken words. Finally Nick clears his throat and offers, "This time last year I was preparing to go off to war."

"Yes, thank God we've nothing like that facing us this year," says Dad.

"Did you make it to Cuba?" Roman asks.

"No, it was over before I ever got outside Texas, but I would have gone and served my country. What of you?"

"I had no part in it. It was a silly little skirmish, to my mind."

Claire looks anxiously from Nick to Roman. "Did you read in the paper they're getting ready to do some extensive repairs on two of the wharves?"

"Yes, seem to be improving on them all the time . . . government grants for deeper water dredging, one thing and another," says Dad.

"Did you know," says Nick, "I read the other day ours is the first primary cotton port in the world, and that we rank with New Orleans as third wheat exporting point in the country, and our foreign import business is growing steadily. I happened to be looking up a telephone number in the directory, when I noticed that information in the statistics section up front. I'll tell you, nothing is going to stop this city. A better place to live won't be found around here."

"To think, my husband based almost his entire campaign for the mayor's race a few years ago on the fact the Wharf Company would kill Galveston as a port. I tried telling him then it just didn't follow, that Galveston's future was sealed," says Claire. "Even Houston will never be able to dredge enough out of that craggy series of bayous running to it, to have anything like the port we've here. Don't you agree, Rubin?"

"Of course it would seem you're right in retrospect, Claire. However, I'm sure Charles was making a valid point about the wharf monopoly. Perhaps in time history will prove him correct. . . ."

Dad to the rescue again. This time as Charles's best friend, listening to his widow make disparaging remarks about him. I feel sorry for Charles, unable to be here to speak up for himself, and wonder whether Claire was so wise in her view of the port a few years ago, or if she is only now trying to shine, sacrificing Charles in a desperate attempt to keep the evening from coming apart in her hands . . .

"Bosh," says Nick. "When you have the kind of facilities we're getting here, you can name your price to anyone wanting to use them. That's just business."

"Oh, I don't know about that," says Roman. He is fingering his empty wineglass, looking into its crystal design as though his mind were many miles from this table of fine china and forced conversation. "It was interesting, to me at least, to learn several days back how your population is decreasing, rather than building. Now, why, I wonder, are people leaving Galveston at a faster rate than they're coming? Couldn't that be saying something about the future of this city? Of course, I'm due no opinion, not being from here myself. All the same, I thought it was pretty interesting."

"In any case, Charles had other good points to his campaign platform that certainly proved true," says Dad. "Look at his ideas about water supply—he certainly proved right there. We're doing just what he said we ought to— pumping our water in from the mainland. Our method of getting water where it's needed, and quickly, has also proven satisfactory. Thank God, we haven't had another serious fire since the one in '85. I shall never forget that one."

"Of course, there was the Beach Hotel, just last year," says Nick. "Scarcely much they could do for that."

"Oh, yes, I remember that one," says Roman. "I don't think I ever saw anything come down so fast as that hotel, like a big pile of kindling wood."

"Anything built entirely of wood, and located down on the beach, is a risk though, isn't it?" says Claire. "I mean, it takes time to get the fire wagons down there, and wood does burn so fast, doesn't it? Isn't the Seaside Pavilion built entirely of wood, Roman, just like the old Galveston Pavilion, which burned a few years ago?"

"Yes, it is."

"And it's so remote, isn't it? Much more so than the Beach Hotel?" she says, then begins on a new tack, shifting the subject with her usual dinner party savoir-faire. "Serena, are you still having the run of the Fischer place down there?"

"Yes, ma'am. The Fischers left for Europe the first of the summer. I got a card from Marybeth yesterday mailed in Belgium. I've had a letter from London, too, and one from Paris."

"How nice you're able to go there. So secluded, private."

"Yes, but of course Porky is always along, and lately, James."

"You know, James really ought to try and make more friends his own age, don't you think? I mean, there are the Baker children down the street and other children around."

James scowls. "I don't like the Baker kids. I've tried to be friends with them, but they have their own little group, and don't care for outsiders interfering."

"You must be patient," Claire tells him. "Some things take time."

There is another break in the conversation then, and suddenly Nick looks across at Roman and says, "I just know I've seen you somewhere before. Where are you from originally?"

"St. Louis."

"Oh? I'm from Cleveland, but I was in St. Louis three months for a seminar a few years back. How long since you've played there—assuming you have?" He speaks the word, "played," as though it were something evil.

"Some. But I spend most of my time touring and in New York. I don't get back to St. Louis often."

"Hmm. Well, I know I've seen you. It'll come to me eventually."

"Serena tells me you're quite a good organist," says Roman. "I understand you're planning your career around liturgical music."

"That's right. I'm off on a special area of interest now— Buxtehude. Do you know him?"

"Only a few things I've heard from time to time. I've never done any of his music."

"I didn't suppose you had, I mean, being in popular stuff and so forth. He wrote some marvelous works. We're going to attempt some of the less difficult ones at the church pretty soon. Of course, with the small choir, and no professional musicians except myself, I can't expect a lot. I have to be content to tailor my selections for music to the easier things."

I look across at Dad, who doesn't look up at Nick, and I wonder if he realizes the sham of the remark.

"How nice," Roman says.

"What do you play?"

"Trumpet, mostly."

"He plays better than anyone I've ever heard," says James.

"Anything else?"

"Piano, drums, a little clarinet."

"Drums? I once knew a drummer," says Nick with a laugh. "He wasn't much of a sport, poor fellow. Got too much to drink one night, and punched a hole through his snare head."

It was a poor choice of words, and Nick grabs his napkin and fastidiously pats the corners of his mouth.

"What do you play besides organ?" Roman asks.

"Only piano. I teach piano."

"Good thing, then."

"What is that?"

"The way you smoke. You'd scarcely have the breath for any of the wind instruments."

There is a chilling moment.

"Shall we go into the parlor?" Claire suggests hurriedly, and we all get up from our chairs like obedient children in school. I am looking down as Nick helps me from the table, so that no one will see the smile of satisfaction on my lips.

When it is finally late enough to take our leave without being rude, Claire suggests a curious thing. "Serena, won't you see Roman to the door, and I'll put these other men to work helping me, so Helga won't have it so hard tomorrow?"

"Of course," I say, wondering whether it's coincidence she should request of me the thing I am longing to do. Could she be a comrade-in-arms?

We walk silently to the front door and out onto the porch. "I shouldn't stay away too long, or it will look odd," I tell Roman.

"Yes, and we wouldn't want that, would we? There're enough odd ones around here already."

"I'm sorry to have put you through this. I know how grueling it was. I don't know why you wanted to come, but I'm grateful. At least now, my father has met you and couldn't say my seeing you was improper or anything."

"Oh? Are we seeing each other?" he asks, his eyes full of mischief.

"Well, I didn't mean—"

"It's all right. I do want to see you again. Will you be at the beach tomorrow morning?"

"Yes. Nine o'clock."

"Will the boy be with you?"

"I hadn't thought . . . but now you mention it, I guess it would be best. It might seem funny if I suddenly had nothing more to do with him, and besides, if my father thought I were meeting you alone somewhere, he certainly would object."

"Really now, are we always to be stuck with a pint-sized escort?"

"I don't know. I hope not. Maybe later, when I know you better—"

"Okay. But the summer is a short season, you know."

". . . Besides, I really do care about James and have to figure out some way to keep from hurting his feelings. He's had a bad shock—both his parents killed—it wouldn't be fair to hurt him unnecessarily."

"Good old altruistic Serena. All right. But your unwillingness to hurt people to whom you owe nothing may one day cause you a lot of heartache. Nobody is going to worry that much about you. You've got to look out for yourself, and if you can help someone along the way, fine. But don't make a career of being a young boy's companion. He'll soon become like a barnacle stuck to a pier, and in the long run, you won't be doing him any favor."

"You're right, of course, however—"

"Besides, there are older ones who need you more," he says, taking my face in his hand. He kisses me quickly and hard, then lets go and starts down the stairs.

My face smarts from the tightness of his grip, but the kiss was a warm, welcome thing and I stand for some moments on the moonlit porch, savoring it.

Roman wasn't on the beach the next morning, and James must have sensed my disappointment as we sat on the Fischer pier, for he kept trying to make up excuses as to why he hadn't come.

"Perhaps they called a special rehearsal or something."

"The other musicians were out there."

"Some of them. I know, maybe he's rehearsing alone. He is the star, you know."

"Perhaps."

"Maybe he got word something happened to his mother, and he had to go to St. Louis."

"Oh, James, don't be so dramatic."

"Nah. He'd have let you know if he were going off somewhere."

"How do you know?"

"He likes you. I can tell."

"How?"

"I don't know. I just can."

"Have you ever had a sweetheart, James?"

"Only once, a few months before my—before I came here."

"Tell me about her."

"She was very good at arithmetic, and she would help me sometimes. She had long brown hair, beautiful, silky; but there was a space between her front teeth. Probably that's the only reason she'd be interested in me."

"Don't be foolish. You said she was smart, didn't you? She knew a good man when she saw one."

This last remark bolstered him. He tried to hide a smile of pleasure by turning away to look at a gull soaring high above. "Oh well," he said at last, "it didn't work out anyway. Her family moved to Dallas."

"Don't worry, there'll be lots of other girls in your life."

"Maybe. . . . But you've found your beau, haven't you? I mean, it's plain he likes you."

"You're kind to say that, James, but I don't know. He didn't bother coming over this morning, did he? Let's get into the water for a while. Hang the freckles."

When Roman failed to appear again on Saturday, I was certain this was the end of it, that I'd never see him again. Practical thoughts had begun to edge into my mind. What did he want of me? With virtually every available girl on the island at his disposal, wasn't it a little foolish to waste time on a parson's daughter, who must always be treated with at least a modicum of prudence, even by Roman Cruz? Parsons' daughters were good girls, who grew up and married young men active in the church. Perhaps people like Marybeth could have a fling or two and get away with it, but it was hardly possible for a girl like me to consider such behavior.

I probably should never have pressed about James, though. Roman was looking for a way to see more of me privately, and, stupidly, I held James over his head, when I should have promised to find a way of getting free of him. He had tested me, and I had failed.

Then again, how could I have offered to see him in private? What would he have thought of me then? How long before we would be discovered, everything ruined?

I lay across my bed for a long time that Saturday afternoon, wondering why I should be doomed to miss all opportunity for happiness. Marybeth wouldn't have let him pass her by. Even if it had been no more than a summer love affair, she would've tagged on and ridden the tide all the way out. If I were ever to tell her how clumsily I had lost Roman, she would throw her hands up once and for all. I was thankful, lying there on the bed, I hadn't mentioned Roman in my last letter to her after all. She need never know how badly I bungled things.

Yet, he did kiss me.

Perhaps only as a parting gesture, though, so that later I could remember it and not feel so bereft in his absence. Better, perhaps, for it to end now, before it was serious enough to cause tears and misery.

I got up finally, washed my face and straightened my hair. There was nothing to do but make the best of it. Nick

would be coming tomorrow afternoon for the inevitable
Sunday dinner. Perhaps, when he came, I could make an
effort to be kinder to him. True, he behaved abominably at
the party, but then it was clear he was jealous. I could
hardly blame him for lashing out at a threat to his happiness.

He was in bad humor on Sunday afternoon because, as
he explained, the music hadn't gone to his satisfaction during services. I was sitting in the congregation and heard it
all, and could find no fault beyond the fact Alice Michael-
son's voice was screechy. Alice is the soprano soloist. As
far as I'm concerned, her voice is always screechy, but
Nick thinks otherwise, so I never argue.

"Oh, it was a lot of things," he told me peskily. "The
acolytes started down the aisle too soon on the reces-
sional—I've told them time and again to wait until we begin the second stanza—and the baritone section was too
loud on the Brahms, near the end. Did you notice?"

"No, but if you say so . . ."

"Well, they were. I guess we'll have to work on that next
rehearsal. It doesn't matter, though, only ten per cent of
what I say ever soaks in anyway."

"Maybe you shouldn't be such a perfectionist. After all,
they're only volunteers. Maybe they sense your displeasure,
so they don't try as hard as they might."

"I just wish we could have maybe three professionals,
like some churches. They'd provide the kind of backbone
we need."

"We can't afford them, you know that."

"How well . . . Let's not discuss it anymore."

"All right, if that's the way you want it."

"Aw, Serena, don't be that way. You know, after we're
married you're going to have to be my sounding board
about the choir and everything. A husband has to tell his
problems to someone, and that's what wives are for, listening. Don't let me bully you into getting mad."

"Nick, I do think it might be well if you didn't take for
granted I'm going to marry you. After all, I did say I
hadn't made up my mind."

"If not me, then whom? That smart aleck trumpet
player, or whatever, who ate with us the other night?
Surely you wouldn't find him more palatable than me."

I said nothing.

"Then you would? Well, that's just fine! I suppose there's no need in me staying around here, if you're busy pining after him."

"I guess not, if you feel that way."

"Let me tell you something, Serena, men like that are not as great as you might think. He'll never belong to anyone, mark my word, and don't get your hopes up."

"As you said, feeling that way, you might as well go. And don't bother ever coming back."

He softened then, as I knew he would. "Oh, let's not be silly. Look, I'm a bit on edge today. Maybe I ought to go home a little early. I'm not good company when I've problems with my music. Forgive me?"

"What is there to forgive?"

"I knew you'd understand. Well, see you next week." He leaned over and brushed his lips across my cheek. "I've every confidence you'll come to your senses like a good girl, Serena."

He didn't appear to mind seeing himself to the door.

Monday: the beginning of a new week, and new hope.

As we passed the band members' beach playground, James reported, "No one over there." My heart fell. Hard as I'd tried not to expect to see Roman, I knew I wouldn't take another deep breath until we'd spent our morning at the Fischer place and returned home. Dazedly, I put the key into the lock, yet it wouldn't turn. "Here, let me," said James, and gently worked it to the right, then pushed the gate wide open. He looked up at me. "Nothing wrong with the lock."

Porky, anxious for a run today, pulled away from him then, and took off across the lawn.

"I'll get him," he said.

"Please do. I wouldn't want him trampling the flower beds, heaven knows."

"Don't worry," he called, already halfway across the yard, and I wondered why it was that, when one important matter goes awry, everything else must go the same way, like a deck of cards blown by the wind. I walked down the pier and carelessly threw down my bag, which landed on its side, dangerously close to the edge. The bag was a gift from one of Marybeth's European trips a year or so ago, part of it leather, part some sort of heavy black carpet with a brushed velvet design interwoven. It was really too fine a piece of luggage to be thrown around, taken to the beach or to dancing, yet it was the only bag I had. I righted it, pulling it far over to keep it from getting wet, then pulled out my swimming cap.

Now we were here, I just wanted to go home. I would, I decided, stay long enough only for the refreshment of a quick dip in the water. Somehow, even this place I loved held no attraction for me now. It would be just as well when Marybeth came back home and winter blew in, and I went back to spending my mornings crocheting for the annual fall bazaar at the church.

There was a sound, coming from the fence. Probably nothing, yet . . .

Again. I kept looking ahead. If it was Roman, I wasn't going to appear anxious.

"Serena, this confounded gate is locked again. Do I have to climb over?"

A chill went up the sides of my neck, and I wanted to shout and run and laugh all at the same time. Instead, I walked calmly across the lawn and opened the gate.

"Oh, I didn't know you were coming by."

"I could make excuses for not coming before, but I won't," he said, and we walked together back down the pier. I wanted to tell him it was all right, that I understood, that I was so happy he was here now it didn't matter a whit what had kept him away before.

"It's all right, you don't have to. We didn't have a scheduled date, or anything."

"One thing I like about you, Serena, you're not demanding," he said, and sat down beside me on the towel. "I can't abide demanding women, and you can always tell in a hurry if they're that way."

"Maybe you just didn't want to come," I said, looking ahead at James, who'd apparently seen Roman enter the yard, and circled around the other way to go into the water.

"You're right. I didn't want to come. But not for the reasons you might guess. I've been doing some thinking for the past few days. I decided it was no good for us to try and make anything of it. You'd only wind up being hurt because I won't be around that long, and I couldn't even promise to be back next summer. That isn't much to offer, is it?"

"No. Is that what you came to tell me?"

"Yes. I had it practiced, all for presentation in my usual

fickle manner. And you would go on looking straight ahead—I expected that—and say it didn't matter, why should I think it did? Then I would make my exit, as I have many times before . . ."

Porky now came sniffing up to Roman, and, satisfying himself everything was all right, trotted up the pier a few feet and jumped into the water, gliding out toward James. The morning sun moved away a cloud, and trekked across the water's surface toward us, warming my arms. I kept looking ahead.

"Well, I guess it's obvious my plan didn't work," Roman said finally, "which is curious because it always has before."

I couldn't look at him; had no idea what to expect.

"Will you look at me?" he said, so then I looked.

"Now I see you, slumped down on this pier with your ridiculous ruffled headdress and wearing that bathing suit designed to tantalize the hell out of me, I can't—come here."

Then he put his arms around me and kissed me in a way I'd never been kissed before, and I was left breathless when he finally released me, and could do nothing but stare at him.

"There," he said. "Now you know all my resolve has gone out with the tide. Oh, why did I ever have to—?"

Then James, who'd swallowed too much salt water in one gulp, began coughing loudly, trying to hold Porky at bay while he cleared his lungs.

"The barnacle," said Roman to me, then called to James, "Careful, old man, don't try to drink up the Gulf of Mexico all in one day." Then to me again, "He really is a good kid. I just wish . . . could you walk me back to the gate?"

"So soon?"

"We've a special rehearsal this morning, something new on tonight's show."

We walked to the edge of the yard, and looked at each other through the iron bars of the fence. "Look, I'm not the milk-toasty type, like your friend Nick," he said. "If you're afraid of someone less gentle and certainly less stable, you'd better forget me and latch onto him. I can't offer you the same things he can, things women generally want, and wouldn't if I could because that kind of life just isn't for me."

"No."

He smiled and said less forcefully, "All right then, I'll see you in the morning." He has a mysterious smile that tells nothing of the thoughts behind it.

"Yes, after class."

He turned and walked away then, and I brushed a tear from my face. I remember looking down in wonder at the wet place on my hand, for I hadn't realized I was even close to crying.

Tuesday, Wednesday, Thursday, Friday, I saw him briefly, in much the same manner. He pleaded rehearsals, some trouble with the new music, but I think I knew even then it was James's presence that kept him from staying. Maybe, too, a reluctance to go too far too soon. Anyway, it didn't matter because he kept coming every day, and he needn't have if he didn't want to see me.

By Friday I was trying to figure a way of getting down there without James, yet avoid revealing anything to him or anyone else about why I now wanted to go to the beach alone. But then on Friday night, Dad stepped in, and everything blew up in my face.

Chapter 7

Dad had been drinking before he came home that evening, probably to bolster his courage, for he never found it easy to argue with me or anyone else. I was taken completely unaware, happily making a pot of stew in the kitchen, when I heard him come into the door.

"Oh, hello, have a seat. Mail's on the counter there—something from Blum Hardware, and a bill from Magnolia Meat Market, I think—have a good day?"

"Nan, I've got to talk to you. Please, come and sit down."

I looked around at him then, and saw the flushed face, the glassy eyes.

"What is it?"

"Before I begin, I hope you'll appreciate how hard it is for me to say this to you. You know, I love you more than anything in the world except your mother, and—"

"All right. Go on."

"I want you to promise me something, Serena. That you won't see that young musician anymore."

I was too stunned to answer at first, and after a moment, rose from my chair and walked back to the stove. Best not to show my face. "I don't know what you're talking about," I said.

"Simply that, Nan. You see, that young man has a rather—well—unsavory reputation around here, and I don't think it would be well if you were to be seen with him."

"But how—?"

"Never mind. I didn't check on him intentionally, I want you to understand that. I respect your judgment far more than that. Just believe that I heard from a reliable source some goings-on that took place a summer or so ago, and I don't want to relate them to you. They're, well, indelicate. Believe me, if you knew, you would readily agree he isn't the sort you ought to be involved with."

"How can you pass judgment on Roman Cruz? As far as we're concerned, all he has done is to rescue a boy being attacked by a group of man-of-war, and that was an act of common decency."

"I'm not passing judgment, Nan. I know that, like every man, this young fellow has some good in his character. It's only that, you know what could happen if it got around you were seeing him. Think of my position in the Church. I simply cannot afford to do anything to jeopardize it. We have to live on my wages as a priest, you know."

"I can't believe you're saying this to me. Of all the unfairness! You're doing the same thing that you would condemn in others. All we've done is talked a few times down at the beach. James has been right there, within earshot and sight, each time.

"Who's been talking to you? Was it Nick?"

"Please, Serena, don't act this way. It's none of your affair whom I've been speaking with. I had no idea you would take it so hard. After all, you could hardly have gotten to know him well at this point. Surely it won't be so difficult to—"

"Claire, then. Has she been snooping around?"

He put up a hand. "I can't betray a confidence, you know that. Can't you trust my judgment, Nan? You always did before. . . . No, it isn't to be, is it? I can see it in your face.

"Very well, then, consider it an order if you want. I'd

hoped it wouldn't come to this, but maybe now you can see the importance in what I am telling you."

When I failed to reply, he tried to mitigate the blow. "Besides, I know you wouldn't want to hurt Nick, and what would he think if he knew about your seeing someone else?"

"I've a feeling he already does," I said, but he didn't seem to hear.

"You two are the perfect couple—everyone says so—and you'll never find a finer man or a better Christian than Nick Weaver. We're fortunate to have someone of his talents at St. Christopher's, and I've felt so lucky that you two seem fond of each other."

"Why don't you say what you really mean, Dad? In time, we'll marry and move in here with you and Mother, and everything will be just dandy, because I'll be around to take care of her—"

"Serena, how dare you say such a thing! You owe your mother every bit of kindness it is within your power to give, and don't ever forget it," he said, then paused before continuing. "Of course, I had entertained the idea of you and Nick staying here awhile. There's plenty of room, and lots of other young couples do this sort of thing when they're first married, and trying to get their feet on the ground.

"But the very idea—you almost seem to accuse me of using you, as though you have no obligation whatever toward your dear mother."

I could see it getting out of hand then, and knew before long we'd both be saying things for which we would be sorry later. His mind was made up about Roman. There was no use trying to change it, or throwing a fit in hopes of getting my way.

"I know, I know. I'm sorry, Dad," I said. "Here, the stew's hot. Have your supper now. I'm not very hungry. Think I'll sit out on the front porch in the swing for a while."

He made no move toward filling his plate, and I suspected he probably had no more appetite than I had as I walked away from him. Soon he'd probably go instead for the bottle of whisky in the cabinet.

It was a pleasant change sitting on the porch after being in the hot kitchen, and the rhythmic screech of the swing as it rocked to and fro always calmed me. It hadn't been such a bad argument, really, and I had—luckily—managed to control myself, and keep from betraying anything of my feelings for Roman. I don't think I had ever imagined he would approve of my seeing a stranger all the way from New York, no matter what his background, and that was why I worried from the beginning over someone finding out about us.

What had just happened between Dad and me was almost unheard of, though, even if it hadn't ended in screaming or hitting, like some arguments I'd heard of at Marybeth's house. We'd always been close as father and daughter, probably because of Mother's accident happening so early in my lifetime. We'd spent many an evening together in the swing where I now rocked alone—the swing he'd given my mother so many years ago as a present for something or other, and where she would probably never sit again. He'd read me stories from books there, and often made up stories, which I always liked better. He'd gotten up early to take me to see the circus animals being led into town when I was a little girl, and bought me stuffed toys and dolls clad in gaudy net and feathers, all of them long since lost and forgotten. He had always been there when something was troubling me, and always understood. And when I was bad, he had always scolded me gently, never letting me doubt he loved me just as much as he did when I was good.

How could he be so totally lacking in understanding now, when it meant more to me than ever that I have my way? How could he presume on Roman's character, basing his condemnation on pure hearsay? It didn't fit with my father's sworn philosophy. Saying what he had just said, he wasn't like my father, but rather like some judge sitting high above a courtroom, arbitrarily handing down sentence on a criminal he'd never seen before nor would again.

I sat in the swing for a long time, and Dad never came out to join me. No matter how much thought I gave it, I knew there was but one answer. I had to tell Roman, and leave it to him to figure a way. All the confidence I'd once felt in Dad now transferred itself to him, leaving Dad as merely an obstacle to be somehow dealt with. And though I regretted matters coming to this, I realized for the first time in my life I wasn't always going to be able to live in a way that would please my father, or anyone else.

Next morning I set out for the beach, firmly resisting

James's pleas to go with me. "I have to talk to Roman, because my father has forbidden me to see him again. You understand, don't you, that we want to be alone?"

"Yes, but how did your father find out?"

"That's what I'm wondering. You didn't say anything to Claire, unintentionally?"

"No, I'm sure I didn't. I don't talk to Claire about things like that."

"Good boy. I knew I could count on you. Now, go down and try to make some friends your own age today, and tonight I want a full report as to how you made out."

"All right," he said, and stood taller. "May I take Porky along? He needs a bath, and I used some of my money to buy him a brush yesterday afternoon. I want to try it out on him."

"Sure. You know, I think you're the best friend Porky ever had."

Halfway to the beach, I began to worry Roman might not come that day, and wondered what I would do if not. Would I have the courage to walk up to the Pavilion and ask for him? Would all the fellows snicker behind my back and think I was just another foolish girl on Roman's lengthy string? Was I just that?

Maybe, just maybe, it was one of them who had leaked the news Roman was seeing me. But to whom? Did any of the band members know people in Galveston who knew me as well?

I went straight to Marybeth's and waited. A side glance as I walked by the Pavilion told me at least a few of the musicians were free to play ball this morning. Oh, if he'd only hurry and I could get this matter off my mind, and let him handle it. It was curious to feel a sense of protection by one such as Roman Cruz, yet I did, whereas I'd never felt protected by Nick, no matter what he did to prove his worthiness. Roman would know how to get on Dad's good side, probably go right up to him and deny the charges made so unfairly against him. . . . Then Dad would see how he really was.

I wonder now, how I could ever have been so mistaken.

He never came, and after almost an hour on the pier I picked up my things and walked to the Pavilion. I loathed doing it, yet it was clear this was the only chance I would have of getting things settled.

The musicians were now absent from their playground;

the beach around the building was deserted. I walked up to one of the front doors and pulled it open slightly. Cool air from the big hall wafted toward my face. After the brightness of the sun, it was hard to make out exactly what was going on inside, yet the cacophony of notes suggested that a practice was about to begin, and this was probably the worst time for intrusion.

My eyes focused better after a few moments, and I could make out Roman seated at the piano, in the center of the stage.

I lost my nerve when I saw him, and was about to let go the door, when it swung out with a suddenness that almost pulled me through it. A chubby, curly-headed man I recognized as one of the players asked, "Is there somethin' we can do for you?"

"I—well, oh no, you see—"

"I know who you are," he said, and popped a wad of chewing gum. "You're lookin' for Roman. Wait here. I'll tell him you've come."

"I only want to deliver a message," I said stupidly.

He was off and through the lobby without hearing my last statement, though, and I had a feeling it gave him satisfaction to see me looking like a little idiot. I stepped out on the porch and wondered just how many girls had come looking for Roman Cruz. How many had he flirted with for a while, then jilted when he was bored with them?

Soon he came out, a scowl on his face, so I began by apologizing. "Look, I'm sorry to have interrupted. I was about to leave when that fat fellow came and pulled the door open—"

"It's all right. You're here now. What is it, anyway?"

"I've got to talk to you, but if you haven't time I'll meet you another time . . . if I can."

"What d'ya mean, if you can? It's all right. I have time. We've been working on music for a benefit performance later this summer, but we're just finishing. Come on around to the back, where we can talk privately."

He took my arm and led me round to the back side of the building, facing the shore. We sat down on a back stoop below a stage door I hadn't realized existed.

"Well?"

"My father has forbidden me to see you."

"Oh, he has, huh?"

"He says you have a questionable reputation in Galveston, and that I shouldn't be seen with you."

"Quit staring down at your feet and look at me," he said. "Have you been telling him we're meeting?"

"No, I don't know how he found out. It might've been Nick, or someone else. James denies he told."

"No, I doubt it would be that kid. He worships you, that's obvious enough. Hmm . . ."

"Well, what do you say? Can't we just go and tell my father how ridiculous this is? He's a reasonable man—"

"I'm afraid not, for you see, it isn't ridiculous at all."

"Oh."

"Well, did you think I come here every summer and gather seashells during my off-time?"

"I guess I never thought."

"Yes you have. I've let you know I've had a few girls here and there. I've even gotten in dutch a couple of times, if you want the truth."

"Oh, I see." I wondered how far "in dutch," but was afraid to ask.

"Look here, if your father forbids me to see you, I guess that's it. I don't know what to tell you. Oh damn, don't start crying."

"I'm sorry. I know I must seem like a stupid little girl to you. I don't know why you ever bothered with me in the first place. But I've never felt like this about anybody else. Nobody."

"In your long and varied experience, eh?" he said with a chuckle, then added more seriously, "Nor I, Serena, nor I." He put an arm around my shoulders. "Listen, you've got to understand something. I won't apologize for anything I've done, to your father or anyone else. I've had no strings attached, nobody to answer to. And believe me, I never forced any woman into being involved with me. If we're going to go on seeing one another, we'll just have to be discreet, that's all. Have you never sneaked about anything in your life?"

"Not before this summer."

"You *are* lily white, aren't you?"

I raised my head and took a deep breath. "Yes, I'm probably not your type at all."

"You're right about that, sister. I guess that's what I like about you," he said, and pulled me over on his lap. His voice became low and soft; he pulled my hair back and kissed my neck lightly, playfully. It sent chills up my back, yet it frightened me too, and I said, "You don't understand about me. I've never . . . never . . ."

"You talk too much. Did anyone ever tell you that?"

"But I've never even—"

"I know," he said, "don't worry about anything," and kissed me hard on the mouth. If he would have kept at it then, I would probably have wrenched loose and gone running down the beach. But with true musician's timing he pulled away, as though something had just occurred to him.

He folded his arms and looked out toward the sea. His face was flush. "What do you want, Serena? Hm? It's up to you. Lord, if you haven't got me hamstrung. But with me it's all, or none of it. So make up your mind and stay here, or get out of my life for good."

I sat there for a moment, sorting out his words. I knew exactly what he meant, knew suddenly that one did not dillydally a summer away, taking an occasional kiss, a handclasp, and expecting Roman Cruz to be satisfied with it. Yet I also knew there was no thought worse than a summer without him, this or any other.

"I could never walk away from you," I said finally, afraid to look into his eyes. I felt his hand cup my chin and turn my face toward him. He wiped away two wayfaring tears with the back of the other hand, and looked at me for a long moment. "I want you, Serena, have wanted you from the beginning . . ."

My mouth was dry. I nodded.

I remember thinking, as he carried me inside the dark hallway and up the isolated tower stairs, that it wasn't going to be as I had always imagined. If for no other reason than that he, Roman Cruz, had his own way of doing all things, it would be different than with any other man. I held him tightly as we spiraled up toward the door. It was a time to fear what was about to happen, yet it was a time, too, for holding close, for trusting.

"It isn't a thing to be rushed," he said when we were in the tiny room and sitting side by side on a makeshift bed in the corner. And I thought, oh no, he's going to send me back home after getting this far—afraid of soiling the reputation of a preacher's daughter. But he sat without touching me and looked away. "You look upon this act of love-making as a surrender, a kind of obligation you always thought you would have, to the man who married and supported you, don't you?"

I nodded, and in that moment felt the stupid tears smarting behind my eyes again.

"This is so silly, I don't know why I always cry around you—"

He took my face in his hands gently, and said with logic, "It isn't quite fair that it should be that way, is it?"

I nodded again, my mouth still dry as harvested corn, first yes, then no, for he had been so right in my assessment about love-making. My hair had gotten caught inside my collar, and he pulled it free and kissed it softly, and said, "Don't be afraid, darling, or shy or embarrassed . . ."

He stood me up then, gently as though he handled a china doll, and found where the buttons began on the ill-fitting bathing dress. And when he'd reached the last one and moved his hands to open it wide, I grabbed his hands and said, "Roman, I'm frightened, truly I am."

"Hush, darling, you've no more to fear than I," he whispered, and continued to shed the clothes from my body until I stood before him as a bride on her wedding night. Then he said "By God, you're even more beautiful than I expected," and swept me up against him. Soon after there was the feel of the rough bed linens against my back and his own body, warm and strong, fine as a god's, bending above. . . .

Afterward we fell asleep under the square of sunlight streaming through the tower window, and I dreamed an endless dream of lying on the edge of the shore and having skeins of colored silk, reds and pinks and greens and blues, washing over me again and again.

When I awoke and opened my eyes, Roman was raised up on one elbow, looking down into my face; not in a crooning, loving way, but rather detached, as though he studied me. I panicked for a moment, and my eyes shot down. We were both covered by the bedsheet.

"What time is it?"

"What difference? Time means nothing."

"Yes it does, because if anyone finds out I could never come again and—"

"And you want to come again?"

"Oh yes, more than anything—"

"Good, then, come again tomorrow."

"No, I can't come until Monday. It isn't that simple—I could never get away on a Sunday."

I rose from the bed, as shy as before at being unclothed, and pulled my swimming dress from the floor. He went on lying there, watching me.

"You're very lovely, you know."

"Oh, I . . . it's nice of you to say so."

"There are some things I never say out of nicety. Come back here and kiss me again. Why should you be so anxious to go?"

I went and sat on the edge of the bed. He kissed me once, then pulled away. "No guilt feelings or anything?"

"No, not right now. Only a fear I'll get caught."

"The light of day . . ." he said, smiling. "Just a piece of information for you, Serena dear. Don't ever feel guilty about what happens between us. It's all a hoax, this demand put on people by society, that nice girls mustn't ever enjoy themselves.

"And also, you were wonderful today, so much better than I could have imagined, but you'll be better in time, just as I will be for you. You needn't pretend it was perfect.

"You may be a little uncomfortable for a day or so, but it won't last beyond that, and—"

Why did he have to analyze it, bringing it all down to simple facts, indisputable things that could prey on my mind? "Oh, Roman," I said, and buried my head on his chest. He didn't reply, just stroked my hair and let me stay there until I was ready to get up.

At the door, I turned and told him, "It's going to be a long time till Monday, and how I shall loathe Sunday."

"Will you have to see that self-righteous prig, the organist?"

"I'm afraid so, unless I break it off with him, which perhaps I may—"

"Watch out, darling. Don't be overly daring yet. Best to go along with your routine, to act as though nothing unusual is going on. If you think you can trust the boy, bring him along to the Fischer place every day. I'll meet you there, and if the coast is clear we'll come back here. No one ever enters this room except me. I have the only key."

"Not even the manager, or the professor have—?"

"Only me."

"You must be quite important to have such a privilege."

"King has no choice but to put up with me. I'm the only star he has."

"You sound as though he doesn't like it much."

"He doesn't. But not every good musician is willing to put up with a traveling show, either."

"I suppose not. Roman, have you had this room every summer since—?"

"Yes, indeed. This is where I bring all my beautiful captives and torture them, didn't you guess? Now I'd better walk you down and see if anyone's outside."

We went stealthily down the stairs, and once outside he looked around and announced it was safe for me to come out: "Go on, darling," he said, holding my hands. "Be careful, and don't ditch me now you've got me all tied around your finger."

"Roman, you don't think me . . . easy, do you? I mean, that I just . . . with anyone . . . that I was just putting up a front?"

"There's no question," he said. "I would have known up there, if there was."

Strangely, though there were bound to be obstacles confronting us and although what I was doing was contrary to everything I'd ever been taught, I didn't worry over these problems as I walked back from the beach. I had an exhilarating sense of freedom that not even the sea had ever given me. It was as though all the frustrations awaiting me at home no longer existed.

I should no longer mind all the hours of being pent up with Mother, if I had the following morning with Roman to look forward to. I could even endure Nick a little easier, now that Roman had made himself a definite part of my life, secure in the knowledge that, no matter what Nick let himself believe, we would never be anything more than friends. For I was now certain I would never marry Nick Weaver. If Roman left and never came back, and I must spend the rest of my life looking after Mother and attending church bazaars, an aging spinster having only the memory of love to sustain me, I would never marry Nick. He would not snatch my happiness from me. No one could take the morning from me, even if it were never to be repeated.

In the afternoon I sat in front of my vanity and studied my face in the mirror. As a rule, I didn't spend much time doing this, not like Marybeth, whose dresser was lined with exotic creams and powders, and French perfumes, but that day I felt as though I must somehow look differently. Surely my cheeks had more color, there was more light in my eyes. Was I really beautiful, just as he had said? I'd never thought of myself as beautiful, had even taken James's notions of my being so as childish prattle. But to be told by a man one is beautiful, a man like Roman Cruz . . .

Yet another disturbing thought occurred to me as I sat there. Suppose I should become in the family way? Marybeth had told me long ago it took only once, and had said something vague about "certain precautions," yet I hadn't paid much attention, never imagining I might be faced with such a problem. Now I wished I'd listened more attentively to her, asked questions . . .

Of course I couldn't discuss the matter with Roman. He'd given me a chance to back out. Now that I had chosen not to, he would expect me to be intelligent enough to know—or at least to find out—how to avoid this problem. If I even brought up the subject with him, he'd probably be put off, bored with my ignorance. And even if not, I'd be far too bashful to tell him what was on my mind. Oh, it was silly, I knew, but I just couldn't . . .

There was one saving grace, which dawned on me then. Often I'd heard women say that if a woman has trouble becoming pregnant, most of the time her daughters will be so afflicted. My mother and father were married almost seven years before I was born, and another six before Donnie came. So it followed, didn't it, that I could not conceive a child any more easily than Mother had?

That thought put my fears at rest. Assuming Roman Cruz were to go on wanting me (oh, please, God, don't let him tire of me!), I could perhaps try to find out what Marybeth meant by "certain precautions." Yet it all seemed so foolish when I thought of Mother . . .

Later, after I'd finished cleaning my room, which I had done out of an urgent need to be busy, Dad knocked lightly on my door. "Yes, come in."

"Hello, dear Nan, how are you?"

"Fine, and you? How're things down at the church? Did Claire work on the garden today?"

"No, I haven't seen her all day till just now. She called from the fence to invite us to dinner, so you needn't bother fixing anything. I said we'd be there around seven."

"Oh? Would you mind going without me? I don't think I feel up to it tonight."

"Are you ill, Nan, anything wrong?"

"No, I'm fine, just don't feel like going."

"You're not angry, or disappointed, about last night?"

"Of course not. As you said, how serious could things have gotten between Roman Cruz and me at this point? What you said made good sense. Don't worry."

"Good. I knew you'd see it once you had thought about it. But Claire will be disappointed about your not coming. It wouldn't hurt to leave Mother alone for just a little while, I don't suppose."

"I know. Really, I just don't want to go."

"All right. I'll stop by and tell her on my way down to Schott's, to pick up Mother's medicine. Can I get you anything?"

"No, thanks," I said, and he left, shutting the door again. I looked in the mirror to be sure nothing showed in my face. It was something I would often do, over the remainder of the summer.

James knocked on the door at five o'clock, while Dad was sitting in his chair reading the *News*. "I'll get it," I said, anxious to get alone with James before he'd gotten in the house.

"Well, how did it go?" I asked him as we sat on the steps.

"As a matter of fact, it went well. I met a new friend—Tommy Driscoll. He lives down the street on the corner. His father's an undertaker."

"I know."

"Anyway, he asked me to go crabbing with him early tomorrow morning. Gets twenty-five cents a dozen for the catch. He explained to me all about how he does it, letting down the line and so forth. Of course I'll be back early enough to go down to Marybeth's with you, that is, if you want me to. . . ."

"James, that's something I've got to talk to you about. How are you at keeping secrets?"

"Foolproof. Even Mother used to trust me with secrets from Dad. You know, like surprises for his birthday, and that kind of thing."

"I see . . . that's good. As you know, my father forbade me to see Roman again."

"Yes, although I don't see why."

"Trouble is, I'm afraid I've fallen in love with him—that probably sounds silly to you, but remember, you're my closest friend and I have to confide in someone."

"No, I don't think it's silly. People are supposed to fall in love. Mother always said so."

"It isn't a bit fair, what I'm going to ask you, but I've thought it over and there's no other choice."

"You're not going to let me go to the beach with you anymore, is that it?"

"On the contrary. I do want you to go with me every time you can. You see, it's my only hope of seeing Roman. I know it isn't right, seeing him without Dad's permission . . . but someday I hope to make him understand about us, and in the meantime . . . Well, anyway, Roman will come round to Marybeth's to get me, and I'll go with him so we can be together for a while. Do you understand?"

"It might look funny if you don't take me along, is that it?"

"Yes, that's part of it; if we're to be honest with each other as we promised, then I must be honest now. Sometimes a girl needs to ask a favor of her best friend. But there's more. I want you to go because Marybeth's place is such a wonderful spot for bathing—whether or not I'm around—and you couldn't get in there without me."

"Where will you and Roman go?"

I hesitated for a moment, then answered, "I'll be able to watch him rehearse sometimes. And there's a little room in one of the towers of the Pavilion where we can . . . talk in privacy sometimes. Or we can walk on the beach together. You see, we may have no more time than this summer together, so it has to be this way. Don't think I'd condone lying to my father about anything else, James. I don't believe in sneaking. Only this once . . ."

"I understand. Parents don't always see what's best, even if they should."

"Oh, I feel awful about this, James, but what else can I do?"

"Don't feel that way. I won't let you down. But you wouldn't run away, would you?"

"Of course not. Why do you ask?"

"I don't know. I was thinking of something that happened in Grady last year. It isn't important."

"No, tell me."

"There was this girl, Lucille Carlson. She was pretty. She

even had a natural beauty mark on her right temple. She lived down the street from us, and was always sneaking out when her parents weren't looking. I would often see her, at nighttime.

"Anyway, she met up with a handsome gambler named Alexander Polk, who drifted into town one day like a lot of gamblers do in Grady. I'd shined his shoes one morning outside my father's store, and he'd told me his name— seemed to be proud of it. Then later I overheard Dad telling Mother that Lucille had taken up with him.

"One day Lucille disappeared. Her mother found a note saying she'd gone off to marry Alexander Polk, and not to look for her for they'd never find her."

"She found the man of her dreams, then?"

"Not exactly, because they did find her. A few days later some hunters found her body lying face down in a ravine outside of town. She'd been beaten, then drowned."

"Oh . . ."

"So you can see what I thought of today when you said what you did about you and Roman. It's silly, I know, because if Roman Cruz would rescue me from those creatures, he certainly couldn't be the sort who would do anything to harm anyone. But then, we did say we'd be honest."

"Yes, I see."

I chatted on with him, but the story of Lucille Carlson hung in my mind. It wasn't that I connected it at all with Roman, only that it seemed so hopeless for a girl ever to find real happiness without taking a risk. Even Marybeth found her happiness in risk. Her mother and father must have tried to marry her off to six different wealthy bachelors from time to time, but she'd have none of it. She would rather meet someone on the sly for a few stolen moments, and run the risk of never marrying, rather than to compromise.

I was only half listening to James, when something he said about Helga caught my full attention.

"What about Helga?"

"Today at lunch. Cousin Claire suggested she ought to go for a visit with her brother in San Antonio, maybe stay a couple of weeks."

"Oh. What a nice gesture."

"Well, it's funny, but Helga didn't like the idea. I could tell that. It was odd to see her looking kind of sad, you know, when Claire mentioned it, because she never laughs or smiles or anything. But she did look sad."

"Didn't she and her brother have an argument when she came back here to Galveston with Claire? It seems I heard Dad mention it once."

"I don't know. If they did, that would explain her refusing the paid vacation Cousin Claire offered her. But you know Claire, she just keeps pressing on, not worrying she might be interfering with someone else's wishes. I heard Mother telling Dad once that she was bad about that."

"Yes, she is. Did she give up the idea though?"

"No. She made Helga promise to think it over, and kept telling her it was really what she ought to do."

"Hm . . . let me know what happens, will you? Sometimes Claire's acts of kindness are a little misguided, though I'm sure she means well."

"Yes, that's what Mother always told Dad. Well, I've got to go now. Can't you come to dinner? Helga's made spice cake with nuts and raisins. I bought them on special at Cook's earlier today."

"Sounds tempting, but I can't make it tonight."

"I guess she invited you and Father Garret when they were out riding together today."

"But I didn't know they went riding together. Dad said—"

"Yes, I saw them when I was with Tommy Driscoll, going up Avenue K in her rig. Of course I saw them from behind and the sun was in my eyes, but I'm sure it was them.

"Anyway, I wish you could come tonight. It'd be so much more fun."

"Another time," I said absently, wondering why Dad had lied about not having seen Claire all day. Oh well, perhaps I just misunderstood him, my mind being on Roman Cruz during our conversation.

Chapter 8

Sunday night it rained, and Mother became ill.

I'd written entries for the past three days in my diary, then gone to bed at ten, too excited to sleep, and lay awake until twelve, when the wind began to rattle the shutters and the rain came like dancing feet upon the roof.

Rain was something I hadn't counted on. Never, in considering the dangers of giving myself away, or being discovered by someone, for doing the unforgivable act for a young lady, had I thought of the simple, irrevocable problem of rain. Rain could keep me from the beach, steal away precious time with Roman. What if it should keep up for days? It often would, once it began, and we hadn't yet had a good shower this summer.

I lay there wondering whether I could manage to go to the beach anyway. If I could not, would Roman understand why, or would he say to himself, "Well, if she lets a little rain get in her way, forget it."

Oh, surely he couldn't be so unreasonable. Yet at this stage he must have wondered a time or two whether I'd have nerve enough to return to him again. . . .

At twelve forty-five Dad knocked softly at my door, and opened it. "Serena, are you awake? Mother's taken sick, I'm afraid she's pretty ill."

"Yes, what's wrong?" I got up, reached for my robe.

"She's been vomiting. I'm going to fetch Doc. Will you stay with her?"

"Of course. Go along, but wear your mackintosh. You can't take a chance on getting a cold and being sick, too."

"Yes, Nan. That's thoughtful of you," he said, and closed the door. It hadn't been thoughtfulness, really. I only dreaded the idea there might be one more obstacle in the way of my seeing Roman, for with the sound of the rain had come the startling realization there were many things which could happen to ruin my plans. If Mother and Dad were both ill . . . I scolded myself for selfish thoughts, and went to Mother's room.

The stench was deplorable, and it occurred to me she must have been sick for some time before Dad heard her and came in to check. How pathetic to lie in misery, unable to form words for seeking help. He'd put a porcelain pan by her bed and she'd filled it with the undigested food of her stomach, and now lay back limply. Her hair was wet, her forehead covered with perspiration. Some of the nasty liquid had dripped down the side of her mouth, and now stuck at the edge of her chin.

"Mother, poor dear, let me empty this and I'll come back and change the bed and clean you up," I told her, picking up the stinking pan. It is frustrating to care for a sick person who cannot tell what is wrong, or say what they think might help them feel better. I'd fed her a supper of ham and potatoes and peas around six o'clock, and had eaten the same food myself, so I knew this couldn't be what was making her ill. I emptied the pan and filled her pitcher with water, then cleaned her face with a wet cloth and changed the bedclothes. There was little more to do, then, except wait for Doc. All the while I sat beside her bed, I kept thinking I might not be able to go in the morning to see Roman, and hating myself for the thought.

"Mother, I wish you could tell me if there's anything I can do," I said finally, impatient for the doctor to come so I would know.

She looked at me vacantly, and a small smile crossed her lips. One never knows why Mother may smile, or why she cries. You can only guess something has pleased or displeased her, real or imagined.

She put out her hand and I reached for it, held it in my own. Her fingers are skeletal things, the thin skin of her hand embossed with the complex of veins underneath. It felt clammy that night, and somehow the feel of it saddened me and I wanted to bury my face in her breast and cry as I had when I was a child. How many times over the years had I cried in frustration, wondering when she was ever going to get well, before I finally resigned myself to the fact she'd always be the same woman who came home from the hospital one day and didn't recognize me?

Year after year, there has been almost no change in her demeanor. Mother's hand is warm and soft, or it is clammy. Mother's hair is clean and limp, or wet, from a night of bad dreams, perhaps, hanging in cords around her shoulders; Mother eats her supper or refuses it; she looks out the window and writes meaningless words across a piece of paper in an almost indecipherable scribble; she smiles or cries, shivers from the cold or perspires from the heat. She is a fragile will-o'-the-wisp of bones and skin, existing in a faraway world of her own. . . . I sighed and gave her hand a squeeze.

The clippity-clop of horse hooves rose to the window, and I went down to let Dad and Doc in and hang up their coats. Doc is very good about coming when needed. That night his hair was mussed and he wore his pajamas and robe. He'd hurried here from his own bed to care for a retching invalid.

"Well now, what's the matter with you, Janet?" he asked matter-of-factly, pretending as always that she understands what he says. He took her temperature, asked me what she'd eaten, then did a curious thing. Claire had left a vase full of pink oleanders next to Mother's bed the day before, and he began to examine the blossoms and leaves. I was puzzled by his actions, but Dad seemed to guess what Doc was doing.

"Say, you don't think she might have eaten off one of those blossoms, do you?"

"It doesn't look that way, but then I wouldn't leave them so close to her bed." He handed the vase to Dad, who, at a loss as to what to do with it, finally placed it on the windowsill across the room.

Doc removed the thermometer, screwed his eyes up to read it, then reported, "Temperature's normal. I would guess she ate something today that disagreed with her. Probably no call for alarm, though. Got some medicine in my bag here she can take every four hours—one spoonful—and she might drink some cool water, and maybe some broth tomorrow. I'll stop by then and see how she's doing."

He went to his case and pulled out a medicine bottle of white liquid. "Looks like a gully washer out there," he said, directing his gaze across at the window. "Always hate to start off a week with rain . . . something disheartening about it. Now, open up, young lady, there you go."

Mother seemed to trust Doc Monroe, and never gave him trouble when he looked after her. He'd lived down the street for a long time, and perhaps been kind to her before her accident. Funny how I can sense how she feels about various people, something about her eyes. I think she liked James right off, and she seems to feel content with Mrs. McCambridge. Regardless of how she feels about Claire, she was fond of Charles Becker. I could see that readily. He came by often before his death, and many times stayed with her so that I could leave during the hours I normally spent with her. To Dad she has almost a pathetic attachment. She'll clasp his hand sometimes, as he sits with her, and hold it and fondle it for as long as he'll stay.

Before Doc left, he gave me the medicine bottle, as though he entrusted me with her getting well, and said,

"Now, don't forget to see she gets this on time. It's very important, missy."

Did he know I had other plans for the morning? Was he the one who'd alerted Dad I was seeing Roman? Surely not, I told myself, and thought how easily I could be driven beyond reason about finding out. I could get where I trusted no one, suspected everyone was against me, and all because of my own guilt feelings trapping me.

As Dad and Doc Monroe left I counted the hours. Next dose at five o'clock, then one at nine. My heart leapt. It would be perfect. I could give her a dose just before I left; that is, if she was feeling well enough for me to go, and besides, Mrs. McCambridge would be here to look after her. Surely it wouldn't look too awful if I left, unless, of course, she was still very sick, and unless the battering rain failed to stop as I had begun to pray it would.

I looked in on her once more before getting into bed at two. She was sleeping peacefully, defying anyone to guess she'd ever been ill at all. I believe the sickness must have been all but past before Dad woke me.

I heard his footsteps on the stairs, just before I dozed off, and wondered, as I have many times, whom he has to look to for comfort. Is it enough, having only God in heaven to give consolation, or must one have something more tangible here that he can see and hold? Was I enough, as Dad had always tried to make me feel, or could anyone ever replace what he'd lost in his wife? Then another thought flashed across my mind: just a few days before I'd found another Old Saratoga bottle on the kitchen table, emptier, even, than the last.

At five o'clock I awoke and gave Mother her medicine, disappointed to notice the rain continuing. Then for the next two hours I slept fitfully, dreaming that Roman came over and he and Dad sat at the kitchen table and grew drunk together.

At seven o'clock I was awakened by the pleasant twittering of birds, and opened my eyes to face a room brightened by sunlight. I thought perhaps this was a "sign," as Dad might have termed it, of God showing me he wanted me to be with Roman, that he condoned everything and wouldn't punish me. For I was afraid even then of being punished.

Roman never changed from the gentle, tender loving partner he was at the beginning. Each time I left the house in the morning, with Mother in the safekeeping of Mrs. McCambridge and Dad off on his church duties, I felt a sense of relief and an anxious stirring inside, an impatience to get to him. Although James sometimes walked with me as far as Marybeth's, often he did not, spending time instead with Tommy Driscoll. When I went alone, I scarcely ever went all the way to the Fischers', running instead straight to the back door of the Pavilion and into Roman's waiting arms.

He always made me feel as though he waited as anxiously for me as I had awaited the appointed hour to go to him, and I began to have the reckless feeling that this interlude in our lives could go on forever, without our ever being found out, or his growing tired of me.

Even on the days of his darker moods, when we were as likely to do nothing more than stand on the beach and talk, or talk upstairs in the tower, as to wind up locked in each other's arms, he made me feel as though he needed me. One morning I found him at the surf's edge, arms folded and feet slightly apart, so that when I saw him I thought of the god Apollo, and said playfully behind him, "It is the god Apollo, god of the song and the lyre."

He turned on me almost angrily, as though his mind were miles from the beach and the rolling surf, and me. "Oh, it's you. You're early, aren't you?"

"Maybe. Did I bother you?"

"No, come here," he said, and I went to him and he put an arm around me, and we stood together for a long time without speaking. Then he said, "That so-and-so boyfriend of yours came to the show last night. Sat right up front where I could see him."

"Nick, at the show? I didn't know he was going, haven't seen him for a week."

"That Bible-toting, high-minded bastard. I felt like yanking him out of that chair and beating the hell out of him. Excuse the unfit language."

"Roman, you couldn't do that—then everybody would find out about us."

"And that would be terrible, wouldn't it?" he said coldly. "Would bring your reputation among the Galvestonians right down to the ground."

"It isn't that, darling. It's just that if my father found out we were seeing each other I'd probably never get away to the beach again."

"Maybe it would be just as well, at that." The wind was stronger suddenly, blowing our hair as though to coax us away from the water.

"No, don't say that, please."

"All right. Let's go for a swim," he said, then playfully added, "Besides, your bathing attire looks far better wet."

As we splashed around in the warm salty water I said, "By the way, what's happened to the boys in the band? I never see them playing ball around here anymore."

"Morning rehearsals have been cut to almost nothing as the summer wears on, and the boys have scattered in all directions. Some go to the public beaches, where they can meet girls. The Professor isn't around much anyway. He has a friend in town."

"Oh, I see."

"Yes, that kind of friend, dearie."

"Roman, this is July. It's been almost a month."

"I know. Only two more to go."

"It's a long time between the end of this summer and next June."

"Yes, a very long time. And I still don't know whether we'll be back."

I'd been floating on my back, and now raised up and stood in the water. "You mean they haven't renewed the contract?"

"It's too soon to tell how the receipts are going to run."

"But what'll we do if—"

"Let's don't talk about it, for God's sake, can't we just make the most of what time we have together?"

"Of course, I'm sorry. I shouldn't be pushing ahead like that . . . don't know what got into me. Time is too precious to spend it worrying. . . ."

The first of a legion of leaden clouds passed above and sprinkled us with rain then, and we ran toward the stage door for cover. "Oh gosh, I can't stay long," I said as we ascended the tower stairs. "It would look funny if I stayed while it was raining."

"What would you do if you were at the Fischer place?"

"Go into the bathhouse, but only for as long as it took to let up a bit. You know, rain down here has a way of going on and on."

It was dark in the tower room. I sat on the edge of the bed, shivering, and Roman lit a candle and set it in front of the window facing the beach. "It's going to get rough down there," he said, looking out. "A person could get lost in that ocean and never be found, you know."

He looked across at me, his eyes somber. Something about the way he looked frightened me, and I sat silently, waiting for him to speak again. "Either he would be caught by an undertow, or attacked by a shark or something, and that would be the end for him."

I couldn't understand this maudlin train of thought, and walked over to stand beside him. "Everyone has to die, Roman. But if we have faith in God, there's no reason to fear death. . . ."

"You sound like a Sunday school teacher. I didn't say I feared it. Look, life is like this," he said, drawing out a match from the box on the windowsill and striking it on the rough wall. "When we're born it's like the spark that ignites this match."

The match fire caught, crept down the stalk, leaving a curl of charcoal above it. "While we're alive it burns like this." I watched his eyes, sparkling above the tiny flame. "When we die it goes out, poof!" he said, blowing it out just as the flame reached his finger. "We simply cease to exist."

"Is that what you believe?"

"That's all there is, baby. That's why I live for the moment. Whether you know it or not, you believe it, too, and that's why you're here with me right now."

He kept looking at me, through me. I wanted to help him, to find out why his mood should become so bleak. "Come into my arms, Serena," he said finally. "Oh, God, how I need you!"

Roman always encouraged my dancing, and when I suggested one day I might skip a class, in order to come to him sooner, he wouldn't hear of it. "Certainly it would look strange if you suddenly began missing lessons, and anyway, dancing means a lot to you, doesn't it?"

"It was everything . . . till you came along."

"All right. I'd be the last one to have you give up what you love most for me. I'm not worth it in the first place, and anyway, every person—man or woman—ought to live up to his greatest potential, if he can."

Truly I had never considered dancing in that light, although Madame praised my ability often and had even broached the subject of my going to a school for advanced training far from here—up East somewhere. Such an idea was out of the question, though, because Dad couldn't afford to send me—how he managed to scrape up the money for me to dance with Madame was an item never discussed between us, yet one about which I had idly wondered a few times. Besides, Dad didn't take my dancing seriously, and only gave me the lessons because he felt he owed me something extra for the time I spent with Mother at home. Then, of course, there was the problem of Mother, always lurking in the background. There were so many reasons why it was impossible for me ever to study away from home that I had soon closed the subject once and for all with Madame, telling her one day, "I'm sorry, but you see it is absolutely impossible."

That same day I'd walked home downhearted at the finality of my own remark, even though I'd never dared hope her idea might become a reality. And on that day I'd silently adopted a philosophy toward dancing, uttered in a prayer that God would see fit to allow me to go on taking lessons for as long as I wanted—years and years, even until I was older than Madame herself—and if he would, I'd not ask for more into the bargain.

From the first few weeks of urgent meetings with Roman in the tower, my dancing ability seemed to blossom, for I now approached each routine or exercise with new and deeper feeling, whereas before I'd been a less inspired, though fairly meticulous, student. Knowing Roman felt my dancing important gave me a new sense of freedom in it, and each movement, each turn of the head or hand, became a thing born of love rather than of concentration and study. Madame, always quick to notice any change in what she called her dancers' "bearing," said one day, "See how much better you do when you relax, Serena—now you look like the real dancer I know you can be!"

One morning, when I'd gone straight to the Pavilion from the studio, breathless from hurrying because we'd stayed over for a long practice on brisé volé, Roman took my carpetbag from me and said, "You've never danced for me, and here I am your most encouraging fan."

He sat down on the bed and began to dig through my bag. "What's this filmy pink thing?"

"My practice outfit."

"Oh . . . I don't think my sister practices in outfits like this. They're more sophisticated in New York, wear less on the dance floor and at the bar. And these are your shoes," he continued, pulling one out and nudging his hand down inside it. "Your feet are long—more narrow than I realized."

"Yes. As you see, I ought to replace the ribbons on those shoes. They've grown ragged."

"You're ordinarily careful about such details, are you?"

"Yes, but lately I haven't—"

"I know. Someone has been occupying too much of your time."

"I wouldn't say that. But I do think of him a lot when I'm not with him, and less about making a trip to Lalor's to buy dancing shoe ribbons."

"Do you practice at home?"

"Yes, on the back porch. I use the railing as a bar."

"My sister's always practicing, has a bar in her apartment."

"What's your sister like?"

"Hannah's two years older than me. She's been in New York four or five years. She's never married, unless you could count being married to her work in the ballet corps. I don't see her very often."

"Did she go to New York before you?"

"Long before. I went only three years ago, to join the King's band."

"What did you do till then?"

"My, aren't we inquisitive today?" he said, the look of mischief coming into his eyes. "What's the difference? Would I ask what you were doing three years ago?"

"If you did, I could probably tell you, and it wouldn't be much."

"Well, it's the same for me. Here, I have an idea. Put these things on and dance for me."

"Oh, Roman, not here. The room is too small—I'd probably run into the wall."

"Not here, silly, downstairs in the main hall. I'll accompany you at the piano."

"But I wouldn't know what to have you play. We dance mostly to classical music, and I'm not too familiar with the titles."

"Come now, quit stalling and put these on. You can just begin something, and I'll pick out music to go with it. What kind of musician do you think I am? Go on, don't stand there fidgeting. I want to see you dance."

"All right. But what if someone should come in while we're in there?"

"So what? It would only be a band member, come to pick up something or other, and they all know better than to interfere with me."

I put the costume on, and the shoes, and sat obediently on the edge of the bed while he laced up the ribbons. He was insistent upon this small act of chivalry, and I loved the warmth of his hands as they wound the ribbons tightly around. His manner was businesslike as a shoe salesman, and when he was done they were wrapped as snugly as though I had wrapped them myself. He patted my knee and said, "All right, old girl, let's go." I stood up, but as we reached the door and opened it I hesitated again.

"Serena, don't act as though I were sending you to the guillotine. After all, who else do you know who is even interested in your ballet?"

"No one, except Madame D'Arcy."

"And old Nicky boy, what does he think?" he asked as we spiraled down the stairs.

"Just about what you would guess . . . that someday we'll be married and I'll forget such foolishness, or so he hopes."

"See how I corrupt you? Putting ideas into your head about really being somebody? My, how scandalous, tsk, tsk."

I wanted to put my arms around him when he said that. The floor of the Pavilion hall loomed larger than ever, with the chairs moved out of the way since the last cleaning, and no one to take up the vast space except Roman and me.

"Now, now," his voice echoed as he reached the piano. "What will it be? Can you remember the name of *any* tune you dance to? Surely you can. Nick would be outraged if he knew his best girl couldn't name all the classical works."

"I am not Nick's girl, and I'd appreciate your not saying that, if you don't mind."

"Yes, of course that's true, although he has yet to realize it. Now, come on. Think of something . . ."

Today he was a new Roman—exacting as a class instructor. I wondered how many sides there were to his personality, and whether I would ever know all of them.

"You probably wouldn't know it," I said finally, "Mendelssohn's 'On Wings of Song.' We learned a dance to it last spring that I loved, so I still remember all of it, I think."

"How dare you accuse me of being so lowbrow as not to know, 'On Wings of Song.' "

He opened the piano cover and ran his fingers over the keys. "Now, get down there in the center, where I can see you. Shall I turn a spotlight your way?"

"Don't you dare," I said, and padded softly across the floor. I had never felt so gawky as I did that day, standing there before the music began. In Madame's studio, the only place I had ever danced except in the privacy of my own back porch, no one need feel foolish because everyone was doing the same thing. Everyone was dressed alike, and all were taking the same steps, whether or not they executed them properly. Here, I was like a star about to perform before an audience, and suddenly I thought I could imagine how Margueretta Sterling might have felt as she began the execution of her dance from *Swan Lake*. I took a deep breath and struck the beginning pose. "Ready," I said. "The tempo is rather slow."

"I'll follow you," he said, and began the long, elegant passages of the music with the sureness of the concert pianist. The dance began slowly, dreamily as the music to which it was set. I moved stiffly at first, rather like a marionette fresh from storage, but as the music lilted on, more crescendo with each measure and vaster in range, I forgot my misery at being a spectacle, and danced the routine with confidence and joy. When Mendelssohn's masterpiece wound to its quiet, peaceful end, I made the final movements and lowered myself into a bow to the floor. Roman shouted, "Bravo, Bravo, she can really dance!" and his applause rang through the empty hall like the clapping of many eager hands.

Then a voice rose deeply from the rear of the hall, "I fully agree."

I turned around to see Professor King standing just inside the door. "Good day," he said politely. "I didn't know they had ballet here in the Pavilion."

"Oh, they don't. Please forgive us, if we were in the way—"

"Nonsense. I thoroughly enjoyed it. Please continue. I'm just here to pick up some papers from the office, then I'll be off to town. Roman has excellent taste, I can assure you. Perhaps I can watch you again, at another time."

Roman made no comment all this time, and when the Professor was gone I said, "Well, thanks for leaving me to explain by myself."

"Explain what?" he asked innocently. "I owe him no explanations. It was you who were so anxious to excuse yourself. Ah, Serena, sometimes you remind me of a little mouse who's come timidly out of his nook in the dining room, just in time to frighten a dowager passing by in her trailing skirts. He runs back into the safety of his nook, never realizing he has frightened the dowager just as much as her screams have frightened him."

"But doesn't that prove what I'm saying? I've no right to be here, any more than the mouse has a right to be in the dining room."

"On the contrary. I'm only saying that you are not a little mouse, so stop behaving like one. You've as much right to be in this hall as King."

"All right. But for that, you've got to play some more for me. This time I'll be the one to sit and watch. I had no idea you played so beautifully."

"I haven't always been a traveling musician, dear," he said, and began to run unhesitatingly through tunes from Bach to Beethoven. I shall never forget that day, for it gave me a new confidence in myself that all the talking and encouraging could never have given. I'd actually delivered a good rendering of a dance routine, and if I could do it before Roman Cruz, obviously accomplished in the field of music, perhaps I could do it one day in front of others.

It was dispiriting, then, to go home and face the problems there.

Mrs. McCambridge stood impatiently at the door as I walked up. "You're late," she said. "You sometimes forget that I must go home and fix lunch for my family."

"All right, all right, I'm here now and you can go. Have you given Mother her lunch?"

"Of course. Don't I always feed her at eleven? I haven't missed feeding her at eleven in all the years I've been here. Not that she always eats."

"Did she eat today?"

"Not very well. She hasn't eaten really well since her sick spell not long ago. Serena . . . I think it would be nice for you to go into her room and spend some time with her this afternoon. You know, I'm certain she's aware when you stay beside her bed. She loves you, even if she can't show it."

"All right, Mrs. McCambridge. I was planning to, anyway. Maybe I'll brush her hair. She seems to like that."

"There's a good child. Well, I must be going now. I told William to put a pot roast in the stove this mornin', and, knowin' him, he'll let it get overdone if I tarry any longer. . . ." She was standing in front of the hall mirror, pinning on her gray felt hat, which she had worn every day since I could remember. "William hasn't been up to snuff lately, runny nose and all. I shouldn't wonder if that boy isn't in bed when I get home, forgettin' entirely about my roast."

"I'm sorry to hear that. Tell him I hope he's better soon."

After she left I went straight up to Mother, and as her room was stuffy I walked over to raise the window a few inches higher. Then an odd thing happened. I wasn't even looking outside the window, just down at the latch, when I became aware of the feeling someone was watching me. I looked across at James's bedroom window in Claire's house. There was no one there, and the window was closed. Yet the curtains fluttered slightly as though someone had only just touched them and moved on.

Chapter 9

Dad was becoming more and more aloof. At first I'd thought it was my fault, because I did take care to avoid him at times. It's hard for me to hide my feelings from him, and I knew the fewer our conversations, the safer I would be.

Yet he, too, no longer sought my company as he used to. Often he had dinner out, and when he came in, would likely go straight up to his bedroom, stopping only to open Mother's door a few inches and look in.

That evening I heard him come in downstairs as I was feeding Mother, and when she finished her tray I took it to the kitchen and found him sitting at the table with his glass of whisky. He didn't hear my entrance, and as I watched him sitting there, looking toward the open back door, I thought perhaps he, too, had some immediate problem which I'd been too wrapped up in myself to notice.

I sat down across from him. "Dad, is anything the matter?"

"Oh, Nan, I didn't hear you come in. No, should there be?"

"No, but you don't talk much lately and stay out a lot. Something wrong down at the church?"

He gazed at me steadily for a moment, then said, "The church? There is little that can happen there at this point. It's all been done, long ago."

I didn't know exactly what he meant by that, except I'd been told once that the mayoral election Charles ran in more than ten years ago had had something to do with it.

"You mustn't give up, Dad. There are lots of other churches in Galveston now, and maybe St. Christopher's doesn't have the best location among them. Maybe you ought to consider moving, closer to Broadway or—"

"Move? No, there's no need for that now," he said, then brightened. "Besides, we're not doing so badly. We still have the loveliest garden in the city, and many loyal parishioners."

"Dad, tell me about what happened when Charles ran for mayor. I know what happened at the church was connected to it somehow, but I've never been sure how."

"Charles can't be blamed for any of it," he said. "There were two things that went wrong. First, I mistakenly tried to be active in his campaign. The bishop learned of it and disapproved of my behavior. But that wouldn't have been an insurmountable problem; indeed, no one in the church would have needed to know.

"The turning point was the fact so many of the communicants were either employed by or somehow connected with the Wharf Company. You see, they were a mighty force. The Wharf Company was naturally against Charles, because he came out strongly against their policies. At that time, politics entered everything—well, I guess that's still true. Anyway, the congregation began dividing into factions, and people began to leave. Imagine, factions in the church! It was all ridiculous for a bunch of Christians, of course, and should never have happened.

"Yet you can't control the feelings of people. Even if I curtailed my own activities in the campaign after the bishop gave me a scolding, everyone knew how close Charles and I were as neighbors and friends. Then of course there was Lucien Carter."

"Who?"

"You wouldn't remember him—you were too young. Lucien owned a shipping company based here, and he wholeheartedly supported Charles during the election. He was also a member at St. Christopher's."

"I see."

"Yes. He left Galveston shortly after Charles dropped out of the race, but there was a lot of bitterness toward me because I was Lucien's friend, too."

"Why did he leave?"

"Oh . . . for the same reason any enterprising business-man leaves one town for another. He felt he had a better future elsewhere. He rather gave up on Galveston, I think, after Charles withdrew."

"The church seems to have suffered worst of all."

"That's true. One of life's injustices, I guess."

"But this could all have been avoided if Charles hadn't given up. Why did he get into it so deeply, then give up?"

"It's a long story, dear, one which I can't tell you in full. Someday, perhaps you will know all of it, but not now. It's enough to say he was sickened by politics by the time elec-tion day neared. He was a gentle man, Charles, not the sort to become entangled with roughshod bullies throwing their weight around."

"Did the Wharf Company threaten him in some way?"

He didn't answer for a moment, but instead took another sip of whisky. Then: "They—let us say, his opposition—used its influence against him as best it could."

What Dad told me that day as we sat at the kitchen table didn't bother me. What nagged at me were the parts he insisted on leaving out. I kept wondering about Charles's reasons for backing out, all through the rest of the evening as Nick and I played two hands of casino, and later, still, as I sat with Mother a few minutes before she went to sleep.

How I wished that night she could talk to me. I had a feeling so much was locked up inside her that would never come out. As I rubbed her arms and elbows with cream, trying to soften the skin that rarely touched anything ex-cept rough cotton bedclothes, bits and pieces of a conversa-tion overheard long ago, before her accident, began to come back to me.

She and Dad had come from the Beckers' one night, and talked in their bedroom for a long time. I was supposed to be asleep, but had lain awake, wondering as I did nightly when the new baby—due at any time—would come.

Dad seemed to be put out with Mother because she'd behaved so strangely in front of Claire . . . in fact, it was probably his unusual tone of voice that first made me listen. "I know how uncomfortable you feel, but you must make a better effort not to show it," he said.

"But when she gets to talking about that summer, I just want to go through the floor. I feel so deceitful."

"Hush, darling," Dad told her. "What happened wasn't our fault, although heaven knows we've profited all these years. What we did was a favor to Charles, and can't be looked at any other way."

Then Mother said, "Why not, Rubin, because then we couldn't live with ourselves?"

I must have been staring hard at Mother, rubbing her arms in a frenzy, as the memory took hold, for she began to look at me fearfully and press back against the pillows. "Oh, I'm sorry," I told her. "I was thinking of something and got carried away, I guess." I kissed her cheek and began brushing her hair, trying not to think of the conversation any more until I could be alone and sort it out.

Later, in my bedroom, I pulled out her poems. I remembered them as soon as I thought of Mother saying she felt "deceitful." The clue must be in the poems somewhere.

The more I read of them, though, the more puzzled I became. They were such vague things. Perhaps all poetry is vague; perhaps only the poetry of a mad person . . .

Had Dad's words about profiting handsomely meant they'd stolen money from Claire? Certainly not, it would seem, for she had no money except what Charles gave her. Besides, why steal money in the first place? It simply didn't ring true, and the thought of Charles Becker doing anything not strictly aboveboard was impossible to entertain. He was one of the most honorable men I've ever known and from all appearances, was totally devoted to Claire.

Besides, Dad would never take money that wasn't rightfully his. Yet he had said, "profited."

None of it made sense, and there was no one left now to explain it except Dad. I was sure he would continue to evade my pointed inquiries as he had earlier, at the kitchen table. Dad is quite apt at getting around things when he wants to be.

. . . Unless Helga Reinschmidt knew something and that was why Charles would never let her come here while he was alive. Over the years Claire has often mentioned Charles disliked Helga, but never, as I recall, has she said why. Yet even Helga's involvement wouldn't fit because her only contact with the Beckers was through Claire, and Claire was the unknowing victim, not one of the conspirators. Still, everyone knows of Helga's almost unnatural attachment to Claire. Perhaps Charles was afraid she might guess what had happened, and tell. Yes. She would almost certainly tell Claire anything she knew . . .

My mind spun through the labyrinth of unanswered questions, of open-ended clues leading nowhere, until I finally gave up pursuing it and fell asleep. No matter how many times I've told myself since then that the whole situation probably amounts to nothing—maybe even just a dream on my part, rather than something actually overheard—I've never stopped wondering.

James was doing nicely on his own these days, and didn't go to the beach with me over once or twice a week. He and Tommy Driscoll had made quite a success of selling crabs, and often he didn't return in the mornings from the catch and the sales trip following in time to go with me.

He worried about this at first, but I told him there was no need. As long as he obviously had something else he wanted to do during the time I went to the beach, there was no reason for anyone to wonder why he wasn't with me. Besides, most of the time I still took Porky, who sat obediently at the back steps of the Pavilion stage door until I returned from the tower to walk him home.

One day James met me at the gate, his eyes full of excitement. "I'm going to do something I'll bet you've never done," he told me.

"What?"

"Going to a séance."

"Séance?" I repeated. I'd heard stories of such goings-on, but had never known much about them. "Where is it to be held?"

"You know the house where the Madisons used to live, down the street?"

"Yes. They haven't been here since May—I don't understand."

"We're going to have it under their house. I've just been

down to make sure there's an entrance through the lattice-work."

"Who else is going to be there?"

"Delta and Joe Baker, and the rest of them. Delta has an aunt that used to be a clairvoyant and taught her just what to do."

"But I thought séances were for calling forth dead people—spirits. Whom are you all going to call on?"

"My parents," he said, and I knew then I should have realized. It was clear the Baker ring was up to no good, and it wasn't the first time. They'd been pulling pranks on people since I could remember, and were disliked all over the neighborhood.

"James, I wouldn't want to ruin your plans, but don't you think you'd better give this some thought? You know, most of these things are just tricks, theatrical jokes. You read now and then in the papers about people who paid for them and got cheated."

"Yes, but I didn't give Delta a dime, you can be sure of that, only a picture of my mother and father. That way, she'll be sure to know what they look like so she can find them among the spirits."

"You gave her a picture of them?"

"Loaned it, till after the thing is over."

"When is it going to take place?"

"A few nights from now. They're going to let me know as soon as they find out what night they can get away without their parents finding out. I told them I could get out any old time."

"Oh you did, huh? Well, just supposing you can, young man. I wonder what you think you're going to prove by all this?"

"Prove? Why, that Mother and Dad are really gone, I guess."

"But James, James, you already know that."

"I told you, they wouldn't let me see them. I never saw them after they left on their ride that morning. Just talking to them again would make me feel a lot better, see?"

"Oh, all right. But let me warn you not to expect anything. I wouldn't trust Delta or Joe either, as far as from here to the end of the block, and I just hope nothing happens to that picture."

"Do you really think she'd do harm to it?"

"Probably not, but be sure you get it back as soon as possible. There's no way of replacing it, you know."

"Yes . . . but then there's no way of replacing them, either."

It was the following day I became involved in my own bizarre scheme, as innocently as James in his, by making a half-serious suggestion to Roman which he then dared me to follow through. It all started with a silly, romantic notion I had one morning as we lay next to each other in the tower room.

"This is all wrong, you know," I said.

"What? Your coming here?"

"No. I mean, don't lovers usually meet in the dark, at night? Do you realize I've never even seen you at night, except the evening I watched you play, then the one at Claire Becker's dinner party? Wouldn't it be fun, just once, to meet at night?"

"Name the night," he said. "No one's around here after eleven. I'll meet you whenever you like, if you're sure you can sneak out without being caught."

"Oh . . . I hadn't thought. Oh well, we might as well forget it."

He turned over on his elbow and looked down at me sternly. "You mean you haven't the nerve, fair maid, after what we've pulled off in broad daylight the past month or so? You slay me!" He heaved an exaggerated sigh, and lay back on the pillow.

"Well . . . I probably could. If we did it late enough, that is. Just think, we could go walking on the beach in the moonlight. I've always dreamed of doing that with the man I love . . ."

"We could do other things too, my dear," he said, and began to kiss my neck.

"Oh, Roman, your mind always—"

"Um?"

"Nothing, nothing . . ."

We set it for midnight on the next Thursday, a night of no performance. After I gave it more thought, I decided it was an even better idea than I had at first imagined. Luckily, the only window in the tower room—the one Roman called a "faker" because it didn't really open—faced the beach, and he could set a lighted candle there, its glow unseen except by people on a boat far out in the Gulf, or someone taking a midnight swim, both improbabilities.

The only problem lay in getting away, then back home safely. Roman offered to meet me somewhere near home, but I told him that surely would be more dangerous than if he waited at the Pavilion. No matter where Dad went, he was normally at home and in bed by ten-thirty or eleven, so unless Mother were to become ill in the night, it would be easy enough for me to leave my room, pass unseen down the hall, down the stairs, and outside. Once I was outside it would be even easier to get down to the beach, unless someone were out there. That was highly doubtful too, for there were no young people of my age group around Avenue L, who might be spooning on a front verandah or taking evening walks together that late. All the kids on our block were too young to be out after dark.

Still, as the night approached I became nervous and fidgety, and could I have notified Roman, I would have called it off. It was curious, but I could never seem to remember to tell him that, should I fail to show up for any of our meetings, it was because Mother was sick or something unforeseen had occurred, and I would be with him as soon as I could. I was always intending to mention that, then as soon as I reached his arms I would forget anything else existed. He had that effect on me from the beginning; he still does.

Therefore, with no advance explanation working for me, I had to go. If I didn't he might take it wrong and be put out with me, something I could not allow because I could never be sure how tenuous a hold I had on him.

At ten-thirty on Thursday night, I lay across the bed to wait. Dad was in bed and Mother was sleeping. It looked deceivingly simple to sneak away, yet I kept reminding myself how foolhardy it was to tempt fate. Hadn't we been lucky all summer long? Was my sudden thirst for adventure, gone wild, now to ruin it all?

I rose from the bed at eleven forty-five, and that was when it happened.

I felt a trickle of menstrual blood escape. I gasped in horror, then keened my ears to be sure I hadn't awakened anyone. I was already overdue a few days for the monthly showing, yet before then hadn't given it a thought.

By the time I'd made a detour into the bathroom, then slipped back into the bedroom, it was eleven fifty-two. I was to meet Roman in eight minutes. What could I do? What did one do when something like this occurred? It struck me then as a horrible irony: had I waited till morning, perhaps I could have figured some way to get out of going to meet Roman—sent James or something, to tell him I was ill and would have to stay in bed for a few days. But what could I do at midnight, except go? Perhaps I could persuade him all that time would allow was a walk on the beach. I prayed so.

Except for the hollow, rhythmic tick of the clock on the landing, the dark hall was silent. I walked slowly down the stairs, holding my skirt high and watching every step. When I reached the front door I remembered it sometimes will stick when there's dampness in the air. I turned the knob and pulled as gently as possible, and it came without hesitation. I felt better then. Perhaps this bit of luck would steel me for what lay ahead.

There was no one to be seen on Avenue L, and only the glow from an upstairs window here and there along my way indicated anyone might be awake. I had purposely worn dark navy, in order to remain unobtrusive, and I was thankful I'd thought of doing this, because the moon shone unusually bright. It would be so perfect for a walk along the beach.

It was a long way to the Pavilion, longer than ever it had seemed during the day, and by the time I neared the beach I was no longer walking, but running as fast as my legs would carry me, fearing all the time that Roman wouldn't be there when I arrived. This possibility always occurred to me as I walked to the beach by day; by night it seemed all the more threatening.

When I reached the stage door I looked above. The candle glowed warmly from the window, and I felt safe, like a sailor who spots a glowing lighthouse beacon in a foggy harbor. Yet as I opened the door and mounted the stairs, the feeling of safety ebbed away. The difficult part was yet to come.

He was standing in the open door at the top of the stairs, holding his arms out. "That's my girl. I knew you had nerves of iron, by God. Come here!"

I went to him, let him hold me for a moment, drawn by the warmth of him, then said, "You know, the moon is at its most beautiful just now. Why don't we go down for a walk?"

"Now? No, later, darling. I've been longing for you all evening . . . Look, I even swept the floor in honor of the occasion." He'd already pulled me through the door and closed it, and now fiddled with the buttons of my navy dress. I was nearing panic.

"No, please, Roman!" I said, and grabbed his hands.

He let me go. "What is it?"

"Nothing, only time is short and I did so want to walk, I—"

"Come on, don't try to fool me. What's the matter?"

"Please don't ask."

"Serena, your face is glowing brighter than that candle over there. Now, tell me."

"You would make me, wouldn't you?" I said, and turned away. "You would have to pressure me into telling you—"

"As a matter of fact I would. Curiosity is one of my greatest shortcomings," he said calmly, turning me back by the shoulders to face him. The mischievous look stole into his eyes.

"All right then. It's a—a—period. A period, if you must know!"

At this he slapped his knee and let go a shout of laughter. "You are so funny, Serena Garret. I knew as soon as you pulled away from me. Now, was it so bad after all? For heaven's sake, why make such a big to-do over nothing? Do you think I'm totally ignorant? As a matter of fact, I'd been wondering just when . . ."

"It's several days late, but that's not unusual for me," I said, trying to match his offhanded tone. Yet I was looking away again as I spoke. In a moment he put his hand under my chin and made me look at him.

"I've tried to tell you not ever to be embarrassed about anything in front of me," he said gently. "Serena, Serena, when will you drop these silly little-girl worries and become totally grown up? Come now, let's have a walk so that you can get back before anyone notices you're gone."

We walked arm in arm down the stairs and out into the moonlight. I felt as though I'd just been through a hot tub bath, and my skin tingled with relief as we padded barefoot through the softness of the sand. When it was time to go, and we were at the edge of the beach and L, he said goodby and kissed me gently.

"On the other hand," he said, "don't ever grow up fully. I like you just the way you are."

My steps back home were more assured, and I had a pleasant feeling it had been a good thing, meeting in the moonlight. As Roman had said, a person has only one life to live, and he must make the most of every moment. That was the way I felt as I walked down L, as though I'd taken my moment, had dipped into the milk pail and skimmed the cream right off the top.

I wasn't watching where I was going, basking in the afterglow of what had just passed. Suddenly I felt myself hit from the side with a thud. It surprised me so I just did stifle a scream, then realized it was James, in the same instant that he, out of breath from running, discovered he'd bumped into me.

His face, now visible in the moonlight, was wet with tears. "It was the stupid séance," he said. "They never came. They never came, the dirty, double-crossing, two-timing rats—"

"Oh, that . . . James, maybe they were found out by their parents. Did you think of that?"

"No, no . . . I was just sitting so long under the Madison house my back got stiff as a boot tree and I got cramps in my legs, and it finally dawned on me I'd been made the butt of a huge joke. It's happened to me lots of times, you know. I never thought they might have been found out."

"Well, you'd best give them the benefit of the doubt," I said, though I was convinced he was right in his first assumption. "You can find out tomorrow. Don't worry about it."

"And you—where have you been?"

"None of your business," I told him, and pulled his ear. "Get to bed now. We'll talk about this séance matter tomorrow."

"Gee, Serena, you know, you're really swell."

Later, in bed and unable to sleep, I looked out at the big benevolent moon which had led my way to and from the beach, and thought of the almost uncanny coincidence that I should meet up with James that night . . . how much he was like me really, reaching out to people in his loneliness.

I'd known from the beginning his hopes for the séance were no more than a pipe dream, and I only prayed that night my hopes for something lasting with Roman would not, in the end, amount to the same.

In the morning mail was a brief letter from Marybeth.

". . . and how are things in quaint little old Galveston?" she wrote. "We're back in Paris for a few days, as you can tell from the envelope. I've met a new man, named Peppi (the last name I would not even attempt to pronounce, much less to spell—he's Austrian, I think). Last night we had dinner at a cute little sidewalk cafe, then took a stroll down the Champs Élysées. . . .

"To tell you the truth, the food was no better than at the Ladies' dining room at the Bon Ton at home, but Peppi was a delight—very handsome, with thick moustache and curly black hair. It rained (it always rains in Paris when we're here) and absolutely ruined a new pair of shoes I got in Marseilles. . . .

"Is *anything* exciting happening there? Hope your little friend hasn't had any more man-of-war stings. I told Dad, and he was furious a thing such as that could happen right off our property. The nerve of the little rascals!!!

"We're coming home in September, don't know which day yet. I considered staying here to go to school, but changed my mind. Europe is fine for visiting but every place becomes boring sooner or later. I'd as soon go to school in the States, or maybe not go at all. Life is wonderful, so full of options. . . .

"I've bought you the most darling music box, can't wait to give it to you. It plays 'The Blue Danube Waltz,' and the little dancer on top looks almost as graceful as you. Certainly she looks nothing at all like me!

"Well, darling, do write if you have time. Just send the letter to the usual address in London, and Dad's agent there will have it forwarded. Love and kisses to you . . . see you in the fall."

The letter was typical Marybeth: breezy and light, reflecting her personality so vividly she might have been standing two feet away, telling me the news. The first line of this one, though, prompted my immediate reply. I would tell her a few things that would show her Galveston was perhaps not quite so quaint as she thought.

Yet, when I sat down to write, there was so little to say, without betraying more than I wanted to. I decided to tell her straightforwardly about Roman, with none of the coquettish little phrases I'd tried to insert the first time I wrote to her, earlier in the summer. I could not resist, however, mentioning that Roman was going on thirty years old, had a rather doubtful background, and that I was seeing him without knowledge of anyone except James. I told her I knew she would never betray my secret to anyone, although I must admit I recognized all too fully she was hardly in the position to anyway.

I wanted to tell her how far things had gone, yet when I tried to write it, it seemed too much like parroting things she'd done many times. Our love was meaningful, not like the times she'd given favors to men just for the excitement of it. Yet it was difficult to put this into words. Perhaps the subtle approach, telling her only that we met on the sly, would be just as effective . . . let her guess the rest, if she chose.

In the afternoon as I was practicing ballet on the porch, James came out the back of Claire's house, slamming the door behind him, and walked around toward the front yard.

"Hey there, you look awfully busy, what's up?" I called to him.

"I've got problems with the Bakers," he said hurriedly, and walked on. His manner made me uneasy and I went to the porch edge and called him back. "You're not going over there to start a fight about last night, are you?"

"They did just what I expected," he said. "Today they pretend they never heard of any séance, and Delta's got my picture. I'm going to get it now, or else."

"James, wait! Look, at least let me change and go with you. If those hooligans tie into you, you'll wish you had stayed home. Perhaps I can help."

"No. It's my problem and I'll work it out for myself. Besides, I know better than to pick a fistfight with them. I've something else in mind, and I think it'll work very effectively. See 'ya."

It was an uncommonly hot day for practicing. I wiped the perspiration from my neck and face, took a sip of lemonade, and continued. Practicing had taken on new importance these days because, though I still knew of no outlet for my dancing in the end, now that Roman had been so encouraging, I had a feeling it would be wise to be ready at all times, in case opportunity ever presented itself. I was afraid to dwell on the possibilities very much, however; just practiced, knowing it certainly could do no harm . . .

It was some fifteen minutes before James ambled back, hands in pockets, whistling a tune. I went to the porch edge. "Did you get the picture?"

"Right here," he said, patting his shirt pocket. "I knew Delta Baker wouldn't be able to turn down my offer."

"What, pray, did you offer?"

"Five dollars. I told her if she could somehow manage to locate that picture I had lost around her place, there would be five dollars in it for her."

"You're pretty smart," I said, laughing. "But I do think you might have gotten off a good bit cheaper than that."

"It's my only picture. I'd have given my last penny if necessary."

"Of course, I understand. I'm sorry . . . . James, how would you like to have the portrait of your mother that we have? I'm sure it would be all right with Dad, and I can't think of a better place for it to be than with you."

"That would be swell. But could you just keep it at your house until I leave Galveston? I mean, I don't want to take it to Claire's house."

"Why not?"

"Well, when Mrs. Reinschmidt was cleaning the other day, she took down every painting your mother had done for Claire, and she and Claire stored them in the attic. Claire's gone right now to buy some new ones."

"That's odd."

"I told you those two were rather queer. Did I tell you, Mrs. Reinschmidt's trip is all set? She leaves at the end of August. She's gonna stay a couple of days in Houston with friends, before going on to San Antonio. While she's gone, Claire says we get to go out for dinner twice a week."

"That's nice. Funny about the pictures, though."

"Yes, and the walls are faded behind. All over the place it looks like someone painted squares on the walls."

"Well, maybe she just wanted some new paintings to look at."

"Yes, maybe so. I don't know, I never ask questions. I'm just a visitor, after all."

"But, James, don't you think you might consider staying in Galveston for good?"

"I couldn't do that. Only till my grandfather can send for me. Besides, Cousin Claire doesn't really want me here. She's gone all the time—even at night—and when she is at home she and Mrs. Reinschmidt share secrets from me."

"Oh, James, your imagination again—"

"It is not," he swore. "They never talk to me."

"But you just said Claire promised you two could eat out twice a week together while Helga's away."

"Yes, but she'll probably back out on that because of some meeting or other, downtown."

"Oh?"

"Yes, she has them all the time at night, and comes home very late. That night of the séance I had to wait till she came in and had time to go to sleep before I could get away. She almost made me late . . . not that it mattered."

"Well, Claire has always had her circle of friends, and if she wants to go out at night, it's certainly her business," I said, but in truth wondered myself just where she went at night.

Was there some connection between her nights out and Dad's? Surely not, because, although she had often displayed more than a neighborly interest in my father, especially over the past few years since Charles's death, I'd always felt certain he didn't take it seriously. Yet there was that day not so long ago when James spotted them together in her rig . . .

Chapter 10

August approaching. I awoke to a dull, dreary excuse for a day, and looked at the calendar. It was easy enough to fool myself that summer might last forever as long as the pages of the calendar were headed up "June" or "July," but in just two days, I'd have to turn the page and face the finality of the word "August." The thought cast a shroud over my spirits.

Worse still, today was Sunday, and I had to spend it with Nick and Dad over roast beef for Sunday lunch, and probably dull parlor games in the afternoon. It was the usual routine. How long had it gone on? Only about a year, yet it seemed an eternal game of appearances we must play in which Nick, the eager suitor, played up to Dad rather than to me. . . .

Yet Sundays had never depressed me as badly as this one. I felt unusually tired as I left the bed and dressed for church, and after fixing my hair, sat down again on the edge of the bed and stared out the window. Only one more month, and it would all be over, and what then? No matter how hard I'd tried not to, I had begun to count on Roman to pull some magical trick that would solve everything and bring us lasting happiness together. More frightening than that, I could never be sure whether he wanted me always with him. He had that maddening evasive way, and he'd never said, "I love you," in those words, though I'd longed to hear them from the beginning of summer.

Often I'd thought he might say them, thereby sealing the pact between us, yet he hadn't seen fit to do so, so how could I be sure he felt them? Perhaps I was to him, just as I surely would be to any other man who knew about this summer, nothing more than a cheap pick-up, good only for a summer fling.

I was thinking of this later in the day, when Nick spoke up at the lunch table.

"Serena, come down to earth," he said jovially. "You look a thousand miles away."

"Do I? Sorry . . . have another helping of corn?"

"No thanks," he said, then directed his attention to Dad. "Father Garret, you really have a prize here. A beautiful little woman who can cook and sew. If she ever decides to settle down and marry, the man who gets her will be one lucky fellow, yes, sir." He sat there waiting, picking his teeth with a match.

Dad lit his pipe and pushed back from the table, then asked in mock surprise, "Oh? You know someone with designs in that direction?"

"I sure do. Not that any young eligible man wouldn't, who got to know her just a little. But one has to consider background in those things. Serena, here, has a whole lifetime of experience in Church affairs. She'd be a great asset to any man who worked in the Church, don't you think?"

"I surely do . . . a great asset to any man, no matter what he did for a living."

Strangely, I believe Dad really thought he was pleasing me by giving his blessing to Nick's proposal of marriage in this subtle way. He simply could not believe it possible I didn't want to marry Nick. In truth, the conversation sickened me. My head was throbbing.

I stood up from the table and said, "I have work to do, and even if I didn't, I wouldn't sit here and be bartered like a sack of flour. If you'll excuse me, please."

Nick looked up at me, the picture of innocence. Dad's mouth gaped open. "Of course, Nan, I didn't mean to imply any such thing," he said.

"Certainly not," Nick added, looking at him. "Uh, well,

I've got some practicing to do this afternoon for confirmation services tonight. I'd better be getting back to the church now."

"I'll see you out," said Dad, and followed him from the dining room and into the hall. I have no idea what they said to each other then, although I imagine they spoke in tones of bewilderment at my unorthodox behavior. I didn't care. I cleared the table and carried the dishes into the kitchen.

Dad soon followed me through the swinging door, and I knew this was to be a confrontation about Nick that had long been brewing. He leaned against the counter. "Serena, please forgive what just happened. I didn't intend to be such a boor."

I looked at him. He was obviously pained by what had occurred, and seeing it in his face softened my anger toward him. He was so like a little boy, innocent in truth as Nick only pretended to be.

"It's all right. Forget it. Maybe I'm just touchy."

"No, it was unforgivable, talking that way, only, you can understand how a father feels about his daughter when she reaches your age. More than anything, he hopes and prays she'll marry someone who is kind and will provide well for her, give her a good life. Because once her father is gone, she'll have no one else to lean on for support."

"But you're not leaving us any time soon . . ."

"Even so, I was thankful when you and Nick began courting. He's a good fellow, Nan, and would always take care of you. He can have the organist's post at St. Christopher's for as long as I'm around, and if he should ever aspire to a higher post—well, nothing would please me more."

I didn't say anything. Dad continued.

"You've seen so much of each other, I couldn't help believing you had some feeling for him, and I was afraid you might be reluctant to accept his hand in marriage because of Mother's condition. I know it's been rough on you, kept you from having as many friends and as many good times as you would, had she been well. I felt it would be a good future for you, were you to marry Nick, and when he first approached me about it, I—"

"He's spoken to you about it?"

"Well, yes. That young man is very fond of you, darling,

and, of course, anxious to proceed as a gentleman would."

"Well, I'm not very fond of him. I don't know how many different ways I can tell you that. I thought you understood at the first of the summer."

"First of the summer?"

"Yes, when we discussed that man from the band."

"Oh yes, I'd quite forgotten about that. What was his name—Cruz, something? Well, of course, I knew that was just a passing fancy. Surely you could have had little in common with a person like him. I thought you truly cared for Nick."

"Now you know."

"But, Serena, let me tell you one thing more. You may not believe this, but when I married your mother, I had no idea what love really was. Of course I *thought* I loved her, but as the years went by I could feel that love deepening, could realize all we had for each other at the beginning was a kind of fondness. Through marriage and all the good and bad times that go along with it, one builds true love that is lasting. It has gotten me through all these years since her accident, that, and nothing else."

"Oh, Dad, I'm sorry. But you both at least had something to build on, did you not? How do you begin if there is nothing? Nick can never be anything more for me than a good friend. You wouldn't want me to lie, would you?"

"No, no, of course not." He sighed. "All right. But don't do anything hasty. After all, you've plenty of time for deciding where your heart lies. Perhaps one day your feelings for him will awaken . . ."

I stared at him. Why couldn't I make him understand?

"Please believe me, Nan, a woman alone is at the mercy of society. I have only your interest at heart when I attempt to persuade you toward marriage. Be it Nick Weaver or some other fine man, no matter. It's your happiness that concerns me."

I went into his arms then, the first time I had for a long while. Somehow even with this ever widening gap between us, it was comforting to lay my head on his shoulder and be held by him. Despite his mistakes on my behalf, I shall never doubt he loves me, and as we stood there, two afternoon shadows against the kitchen wall, I wanted nothing more than to tell him everything about this summer.

How thankful I am I did not.

In those first few days of August, and even more so as
the month wore on, there seemed to be a kind of impa-
tience growing all round. It hadn't rained since the night
Mother was ill in early July. The grass was a dirty yellow
color; the dust in the street seemed to kick higher than
usual when a carriage passed down or a group of children
gamboled toward the beach. The water pressure was low,
and people up and down the street complained to one another they couldn't get enough from their hoses to water
the gardens properly. Good vegetable crops were growing
dry; flowers drooped their heads like dancers after a tiring
routine.

Claire, who often left in her buggy nowadays a little earlier than I left for the beach, would stop regularly at the
barometer on her back stoop, narrow her eyes, and tap it a
couple of times to see if it were dropping. Helga seemed
more irritable than usual, and I would often overhear her
tersely instructing James about something or other, when
Claire was away from home.

I would awaken mornings, the bedclothes clinging to my
back, perspiration all over my face and neck and arms, and
I couldn't be sure whether I felt worn out because of the
heat, or because of something else. By the time I was up
and dressed, I was in an angry mood, and sick and tired of
keeping secrets. The uncertainty of what was to come
welled up inside me like a festering sore. . . .

"You haven't said anything about the contract," I told
Roman one day as we sat on the beach eating apples.

He finished paring a piece of fruit and took a loud bite
before answering. "It's still not decided," he said.

"Are you just saying that, to put me off?"

"Of course not. Why should I?"

"I don't know."

"I'll let you know as soon as King gives the word. He's
negotiating it this morning, I think."

"Well, that sounds like a good sign, anyway. No hurry,
you understand, August has just begun. It's only that—"

He stopped eating his apple and put a finger under my
chin. "You're not going to cloud up and cry, are you?"

"Certainly not. Why should I? Live each moment, as you
always say. It's been a great summer. What difference what
happens when it's over? No strings."

"Right. By gosh, that's what I like about you. You understand how things must be."

"Of course."

"Tell you what. Let's go for a swim. Fine day for it."

"Yes, let's. I need something to cool me off."

He pulled me up from the sand and we ran into the surf together, ending the conversation that obviously made him uncomfortable.

All the month long he was like a little boy on holiday, wanting to play as much as possible before it was over. And if I ever looked too serious, or began to say something about us, he would quickly change the subject or kiss me into silence, and I wondered whether he was having as hard a time facing the end as I was, or whether he looked upon it with relief, and was merely letting his latest conquest down easily before boarding the train for New York.

Day by day I seemed to have less energy. In dancing I could manage only half as many fouettés as usual, and the heat couldn't be entirely to blame, for Carlotta Maxwell, never a particularly promising or energetic student, was now doing ten or twelve of the pinpoint gyrations to my six. Madame said nothing, but began to look at me a little differently, as though she wondered at the cause of my lackadaisical behavior.

Often I was panting heavily by the time I reached Roman on the beach, and once he commented, "Heat getting to you, old girl? You've lost some of your bounce lately."

I'd gone home that day and looked at the calendar. It was the second week of the month, thirty six days since our twilight meeting, and yet there was no sign of the monthly bleeding that had so mortified me on that daring night.

I told myself it was a case of nerves, and tried to pass it off and to relax, to see whether the period would come. I had never before missed one as far as I could remember, yet Marybeth used to miss one occasionally, and wouldn't let it bother her.

I was, therefore, anxious to become involved in something new and interesting about that time, to get my mind off the prospect facing me. James and Claire provided just the thing.

"She's going to give me a birthday party," he told me one day. "My birthday's on the twenty-fifth, the day before Helga leaves, and we're gonna have an oyster roast in the backyard, and cake and ice cream." His face was beaming.

"How marvelous. You see, Claire's not such a bad sort after all."

"I guess not. She asked me out on the porch last night just at dusk, so we could watch the sun go down together. 'James,' she said, 'there isn't much left of summer . . . there is something so altogether *final* about the end of summer, don't you think?'

"I didn't know why she was telling me that. She seemed to be thinking of something else, you know, the way grown-ups do sometimes."

"Yes?"

"Then she looked at me, put her hands on my shoulders, and said, 'I want to do something special for you, to wind up the summer. Your birthday is on the twenty-fifth, isn't it? Let's have a party. You can invite anyone you want, and Helga can make all the fixings.'

"Just like that! I told her I'd be everlastingly grateful."

"That's a mouthful. Only James Byron would say thank you that way. Truly, though, I think it's wonderful. Tell me now, what can I do to help? I'd be so happy to do something . . . anything."

"Gee, I don't know. Just come. You will come, won't you?"

"Try and keep me away. But you be thinking about something I can do. Maybe write out invitations. Yes, I could do that, couldn't I?" He was swinging on the newel-post.

"I'll have to ask her," he said. "There isn't much time till then, is there?"

"Yes," I said quickly. "The end of August is a long time off yet."

"No, only a couple of weeks."

"That's a long time, James," I said, and thought, Oh, please let it be a long time . . .

Day by day, the conviction grew stronger. I tried relaxing more, getting more sleep, taking more walks, but nothing worked and my nerves became tighter than a drumhead. One thing I couldn't do was voice my fears to Roman, for even after a summer with him I couldn't be sure how he might react to the news I was expecting his child. He might be gentle, say we'd marry at once, settle in Galveston, or better, move somewhere else together.

On the other hand, he might be angry, might say it was all a bore, and demand I go somewhere and have one of those horrible operations Marybeth told me about, to get rid of the child. How could I know someone so intimately, yet not really know him at all? Oh, how could I have been so foolish as not to find out how to avoid a pregnancy before it was too late?

He sensed immediately, of course, that something was the matter. If he should touch me unexpectedly, I would jump as though someone had put a piece of ice to my neck.

"What's bothering you?" he asked one day as we lay together on the little bed.

"Nothing. Why should there be?"

"You've got me, baby. Say, King mentioned this morning we'd probably renew the contract."

"Wonderful."

"You don't sound as though you mean it," he said, and looked at me in that daring way of his, commanding me to prove what I was saying.

"Of course I do. It's just . . . well, it's a long time till next summer."

"Yes . . . much can happen between now and then. You might find someone else, marry, and have a kid on the way by then."

There was a tight lump in my throat. I couldn't speak.

"Look, baby, one thing I've always liked about you is you don't ask for commitments. A year away from each other might be the best thing for us. Give us time for thinking. Then, if things go right, we might pick up again next summer."

"That would be convenient, wouldn't it? I mean, to have me waiting here at your beck and call."

"No, that isn't what I meant. You're free to do whatever you wish. You will aways be free."

"So if I find someone new, or even marry someone I already know, before next year, there'll be no hard feelings."

"None, except that I'll probably murder the scoundrel," he said, laughing, and pulled me closer to him. "Don't think I'd be doing you any favor by holding you. Traveling all over kingdom come is practically all I do anymore. It isn't any decent life for a woman. Anyway, I'm not the sort a girl becomes involved with permanently. Thank God, you seem to understand that."

"Roman—I—"

"Sh. Don't talk anymore now. Let's make the most of the time we have left. My God, you get better every day."

And so it was for the next couple of weeks. Just when I would get next to telling him, I'd lose my nerve or he would interrupt, and I'd wind up hoping the period would start and end all my troubles, and I would still be the same next summer for him to come back to, would be summer after summer, I didn't care for how many summers.

I went right on dancing, afraid to stop lest someone might guess what was happening to me. And there were days when I even felt totally myself, with all the old energy returning so that I'd finish a series of steps for Madame, and she would clap her hands and say, "Bravo, bravo, Serena! Show us again, and you there, Sheila, pay attention. . ."

I took great care to avoid Dad as much as possible, and he, fighting some private battle of his own, was not given to involved conversations either. I came home one day to find him drinking whisky in the kitchen, and since we both knew it was early in the day for him to begin drinking, he half rose from the table as I walked in, then sat down again. His face was flush; the bottle beside the glass was all but empty. He picked it up as though he would pour another, then changed his mind and replaced it on the table.

"Dad, you seem to be—uh—drinking a little more lately. Is anything wrong?"

"No, nothing new . . . A man just likes his whisky now and then, even a priest."

"Have you been up to see Mother today?"

"Not since this morning. Perhaps you'd better look in on her."

"I'll do that now."

I walked around the table and started out of the kitchen, then looked back at him. His big shoulders hid the bottle from view, and one might have thought he sat poring over next Sunday's sermon, or studying some Bible verse. How I wished we could confide in each other as we used to. Instead, we became more alienated by the day. My problem was one which would break his heart could he know of it. What hounded him must be something he dared not confide to me. Was this the meaning of growing older, becoming withdrawn into ourselves, unable to seek help in another human being for fear of betraying some secret?

"Nan," he said as I still hesitated.

"Yes, Dad."

"Don't ever do anything you'd regret later, no matter

how right it may seem at the time. If your instincts tell you
it's wrong, don't do it. Steer clear of it at all costs."

As he said it, I was caught between a burning curiosity
as to whether he'd done something himself lately to prompt
him to relate such a lesson, and a fear he had an idea what
was going on between Roman and me. Therefore, I
couldn't afford to ask him the reason for the sudden piece
of advice. I had to remain offhanded about it.

"That's a good point, Dad. We always have a feeling
when we're doing something wrong. God shows us."

"Yes, Nan, *listen to him.*"

My mouth was dry. "Of course. I'd better look in on
Mother now."

Chapter 11

I shall never forget the day of James's birthday party. I
awoke to feel a spot of blood escape, and went tripping
around the bedroom like a fool, consumed with joy. I resolved to find some way to get hold of a book telling me
how to avoid unwanted pregnancies. I had overheard
women talking from time to time about certain days of the
month you must abstain. Perhaps those days for me
wouldn't come until Roman was gone from Galveston the
following week.

Throughout the morning, I was light-headed with relief,
and began to look positively at the year ahead. The best
thing would be to throw myself wholeheartedly into dancing. Maybe I could persuade Dad to give me an extra lesson each week, to make the time pass even faster. Then a
new thought struck me: what if, by the time Roman came
back next year, I could be ready to audition for the school
in New York where his sister had studied? Maybe he could
fix it for her to help me enter the school, and I could get a
letter from Madame. No one need know anything except
that Madame was helping me get into the school. Perhaps I
could get some sort of scholarship to pay my way. Perhaps
we could find someone to look after Mother after I left.
There were many stones to turn along the way, yet hadn't I
faced and overcome obstacles all summer?

At last I would have something to look forward to, to
give me hope in the coming year. . . .

With soaring spirits, I told Roman of the idea later that morning. "It might work," he said, "if there's an opening in the school. Tell you what, when I get back to New York, I'll check into it. Your teacher would have to write a letter, just as you say, and you'd almost have to have that scholarship because otherwise it would be too expensive. My sister would have never gotten through without her scholarship."

"I'll find a way. I doubt I'm ready yet, but perhaps by next year I will be. I'll speak to Madame about it tomorrow, and if she thinks so she'll coach me this year."

"But how will I let you know?"

"Oh, I hadn't thought. I know . . . you can send word through Marybeth. She'll be back in Galveston in a week or so. I'll give you her address, and you can write to her. I can trust her, I know," I said, sloughing off the fear that his letter might land in the wrong hands because truly it seemed the only answer.

"All right," he said, but he looked troubled and I wondered whether he felt I was trying to tie him down by entering the school. Maybe he wanted me as long as he was in Galveston, but there was someone else in New York to occupy his time there.

I didn't pursue it any further. When I reflect on this summer, I see myself as Román's little mouse, too frightened to pursue anything of importance, always afraid of having the door shut in my face. It was like walking a tightwire all the time, ever within view of the end, yet too far away to be confident of reaching the platform before falling from the wire.

The party for James was a great success, both for him and for Claire. I had a warm feeling inside as I watched him greet his guests and accept their gifts, and blow out the candles on his monstrous cake, for I believe he had at last found acceptance among the people around him, and was probably one step further toward facing the fact Galveston was to be his permanent home.

Tommy Driscoll came, spruced up in a suit, with bow tie around his neck, his face clean for the first time I'd ever witnessed. The Baker kids came too, their proverbial group of hangers-on straggling along. The only one of them to bring a gift was Delta, and I watched as she presented James with a small box, telling him proudly that her present had cost five dollars. I do believe Delta is sweet on

James, and perhaps with time, a real friendship will develop between them.

Claire, in her true dramatic fashion, saved her gift for last, and I have never seen anyone so pleased as was James when he opened the wrapping and discovered a Kodak camera inside. With that one small token, she'd won his affection for good. I could see it in his face. He thanked me for the light cologne I'd brought him, and opened the bottle to dab some along his face. He seemed to understand the gift was my way of telling him I thought he was truly growing into manhood.

The camera, however, was positively his greatest prize, and after everyone eagerly inspected it, and went off to enjoy hot roasted oysters and corn on the cob, birthday cake and ice cream, he busied himself reading the instructions included in the box and loading the camera with film, trailed all the time by Tommy Driscoll, who was as eager to watch the new contraption in action as James. It was too dark for snapshots that night, though, and James, at first disappointed, finally said, "Well, I'll just have to get up early in the morning and use up the roll then. I can have it off in the mail by noon."

Nick Weaver came, bearing no gift, and kept a hand on my elbow the whole evening long. He was overprotective that night, even for Nick, and I made sure we stayed within the crowd all the time, sitting in the wicker chairs near the table of food, so that he couldn't get me alone, for I felt he was on the verge of bringing up the marriage business again, and I could not have taken that.

Helga was kept busy replenishing the punch bowl and seeing everyone had all they needed. Once, as she passed by, I wished her a good trip. "You'll be off to the station tomorrow morning, won't you?"

"Yes'm. But I'll be back, and soon. You can be sure of that."

"It'll be nice, though, having a rest and visit with friends and family."

"There'll be a better time for resting, later . . ."

She shuffled off in her black dress after the cryptic remark, and I wondered, not for the first time, if anyone had ever fathomed the depths of that guarded, confined personality. Did Claire know her as intimately as she thought? Did anyone really know Helga? Had she lost out at love sometime or other, and the experience calcified her soul?

Or, had she always been cold as a corpse? I shivered at the thought, and turned my attention to Nick, who was shoving a bowl of ice cream under my nose.

Dad was in one corner of the yard, talking with Claire. She was dressed head to toe in white gingham that night, her dress altogether too frilly for one so small and buxom. I could tell Dad was trying to get away, for he kept stepping back and nodding and smiling. Still, she kept him there for a long time, talking of heaven only knows what—probably her beloved garden at the church. Claire has a way of dominating conversation to suit herself.

I thought of Mother then, and glanced up at her window. She'd rolled her chair within view of the party, and her body was outlined by the half-light of the bedroom beyond. Her face was encased in shadows, and I wondered as I watched what she might be thinking. Did she simply watch mindlessly the movings of the people below, puzzled by the presence of so many people? Was she thinking of nothing at all?

Or did she, even in her present state, suspect Claire of occupying too much of my father's time? Had she kept an eye on them as they chatted in the corner?

Chapter 12

With the dawn of the next morning, the summer's pace doubled itself, as, near the end of the race, a horse speeds his gallop at the feel of the whip across his flank.

The period was over. It had been unusually light, amounting to only a scant showing the day of the party, and when I awoke I was tired again and half relieved this was the day Roman and his fellow band members would be in Houston for their benefit performance there. They wouldn't return until the night train pulled into Galveston.

It was a pleasant morning, a cool breeze rolling in off the Gulf, and by ten o'clock I'd decided to put on my practice clothes and go through some steps on the back porch. I'd forgotten about Helga's leaving until I saw her go to the barn and bring the rig round. A fickle wind loosened the ribbons on her black bonnet, sending her hat aflight across the yard, where it landed among the craggy edges of a shrub. I met her there as she went to free it.

"Have a good time, and don't worry about anything," I said. "James is a good boy, and will help Claire see to things while you're gone."

She nodded stoically and started back across the yard. I felt foolish for having opened my mouth, and went back to practicing. I kept stopping in the middle of steps, taking sips of water or resting. What had sapped my energy I couldn't guess, but supposed at the time it must be a combination of all the summer's events coming down on me like a thousand pressing fingers.

I'd been out an hour or so when I heard James and Claire returning in the rig. James jumped out before they reached the barn and said, "Cousin Claire wants you to come for lunch."

"All right, but I'll have to change first."

"No, wait. I want to take a picture of you in your dancing outfit. I haven't got to use my camera yet, because Helga wouldn't let me take her picture at the station." He had the camera hanging from his shoulder by its leather strap. "Would you mind, though, if we do it on your front verandah? I've studied on it, and think I can get a better shot from there because of the light."

He wouldn't have, I thought to myself, if I hadn't finally persuaded Dad to cut back the giant oleanders last summer, which had for so long enclosed the porch in darkness. I'd never been able to guess why my mother would have wanted to allow them to grow to such immense proportions . . .

"Now," said James. "Do one of those things where you curve your arms around and lift your leg in back."

"An arabesque."

"Yes! You look so pretty when you do that. There now, stand up on your toes and pretend there's an audience out there, cheering you."

"Good gracious, James. All right. Let me know when you're ready."

"Yes, but don't look directly into the camera. Look away, like out at the audience, when I take it."

"All right," I said, and when I allowed my mind to wander I could almost hear the shouts of praise, conjure up the glorious feeling of performing before hundreds of adoring fans. This is how it would be, then, to . . .

James clicked the camera once, then said, "I'd better take two or three more, just to be sure." He didn't seem to trust the little black box, and as it was a model new on the market, I didn't much blame him. You could never guess how long some newfangled gadget would last. I hoped, for his sake, that all his pictures would turn out well.

"All right, that's it. I think it takes a couple of weeks to get the pictures back," he said. "Hope the mail hasn't been picked up yet."

"No, I don't think I've seen the postman."

"You will hurry, won't you? Claire says lunch is almost ready."

I should have known better than to subject myself to Claire's prying that day. Before finishing the first course of oyster stew, I was tired of trying to satisfy her curiosity while avoiding a betrayal of myself.

". . . It was nice of you to bring your young man Nick with you last night. I suppose we'll soon be hearing wedding bells pealing at St. Christopher's. Perhaps I'd better bone up on raising appropriate wedding flowers in the garden."

"No, ma'am. We've no plans to marry."

"Oh? That's odd, I mean, seeing you've been keeping company with him so steadily. At least, before this summer. We haven't seen quite so much of him this summer as usual, have we?"

James cleared his throat, and kept his eyes on the bowl of milky liquid in front of him.

"Well, he has five or six students now," I told her. "They keep him pretty busy when he isn't practicing organ or coaching the choir."

"Hm. But you say you're not serious about Nick?"

"No."

"Well, there must be someone else then. After all, a girl your age, pretty as you are, must have a beau hidden somewhere. Charles used to say when you were a child, that you were so pretty some young man would snatch you away from us before you turned eighteen."

I looked across at her, trying to see behind the words. "No, no one."

"I see. Well, I wasn't married at your age either, although James's grandmother Betsey was, and his own mother was on the verge of marriage at nineteen, I believe."

"Yes, ma'am."

"It's a lovely thing, two people finding each other and

striking out together. Of course . . . it doesn't always
work out beautifully in the end. Yet if one is careful to look
for the right things in another . . . Ah well, dear, you
don't want to hear my philosophies on marriage, do you?
By the way, you know I haven't gotten down to the Seaside
Pavilion one time this summer, to see that band play, much
as I intended to after meeting Mr. Cruz. And only the
other day Jassie Norton, on the gardening committee, mentioned how much she and her husband Howard had enjoyed their music this summer. Oh well, I suppose they'll
be back next year. But then, perhaps I might still go before
they leave. Have you any idea when they return to New
York? I had lunch with Esther Harrington last week . . .
you know, Stuart Harrington owns the Pavilion . . . but I
didn't think to ask her. Wasn't that silly?"

"I . . . believe I read somewhere, less than two weeks
from now. I don't know how many performances it said
between now and then."

"Oh? And where did you read that?"

"I don't know. The *News,* I guess, or maybe the *Tri-
bune.*"

"Funny, I didn't notice any ads in the papers. You
know, since Charles and I came here we've always taken
the *News.* That paper was kind to him when Charles was
running for mayor. But I do find most of the time, ads
about amusements are duplicated in both papers, don't
you?"

"I guess so. Perhaps I saw it somewhere else. I don't
remember," I said, wondering with disgust why I hadn't
been bright enough to have told her I didn't know, instead
of allowing her an opening . . .

"I know. Maybe it was *The Opera Glass.* Do you take
that paper? Mine hasn't been brought around in two or
three weeks, and I've been meaning to call them. Lands,
when one pays two dollars a year for something really elite
and cultural, you would think they'd see it got delivered,
wouldn't you?"

"Yes, ma'am."

"Oh, Serena, I've been meaning to tell you how nice
your skin stays—I mean, the coloring. Are you spending
much time at your friend's place lately?"

"Some."

"James has been busy crabbing with that Driscoll boy,

or I'm sure he'd have accompanied you down more often. That would have been nice, wouldn't it, James?"

James nodded and sipped his stew.

"I don't know why this boy prefers the company of that undertaker's son to all the other kids around the neighborhood. You know, he comes from a long line of undertakers. What a thing to be!"

"Someone has to do it, I guess."

"I suppose. When I'm gone, though, I shall fix it so there won't be anything left for an undertaker to prepare. I've been having some changes made in my will lately, and I've had it put in that I want to be cremated. When Charles was alive he wouldn't hear of it, but it's something I've always wanted to do. I won't have anyone touching me after—"

"Yes, some people prefer it that way. Everyone ought to have his choice."

It was stifling conversation, and something about the stew was repelling me more with every spoonful. As we proceeded along through crab salad and ice cream, I was unsure whether Claire knew what I had been doing all summer, or was only making conversation in her usual way.

But then she did an odd thing. As we were about to leave the table, she spotted something on the windowsill behind me, and walked toward it. "A spider's web," she announced, slicing through it with her arm. "Busy things, spiders . . . they can build a web within twenty-four hours that will make it look as though you haven't dusted your house in months. Seeing one always reminds me of the old adage, 'Oh what a tangled web we weave, when first we practice to deceive' . . ."

She looked at me then, and I was convinced she knew.

"I'd better be going soon. Let me help you with these dishes," I said.

"Oh dear, I wouldn't think of it. James, see Serena to the door, will you?"

When we were out on the porch he said, "Do you think she knows?"

"It looks as though she might. But how?"

"Who knows?" he whispered. "I haven't said a thing. But Helga might have been snooping. I never know where I'll find her next, and she often peers at me when she thinks I'm not aware. Oh well, that's irrevelant, no, I mean irrelevant, I always mess up that word. Helga's gone now, and if

Claire knows anything, what could she do about it anyway, except just love knowing? That's how she is, you know."

"She could tell my father, and probably would."

"Oh. Maybe she already has."

"No, I don't think so. I could tell . . ."

"Yes, probably. Well, think what she said about young love, though. Maybe she thinks it's very romantic—like a fairy tale—and hopes you'll tell her about you and Roman so she can help."

"Maybe. No matter, though. Don't act as though anything were wrong. I've got to talk to Roman."

"Serena, you're not going to run away, are you?"

"I don't know. I don't know what to do."

"Maybe I could pry it out of her."

"No, don't say a thing. We might both be wrong. Perhaps she doesn't know anything, and is just being meddlesome," I told him, trying without much success to keep the alarm from my voice.

Chapter 13

Madame D'Arcy's office is but a small nook just off the main floor of her studio. Centered there is an oversized desk, usually piled high with papers and odds and ends she never gets around to putting away. On the walls are pinned pictures of former students, many of whom have gone on to bright careers in ballet, either following their instruction from her here in Galveston, or in a studio she used to own up East somewhere, before coming here twenty years ago. There are, among the pictures, several of her, taken many years ago, when she herself was a professional dancer.

I was gazing over the pictures on the day she asked me to wait for her after class, the same day I'd chosen to speak with her about the school in New York. I remember how it surprised me, her calling me while I was changing clothes, almost as though she'd guessed in advance I needed to speak with her.

How foolish we look to ourselves in hindsight.

I was anxious to tell Roman about Claire. He would be back at the Pavilion today, and I would go to him directly from the studio. The fact of Claire's possible knowledge of our summer together made it all the more urgent I get all the loose ends tied up, get something definite worked out about what we would do. There was the slight possibility Madame would feel I was even now ready to audition in New York, and if so, I might be able to persuade Roman to take me there within a week, rather than a year from now. My stomach was churning as she entered and closed the door.

"Serena, dear, this won't take long," she said, sitting down across from me and wiping the perspiration from her brow. She looked older from this distance, more gray strands showing in her dark hair, her face a little longer and thinner, her eyes not quite so bright as they seemed on the studio floor. Her firm, muscular body, though, defied the years at any distance. She put her hands together and hesitated as though she hated to begin.

"I've been wondering whether you're having some difficulty at home."

"No, why should you—is my dancing not good? Am I losing ground?"

"No, no, hardly that," she said, and looked down at her desk. "It's your fees, dear. Your father has paid me nothing since last April, though I've sent many notes to his office. No answer ever comes. . . ."

I could scarcely speak. "I'm sure there must be some explanation. Please forgive—oh dear, I'll talk with my father first thing."

"I'm certain it must be some sort of misunderstanding, dear. I'd hoped to spare you this . . . put it off as long as possible. Serena, you know I adore you, feel you're one of the most talented students I've ever had. If I could afford to teach you free of charge, believe me I would—"

I rose from the chair. "Of course not. I'll go to his office right now. I'm so sorry, I—"

"Now, now, don't worry. Just let me know. Nothing more need be said about it. I'm only sorry I had to come to you with this. . . ."

"Please, madame, don't apologize. Let me get it straightened out. You're right, probably some mistake. I'll let you know."

I ran all the way from the studio to Dad's office at the church, too incredulous to think straight. He was seated inside, reading the morning mail. "Why, Nan, what a pleasant surprise. Come to ask your old Dad to lunch?"

"No," I said, panting. "Dad . . . I've just spoken with

Madame D'Arcy. She says you haven't paid her since April. Can . . . can this be true?"

"Oh." The color drained from his face. He cleared his throat. "I'm afraid so. You see, we've been in a bit of difficulty lately over finances. . . . I've been intending to get a payment over to her. Perhaps I could scrape something together today."

"Why didn't you tell me before this happened? I was mortified. I had no idea you were in trouble financially. What has happened?"

"Nothing at all, dear. It's just that, well, I did have a kind of reserve fund for a while, for things such as your dancing, you know. But it has . . . well, dwindled, over the past year or so.

"I'm afraid we're going to have to cut some of the extras we've enjoyed, that's all. Nothing we can't resolve in time. I've been trying to figure a way of telling you, but I know dancing means such a lot to you.

"I had an idea the other day, though," he said, brightening. "Perhaps you might take up lawn tennis. A fellow in our parish—Ned Stevenson, do you know Ned?—is building a new court not far from here, as an experiment. But he believes the game will catch on here soon. . . ."

"But, Dad . . ."

"Or, if you don't like that, you might be able to go to the YWCA. They've a fine gymnasium there, and you could get your exercise. I think we might be able to afford it, after I've paid off Madame. It's nowhere near as expensive as the dancing lessons. I'll go and see her today, and set up some sort of program."

As I listened to him I realized the mistake I'd made by never bothering to find out how we were able to afford the dancing lessons. I should have pressed him on the matter, rather than shuffling it to the back of my mind all these years. He made little as a parson, had not had an increase in wages for years, and there was Mrs. McCambridge to pay and the grocery bill, and medicines and lotions for Mother.

"Is anything else behind?"

"Not a thing, I assure you. The bill at Moore Brothers Grocery got out of hand for a while, but Fred Lindsay was very kind about it, and I've got it under control now."

I sat still, staring at him, wondering whether he was even now evading the truth.

"Serena, you've no idea how badly I feel about this. I wouldn't have embarrassed you in front of your teacher for anything in the world. I kept intending to send a note telling her a payment would be forthcoming, and I was going to try and get one over to her next week."

"I can never face her again."

"Yes, of course, and you needn't. Please forgive me, darling. I'll try and make it up to you."

"There is no way you ever could. I'll see you later at home."

There was no question then, after our discussion, that I would have to persuade Roman to take me with him. And if he refused, I would at least not be floundering any longer. I could begin making some other plan to extricate myself from the crumbling ashes life had become. I could no longer be content to hope for the best, hoping Roman would say the right thing, hoping he would care for me in the way I cared for him. There was no choice now except to find out once and for all, and I went to him from Dad's office with a determination greater than any I'd ever had.

He was in a pesky mood, standing just at the edge of the surf behind the Pavilion, arms akimbo, looking out to sea. I walked up beside him silently. There are times one is better off not approaching Roman Cruz too abruptly.

"Oh, hullo," he said, more quickly than I'd expected.

"It's only me."

"Only you," he repeated softly, and kept looking out to sea. I felt instinctively this day of all days was ill timed for what I needed to say, yet at this hour of the game, one day might make a world of difference in planning. There was but a week before Roman's train pulled out of Galveston and headed for New York.

"Well, fair maid, how does this day find you? Shall we go for a swim now?"

"Not now, and how I feel depends on you."

"Oh? Then I'm afraid you're leaning against the wrong post. We got the final word this morning. No contract. Something about the price we demanded. Galveston is out next summer. But I've a strong feeling King didn't negotiate too hard. Every year he shows a little less interest in the band. I think he'd rather keep all the engagements near New York; he's always complaining about the long-distance traveling . . ."

I was filled with hope. "Does it disappoint you?"

"Damn right."

"Why?"

"Why the hell do you think?"

I stood still. Everything had changed. If he knew there was no coming back, my chances might be better than ever. I took a deep breath and began. "Roman, I've got to talk to you. It's important."

"All right. Want to go upstairs?"

"No. Things have a way of . . . happening . . . upstairs."

He laughed. "All right. Let's have it then. You've found someone else, is that it? Going to marry that organist and settle down like a sensible girl?"

"Stop teasing, Roman. This is serious," I said, and looked down at the foamy water swirling around my feet, unsure what to say next. "One thing is . . . I think we've been found out."

"By whom?"

"Claire Becker."

"The old girl who gave the dinner party? She did strike me as a busybody. How?"

"God only knows. She's a devious soul, and I'm sure she has ways. Not James, though. I'd almost trust that boy with my life . . ."

"Careful not to ever trust anyone too far, Serena. You know, a person can only be trusted as long as it doesn't hurt his interests to act on your behalf. Remember, people have divided loyalties. No one can be trusted completely."

"Yes, I seem to be finding that out this summer. . . . Anyway, I was all ready to come and tell you about it, to see if we couldn't figure out something to do before she spills everything to Dad, then before another day passed something else happened. My dancing lessons are at an end. My father owes Madame quite a lot of money. She told me this morning."

For the first time I think I had reached him. He looked down at me for a moment, then pulled me close to him. "Poor, poor Serena. Everything seems to fall apart at once, doesn't it, baby?"

I don't know what had held back the tears before, but the showing of tenderness, the unexpected gentleness in his voice, dissolved all courage and determination to be brave, and I cried as I have not cried since the day I finally realized my mother was never going to be well again, when I was eight years old.

Roman ordinarily detests tears, but that day he let me alone as I wept. I kept trying to apologize, catching my breath in gulps, yet I couldn't quit crying and he held me and stroked my hair.

"It's my fault," he said. We'd walked away from the surf and sat down together on the stage door steps. I wasn't crying hard anymore, only shivering a little as the tears waned and dried upon my face. "I should've never intruded on your life. You'd have been so much better off, had I stayed away."

"No, no, you've brought me all the happiness I've ever known."

"The worst of it is, I knew from the beginning better than to fool with you. Knew it the first time I walked to that fence and saw you there on the pier with your dog and your little friend. You were not the sort for me, and I should have stayed away. You know what? I came very near doing that."

"But you didn't. You must have cared a little, even then."

"No. I won't lie to you, Serena, especially now. You were but a new distraction from the dullness of the summer, just like all the others. I didn't care for you except that I thought you damned attractive, and I found your confounded innocence new and refreshing."

"But surely that isn't all it's been this summer?"

"No, only until the first time I brought you up there," he said, glancing toward the tower window. "I felt awful after it was over. I've never been the first for any girl in my life. I thought that day if you never came back it would be the best thing all around. I'm destructive, you see. Look what's happened to your life since I moved in." He picked up a stick and traced a path through the sand, then broke the stick in half.

"No, don't say that. You know how I feel."

"But you did come back, and I was as hooked on you as a schoolboy on his first grade schoolmarm. Damn, I didn't have the guts to call it off because I couldn't get enough of you."

"I'm so glad you didn't . . ."

"Look, there's no use making things any more painful than they are now. Let's just end it. We'd have to anyway, because our time's run out. Let's not hold each other with commitments to meet again next time I'm in Galveston . . . if ever I am again."

I must have looked as stunned as I felt, because he turned away and continued, "Take a good piece of advice. Go back to your organist friend, marry him, have his children. You'll have a better life than if you cling to me. Believe me, it's best."

"I could never marry Nick Weaver after having known you. The idea sickens me."

"But you know nothing of me, you little fool. Do you realize that? I'm one of those people nice fathers don't let their daughters have anything to do with. Do you know why I came when your neighbor invited me to dinner? Because it was a novelty, being invited up into a respectable neighborhood in Galveston.

"I've done things you wouldn't believe, dearie, and you wouldn't want to know what they are. My background is what people call 'questionable,' as you once so aptly put it. I told you I haven't always been with a traveling band.

"Just tell me something. Haven't you thought all along that Professor King's band was just the ultimate? Being its star was the zenith in the music world? Well, it isn't. It's an opportunity for someone who has nowhere else to go but down. It's for losers, Serena, for losers."

"No, I won't let you say that. I don't care what you've done in the past. All I care about is what has happened this summer. You can't go around all your life paying for what you did in the past, denying yourself any chance of happiness because you feel you don't deserve it. When I met you, I decided I was due some happiness, after having been tied down to a sick mother and a dull, dull existence all my life.

"You made me see there was a chance for something better. You made me aspire so much more toward being a dancer. You made me believe in myself. How can you turn around now and downgrade yourself? I know you haven't been any angel, what man has? And how many would be so honest about admitting it?"

"By God," he said with a half-smile, "I had no idea how much you were influenced by the likes of me."

"I didn't either until now, when you got me stirred up."

"You know, you're twice as fetching when you get stirred up. You ought to get that way more often."

"No, I'm trying to be serious, to figure out what to do. I need you to take things in hand."

"What you're really saying is you want to go away with me."

"I guess that's what I'm saying."

"Well, I'm sorry, doll, that's out. There isn't any way for that to work. It would be disaster from the beginning, and you'd wind up being more unhappy than you ever thought possible."

"No, I wouldn't. I could travel with you, help you, oh, Roman, I'd do anything for you. I love you so much . . . I never knew I could love someone as I love you . . ."

I'd said too much, put him off. He looked down at the steps in silence for what seemed an eternity, and I awaited his decision as a helpless criminal awaits a jury verdict.

"No," he said finally. "No. Go now. Go away. Don't ever come back."

"Roman?"

"You heard me. Go. It's no good. Go on, now. I don't want to see you again."

"Roman?" I said again, backing down the beach. His mouth was set and he stared straight into my eyes. Finally I could bear the look no longer and turned away.

I stepped unevenly down the beach. As though nothing had happened, the gulls kept on winging back and forth above, the edge of the waves flirted with my feet as I passed. I shaded my eyes from the glare of the sun with one hand, and tried to think only as far as the next step. It could not be over, yet it was, because his look was unequivocal, branded on my mind. I would go back home and try to act out the rest of the day. Later, I would call upon a reserve of strength that must be waiting somewhere within me, to help me through the week, the month, the rest of my life. If I were pregnant, as I now feared more each day, I would be forced to commit murder on the child growing inside me, for there was no way to get away, no way . . .

There was a point, not more than a hundred yards or so from the Pavilion, when the thought struck me it would be so easy to turn to the right and continue walking toward the water, and to let the Gulf take me for its own. Hadn't James said I was a child of the sea? Aphrodite would eventually return to her birthplace, would she not? One could so easily walk into the surf as though for a swim, yet then to wade a little further, a little further . . .

Chapter 14

How long had he been calling?

He was running toward me now, fright written all over his face, the beautiful Apollo running to save what might have, should have, been his. He'd never run to me before; how strange to see him spatter like a panicked animal across the water, then to glide with muscles taut the last few feet. I treaded silently, waiting.

"You crazy little fool," he shouted, grabbing me first by the shoulders, then lifting, carrying me. "I start calling you, and you run into the water. Would you have the sea before me?"

It was all a dream, of course, and I was but a limp puppet being handled by its master. I gave no resistance to his pulling me back, yet had he let me go I would have contentedly given myself to the sea.

Back on the beach he sat me down roughly and shook my shoulders, bringing me out of the daze. He was angrier than I have ever seen him, for I had frightened him. "Damn you, don't you ever let anything happen to you, you little idiot!" he said, then took me into his arms and held me, rocking back and forth, and kissed my face, till the breath went out of me.

Later he carried me back up to the tower room, just as he had the first time I ever went to him for loving, laid me down on the bed, and pulled covers around my quaking body.

He was kneeling beside the bed and rubbing my hands. "Look, whatever you want," he said. "I'm not the prize you seem to think, but by God, how I'd ever live a day without you, I don't know . . ."

He laid his head down on the bed next to mine then, and I stroked his hair. It was strange, my comforting him. He was a man always in command of me, yet now he came to me as a small boy comes to his mother, frightened of a storm during the night. My body continued to shiver, yet I had a warm, overflowing feeling inside. I wanted him now more than ever, and raised the cover and looked into his eyes. It was the first time I had ever made the move toward love-making, and as he moved in and began to kiss me I felt I would never be afraid of anything again.

Later I thought of it all, walking home from the beach.

He hadn't told me how we would work it out, only that he would fix it and for me not to worry any more. Just as I was leaving him I'd turned and asked the questions which had nagged at me all summer long.

"You're not already married or anything, are you? I mean, I've always had this fear you might have a wife back in New York. Are you . . . married?"

"I have been."

"And now? What about now?"

"No. There is no one."

"Roman, could you just say . . . do you love me? Tell me the truth now, please. I have to know."

"You little fool. There isn't an inch of you I haven't loved since the beginning took place right in this room. Haven't you realized that?"

"Then, will you say it?" I was at the door, looking out into the hall. I dared not face him at that moment.

"All right. It's only that . . . I've said it so many times to so many women, it has a cheap ring to it by now. I didn't want to cheapen you by saying it. Can you understand that?"

"Yes, but it wouldn't be cheap to me. It would be like music."

He hesitated a moment, then said, "I love you, Serena. I love you by day and by night, as I never intended to love anybody. Is that what you wanted to hear?"

I turned and looked at him. It was so much more than I had hoped for.

There was much excitement on Avenue L when I returned, and I feared I must be awfully late and Mrs. McCambridge was having a fit, readying a search party to drag the ocean for my body. Yet why was everyone walking away from the beach?

When I reached our gate I saw James come from the crowd several houses down, and run toward me. His face was tear-strewn as he tried to tell me. "Oh, Serena, Serena, it's so awful. I don't know how to tell you, I don't know."

He was crying and talking at once, and I knelt and tried

to calm him. "James, what is it? Has someone been hurt? Mother? Dad?"

"No, no. It's Porky. He's down the street in the Madison yard, and he's dead."

"Dead? How can he—where?"

"Down there," he said, pointing toward the people. "You mustn't see. I don't want you to see him. They're going to bring him back in a wagon."

"No, I have to see," I said, and ran down the block. Even as I approached the scene I couldn't believe it. Porky never got out of the yard except at the end of a leash. What would he be doing down the street in someone else's yard?

When I got there Dad was leaning over him, and I knelt down beside him. Porky's body was perfectly still, lying on its side, showing no marks at all. He might just as easily have been sleeping, his legs stretched out in front of him, his eyes closing out the sunlight. I felt nothing, then, except disbelief.

"But what happened? He doesn't look as though he's been touched."

"Poisoned, no doubt about it. You can see it around his mouth."

I didn't want to see his mouth. "But why? Who?"

"I don't know. Maybe some mischievous prank. Some kids, or vicious grown-ups. Poor old boy, he never hurt a soul."

Something about the endearment clung to my heart and I felt the lump come into my throat. "Just let me stroke him," I said, "tell him good-by. I haven't been the best mistress lately, have I? Poor, poor Porky. He's so beautiful, so beautiful . . ."

"Come away now," said Dad, pulling me up. Tommy Driscoll, a junior edition of his undertaker father, stood by with his wagon, and Dad gently picked up the lifeless form. James appeared then, and said, "Please, Father Garret, I want to help pull the wagon home."

"All right," he answered, and allowed James to help him get Porky into the wagon. Over the summer Porky had been James's dog more than mine. It was fitting, then, that he should be at the lead of this queer entourage of people, making its way back up Avenue L . . .

Porky was the final living evidence of Charles Becker. Everything else he had given me during his lifetime—the

countless bijous purchased here and there, and given for
little or no occasion; the dolls in the doll chest in my room;
the sewing machine on which I had learned to sew; the
wooden rocking horse; the mounds of books he'd brought
to me—all were still around. The books were in St. Christopher's children's library and even the rocking horse, his
mane lost somewhere along the way, his paint job in bad
need of repair, was housed in our attic. Yet Porky was the
gift he took the most delight in giving. Now that Porky was
gone I found I missed Charles more than I had following
his own death three years before.

I think now that if Charles were around, everything
would be different for all of us today. Dad would find it
much easier to handle his problems, for, contrary to the
opinion of most people, Charles was the stronger of the two
men. People found strength in my father because they expected it to be there, and never bothered wondering
whether it really lay inside him, or whether his manner of
self-assuredness was really only a thin mask imposed by the
priesthood. My father leaned on Charles a great deal, and I
don't believe it was until after his death that Dad began to
take his whisky so frequently.

Were Charles here now, I might have gone to him, confided in him about Roman. He would have known how to
reason with my father, there being no question he would
have sided with me . . . why, I don't really know.

They buried Porky in the side yard, opposite Mother's
window and Claire's house. I took a book and read to
Mother as they turned the ground. We didn't want her to
see what had happened, and felt it might be better if she
discovered him gone one day and thought he'd run away.
Of course, one never knew about Mother. She might not
even remember tomorrow that Porky ever existed and had
sat sometimes at the foot of her wheelchair out in the sunshine.

James came over in the evening, and asked if I could
come out on the verandah and talk. We sat on the swing
together, smelling the sweet scent of blooming oleanders in
the moonlight. I had shed my tears for Porky in the afternoon, and I remember as we sat there the contentment I
felt, as though no matter what happened between now and
next week, everything was going to be all right. If I had
Roman's love, I could make it through anything.

"Serena, I want to tell you a proposition," James began.

"Yes?"

"It was so terrible about Porky . . ."

"Yes. He was such a good dog, and I shall miss him. I know you will too, James. He was quite fond of you, you know."

"I never had a dog of my own. Mother and Father promised me one for this birthday, but then of course they were killed."

"Yes."

"Anyway, with Porky gone now I thought we might get another dog. Not that any could replace Porky, but at least he would be a dog. I looked in the directory just now, and there's a pet shop downtown, right off the Strand. I think I've enough money saved to buy a puppy there. We could go down together and pick him out. He would be your dog, and I'd only ask to be able to play with him the way I did with Porky."

It was one of the greatest kindnesses anyone had ever paid me, and I couldn't resist a sudden urge to hug James's neck, a fact which dismayed him terribly.

"Don't get all mushy," he said, wriggling loose.

"All right, I won't. But, James, you'll never know how much I appreciate your thoughtfulness."

"Does that mean we can do it?"

"I'm afraid not. James, you've been swell at keeping secrets all summer. Now I shall tell you another, if you think you can stand it, and this is the biggest one of all. I'm telling you because it will explain why I can't let you buy me another puppy."

"I think I know. You're going away, aren't you?"

"Yes, did I give my secret away?"

"Only just then, when you said what you did. You really love Roman, don't you?"

"You sound like a little old man, James. Of course I do, more than anything in the world. And he loves me. We're going to be together always."

"Yes. I was afraid you would decide to go with him."

"You do approve, don't you? Look at me. I wouldn't want you disapproving, because you mean too much to me."

"I guess so. If you're sure he can be trusted."

His words puzzled me until I thought back a little. "Oh yes, you're remembering that girl Lucille, in your hometown. The one killed by the gambler."

"They never said for sure it was him, only assumed it was. They never caught him, you see."

"Surely you know Roman wouldn't harm anyone. Didn't he rescue you that day, carry you all the way home?"

"Yes, and I believe he's a good man. I just wouldn't want to ever take any chance when it comes to you. You're too special. And don't get mushy again."

"All right. But don't worry about me. Just be grateful I'm finally going to get my chance at happiness. Someday you'll get yours too, only it won't be like this—clandestine meetings, running away without letting people know where you're going. You'll meet some lovely young girl who just might be deserving of someone as dear as you, and you'll have a huge wedding attended by everyone in town, and live happily ever after in a cottage up on a hill somewhere."

"I don't know. I may not ever marry. I might be something else, might sail the seas or something, like Cousin Charles's brother. Claire is always talking about him, and how exciting his life was."

"Oh, I can't really see . . . Is that what you want to do, really?"

"I guess I don't know yet. I've had several ideas, but always change my mind."

"You'll probably do that many times before deciding."

"Will you ever come back?"

"I don't know. Roman hasn't yet explained all the arrangements for leaving, and I haven't thought far enough ahead to consider whether we'll come back. Someday . . . perhaps not right away . . . he'll help me get into a ballet school in New York, the one his sister attended."

"You'd let me know, wouldn't you, if you were ever stranded or needed me, or anything?"

"Certainly. Tell you something else. If you were about five years older, I should be very tempted to set my catch for you, if you'd have me."

"That's the nicest thing you've ever said to me."

It was the last conversation we had. Yesterday morning James came by and brought a slip of paper, but didn't stay as Tommy Driscoll awaited him for their morning crabbing trip. When I opened the paper I read his full name at the top, James Randolph Byron. Underneath in bold lettering was first his Galveston address, 707 Avenue L, then his former Grady address, Number 2 Blackburn Place. I doubt seriously I'll ever have need of either of them, except perhaps to write to him someday. I am touched by his concern for my welfare, however, and have slipped the paper down into the pocket of my carpetbag, alongside the other things there.

It is seven o'clock. The dawn is creeping upward, bathing the sky in new light. Surely nothing can happen in the last five hours, yet why does this uneasiness loom above me like a sword of Damocles?

Minutes from now, Dad will arise and Mother will awaken, and soon after Mrs. McCambridge will come into the hall, take off her hat in front of the mirror, fluff her hair, and see to Mother's breakfast. I shall go down to the beach at the usual time, so that no one will suspect anything. There I will meet Roman in the Pavilion tower room, where we will wait until almost noon, then go to Union Depot in the rented rig and join the other band members, who've come straight from their downtown hotel.

Tomorrow a group of men I've never met will board up the windows of the Seaside Pavilion, making it safe for the coming storm season. Even our tower window will be denied its patch of sunlight, and the place that was ours will be vacant till a year passes and a new season of summer entertainment begins. Will our room be used by two lovers, who will take joy in their secret hiding place as we did? I hope so, and wish them happiness that will last far beyond the brief interlude of summer. . . .

Once in New York, Roman and I will be married, and I will go wherever he goes for as long as I live. And today as our train speeds along, I will voice to him my conviction that I am carrying his child. I'm no longer frightened of doing this because, knowing he loves me, I cannot believe the news would not delight him as much as it now does me.

Last night I sat with Mother for a long time. I wanted so much to tell her everything, to say I loved her and was sorry to desert her; yet, instead, I held her hands in mine and looked silently into her eyes. When I rose to leave she gripped my hands tightly, and as I gently tugged away I saw a tear escape from her right eye and trace a path down her cheek.

The only thing left to consider now is the box of her poems. They are still unsolved riddles that only provoke questions with no answers, and I believe I'll burn them in the hope that destroying them might help me forget that my mother and father ever did anything to cause them shame, foolish as those feelings probably are in the face of what I'm about to do . . .

After this task is done, I'll go down to the kitchen and put the coffee on, and it will be, for a while, just like any other morning.

~ *Willa* ~

December 20, 1920—December 26, 1920

Chapter 1

Sundown.

I've traveled almost a thousand miles in the past week, yet this fifteen-minute drive between Union Station and Heights Boulevard seems the longest journey of all. There may be nothing at its end except an empty house with a For Sale sign posted out front. And what would the buyer find? A rambling house with fresh paint job, maybe even some furniture for sale inside? An undercroft that once frightened a girl so as she descended into it, she almost tripped over her own feet, scurrying up to the entrance door at the top?

Lord, it sounds like a haunted house in a mystery story.

Yet the biggest mystery now is the question of whether I can get it to work this time, whether I can sell myself to Rodney Younger again, whether he'll believe that I am finally telling the truth, whether he cares what I'm telling anymore.

He shouldn't care, of course. By all rights, if he is there in the house and answers my knocking, he ought to slam the door when he sees who is on the porch. And I wouldn't blame him. I'd be like a puppy who just wet on the carpet and had the paper taken to him, his head hung low because he knew he'd gotten what was coming to him.

But I would probably knock again, and keep knocking . . .

Now see here, Rodney (I would tell him), you're at least going to hear me out, if I have to stand out here on the porch and shout the whole story to you, and tell all the neighbors in the bargain.

What would you have done in my place?

There I am, about to sign away the rest of my life to a man I'm not even sure I love when I happen to find this Godforsaken-looking carpetbag that I've an odd feeling I have seen before. And when I look inside and touch the material of the nightgown lying on top, my memory is like an arrow hitting target: within the space of a few moments, I relive the catastrophe which followed my first discovery of the bag, years before, and I know then there must have been some reason why it was so important I not see the bag that first time or ever again.

I pull out the gown, and discover next a pair of dancing shoes, and finally, as though hidden away all these years just for me, a picture of two people I assume to be my real parents, two entertainment programs, brittle with age, and two addresses written in childish scrawl on a slip of paper, for a boy I never heard of. I know at once to whom the bag belonged, and that I have been the victim of an elaborate charade about my real beginnings, and the long suppressed hope rises in me again: my mother may yet be alive and missing me.

Now, I ask you again, what would you have done if you were suddenly possessed of at least a set of clues which may lead you to the answers of questions that have consumed you all your life, questions that have time and again been made to seem unreasonable—almost evil—when voiced?

What if your first acquaintance with the word "prostitute" had been in a snide reference to your real mother?

You'd have set out for the truth like a hound on a fox hunt, and don't deny it. Or maybe you wouldn't, I don't know. But it's what I had to do regardless of wedding plans or anything else, and if you've ever loved me you'll just have to try and understand.

Please?

Oh, God, it's snowing again.

It hardly ever snows in Houston, but there it is, no denying it, settling on the windows of this taxicab and forcing the driver to slow down, making the arduous journey to 1204 Heights Boulevard still longer. I shall take my handkerchief and wipe the clamminess from my hands, then try to sit back and relax, think of other things besides Rodney Younger . . .

Wonder if he's thinking about Rosemarie? Heaven knows, she never did anything to him like what I've done. And even if he is kind, patient to a fault, he'll have his breaking point like everyone else. He might have already decided he'd have been wiser to go on living with her ghost, rather than to become tangled up with me.

Will he have gotten hold of some more of that horrible

bootleg wine, and be sitting before a roaring fire in the Heights house, sipping from a paper cup and thinking of her? Surely he would be there, doing something, rather than be out in his old Ford somewhere, in this weather.

Of course he may have moved, taken an apartment. But I wasn't going to let myself . . .

His old Ford with the Stewart Starter was a real paradox to the society wedding planned for us by my mother and Velma Crosthwaite, her best friend, and I've a feeling Mother had coaxed Dad into a more suitable automobile for us as a wedding present—a Daimler or Duesenberg maybe—being unable to countenance the thought of our leaving Christ Church in an old Ford. It is heated by now, at least, which is more than I can say for it last winter. Rodney always wanted to make a showing in the real estate business before he spent money on a heater for the car. It was a matter of principle with him. Poor practical, sensible man.

I wonder what they did with all the cake and punch, and flowers, and what they told Velma and Carter Crosthwaite and all their other friends? Perhaps the news showed up on the Social Page of the Houston *Post:* "Willa Katherine Frazier, daughter of wealthy oilman Bernard P. Frazier and wife Edwynna, has fled on the eve of her wedding. Plans for nuptial ceremony at the Episcopal Christ Church and reception following at the Rice Hotel Grand Ballroom have been canceled by the bewildered parents of the bride."

It won't have been the first time Willa bewildered her parents.

I can't remember a time when I felt I pleased them both by just being around. It seems there was never a moment of unqualified joy when the three of us were together, never a time when I did not feel like a poor substitute no matter how many times they assured me they'd picked me to be theirs, and loved me just as much as a child born to them.

And other people—friends and relatives—seemed always to be reminding me how "lucky" I was to have been adopted by the Fraziers. I'd grow up wanting for nothing, in a world full of limitless opportunities for happiness. I was asked more than once, "Where would you be if the Fraziers had not come along?"

"I'd give anything to *know,*" I'd reply, and would be looked at sternly and told, "You're downright ungrateful,

Willa Frazier, that's what's the matter with you. You ought to straighten up and count your blessings."

What blessings, I wondered? My father stayed away from home working. My mother wouldn't have me on her lap. Didn't I know she suffered from a bad back, and spent many of her days wearing a confining corset? I should be more considerate of her feelings. Of course she loved me, why couldn't I understand? What an absurd question to be always asking anyway. Little girls should go off and play and remember the closet full of beautiful clothes, the expensive toys, the food on the table, the warm bed, and be thankful.

Well, I was unconvinced they loved me, and thus distrustful when they told me (time and again) the truth was my real parents were dead and they didn't know anything about them. Somewhere, I thought, there must be somebody who loves me, someone I really belong to.

As early as I can remember I stopped trying to please the Fraziers. I threw kicking tantrums to get my way, and they usually worked splendidly. By the time I was fourteen I'd begun cigarette smoking on the sly, and in the following three years I was expelled three times from Central High and wrecked my father's new black Pierce-Arrow. I wonder now how they managed to put up with me. (Could there be such a thing as "un-adopting" a child?)

What a relief Mother and Dad must have felt when Rodney Younger showed up and fell in love with me. Not that I'd caused much trouble recently—the last time I totally dismayed my mother was two years ago, when I refused to go to Galveston as a debutante at the Artillery Ball, or to come out among the society princesses of Houston either—but I had remained damned independent and aloof toward them right up to the night before the wedding a week ago.

Yet to think I would actually wind up with someone Dad termed "good stock," as though Rodney were a cow grazing in a field, and someone even Mother believed had good intentions . . . well, there's no doubt their minds were put at ease. It was Mother who always looked crosswise at my suitors, afraid they were after the money. This question never seemed to cross Dad's mind, although he's the one who struggled to make us rich. As likely as not, the only reason Mother thought money was the motive for courting her daughter was because her daughter was so uncommonly difficult to get along with. Surely no one could

be interested in Willa as a person. She would have shaken
her head and said, "Utter nonsense."

Poor Mother. Whenever she looks at me, her face works
into a mask of resignation. How long has it been this way
between us? Forever, surely. Of course, much of this is her
fault. She always prided herself on being "modern," telling
me at an early age that I was adopted, assuring me then
that she and Dad loved me just as much as if I were their
own blood kin—maybe more.

Not that I wouldn't have soon guessed I was not really
theirs. Mother is small and roundish, with a plump face, and
Dad is short and fat, with pale skin made especially so by
working inside all the time, and a jet black moustache and
fringe of hair to match. I am taller than either of them and
in no way resemble the Fraziers. I have long feet, hands
and fingers, an olive complexion no matter how much sun
I get, and light brown, almost auburn hair.

So there you are. It is not possible I could have been
fooled for long into believing I belonged to them. Besides,
the one who was theirs was named Sarah, and has been
immortalized in a photo with gilded frame which sits upon
Mother's dresser next to her silver comb and brush set Dad
gave her as a wedding gift. Julia dusts the frame and cleans
the glass weekly, and Number One sits there in white christening dress, the lacy thing which reaches twice the length
of her body and drapes across the chair holding her up.
She died an infant, and Mother couldn't have any more, so
they got me, and all my life I had assumed this to be the
whole story behind their doing so.

I only wondered why they'd gone to the trouble, since
they didn't seem to want me once I was theirs. One day,
when I was eleven or so, I spent a long time looking at that
picture in the gilded frame, and when I'd finished I thought
I had the answer. Perhaps when I was an infant I resem-
bled Sarah and it made them happy to look at me and
remember her. But then, as I began to grow up, I didn't
remind them of her any more so they stopped loving me
and wished they'd never gotten me after all, yet it was too
late to take me back.

I realize now they could never have known the torment I
suffered growing up, and if it had not been for the fact I
happened to find my mother's carpetbag a week ago, the
torment would have gone on and on. I would have pro-

ceeded through the wedding, playing the role of happy
bride as best I could, all the while having nothing to bring
Rodney in marriage except a transfer of the unhappiness
I'd doled out to Mother and Dad all my life. He is too
good for that, and I knew he was then, yet I could see no
other direction to take at the time . . .

I met Rodney one rainy day in Clancy's Sandwich
Shoppe, where I often ate lunch because I love roast beef
sandwiches and they have the best in town. It was, in fact,
because of the roast beef that we met.

There was only one sandwich left on the rack, and we
both reached for it at the same time. Actually, his hand
reached it before mine and I knew it, but he was too polite
not to offer me the sandwich anyway, and I was too rude
not to accept it as though it really should have been mine.
We finished filling our trays and looked around for a place
to sit.

The shoppe was packed that day. There were only two
chairs left, opposite each other at the end of a long table.
We sat down and Rodney politely took my tray and struck
up a conversation, which was hard to do above all the loud
voices and clatter of silverware and dishes, and the woman
sitting an elbow's length from him who kept blowing her
nose.

He was something of a novelty from the beginning, because I'd never dated a red-haired boy with freckles, and
anyway, he was kind of cute and terribly proper, and I had
no one else at the time. Right off, sitting there in Clancy's,
I displeased him by pulling out a Camel.

"Oh, so you smoke," he said, raising an eyebrow.

"Yes, isn't it wicked?"

"Don't your parents mind, or your boyfriend?"

"I have no boyfriend, and yes, my parents do mind, awfully."

"Which makes it all the more fun."

I took a puff and blew smoke out to the side. "Exactly."

"What else do you like, besides smoking and roast beef?"

"Oh, several things. I like fast cars . . . I once went
with a guy who had a Stutz Bearcat that would make a
hundred easy. He used to let me drive it sometimes. And I
like good clothes and hats . . . and music."

"What kind?"

"All kinds. I have a phonograph at home and a hundred records or so."

"You play any instruments?"

"No, only the phonograph."

He laughed. "I see." He was older than I. Not that he looked it, yet I could tell by the note of indulgence in the laugh. "Your parents musical, too?"

"Heavens, no. My father has a deaf ear, and Mother is constantly bit—griping because I play the phonograph too loud. Anyway, I'm not really theirs, so it wouldn't matter what they thought of music. I mean, whether or not it ran in the family."

"I see. Any brothers or sisters?"

"None that I know of. Adopted children don't always know who they really have."

"You're probably lucky, having a home and two people who've taken care of you."

"If you mean as opposed to growing up in an orphanage, I guess you're right. I don't know sometimes, though. Not that they're not good to me. It's just, well . . . I don't know. I've spent my life wondering who I really am, you know?" I said, and began to wonder why I should be confiding in him.

"I suppose so. But the people who raise you are really your parents, as I see it. Doesn't matter who brought you into the world. What counts is the attention you got after you arrived, and, from the looks of you, you've gotten your share."

"Well, it does matter . . . to me. Look, now we've covered my life history, how about yours? Do you give out your name, or is it a secret? I mean, that trench coat you're wearing . . . you could be a spy or something," I said, lowering my voice.

"Oh? My coat, huh? It dates back to prewar days. My name is Rodney Younger. And I give you my word, the only work I performed for Uncle Sam was down in the trenches."

"Rodney. Friends call you Rod?"

"Just Rodney."

"I thought so. You seem more a Rodney than a Rod. Something racy about the name Rod, don't you agree?"

"Maybe. I never thought about it. What's your name?"

"Willa Katherine Frazier."

"Friends call you Kathy?"

"No, heaven forbid. Willa."

"I thought so. It suits you. You're sort of willowy."

"Is that supposed to be a compliment?"

"You bet your life," he said, and smiled.

"Well, I've got to get back to work. My father gives his lucky employees only thirty minutes to gobble lunch."

"Oh, family business?"

"Not exactly. I just work in his office when I have nothing better going, and this summer I've had nothing better going."

"I see. Which building? Perhaps it'll be on my way to walk you there."

"Frazier Building, on Commerce," I told him, and awaited the proverbial reaction.

"Frazier . . . then your father is *the* Frazier—in oil?"

"The same. Too bad you had to ask, though. Now I'll be certain you're after my money if you should try to see me again." I was disgusted with my own cattiness even as I made the remark, and I wanted to apologize.

Yet it was too late. "Well, Miss Frazier, it would suit me fine if I never laid eyes on you again, but unfortunately I'm afraid we work in the same building," he said, his face reddening.

"Oh?"

"My father's real estate brokerage is on the third floor."

"Oh."

"You might want to switch to volunteer nursing or something, since you obviously don't need the job," he said, and with that comment put on his hat and left the table, a tall figure disappearing among the crowd, with broad shoulders covered by the most ghastly trench coat I have ever seen. I murmured under my breath he was probably on his way down to Buffalo Bayou, where he regularly washed that coat, but then I was sorry when I could no longer see him, and thought of how his face lit up when he smiled, and how I wished I hadn't offended him so quickly.

Before that day I'd been unaware of the existence of Rodney Younger, though I learned later he had worked in Dad's building for a month, since returning from the service. Now that we'd met, and I had managed to lower myself in front of him, I seemed to run into him at least three times a week. We'd pass on the stairs, or come face to face on the elevator, or by coincidence be leaving the building at the same time. He might nod or open a door for me, but he wouldn't speak, and I thought it was just as well I'd put him off before I even got to know him; sooner or later I'd wind up driving him off anyway.

I kept working for Dad right into the fall of 1919, and though this fact surprised him, he didn't object. He'd lost a filing clerk early in the summer and as long as I was around, he needn't bother having her replaced. He had only a small staff: one accountant, a secretary, a typist, and me, besides the field staff, whom I rarely saw. His employees worked hard because there was much to do and he didn't believe in hiring excess personnel. Miss Daniel, his spindly, bespectacled secretary, had been with him ten years and I think she fancied herself in love with him. Anyway, she'd go to the world's end for him if necessary, and on her tenth anniversary with the company my father gave her a gold wristwatch. I was on my way to Swanson's Jewelers in the Chronicle Building to have it engraved, when I saw Rodney, walking a few paces ahead.

I noticed then for the first time Rodney Younger had a slight limp; his right leg dragged just a little as he walked down the hall. It wasn't much; I had seen some far worse sights in the months since boys started coming home from the war. Yet something about the way he held his shoulders erect, his head up, as though refusing to acknowledge this physical shortcoming, was very touching as I stood watching him getting further and further away. And then I remembered the warmth of his voice that day we first met, his readiness to like me until I insulted him, and I knew I couldn't let this opportunity pass by to try and make amends. I hurried up even with him.

"Hullo."

He gave me one quick look askance. "Oh, it's you."

"Me, the rude one. I want to apologize. I usually don't insult people until I know them better."

"It's quite all right," he said, and kept walking.

"Look, I said I was sorry. Don't you believe in forgiving people?"

"I just told you it was all right. Now, I have business to tend to, if you don't mind."

"Oh, I guess I was wrong then. I thought you were nice, and was wasting all that time hating myself for being ugly to you. I guess you're not so great after all. Good day." I walked a little further, passing him by. Even then I hoped he would change his mind, call to me.

Several moments later, he did. "Wait up, Willa," he said, and I stopped walking and smiled to myself, but didn't look around.

"You're right. I could be a little more forgiving, I guess. We had a big sale fall through out in the Heights this morning, and I'm down in the dumps. Have you time for a cup of coffee? We could stop by the Rice."

"There's just one thing you ought to understand," he said, after we were seated at a corner table. "You may think everyone wants your father's loot, but you can be sure I've no interest in that direction. As a matter of fact, if I were to marry a rich girl—though it's very unlikely—I would take nothing of hers. She'd have to make do on my money."

"Is that so? You'd deny a girl her rightful inheritance?"

"She could do with it as she liked—buy fancy clothes and shoes, give it to charity, whatever, as long as she didn't spend it on anything that included me."

"But as you said, chances of it happening are unlikely. You said you sold houses. Tell me about it."

"There isn't much to tell. I'd only just begun before the war, and when I got back last month I went in with my father. He's done pretty well . . . this is a darned good town for real estate, especially since the war. But we had this deal going for a house out on Heights Boulevard—gorgeous thing, built in '98, three-storied, huge lawn, beautifully landscaped. We've had the deal pending for twenty-five days, and it looked promising. It was my sale, and would've been my first commission. Then the buyer phoned this morning to say he'd been transferred by his company to North Dakota or some place out there, and he'd have to back out."

"That's too bad. How much did you lose?"

"Nine hundred."

"Well, that isn't so much," I said, then regretted it because it was obvious from his face the amount meant a great deal to him. "I mean, it's a lot, but not so much it can't be recovered. Anyway, by the time you get your sign back up in the front yard you'll probably have three more prospects. You do have other listings, don't you?"

"Yes . . . several in South Houston, two in Park Place, three lots on Bellaire Boulevard, and even a house on Lovett Boulevard—a good one—but I'd have to sell several of the smaller properties to make as much commission as I would have on the Heights house."

"Lovett? I live near there, on Montrose."

"Well, I might have guessed—the most exclusive area in town."

"Our house isn't new or anything. We've been there eight years."

"Boy, I bet if your father sold right now, he could make a whopping profit. Property values over there have really gone high. He isn't thinking of selling, is he?"

"Hold on, now! You'll have us moved out of house and home like evicted tenants if I don't watch you. Tell me more about real estate. What else do you do?"

"We take care of rent properties. You know, the tenants come to us to pay their rent, and we draw commission from the owner for taking care of them. But that's a pain in the neck. Dad got into it while I was away. People can be very bothersome. Their pipes don't work or their heater is broken, or someone threw a rock through a window, or the roof leaks—a thousand problems all the time. He was talking for a while before the war about building some apartments here, but now, under the circumstances, I guess the project will never be carried out . . ."

"What circumstances?"

"Oh, nothing. Long story."

"Where are you going now?"

"Out to Harrisburg, to look at a new listing with the owner. It's all right, though. I'd left a little early because I needed some fresh air."

"But wouldn't it be worth your while getting that sign up in the Heights again as soon as possible? I mean, surely properties in Park Place aren't worth as much as that one?"

He raised an eyebrow. "My, my, you have the mind of a businesswoman. I may be able to use you sometime in my firm. No, the Park Place property will probably go for forty-five hundred or so, but I've had the appointment since yesterday and I've got to keep it. I'll have to go out to the Heights later this evening."

"Tell me more about that one."

"Well, it's kind of an ugly mustard green color now, but needs painting anyway. It would really be lovely in white, I think. The roof is deep red. It has a fanlight with stained glass windows, and a steeple on one side, right above the inside staircase so that when you climb up to the second or third floor, you have this feeling of unfathomable height.

"Stairs are polished mahogany—beautiful winding things, with turkey feather graining in the railing and on the base. Oh yes, and the house even has an undercroft."

"What's that?"

"A little vaultlike room beneath the back side of the house. You enter it from a stairway off the kitchen."

"Cellars are pretty unusual for this area, aren't they?"

"It isn't a cellar. Too small. The family who built the house used it for wine storage. But the next family who moved in were teetotalers, and tore down the wine racks to replace them with shelves for food. That's the way it's fixed now . . . You seem so interested in the house. Would you like to go out with me this afternoon and look at it?"

"I thought you'd never ask. What time?"

"Three o'clock?"

"Fine. I'll meet you downstairs by the cigar stand."

"Right. Now I really must get out of here and meet that client. You surprise me by your interest in real estate. Most women I've gone around with never want to discuss business."

"Guess I'm my father's daughter in some ways—I mean, my adopted father. Don't tell him, but what you do is a lot more interesting than what he does."

"Not nearly so profitable, though."

"By the way, something I promised myself I'd ask you, if you won't be offended—and believe me, I'm trying to wait a while before I do that again—where did you get your limp? Fighting for God and country in the war, all that?"

"Yes, shot in the leg. But I don't care to talk about it."

"That's good. The war bores me, anyway."

All the rest of that morning I kept thinking of my off-handed remark to Rodney about being my father's daughter. It nagged at me for it wasn't true, and I didn't want to leave that impression with him. Saying something like that made me feel disloyal to my real father, whoever, wherever he was. I certainly wasn't business-oriented, I told myself. Only a few days before, I'd seen a picture story in the newspaper about the First International Congress of Working Women meeting in Washington, with women attending from all over the world, and the only remark I'd made to Mother at the breakfast table was that the hat worn by the fat woman on the far right was too small for her bulky size, and made her look like a stuffed pig.

After lunch Miss Daniel, who adopted the role of supervisor when Dad was out, put me to work rearranging and updating the index card file on one of the oil fields he has interests in. It was a tedious, monotonous project, more time-consuming than I realized, and when I walked out of the file room and looked at the clock the hands were stationed at three-thirty. I gasped, threw aside the file in my hand, and ran all the way down to the cigar stand.

As I feared, he'd already gone. I rushed to the door and looked both ways down the sidewalks, just to be sure, but no one was around except a blind man selling pencils and a mounted policeman at the intersection, whose horse looked as bored as he did from the lull in afternoon traffic.

"Damn, damn," I said, and a woman walking past with a little boy looked aghast at me and covered the boy's ears with her hands.

Miss Daniel was standing behind her desk when I re-entered the office and said with expectant pleasure, "Miss an appointment, dear?"

"None of your business," I told her, and walked back into the file room. She mumbled something about not wishing to interfere, but I only half listened. It was her standard remark, and its lack in truthfulness got on my nerves.

Later I went to the third floor and wrote down the office room number for Sidney Younger and Son, Realtors. Then I penned Rodney a note and sent it out by inter-building mail delivery. "Remember," it said, "I am a working girl and when duty calls . . . I came at three-thirty but you'd already given me up. If you still like roast beef I'll meet you at noon tomorrow at Clancy's. If not, I'll have to eat alone."

It wasn't really an apology, but then my tardiness was not truly my fault. It is hard for me to apologize when I'm guilty of something, and impossible when I'm not.

I arrived at Clancy's before he did, and picked a table for two against one wall. The place was not as crowded as usual. I wasn't sure my note would set well with him; he didn't seem the sort of person to put up with a lot of people. Was this why he continued to interest me, when I normally became bored so soon? I puzzled over these things for a quarter of an hour before he showed up, and when I saw him come through the door I thought, What do I care what the reasons are? I am interested in this man, so why try and pick it apart? If he hadn't come today I should have had to find some other way to get on his good side.

I concentrated on letting none of this show in my expression as he neared the table. "Oh, you haven't got your sandwich yet. I know what you want. I'll get it."

"You'd better hurry. I only have a few minutes."

When he returned with the laden tray he was the one apologizing. "A man came to the office just as I was leaving. It seems the American Legion is on a drive to get all the soldiers in Houston to join, and they're bucking to get the next convention held here. He went on and on about why I was obligated to become a member, and told me about the proposal for making November eleventh a memorial day for all the dead soldiers, and so forth, which I'd already read about in the papers. I couldn't get rid of him. Sorry he ran me late."

"It's all right," I told him playfully. "I would have been mad if all the roast beef sandwiches had been taken, but since they weren't, I'll let you off easy. Did you join the Legion?"

"No, I'm not much interested in belonging to any clubs just now because I wouldn't have time to participate as I should. I don't feel any obligation, certainly. God knows, I've fulfilled any obligation owed to the country for this last war." He heaved a sigh and took a bite of sandwich. "Well, so we missed out again."

"I was afraid you'd be mad, but I really couldn't help it. Time got away."

"I was impatient, only waited a few minutes. But I can't wait around long for anyone. I'm losing money every minute that house is on the market, and if it doesn't go soon, I face the danger of losing the listing. Owners can be impatient, too."

"Any new prospects?"

"No, but I've got two good deals working in South Houston."

"Well then, your spirits will be a bit brighter."

"Considerably. You know, I was thinking as I walked down Main just now, seeing you is different from anything I've ever done."

"How's that?"

"Well, I keep feeling I've sort of backed into the whole thing, you know? Doesn't it seem backward to you?"

"You may find I am backward in more ways than one."

His eyes were puzzled, but he didn't pursue the point. "When I got your note yesterday I wasn't really surprised."

"Oh, you mean you hadn't thought I'd stood you up?"

"No. I figured you got tied up. But one thing you must understand is that right now, my work is the most important thing. If I'm ever to get anywhere, I've got to hustle. I've already lost three years because of the war."

"How old are you?"

"Twenty-nine."

"I thought you were older."

"And you?"

"Just turned nineteen. I'm a turn-of-the-century child."

"Good Lord, I'll be accused of cradle robbing."

"Oh, I left the cradle a long time ago."

"Are you free tomorrow night?"

"Tomorrow, let me see . . . I have a date already. But I can skip it. It isn't important."

"Oh, no. I'm not going to have you doing that on my account. You go on your date and we'll get together some other time."

"But it's just a date. He's nobody special. I can break it, like that," I said, with a snap of my fingers.

"Don't you dare. He *is* somebody special, who's counting on you. I don't want anything to do with a girl who ditches people when somebody better comes along. I heard too many Dear John letters being read during the war."

"Ever get one?"

"No. My situation was . . . well . . . different."

"Then I suppose you don't want anything further to do with me, since I do break dates now and then when something better comes along. I'm not going to apologize to anyone for being me."

"Let me tell you something, Willa," he said, narrowing his eyes, "That isn't you, at least not all you could be if you wanted to. You love for people to think you're tough, that nothing matters to you, but you're not like that at all."

"How do you know?"

"I just do."

"I don't think I'm tough or anything. Just the same, I prefer that people keep their distance."

"Anyone could see that. One day someone will come along who'll change your mind."

"I doubt it."

"All right, but you go ahead with your date Friday night. I'll see you on Saturday. No, I can't Saturday, for I'm busy. Sunday. Sunday afternoon I'll pick you up and we'll go out to the Heights house. What do you think?"

"Fine."

"By the way, I hope you won't be offended, but I haven't a Stutz to my name, not even a Duesenberg. Only an old beat-up 1916 Ford with a Stewart Starter and no heater."

"How fast will it go?"

"It has been known—once or twice—to make fifty."

"How daring."

It was galling, the fact my lie had fouled me up again.

I had no date for Friday night. I only wanted him to think I did, or rather I had told him that without even thinking. I never expected him to insist that I not break it, and as a result to be left sitting at home alone. Even when Maybelle Crosthwaite, Velma's daughter and something akin to a friend, called and asked me to go see *The Gamblers* at the Crown, I had to tell her no, for what if we should run into Rodney there? He might never speak to me again.

At times I wasn't certain whether Rodney took a paternal attitude toward me, or considered himself a serious suitor. It might have been different without the ten-year gap between our ages, or if neither of us had known about the gap. But he always expected a lot from me, as a father would from his daughter.

Not *my* father, of course, who thought giving money and gifts was the way to be a good father. I can see now it was his way of showing love, but then I resented the lack of attention . . . his Sundays spent working instead of taking me to the park when I was a child; all the school programs and plays attended only by Mother. The gifts didn't go far in making up for his absence, and didn't help convince me I was really loved like "blood kin."

Perhaps, then, I did look upon Rodney as a father type. He made me behave, whereas no other man had forced that upon me, and this unusual aspect of the relationship sustained my interest during the first few weeks, before things got involved in other ways.

That Sunday he drove up promptly on time and we set out for the house he was so enthused about. It was a lovely fall day, with just a chill in the air and plumes of white clouds, soft as underfur, thrust across the blue sky. I had suggested we have a picnic, and even went so far as to offer to bring the lunch.

I was like a high school girl awaiting the hour of her first date. I'd picked a special dress of soft jersey with a large, lacy collar and long tapered sleeves to wear, and pulled my hair back into a twist, with curls left around my face, in an effort to look alluring and feminine. I'd packed sandwiches and fruit, and hot chocolate, and was ready when he knocked at the door.

The fact I was ready on time didn't seem to surprise him, yet he did comment on the dress while he took the picnic basket from my arms and threw the quilt over his shoulder. "It isn't like you," he said, "or at least what I've seen of you so far."

"You don't like it?"

"I do like it. I'm just used to your looking businesslike."

"Well, I'm going to try not to be too businesslike today, because it doesn't fit my mood."

"Nor mine. I can't wait to show you the house."

It was as he had said, large with rambling lawn, dwarfing the other houses around it. A paint job was sorely needed, but I agreed with him as we emerged from the Ford the house had unlimited possibilities.

"Wouldn't the seller have been better off if he'd painted before moving away?"

"Yes, but there wasn't time before he left town. If we can't sell it as it is, we're going to hire a paint contractor and bill him for it."

"This porch is bigger than ours, nice and breezy, but there's too much foliage hanging around it. It ought to be more open, don't you think? To show off the cut glass doors better."

"The house itself is nothing to compare with the one you live in, Willa, but I can see your point."

We bantered back and forth like a couple interested in buying the house for ourselves. Wouldn't a highboy be perfect against a wall here, or two Queen Anne chairs across from each other in front of this fireplace or that, a jardiniere either side of this door, a whatnot shelf in that corner, an étagère here?

"You convince me more all the time real estate ought to be your field," he said finally. "You've a knack for imagining things, and your enthusiasm could be contagious to customers. Next time I have an interested client, I may impose upon you to come out with me."

"I can't see myself trudging around all the time trying to please picky buyers, or putting up with people who back out of contracts. If I made suggestions to your customers, I would expect them to be carried out."

He smiled. "What a lot you have to learn about the public."

"I know all I want to about the public, thank you. Let's look at the undercroft. Through this door?"

"Yes, hold on a minute. I've got the key."

He fiddled with the latch for a moment, then opened the door and turned on a wall switch, yielding only a taper of light. I felt fright clutch at me as I looked down below, but didn't want him to know. He'd think I was silly. I took in a breath. It was stone cold and musty as we descended the shallow stairs and suddenly a feeling of queasiness came over me. I stopped and put a hand to my stomach.

Rodney turned around. "Something wrong?"

"No, no, of course not. I just felt a little dizzy, that's all."

"Okay now?"

"Sure. Go on."

He turned around again and started down. The further we got the more nauseated I became and once we reached the bottom of the stairs I knew I had to get out of there, and quickly. "Look, it's nasty down here. Why don't we go back up?" I asked.

"Sure, if you like. There isn't anything down here anyway but empty shelves, and maybe a hungry rat or two. But with proper lighting and heat, it could be—"

"Please, let's just get out of here, okay?"

He said nothing more and we ascended to the first floor again, but he saw right through me and teased me about my fears back in the kitchen. "Well, you've ruined my chances, I guess. I was all set to keep you down there in chains as a special attraction for clients."

"Look, you don't have to make fun of me. Is it a crime for a person to feel trapped? I don't even like riding in an elevator—it's why I take the stairs most of the time. I don't know why I'm that way, I just am. Let's get out of here and have our picnic."

On the back lawn at 1204 Heights Boulevard we spread our quilt under the moss-hung trees. My mood was now as

damp as the undercroft, and I was silent as we pulled the
picnic things from the basket.

"Hot chocolate?" I asked finally.

"Sounds great. Here, let me open that jug for you."

"No, I can get it," I said, but as I closed my hand
around the cap I had a stabbing pain. I let go.

"What's the matter?"

"I don't know," I said, looking at my hand. "I must have
hurt it doing something else, and didn't realize. It feels like
I'd banged it against a wall," I told him, holding it down
on my lap and trying not to let him know it ached as much
as it did. In a moment he'd begin to think I was daffy.

Later, after we'd eaten the sandwiches and drunk the jug
dry, he leaned against a tree and considered me. "You're
strange, Willa."

"I know, but I won't apologize."

"You put on a show as a self-confident, sometimes even
pushy person, but you're not really like that. I think you're
a little afraid all the time."

"I don't know what you mean. What have I got to be
afraid of? I've probably done things you've never dreamed
of doing. Besides, if my personality bothers you so much,
why do you keep seeing me?"

"I didn't say that. You always jump to conclusions. I was
thinking the other day, now there's a girl who is friendly,
yet cautious. She's nice in a way, but don't ever cross her."

"Oh, so *you're* afraid of *me?*"

"On the contrary. I wouldn't be afraid of displeasing you
at the price of making you mad. I don't owe anybody that.
I just meant . . . well, if I were going to try and remain
on your good side, I should remember how you are."

"And are you?"

"I don't know. It's not in my line. But you do need
somebody, I can tell that. You need somebody more than
anyone I've ever known, Willa Frazier."

"I just love the way you're always sizing me up. Well, I
don't need anybody. I'm perfectly fine as I am, and was
getting along great before you dropped into my life."

"What's eating you, Willa?"

"Nothing, nothing! Why must you pry so? Can't we just
try and have a good day without your analyzing me?"

"Of course, you're right. I'm sorry. It's only that you
interest me."

"Yeah, like a monkey in the zoo. Now, I've a splitting headache. Let's go home."

"I'm sorry. I'm responsible for ruining this go-round. Oh well, at least you did finally see the house."

"Yes, and I did like it, really. I can understand your enthusiasm about it."

"Even the undercroft?"

"I could get used to it. I'm not all that afraid. What I mean is, I'm sure any client would like it, with proper lighting and so forth. Anyway, if it were my house and the room bothered me I would either have it sealed off or send a servant down whenever anything was needed from it."

"It may surprise you to learn not all my clients have servants at beck and call. Some are just plain folks like me."

I was going to say the obvious—anyone who would buy a house that large would surely have help—but I dropped it, and wondered why it was so often we wound up insulting each other. Why couldn't I just get bored with the whole thing and drop Rodney as I had just about everyone else?

He decided to try again the next week, and asked me over to his house for dinner on Friday night. It had been two days since the Sunday picnic, and I'd told myself many times it was foolish to carry on this friendship any longer. Still, I said yes, without hesitating.

The Sidney Younger home, off Caroline, was just as I expected—pleasant and unpretentious. We were met at the door by Rodney's father and a waft of garlic coming from the kitchen. Mr. Younger didn't favor Rodney very much except he was tall and lean, with a trace of freckles that seemed to have faded with age. He parted his thinning gray hair down the center and wore multicolored armbands with bright orange mingled through like fudge in a marble cake.

His skin had a certain pallor, although I attached no significance to this at the time. His eyes were bright, lively, almost laughing as he said, "Well, come on in, children," as though we were tardy for dinner and had come in together a hundred times before. There was no getting to know Sidney Younger. You just met him and knew him right away.

Agatha Younger was straitlaced and far less friendly than her husband. It was from her that Rodney took his red hair, although the years have mellowed hers to almost a light brown. Mr. Younger called her Red that evening. Red is what he almost always called her. A small stout woman, she served us tomato juice cocktails as Sidney apologized, "Red's very strict about upholding prohibition around here, even if it's foolish."

The parlor was homey, full of framed snapshots of Rodney in his military uniform and cheap ceramics, with crocheted doilies on the backs and arms of the furniture. A Packard piano stood in one corner, lit by a lamp with heavy fringed shade that gave the keys a spotlight effect. A huge portrait of Christ, complete with Sacred Heart and faint glimmer of halo, hung above the fireplace. Pinned to another wall was a small crucifix. I stared at it, only then realizing the Youngers were Roman Catholic.

As though reading my thoughts, Agatha began, "And what faith do you profess, dear?"

"Mother, really——"

"Just curious. I'm sure Miss Frazier won't mind telling me a little about herself."

"I was christened Episcopalian, but I don't go to church anymore."

Rodney was scowling at me from the corner, but I could see no point in trying to impress anyone. It was my business if I didn't believe in that ceremonial frivolity. I wasn't even sure God existed.

"I see," she said. "Well, I suppose there comes a time for many when they stray. Of course, I can't recall experiencing . . . Oh well, Sidney, come along and help me finish dinner."

When they were out of earshot I said, "I've insulted her, haven't I?"

"It's all right. Mother goes a bit overboard on religion."

"How about you?"

"I've broken from Catholicism, to her disappointment."

"So you're like me, then?"

"I don't know your feelings. Before the war I thought a person needn't believe in anything, for it had no bearing one way or the other, but after I saw a few guys get shot up within feet of me and spent three years fighting for something I knew deep down was senseless at best, I got to thinking we all need someone or something to believe in. It's the faithless people who've messed up the world—or else those with misguided faith. I guess you could say I'm a former Catholic, converted to religion in general."

I turned and gazed into the dying log fire beneath the portrait of Christ and wished, for a moment, that I could have Rodney's convictions. Maybe then I wouldn't feel so desolate inside. . . .

After dinner we had a sing-song, which, I soon learned, was a Friday night tradition in the Younger household. Sidney's favorite was, "Hello, My Baby," and this we sang three or four times. He had a buoyant voice, which wasn't too loud although he seemed to be putting much effort behind it, and Rodney's sisters Amanda and Jane, twelve- and thirteen-year old look alikes with long brunet plaits and mischievous brown eyes, flipped the songbook pages back and forth between songs, arguing over what we'd sing next.

It was the first of many evenings I spent at Rodney's house, and when I look back on them I recall best the way Sidney rolled his hands over the piano keys as he sang, "Hello, My Baby," his armbands dazzling in the light. I believe now I'll think more often of him, although I never felt a twinge of sadness or spent a tear when he died before the end of the year. He'd had cancer for over a year and had shared the knowledge with Rodney and Agatha all those months. One night shortly after Thanksgiving he was rushed to the hospital in an ambulance.

Rodney and I had tickets to see six reels of Harry Houdini that night, and, being a great fan of the escape artist, I was eagerly looking forward to the show. Rodney phoned as I was dressing to explain why he couldn't make it.

"I'll come down to the hospital and meet you," I said.

"No, you go on to the show—"

"I'll come," I repeated, and when I hung up the phone I muttered, "damn." Mother, who was coming down the hall just then said, "Willa, what in the world? Standing there in your slip like that. What's the matter?"

"No Houdini. Rodney's father is at St. Joseph's Infirmary. I've got to go there now."

"But your father isn't home yet with the car—"

"Oh yeah; will you order me a cab?"

"All right. But do you think you ought to? I mean, do you know the family all that well?"

"Skip it, Mother. I have to go."

"All right then," she said, and picked up the directory. On the way out I tossed the Houdini tickets on the table and offered them to her and Dad.

"But your father has a meeting tonight."

"Well, get Velma to go with you."

"Velma? I hardly think she'd be interested in that sort of show. She and Carter are attending the Houston Grand Opera tonight. You ought to see her dress—"

"Okay, leave them. Maybe we can exchange them if the films play here long enough."

The films did not play long enough, and I had no more than entered the halls of St. Joseph's and found Agatha Younger sitting stoically against one wall near the admittance office than I knew that Sidney Younger would not last long either.

I sat down beside her, realizing for the first time I had nothing to say. I hadn't stopped long enough to consider this after Rodney's call. She'd been crying, for her eyes were red, her cheeks pinched and damp, but she wasn't crying at that moment.

"I'm so sorry, Mrs. Younger. I didn't know Sidney was ill."

"It was a family matter," she said almost huffily. "They gave him six months, but he's survived this long. We are grateful for God's blessings to us."

I looked down at her hands and saw the wrung-out lace handkerchief in one, the black beaded rosary wound around the other. Was this what you did when about to lose someone? Pray for strength, or count the beads along a cold piece of jewelry?

I leaned back against the wall, no harder than the wooden bench that had been provided for the loved ones of patients going through the machinations of entering the hospital. My mother had been right. I had no place here tonight, though perhaps not for the reasons she named. I knew nothing of losing people, what to say, how to cope. I could feel nothing except sudden flashes of resentment when I thought of missing out on Houdini.

I didn't know Agatha Younger or how to understand the roots of her faith. She sat next to me rigidly, as though held together by something so tenuous she feared to move. Somewhere in the distance I could hear Rodney's voice now and then, talking with some admittance clerk whose feelings toward Sidney Younger were no more or less personal than mine. I decided to be practical.

"Maybe they can pull him through again. If he has lived

this long, maybe he has a chance of getting well, even. You mustn't quit hoping."

"My dear, giving up on one's life is not the same as giving up hope for them. God has given me Sidney for thirty-five years. I must appreciate all the time with him and keep on believing he is bound for a greater, happier place than here. If he should pull through, I will again be grateful for God's pardon, and pray that it won't mean a dragging out of suffering for him. He's been so fortunate for having little pain these past few months. I do pray God will spare him that. . . ."

Her voice drifted off. I looked away.

Thankfully, Rodney soon appeared, and he seemed grateful I'd come.

"You needn't have," he said softly. "It was kind of you. Father's been taken to room 201, and Mother can see him now. Are you ready, Mother? Willa, I—"

"I'll go now. Call me at home if you need anything."

He nodded, and I watched as he helped his mother up and put a protective arm around her shoulders, then led her down the hall: two solemn figures, one tall, wearing an ugly trench coat wrinkled from sitting, walking so slowly his limp was indiscernible; the other, slight, wearing a long blue coat with a fur collar and carrying a wrung-out handkerchief and a chain of beads. Why could I feel nothing?

You must find something before being torn by losing it, I decided in the cab going home. How can anything have a value until you possess it? The questions, never far below, began surfacing as they often did. Who am I? Where did I come from? What have I to do with all that is going on around me? Have I a place, and if so, where?

What if I had lost my own mother or father? Would I feel nothing because they are not truly my own? How horrible to think in several years I could be facing what Rodney faces now, and have to shed false tears and feign sorrow because I could call up nothing from inside. How lovely if things could have been simple for me as they have been for him, with a real mother and father to love, to know exactly where he came from and what to expect from himself, what his limitations are. . . .

How wonderful to be no one's second choice, to have no picture on a bureau somewhere of a child in christening gown, reminding him he has not first rights on the intangible property called parents.

Was I alive or dead inside, I wondered? Was the blood running under the skin icy like the wind blowing by the cab window outside? Why didn't the memory of all the evenings when Sidney Younger sat on the piano stool and belted out his favorite tunes bring forth even a sting behind my eyes? Why couldn't even the recollection of other, opposite things bring forth some emotion? The way he sang with vigor but made somehow less noise than might have been expected from a man his size; or, the fact he ate so little at all the delicious dinners. How he'd say, "Ol' Red has done up my favorites tonight—chicken casserole and molded salad—" then hardly touch the plate of food before him, and if Amanda or Jane chanced to make some comment about Daddy not eating all the food on his plate as they were bound to do, Agatha Younger would simply quieten them and say nothing in admonishment to her husband.

The pallor of his skin. The bright eyes glowing from out of the pallor. The man who lived a life of love and generosity to his family, who kept them together as a unit even with the wide age gap between Rodney and his sisters. I could appreciate the man, but I could not grieve for him. Was he at this moment drawing his final breath? Would he live on, come home from the hospital? Would I see him yet again, and if I did, would it be like always? Or would he be a tired, bedridden invalid, impatiently living out his last painful days and snapping at those around him because they had what he'd been denied?

Oh God, I had not thought of seeing him again. Now that I knew, seeing him again. What would I say, how would I act? Could I pull a typical Willa tactic and make my exit from Rodney's life now, while it was safe?

"Ma'am, that's three bits," said a voice from somewhere far away. "Ma'am, are you all right?"

"Oh, of course, how much? All right. Yes, keep the change. Thank you."

I got out of the stuffy cab and shivered in the wind, and, walking up the sidewalk and mounting the stairs, thought of the song:

"Hello my baby, hello my honey, hello my ragtime gal. . . ."

Chapter 2

Within the month Sidney Younger was dead. I saw only brief glimpses of Rodney at the funeral and did not go to the graveside services. Miss Daniel was off with the flu, and I was helping Dad answer the telephones and run the office. I left work only long enough to ride a cab down to Annunciation for the Mass. I had no idea what was going on, but apparently many in the church did, for there were beaded rosaries and dog-eared missals held up lovingly along the pews, as the priest uttered Latin phrases and bells jingled now and then. Thankfully, the coffin was closed, saving me from having to figure out how to avoid being ushered up to the front of the church to view Sidney Younger in death. For a reason I could not name, I knew I would not be able to face that.

When I returned to work, Dad said, "Come in my office a minute, will you?"

Figuring on a project about to be assigned, I grabbed a pencil and Miss Daniel's notebook. "No, I just wanted to ask you about Rodney," he said. "He all right?"

"Yes, I think so, though I didn't talk to him today."

"I sent a big bouquet."

"That was kind of you."

He turned away from me in his chair, and looked out the window behind his desk. "It's a universal sorrow, losing a father. I wanted him to know we were thinking of the family. The flowers were the only way I knew. I think your mother was going to write a note, but I don't know whether she did."

"Yes, that's nice too."

"Tell me, are you serious about this boy?"

"I don't know yet. It's too early to tell."

"Yeah, I guess so. You've been seeing a lot of him, though. He strikes me as being good stock. I don't hold much with Catholics, but then everyone to his own taste."

"Yes, or even no taste at all."

"Yeah, well, nothing more . . . just wanted you to know I was concerned. I hope they didn't forget to enclose a card on those flowers."

"I'll mention them to him, if you want. He'll appreciate it."

"I did it not only for him, but for you, too."

This seemed an unusual remark, yet, anxious to put the interview at an end and get back to work, I didn't bother to question it. "Oh well . . . would you see if you can find the Talyacker field file for me?" he said after a pause, turning around to face me again. "I looked for it but never have been able to understand Miss D's mysterious filing methods. I think she figures if I can't find anything while she's gone, she won't ever be in danger of getting fired."

"She may have a point there, at that."

I left then and found the file. Miss Daniel's filing methods are actually as predictable as she, but my father hates paperwork so much that he won't take the trouble to learn where anything is. There must have been a time when he had to put up with mountains of it, years ago, when he was first beginning in the oil business. He came from Ohio with nothing, and built everything for himself. He is what people call "self-made."

What he'd said about Rodney was kind enough, and his way of voicing approval if I wished to get serious about him. Later that evening Mother did likewise, in her own fashion.

"Rodney certainly seems a fine boy," she said. "In fact, I'm almost surprised he—"

"Stays around a bitch like me?"

"Willa, watch your language! I meant nothing of the kind. But you'll have to admit, your romances don't break any records for longevity."

"Maybe I just hadn't found anybody worth keeping around, before Rodney."

"That fellow who worked for the creamery, he was nice. Whatever happened to him?"

"Cliff and I had a disagreement."

"I see."

"Listen, Mother, if that's all, I really need to wash my hair."

"Of course, but one more thing . . . do you think you'll be here on Christmas Day? The Crosthwaites will be out of town, and I thought maybe just the three of us could spend the day together. It's been so long. Your father promised to take the whole day off."

"I don't see why not. I haven't anything else to do unless Rodney calls."

"Maybe, if he does, you could invite him here? It would mean a lot to me, having you home on Christmas. We have a special surprise for you this year."

"I imagine Rodney will want to spend Christmas with his mother, especially this year, but if it means so much, yes, I'll be here."

I wondered idly whether they'd bought me a car, but I didn't expect so. After I wrecked Dad's Pierce-Arrow, long ago as it was, I was told not to expect a car of my own any time in the future. The surprise this year was more likely a new piece of jewelry or something to wear.

Visiting relatives, tiresome arrangements, things to keep Rodney from calling. Did his mother lean on him more now, I wondered? Would she become grasping, possessive, like some mothers who lose their husbands and are left their sons? Her attitude before her husband's death seemed to indicate she had no intention of letting go of her son very easily. Then she was probably looking to this day of loneliness, and planning her strategy accordingly. Was she plotting her ground the night she questioned me about my faith, hoping early on to weed me out as a prospective daughter-in-law?

Yet why was I wondering? Rodney had never mentioned marriage to me, and even if he had, I wasn't sure I would accept his proposal or anyone else's.

I might grow bored with Rodney Younger and his mother: a comforting thought to keep me from feeling trapped . . . yet I cared when he didn't call for five days, between the funeral and Christmas, although I told myself it was just as well, that if he never called again it would be fine with me.

Yet each time the phone rang, it gave me a start. Once when Maybelle Crosthwaite phoned to ask me to a vaudeville at the Prince, I told her abruptly I was busy, and I think it hurt her feelings. Maybelle really has no one. She is profoundly homely—a big-boned girl with plain features and stringy hair, living all the time in the shadow of her domineering mother—and because her mother is my mother's best friend, I've been thrown into the position of having to be her friend.

When, finally, Rodney did call, at six o'clock in the evening on Christmas, I was busy helping Mother and Julia in the kitchen and didn't even hear the phone ring.

Dad called from the hall, "It's for you. It's Rodney."

I rushed past Mother and Julia, who looked at me in puzzlement, then tried to sound perfectly calm when I reached for the receiver.

"Hullo."

"Willa . . . Merry Christmas!" he said, sending a tingle all through me.

"Oh, Rodney, I thought maybe you'd left town or something," I answered, still trying to sound cool.

"Don't be coy. Can I come over? I have a present for you. It isn't much, but I wanted you to have it. I'm sorry it's been so long, but I'll explain when I see you."

"I'm spending the evening with Mother and Father. Maybe tomorrow. Oh, that's right, back to work. All right, but make it late. About nine."

"Okay. Mother wishes you season's greetings and all that. We've just gotten home from church, and she's sitting here next to me."

"Oh."

"I'll see you at nine."

I hung up the receiver and glanced at the new jeweled watch on my wrist—my parents' offering for the season, which probably cost almost as much as a car. Three hours. Why had I told him nine o'clock? How inane. How could I live another three hours cooped up in this house?

I went back to the kitchen and picked up a stalk of celery. "Rodney coming by for dinner?" Mother asked.

"No. He'll be here at nine."

"He could have come to dinner if you'd wanted."

"No, we'll go on as planned—just the three of us."

"How nice. Get your father from the parlor. Julia, bring out the bird. I'll light the candles on the table." Julia mumbled in agreement and leaned her hulking body toward the oven. Julia is Swedish, with blond braids wound around her head like sausages, and big lips. She is the only live-in servant Mother has, and has been with us fifteen years. She and I have always gotten along just fine because she minds her own business.

"Hurry up, now," Mother directed. "I do hope the turkey's moist. I simply deplore dry turkey." Dry turkey, wet turkey, what difference? Rodney was coming, and this was the first time within memory I'd been excited about such a prospect.

Dad had left the day following Sidney Younger's funeral for Wichita Falls, because there was a big oil fire near the city, in one of the fields where he owns an interest. He didn't really have to go, could have depended on the field-man Buckley Reynolds to look after things, but he could not resist the temptation to be in the middle of the excitement. He'd promised Mother to come home by Christmas Eve, and, for once, kept his promise.

"I'm going out later," I told him in an effort to pry him away from his newspaper. "So we'll have dinner together, you and Mother and I."

"Oh? And where are you off to? Need the car?"

"No. Rodney's coming."

"Oh, yes. Poor Rodney. I know what it's like losing a father. It gets tougher by the day, believe me. Hard to explain the feeling."

As we walked together into the dining room, I wondered if it was anything similar to the way a person felt if she had no idea who her father was.

Rodney arrived a few minutes early that night, and sat talking with Mother and Dad until I was ready. Curiously, as soon as I heard the door open downstairs, and my father jovially extend him season's greetings, I became nervous. What would I say to him? Would he be upset? Why in heaven did people have to be put through these things? Why couldn't death be just like everything else, easy as catching a bus or train? Why all these awkward moments of not knowing what to say to the bereaved? There ought to be a place for people to stay after they lose a loved one until they're completely over their grief. When they returned, no one would be called upon to say anything. There would be no false words of comfort, no pretending to care when you tried but could not.

Rodney looked better than I expected, sending a wave of relief over me as we walked out into the cold night. I even thought, mistakenly, we might not have to launch a discussion on his father.

"I didn't get you anything," I said. "When you didn't call, I—"

"No bother," he said, and opened the door. There was a small beribboned package on my side, and, seeing it, I thought, oh no, this is a ring. What do I do now? I can't marry this boy.

Yet it was a pendant, heart-shaped gold filigree around a small pearl, nothing special but in good taste, just as one would expect from Rodney Younger.

"It's lovely, and really thoughtful after all that's happened—here, will you get this clasp for me?"

His chilly fingers felt like pinpricks on my neck, and I shivered slightly at his touch. When he'd gotten the chain hooked, he turned away and pulled on his leather gloves. "Where to?"

"Where? I hadn't even thought. Have you eaten? Of course you have. What about a movie? Something good at the Liberty, I think—"

"No, I want to talk."

"Oh." It was coming again, the fear. I closed my hand tightly around my bag.

"Let's just drive around till we find a spot."

"We're near Hermann Park. I guess we could stop somewhere over there for just a few minutes."

"Yeah, why didn't I think of that?"

He pulled into one of the drives and stopped near the Ladies' and Gentlemen's rest rooms. I can never remember being so cold as we were that night, and how queer it was, to be sitting out in the frozen park instead of before the fireplace at home. How incredibly "unsensible."

When he'd stopped the car he reached into the back and pulled over a heavy cover of rancid-smelling thick fur, and draped it across both of us. Only then did I realize what I'd gotten myself into. When people drive to places like this at night, things happen between them.

I must get him talking about his father. Even that would be better than the situation bound to develop when the talking stopped, for it was warm next to Rodney under the coverlet, yet something more than that . . .

I'd felt it only twice before: once for Dick Rayburn, with whom there had been nothing else except constant quarreling which finally brought the three-month courtship to a halt, and once with Cliff Wagner, who'd sensed it like a hunting dog and tried to take advantage. It was a feeling my mother would have referred to as, "not nice," and regardless of her opinion, one which frightened me far worse than the thought of being trapped in an undercroft.

"Well, it's bound to get easier from now on—the grief," I said quickly.

"I wonder if it'll ever get much better. Have you ever lost anybody close?"

"How could I? I've never even found anybody close."

"Even if you had, it wouldn't be quite like losing your father . . . or maybe for a girl, it's losing her mother. Anyway, it's like having someone cut off a limb, and you know you're no longer whole, that something irreplaceable is missing.

"It's like having your defenses taken away suddenly, and there's nothing and no one out there between you and the world anymore . . . Oh, Willa, when I saw my dad before they closed the coffin I had this overpowering urge to grab him by the shoulders and pull him out of there, to say, 'You're not dead, you can't be! Get up, Dad, and come out of there. You were just alive, how can you change all that and be dead?' "

He didn't notice his remark had set me ashiver, and turned away and put his head on the steering wheel. I thought he would cry then, or beat his fists against the dash. But he just lay there like a helpless fish, washed up on the shore. I wanted so much to hurt for him, but could not feel anything except an urgent need to get him away from the subject. "Will you go on, take over the real estate business?" I asked.

"Definitely. We talked about that when we first learned of his illness. I was stationed close by at the time, and got to come home on emergency pass. We said when I got out I'd go right in with him, just like I'd sort of halfway planned before I left. But then it took on new importance. I knew I'd have to substitute as a father for Amanda and Jane, and look after Mother some, and the facing up to that responsibility was frightening."

"I see."

"Sometimes it seems life is like a stubborn automobile. It starts and stops, coughs, backs up and goes forward a little, then stops again."

"How do you mean?"

"I want to tell you something, Willa. I don't know if it'll make any difference to you, but I was married once, before the war."

"Oh? No, it doesn't make any difference, but I would never have guessed," I said.

"I was only twenty. She was sixteen. I loved her very much; I always will."

"What happened?" I asked, and could hear the hollowness in my own voice. Second runner in this race, too.

"She died, three years after we married, of diphtheria."

"I'm sorry."

"She was a tiny girl. Somehow she seems smaller now than she did when she was alive. And she was blond, had curly hair that would come loose from its braids and fall into her eyes. Always irritated her, you know. And she had a dimple on her chin, just one, right in the center, and freckles and blue eyes, and—oh, I'm sorry, forgive me for rambling. You don't want to hear all about Rosemarie, do you?"

"That was her name, Rosemarie?"

"Yes. Everybody called her Rosie."

"She sounds totally opposite from me."

"She was."

"Then why would you be interested in me?"

"I don't know," he said, and his eyes searched my face as though he wondered too. "Do you mind, about Rosie?"

"Why should I?"

"I don't know. It was a long time ago. We were so young and I had no idea where I was going, what I was going to do with my life. It's a thousand miracles we didn't have a child or two, although at times I've almost wished we had . . .

"But people change over the years. It might well be things wouldn't have worked out for us in the long run. We were darned young and inexperienced—like two kids ourselves."

"So your choice of mates at this point would be based on something different?"

"Yes, although I'd never make the mistake of marrying for anything but love. I'd look for that first, then let the rest follow."

I looked out the window. "Oh well, it's got nothing to do with me."

"Maybe not."

We sat silently for a few minutes, and I knew that he was not going to end the night on this note. He was going to kiss me. It was time for that at last, time either to forget the whole thing or go a level deeper.

When he did take my face between his hands and pull

me toward him, he did it gently, and I knew the kiss would be a gentle thing, too, unassuming like Rodney, and warm and sweet.

He leaned back then, and I almost asked, "Well, how did that compare with your child bride?" Yet I stopped my tongue just in time.

"We'd better go now," he said, and started the engine. "Sorry to burden you with all my talk about Dad, and everything."

"It's all right. Everybody needs to open up now and then."

"And you? Do you ever open up?"

"Oh, please don't begin probing tonight, and spoil it all."

"Okay, I'm sorry. It's just that I feel so alone now. You don't know what it's like."

"No, nor do you know what it is never to have known your father. You're very lucky for your memories, believe me."

Did Rodney need me? Did I need him? I still don't know whether we did at first, for it was so unlike any experience I'd ever had with a man. I had thought Cliff Wagner was going to be something like Rodney at first, gentle and kind. After all, he did work at the Texas Creamery, home of Morning Glory Butter. What could seem more wholesome, more all-American? The Stutz Bearcat he drove belonged to an uncle he lived with, and I had thought, mistakenly, that when he allowed me to drive it, to test it at a hundred miles an hour out on the open road, it was going to be all fun and nothing expected.

Then one night in the Stutz, he abruptly pulled me toward him and started kissing me and pulling at my clothes, and insisting, insisting (very strange for a boy from the Texas Creamery) until he finally had me down on the floor and I had to fight to get my hand to the car door and open it to freedom. Afterward, I sewed up my torn blouse so that Mother wouldn't find out. I was afraid she might know anyway because as I hurried up the walk to our house, Cliff Wagner was shouting, "What the hell do you think you are, Miss Rich Girl? A prick teaser?" Then he drove off in the fast automobile, and I never saw him again. I thought he'd shouted loud enough to be heard all the way to Lovett Boulevard, but when I got inside the house was quiet and if anyone heard the commotion, nothing was said about it.

Rodney, then, would probably not try to force me into anything. I could afford to relax with him, nothing more expected than a gentle kiss now and then. It was going to be an easy thing, now that the first kiss had signified the beginning, different from anything before it.

Once Rodney got back into the routine of work, he applied himself with a frenzy. He was trying to pull in the reins, to bobtail expenses. He pressed harder than ever for new listings and buyers for the properties he had. He did all his own clerical work, and often toiled until nine or ten at night before closing the office. About the only time I saw him was for a quick sandwich at lunch or an outing on Sunday to look at more properties.

I began to get an idea. I was growing tired of the oil business, and Miss Daniel's patronizing ways toward my father. I offered to help Rodney.

"Oh, I couldn't let you," he said from behind his desk. "I couldn't afford to pay you anything right now, and anyway, it wouldn't do for you to work for me when I'm seeing you on the outside."

"You're hardly seeing me at all as it is now. Look, it wouldn't be like work because you couldn't fire me. You could run me off, but you couldn't fire me. And it would help you get caught up and maybe we could get out together more."

"I don't know . . ."

"We can try it for a month. If things don't work out, I'll take the advice you gave me long ago and try out for the bedpan patrol."

He laughed and said, "All right. But you've got to promise not to take anything personally that happens here. I may be different in business than I am when I'm not working. I might breathe fire over typographical errors—you can type, can't you?—and scream if something gets misfiled."

"You wouldn't dare."

"Okay, but you might be put off by the customers, especially the tenants in the rent houses."

"I'll just take their messages and give them to you."

"But I'm still afraid we might not get along together."

"If you insult me I'll just stick my tongue out at you. I used to be very good at that."

"All right. But don't cry or anything. It gets hectic in here sometimes."

"I never cry. Besides, I can learn something new, and won't ever have to look at a report listed in barrels of oil. Gad, what a nice change."

"You have to be kind to people on the telephone, you know, even when they're tiresome, which they often are. You've got to learn how to filter out people who read the newspaper ads and call just to fish for information, not really interested in buying. You'll get hordes of calls like that every Monday, because Sunday's when we'll be running the biggest ads.

"And on Thursdays, you can take the ads to the *Post* and *Chronicle*. You can even learn to write them, if you want."

"There, see how much enthusiasm I've caused already?"

"Yeah. Now, scoot upstairs and tell your dad. If I hear a rumble I'll know he doesn't approve."

"Don't worry. He always approves of what I do."

"And when do you start?" Dad asked between cigar puffs. I could hear a shuffle outside the door: Miss Daniel getting an earful.

"Tomorrow."

"Good, Baby. Great experience for you. Now, aren't you glad your mother and I insisted you take those clerical courses in high school?"

"Well, it beats the bedpan patrol, anyway."

"What?"

"Nothing."

"You might find it hard, dealing with the public—they can be pretty tough."

"That's what Rodney said."

"You'll have to hold your temper with them. A mistake could cost him a sale, you know."

"I'm well aware of my unbecoming personality. As you said, it'll be good experience for me. Maybe I'll even become pleasant."

"Aw, Willa," he said, and laughed indulgently. "Get out of here now, I've got work to do. Let me know how you make out. You gonna be on commission?"

"I won't even be on salary."

When I told Mother that evening at dinner, she raised an eyebrow and took a fastidious sip of onion soup. "It might cause tension, working in an office together all the time."

"Oh, I don't think so. Rodney's pretty easygoing."

She looked across at Dad. "All right, Willa. Do whatever you want, of course. You know how we feel about Rodney."

"At any rate, he'll be out of the office most of the time. I'll probably see less of him than ever, during the day."

She nodded and returned to her soup. I didn't interpret her remarks that night as anything to do with sex, although after what happened a few weeks later I could see what she'd been talking about and knew she had been right.

Chapter 3

I began with the Younger real estate company on Tuesday morning at seven-thirty—half an hour earlier than Dad opens his office. Rodney stayed out on calls most of the time and I answered the phone, collected rents, waited on people who came by for various things, typed contracts, applied for and received my notary license, and occasionally went to the courthouse to have a deed recorded. Thursdays I liked best, when I got to create Sunday ads for the papers, and even Rodney agreed my ads were more imaginative than his. We spent Sunday afternoons looking at properties, because this acquainted me with them and made it easier for me to write intelligent ads and to answer the questions of customers.

I soon learned to weed out the non-serious phone calls, which I would often manage without Rodney's having to return them, and any time a customer gave me a bad time I just waited until he left, or got off the phone, then cursed at the blank wall in front of the Remington. This particular aspect of my job amused Dad, I think because he hadn't known I was capable of such ingenuity.

Working there gave me a feeling of accomplishment that made me realize how much time I'd wasted before. Rodney was always praising my work, and promising to put me on salary as soon as he closed several pending deals, but I didn't care about the money. It was the sense of importance I craved. I came to work early, stayed late, thought of extra ways to help. I know now I must have been twice as valuable to Rodney as ever I was to Dad in his office.

It happened finally, the break. Rodney sold six houses in one month, closing all six contracts before the end of August. The Heights house was not among these, and didn't seem to be of growing interest on the market, although we'd hired a painter in the summer who gave it a bright, new look with gleaming white and Wedgwood blue trim. I picked the blue myself.

The commissions he did earn, however, were over two thousand dollars in total, and sent his spirits soaring. He went out in the afternoon of August twenty-third, and was gone two hours.

It was raining in torrents that afternoon, and I kept going back and forth to the window, looking for him and listening for the sound of his footsteps in the hallway. The thunder and lightning were a constant barrage so that I was half afraid the window glass would come shattering to the floor. I kept thinking of him in the Ford, driving God only knew where.

When he finally returned, he was carrying a bouquet of red roses and a box of candy, and a bottle of wine. His voice sounded more nasal than usual, and by the time he'd announced with great flair that, effective September first, I was to go on seventy-five dollars a month salary, I knew the wine he carried under his trench coat was not the first he'd come into contact with in the previous two hours.

"You could've gotten caught with this, you know," I told him as he lifted the bottle from its hiding place. I had work to do that afternoon, and was not in the mood for an early celebration, especially when he had a head start.

"I know," he said in mock whispers, "it's kind of like your smoking—all the more fun because you're not supposed to. After all, when was the last time—or even the first—we had any booze? I think I've been a fairly decent guy about this whole stupid mess. After all, they'd never have gotten away with prohibition if a few more of us had been around to vote." He ambled into his office, talking over his shoulder.

I stuck the roses in a half-empty glass of water on my desk and followed him. My irritation at his coming back half drunk dispelled any joy I might have gotten from such a thoughtful gift as flowers and candy.

"And did you hear what I said about salary?" he asked.

He was fishing around for a stack of paper cups he kept in a cabinet behind his desk.

"Yes, I heard. It's very nice. I think I'll take part of the first month's wages and buy you a new trench coat."

"What's'a matter with the one I've got? It's still got at least ten years' wear in it."

"Okay. I don't want to argue. God knows I don't want to argue. Just relax in here for a while. I'll close the door so the typewriter noise won't bother you."

"Nothing doing. Here, I've found two paper cups. We're taking the afternoon off to celebrate. Damn if we don't— oops, 'scuse the language—deserve the afternoon, the way we've worked. After while I'm taking you to dinner. I've reversed the OPEN sign outside the door. Now all you have to do is take the telephone off the hook and we'll be set."

I was getting nervous. He'd poured two cups of wine and now thrust one at me, almost spilling it all over my dress.

"Gee, you seem to have had a few nips while you were away."

"How can you tell?"

"Your eyes are red, your voice different, your walk a little crooked—nothing much."

"Well, it's all the fault of the damned prohibition. Gets people out of the habit of drinking, so they get where they can't hold it anymore. I haven't had nearly so much as I used to have without even getting a buzz. Damn war. Damn Volstead Act. Damn."

"Rodney, why should you be mad about anything? You've just had the best month in your career."

He leaned back on the couch where he'd slumped down after pouring the wine. "You're right. You always point out the good things."

"Sure."

"How do you like the wine?"

"It's pretty bad, but then I'm not much of a drinker."

"First few cups, then it isn't so bad anymore. By that time your tongue is numb. Anyway, I figured you'd have had your share of the booze. I'm really surprised you're not a vet'run drinker."

"Oh, so that's what you think of me. Well, I'll tell you something. If I wanted to drink no prohibition law or anything else would keep me from doing it. I just don't happen to like it particularly, and don't need it to have a good time."

"That's my girl. Come over here and sit next to me. I want to put my arm around you."

I edged closer. My hands were getting clammy. I wanted this to be over, for him to return to his normal self. I'd never before realized just how much I had come to depend upon his stability, or how uncomfortable I would be around him if that aspect of his personality were suddenly to disappear.

"Sometimes I need it," he said, and I'd already forgotten what we were talking about.

"Hm? What's that?"

"A drink. Sometimes I need one . . . several." He emptied his cup and poured another for himself, then filled mine dangerously close to the brim. He leaned back again and closed his eyes, and I had this welcome feeling that maybe he would fall asleep. Yet it wasn't to be. "Imagine—six houses in a month," he said after a moment. "A person could almost make a living in this bus'ness."

"As long as he had good clerical help."

"Oh, yes. You're better than the girl we had before, better than I ever dreamed. You know, to be honest, I didn't think you'd be much use in the beginning. Thought you'd go at it like you went at the work in your dad's office. But you've fooled me, turned out to be a real princess. Did you come here when I told you? Why isn't my arm around you?"

I obeyed and moved against him. He was warm. Rodney was always so warm.

"It's stuffy in here, don't you think? I closed the windows when the rain started, but we've just got to have some air." I pulled loose from his grip and crossed to open the window.

"Anybody ever tell you you're damned good-looking?" he said to my back while I fiddled with the latch. I kept working with it although it wasn't stuck, and didn't look around.

"Someone may have mentioned it a time or two, I forget."

"You appreciate yourself least of anybody, Willa. You shouldn't be that way."

"I don't know what you mean."

"My mother always told us that before we could like

anybody else, we must first like ourselves. You know, that's one of the few things she's ever said I could completely agree with."

"It makes sense."

"I like you, Willa."

"That's nice."

"I like you a lot."

"Good. Good clerical help is hard to find."

"That isn't what I meant. Look, come over here by me now and quit faking the job of getting the window up. Let's finish the wine, then go to dinner."

I let go a sigh and obeyed him again. Why was I so afraid of crossing him? It wasn't like me to be afraid of making someone mad, particularly when they'd provoked me as he had. He poured the rest of the wine into his cup and looked askance at mine, still full. "If you'd get a little tight, I wouldn't seem so drunk. I'm surprised at you for not figuring that out."

"Oh yes, how thoughtless. Well, one of us ought to try and stay sober. Nothing to prove by both of us landing in jail."

"We're not going to jail, darn it all. I never figured you for a scared-y-cat. What time is it?"

"After five."

"Hungry?"

"Yes, but I'm not dressed properly to go anywhere special. Why don't I just go to Clancy's and get some sandwiches and coffee, plenty of hot coffee."

"I don't want any hot coffee or any sandwich. I'm sick of roast beef."

"All right. How about the Rice Hotel? I can go down and pick up some food, bring it back. It isn't raining anymore."

"No. I'm taking you out tonight. You look just fine to me, and if anybody says anything about the way you look, I'll belt them."

"I hardly think you're in shape to be going out to dinner or belting anyone either."

"I'm not as bad off as you think. Hand me my coat and let's get out of here. It's almost time to close, anyway."

"Good. That's the best idea I've heard all day."

"Willa, is seventy-five enough? If it isn't, just say. You can name your price."

"That's fine. You probably couldn't afford to pay me what I'm really worth."

"Oh, so you really do have a price, then?"

"I didn't mean that. I just didn't want to be accused of underrating myself."

"Everybody has a price, Willa. Even you."

"You've not making sense. Let's go."

He followed me through the door and I put out the lights. It seemed a long way between there and dinner, and it was.

An edge of the dying sun peered down on the steaming sidewalks as we walked to where Rodney had parked his car, a little awry in a space in front of the building. But car lights had begun to flash up and down the street. The day was nearly spent.

He opened my door with a cavalier sweep, then went to his own. He seemed always to be trying to prove he wasn't drunk or even tight, and I wondered whether he sensed how uncomfortable he was making me, how badly he was ruining my day, which had begun as high as his.

I suggested a couple of places we might eat, trying not to sound nervous or impatient but at this point not succeeding very well. Finally he waved a hand and said, "No, let's don't go for a few minutes. I want to talk to you."

"All right."

"Look at me, Willa."

"What is it?"

"Sometimes I wonder where all this is leading. I mean, about us. We don't seem to ever get anywhere, do we? We just sort of tread water with each other, pussyfooting around, wandering . . ."

"Oh? I hadn't noticed. I thought we were doing fine."

"You've been happy, the way it's been?"

"Happy? I'm not even sure I know the meaning of the word. Content, I guess. Yes, content. I know I haven't wanted it to stop."

"Me either. That's all I've really ever known for sure. But I'm not sure I know why—or even if it matters very much."

"You've been good for me."

"I've only believed in you a little. It was all you needed, someone to believe in you and make you realize you ought to pay yourself the same service."

"Maybe you're right, I don't know. You seem—until today—always to expect the right thing of me. No one has ever 'expected' things from me—good things. Not even my parents. I think they always expected the worst."

"Maybe that's why you've always been so hell-bent on giving it to them."

"Maybe."

"Willa, I think I might love you. A little, anyway."

"I don't know. Maybe it's just that I'm different. You can't tell. You said it was love with Rosemarie. Maybe this isn't the same thing."

"Is that how you feel?"

"I don't know how I feel, Rodney. Look how dark it's gotten. Once it starts, it comes so fast."

"Yes," he said softly, and I imagined the air outside after the stuffiness of the office had sobered him some. Certainly he was talking more coherently, whether or not he'd remember any of it tomorrow.

"Willa, couldn't you just come to me a little? I've wanted so much to hold you more, but you're so aloof. I want to kiss you right now. I very much want to now."

"What's stopping you, Rodney?"

"Maybe nothing at all, maybe everything," he said, and leaned toward me and kissed me like the time before, sweetly, unassumingly. I felt safe again for a moment . . . two . . . then he seemed to have decided something on his own and he kissed me again, only this time more forcefully. I was trying to be responsive, not to mind the wine on his breath or the way he was holding me, but he was getting out of hand. I could feel his teeth pressing behind his lips and he seemed to be gripping me tighter with each moment, exploring me like a high school boy. He kept going and kept going, after things had started out sort of ill at ease and I'd been fooled into thinking it would come to nothing.

Then he was doing something that brought it all back, Cliff Wagner and the Stutz Bearcat and the abrupt way he'd come for what he was after. My blouse was coming undone and he was whispering my name over and over in my ear and I was trying to stop him, God, had his hands ever been so strong? And before I knew it I was screaming in panic, "No, no, leave me alone, let me out of the car!" and forcing with all my might his leg off mine and his hand off my breast, and thinking how stupid I'd been to let it happen again.

He did stop then, I think a little sooner than it seemed, and leaned his head back against the seat. "Oh, Willa, I'm going to be sick. You'd better drive this heap somewhere and let me out."

"All right. Scoot over to this side." I got out and walked around, and the air felt so clean, so refreshing, like waking up after a terrible dream and finding it wasn't real after all. Except that it was. I got in and started the car and we drove home. By the time we reached Montrose he'd decided he could drive on to his house alone, but after telling me that he said nothing else and we rode on through the semi-darkness to the curb in front of my house.

I was angry, and the cattiness surfaced again. I left the car and looked at him through the window. "Don't expect me tomorrow," I said.

How tiresome. A blue Daimler in the driveway. The Crosthwaites for dinner and I'd forgotten. All I wanted to do was bathe my face and go to bed.

Maybelle met me at the door in her inevitable blue middy dress, her usual look of puppy dog anxiousness to please written all over her face.

"Hello, Maybelle," I said with exaggerated flatness. I was in no mood for pretending to be pleased at her presence. Mother and Dad and the Crosthwaites were in the parlor having tomato juice with lemon, the prohibition cocktail at our house when company is around. Though Dad has a "prescription" at the drugstore for liquor as a mild pain reliever, his stock usually remains in the cedar chest unless he is drinking alone or with close friends, and he does not consider the Crosthwaites good friends, no matter what my mother feels.

Velma was holding forth before the fireplace, talking about some committee she was working on for the coming Grand Opera season. Even if I'd not overheard her voice, penetrating as the blare of an alphorn at close range, I'd have known she was up there dominating the conversation. Velma is tall and ungainly, buxom, with wavy iron gray hair and deep-set eyes. She always wears large dangling earrings and lipstick that divides into squares along her wrinkled mouth. Velma has always had a wrinkled mouth. As far as I know, everyone has noticed it except her.

Mother's voice tripped across Velma's deep tones. "Is that you, Willa? Come in and say hello to Velma and

Carter. Dinner's almost ready—Julia's made oyster bisque to kick off the oyster season."

"And lemon pie," Maybelle whispered in my ear, as though imparting some sensuous secret.

"Good evening," I told them, nodding at everyone in a sweeping glance. Carter was seated next to Dad on a sofa across from where Velma stood. He is a slight, balding man, shorter by inches than Velma and henpecked so much by her at home and in public that Dad says, while working at his investment job, he is brash and overbearing, probably trying to make up for the beating he takes from his wife. Dad told me this privately, of course. Should anyone say a disparaging word against Velma in front of Mother, she would be angry for days, and I have often thought even before the days just past that Mother is more influenced by Velma Crosthwaite than by my father.

On any other night I could have made it all right through oyster bisque, but on that evening I simply had to extricate myself from the sheer dullness of dinner with them.

"Mother, I hope you won't mind, but I'm not feeling very well. Upset stomach, you know. I think I'll skip dinner and go straight to bed."

It sounded pretty good to me as I said it, but Velma looked suspicious right away, and Carter shuffled his feet and looked down at the floor. Dad busied himself pulling a cigar from its case on the lamp table.

"Of course, if you're not feeling well," Mother said. "Not even?—oh well, go along, then. I'll come up after while to check on—"

"It won't be necessary, probably something I ate for lunch. All of you go on and enjoy the evening."

Maybelle insisted upon walking up the stairs alongside me. "How could you? Leaving me with the four of them. Oh, you are a cruel and vicious being, Willa, and cowardly too." She murmured this with no malice, only her usual degree of matter-of-factness. Somehow I had to be nice to the pimply-faced, bespectacled girl, the sooner to get away from her and the rest of them.

"Look, I really meant what I said. Sorry. Would you mind letting me by?"

"May I just come in, turn down the bed, visit for a while . . . after dinner, I mean?"

"I'll probably go right to sleep. I've had an exhausting day. We'll go to the show next week, all right?"

"Yes, Mother said you were working in that real estate office with that man. Wish I had an interesting job like that. Oh, but a show would be marvelous. Call me?"

"Of course."

"Good. Hope you feel better. I'll see they leave some lemon pie for you . . ."

This was a generous concession for Maybelle. She was but a year my junior, yet somehow had never grown up. Eating was her favorite pastime, as evidenced by her still pudgy figure.

Cool water rushing over my hot face, soap on a soft washrag.

I checked the blouse to see if anything was torn or any buttons missing, and, finding none, closed my suit coat again. Rodney was not so rude as Cliff Wagner, of course. What he had done was out of . . . well, a kind of longing, I guess, whereas Cliff's advances had been fiendishly calculated.

I changed into a nightgown and got into bed, though it wasn't yet seven-thirty and I wasn't sleepy, or at least was beyond the point of unwinding sufficiently to doze off. So I stared at the wall for a while, and lit up a cigarette, took one puff, squashed it into the ashtray, then turned out the light and stared some more. When I am gone, I thought, my tombstone will read, "Here lies Willa Katherine Frazier [always remained a Frazier], a cold bitch who died as she lived . . . alone." It was funny thinking of that, and I turned my face to the pillow so no one downstairs would overhear my giggling, but then the tears smarted behind my eyes and I knew the only amusing part of the tombstone was its irony.

Why could I not open up to anyone? Not even to Rodney, who saw beyond the mask? I wanted to open up, really, wanted it more than anything. But when matters began to get serious I was frightened, so frightened I would always panic just like today. I could have handled it better, more adult-like, without spouting off about not coming to the office tomorrow. But at that moment I hated Rodney Younger neck and crop. Now, only minutes later, I didn't know. It was as though all my feelings for him—whatever they were—had been muffled, covered over by a heavy quilt and hidden somewhere in the far reaches . . . Was that the door?

"Who is it?" I asked, expecting Maybelle. Worse still, it was Mother.

"Willa, dear, are you all right?" she asked, and sat on the edge of the bed. "Let's feel that forehead . . . no fever, that's good. Is it your stomach? Did you take a powder?"

"No, you know I hate taking things. I'll just sleep it off."

"It's Rodney, isn't it? You and he had a quarrel. Did you work it out all right? You didn't break it off, did you?"

I leaned back against the pillow and considered for a moment. "I really think you'd be disappointed if I had."

"Well, he is a nice boy and all, dear. I just wondered. Of course it's entirely your business."

"Well, the truth is, I don't know yet. But don't wake me tomorrow. I'm taking the day off."

"All right. You have worked awfully hard for him, haven't you? Bernie says he thinks you've become very interested in real estate, as you never were in his business."

"It's nothing, Mother. I just ate something that set my stomach off. Just leave it at that, will you? You'd better get downstairs, they'll be missing you."

"Oh, all right. Don't think you've fooled me, though. I know you're holding back as always." She sighed heavily and moved away. "Sure you wouldn't like Julia to bring you a tray?"

"No. I've no appetite. And don't save me anything. Give all the left-overs to Maybelle. She loves to eat."

"That's unkind, Willa."

"I know. I'm sorry."

She left the room and closed the door quietly, the soft folds of her long dress brushing the floor behind.

I didn't work the next day, nor all the rest of the week. Truthfully, I didn't feel well, though it was nothing one could put a name to. It was easy enough to use the semi-illness as an excuse, though, and not to have to explain any more to Mother. No word from Rodney, not even a phone call. Maybe he felt we'd best stay clear of each other for a while, or maybe he was too busy picking up all the clerical work at the office, or too busy out in the field. Maybe he was just fed up. Why did I wish he wouldn't be so stubborn, and call?

Saturday morning he came.

I was up early and happened to be looking out the window, brushing my hair, when I saw him drive up. I concealed myself behind the fluttering curtain and waited until he'd gone up to the porch. In a few minutes Mother was knocking at my bedroom door.

"I know who it is, Mother. Tell him of course I'll see him. I'll be down in a moment."

She said nothing, and I heard her footsteps down the hall. A week had done my old sense of coyness a lot of good. I should better be able to face Rodney Younger. I felt completely detached.

He was seated in the parlor on the edge of the sofa, looking pitiful. Had he slept since Monday? He didn't look it. I hadn't expected him to have been suffering so much and the surprise of it threw me off guard and temporarily dispelled my determination to be flippant.

"You look terrible. Are you all right?"

I sat down next to him, in perfect command even still.

He looked at me pleadingly. "Oh, Willa, it's been a horrible week. I've missed you so much. Can you ever forgive my behavior? I know I was just awful."

"Forget it."

"No, I can't. There I was like some kind of animal, pawing at you. Lord, no wonder you were put out—anybody would have been. Please say you'll forgive me."

"Of course. It hasn't bothered me. I've been sick."

"Oh, you poor dear," he said, taking my hands in his. "You look fit, though. Are you all right now?"

"Perfectly. I may even come back to work Monday, if you still want me."

"Listen, Willa, that's up to you. But one thing I wanted to try and explain today was the reason for the way I acted the other day. Do you know why I got drunk? Not out of reckless pleasure about what had happened or anything. I'm not the sort for that, never have been.

"It kept gnawing at me, that's all . . . my father. How happy he'd have been to have been a part of it all. One of the houses that sold was a property he'd gotten shortly before Thanksgiving. He worked like the dickens trying to unload it, and the customer who finally bought it had originally talked with him on it months ago. So you see, all the success wasn't mine, and yet he wasn't there to share even a part of it. God, how I miss him. Can you understand that?"

"Maybe I can, a little. But you can't make yourself miserable over it. You can't bring him back, Rodney. You can't live your life feeling guilty over whatever happiness or success you enjoy, just because you think he might have had a hand in it. Do you think he'd want that?"

"No, I suppose not."

"Well, I know he wouldn't. Your dad wasn't that way."

"You liked him, didn't you?"

"Of course. Who wouldn't have? He was kind, straightforward. I liked him or I would have never spent so many of my Friday nights forbearing your mother's probing or her looks of disapproval."

"You just have to try and understand Mother, Willa. She's really not so bad. Just kind of confused."

"I'll give her that."

"She likes you, you know, was really impressed that you showed up at the funeral. Things like that are important to her."

"Well, now we've got that settled—"

"Listen, Willa. That isn't all I came to say. I know it's probably not the time or place and you don't have to answer right now if you don't want to, but will you . . . that is . . . will you marry me?"

"Marry you?" I repeated.

"Yes. You've proven yourself in so many ways, darling, when all the time I've sat back criticizing you for this and that. You weren't warm enough, you didn't open up enough. And all the time, there you were working your head off just for me—no pay—just working like a good scout. And the way you came when Dad died—it meant a lot to me, too. You're so level-headed, and I've come to appreciate that, especially in the past week."

"I'm not level-headed. That doesn't fit me."

"Oh, but it does. And then, the way you reacted toward me the other day. It made me see how really fine you are. I'd never credited you for having such, well, corny as it sounds, high morals. Why, Willa, you're just the kind of person I want for my wife. It took me a while to realize it, but I know it now, and I'm not letting go of you again unless you force me out of your life."

"I hadn't thought of marriage—"

"Sh. Don't make up your mind today. Give it some time.

Tell me when you're ready. Oh, I do love you," he said, and leaned and kissed me lightly on the forehead. "I'm going now, won't bother the household any more. I'll be waiting to hear from you."

"All right then. All right."

"Good-by, darling."

"Good-by, Rodney."

Chapter 4

It occurred to me that day as he left, and I'm not sure even now I wasn't correct, that he'd arrived at the conclusion I should marry him because he was finally able to cast me in the role of Rosemarie, whom he had truly loved but lost.

Everything he said that morning, especially about morals, seemed to hint that in his search for a new Rosemarie he'd finally been able to compromise with me, although heaven knows, Rosemarie and I must have been poles apart both in character and personality.

Still, I viewed the question of marriage to Rodney Younger dispassionately. I don't believe I'd ever imagined myself married, even as I watched my school friends graduate from Central High and each one, in time, marry their high school sweetheart or find someone new, perhaps in an office where they worked or in college, settling down to do all the inevitable things like fixing up a house, starching and ironing curtains, learning to make coffee and to cook, and, of course, to have children as soon and as often as nature permitted.

I simply could not see it for me, mainly for a reason Rodney would have never suspected: what had appeared to him as high morals in the car the past Tuesday, when I'd screamed and fought off his advances like a tiger about to be caged, was instead a basic, nauseating fear of sex.

Poor Rodney thought I was saving myself, determined to remain in my virgin state until I approached the altar and gave myself, once and for all, to the man I loved. Actually, I had plenty of chances for sex even before Cliff Wagner came along, and if I'd wanted to take advantage of any of them I'd have done so long before Rodney ever entered my life.

This aversion to sex would not make me good marriage

material. Night after night—I thought of it then—submitting myself to a man's desires, no matter how much I cared for the man, was degrading. Even when I welcomed the feel of Rodney's body touching mine as we sat close together in the car, or when he leaned down over my desk in the real estate office to explain a certain procedure to me, I welcomed that presence only to a point. Beyond that point I grew panicky. What a fine wedding night I would bring him! What a shock to find Willa would perform her duties with excellence during the day, yet at night would turn cold and demand to be left alone.

Further, even if I was able to grit my teeth and withstand the punishment long enough for Rodney to satisfy his desires for me, there would be the inevitable question and final reality of children: the swelling stomach, the confinement, the painful hours of labor; crying in the night, dirty diapers, ruined furniture and clothes. The whole thing was a vicious circle, and one which I'd never been foolhardy enough to allow myself to get caught in.

Yet one must consider every aspect.

I hated the thought of giving up the work in real estate. Even over the past week I had missed the hustle-bustle of the office, the creating of ads on the properties. I'd wondered how Rodney got on with writing the ads himself again, whether he'd gotten them to the papers by the Thursday deadline. I regretted now that I probably wouldn't be visiting properties with him this Sunday (unless I phoned and invited myself, thus also inviting a confrontation over his proposal, perhaps before I was ready). Should I go back to work on Monday, I would be at a disadvantage with any prospective client who phoned or came by to inquire about a new listing I had never seen.

Oh, why couldn't things just go on as they were? Everything was so perfect between us. I could have been content for years. Why must I always be called upon to take direction, why continually find myself at a crossroads of some sort or another? Why, when I suddenly found a workable daily routine that brought the feeling of usefulness, did there have to be a decision looming in the corner, forcing me to give up something for something else?

What, on the other hand, would happen if I refused Rodney's hand?

My education wasn't superior enough to offer many career options. I should probably wind up back in Dad's office, drifting along for the next few years, wandering through oil statistics and index cards and right-of-ways, choking to death with boredom while Miss Daniel breathed down my neck.

Would I ever marry? Certainly I'd never felt about anyone as I did about Rodney. If there were such a thing as love, then I'd come closest to feeling it for him. If missing him when he was gone or didn't call, or worrying over him when he was out in the rain, or going all out to support him when his father died, not even knowing why, could be classified as a kind of love, then I had it for Rodney as surely as I'd never felt it for anyone else.

It was there to be faced and I faced it that Saturday morning. If I didn't marry Rodney Younger I would never marry. Always frightened off by the same misgivings, no man would ever please me enough to make me give up myself for him. In the years to come the few people I did have contact with would drift away, Mother and Dad would die, and I would be truly alone just as the imagined tombstone had told me, not only in spirit but in cold reality.

My spirit had always dwelt alone.

Maybe I could marry Rodney and save its isolation still. I could play a pretending game, smiling as he came near me at night until he could no longer see my face, then smiling in relief rather than gratitude when he was through with what was to be done. How could he know the difference?

I actually wondered if he would be able to tell the difference.

I could keep putting off having children. There were ways to prevent that sort of thing, even without a husband knowing, if necessary, and I would learn about them before the wedding. We could work together and become a highly successful team of real estate people, and he would love me because I would be a key part of his success, unlike Mother, because she never had anything to do with Dad's accomplishments.

I called Rodney Sunday morning and invited myself to look at properties.

"Great. I'll pick you up around noon. And, Willa, have you had a chance—well, never mind, we can talk about it in the car."

We drove to two lots on Bellaire Boulevard, looked at a

ten-thousand-dollar home in Audubon Place, and stopped by at the Heights house to see how the paint job was wearing and whether the grass needed cutting. We seemed often to migrate to the Heights house, and this is where we finally got around to talking, while we sat out on the cool front porch.

I was surprised to find I couldn't look him in the eyes. "I've thought about it," I said, "and if you want me, I'll marry you."

He put a finger under my chin and said gently, "It's not polite to say a thing like that without looking at me. Willa . . . are you sure this is what you want? I didn't intend to rush you . . ."

"Of course. There's only a thing or two you've got to understand, though. I'd go on working for you."

"Sure, until the time we had a kiddo on the way, then you could retire to the nest and I'd—"

"That isn't what I mean, Rodney. I don't know whether I ever want children. If I should decide I do, fine. For now, I don't."

"Oh."

"See, I'm probably not the marriage material you thought I was."

"Oh, but you'd change your mind after a while, I just know it," he went on. "It's hard for you to imagine having a real family, having grown up an only child, but believe me, it's such a good feeling to be part of a big family."

"You may be right, all the same it isn't fair for you to enter into this blindly. You must be prepared not to ever have any children, if you marry me."

"We won't worry about that now. It's too remote. You'll change your mind, and probably be thankful for the chance to kiss the real estate world good-by."

"Maybe. Maybe not."

"All right. What else?"

I was going to tell him my feelings about sex, going to lay it all out for him so he'd know what to expect, but then something jackknifed inside me and I couldn't do it. My mouth was dry and the words stillborn.

"Come, come, I thought you said a thing *or two*. There is something else, isn't there?"

Still, I couldn't answer. Finally I turned to him, smiled, and said, "How about a December wedding? We could upstage Santa Claus."

"December? Oh, Willa, if you'd said next week it wouldn't have been too soon for me," he said, and kissed me right there on the front porch of 1204 Heights Boulevard, sweetly, Rodney-like.

I thought, a bit uneasily, this can't be so bad after all, can it?

Chapter 5

One does not have a wedding. One is had by a wedding: a victim swimming helplessly in a sea of invitation lists and catering arrangements, seed pearls and lilies of the valley.

When I told Mother and Dad on Sunday night that I was going to marry Rodney, I thought I'd be able to keep everything under control.

"Let's keep it small. After all, I haven't all that many acquaintances, and no one is interested in my getting married."

"On the contrary," said Mother. "All our friends will want to be invited. It would be unkind not to at least have a reception to welcome them. I mean, you couldn't just go down to the justice of the peace."

"That's what we did, honey," said Dad, and as I glanced across the table at him, I knew she'd cut him by her remark.

"Yes, but that was different," she said. "We hadn't the means to do anything more fancy. We can do much more for Willa, and whether she realizes it or not, I want to do the very best by you, dear," she ended, looking back at me. She'd been having pain in her back and legs lately—more so than usual—and had been wearing her support corset for several days. The stiffness of her carriage seemed to accentuate her determined face.

"All right. I didn't say it couldn't be nice, only that we want to keep it small. Okay?"

"Of course, dear. It's your wedding."

Later that night she came up to my room, and what passed between us was one of the most amusing conversations I can ever remember having with my mother, and proved more than anything just how little she knew about me.

"I must say, Willa, you're certainly casual about your

news of the marriage. I mean, it's as if you had told us you were going down to pick up a loaf of bread or something."

"Well, that's rather what it's like, isn't it? Rodney and I could have come to you and Dad together, announced it with a background of flowers and violin music, but that's so corny, don't you think?"

A long sigh escaped her, as though she'd expected something like this, and she lowered herself stiffly to the vanity bench. "Willa, are you doing this because you love that boy, or for some other reason?"

I didn't catch her meaning at first. "Because I love him, of course. Isn't that why everybody gets married?" I said, and picked up my hairbrush to begin the nightly ritual.

"I mean, you'd tell me, wouldn't you, if you were in some sort of trouble?"

It hit me then, what she was leading to, and it was so uproariously funny, so wide of the mark, that I might be in the family way, I burst into laughter.

"Well, you will admit you haven't exactly been an angel in your lifetime," she said, raising an eyebrow. "I'm only getting things straight from the start, so we'll know just what kind of wedding to plan. I'm not going to have your wedding picture plastered all over the Social Page and you delivering a baby, seven months hence."

"Mother, I can't believe you're asking such questions! I never knew you could be so crude. In fact, it almost seems as though you've been talking to Velma . . ."

"Just be honest with me."

"All right. I'm lily white, just as lily white as the day you delivered me . . . oh, that's right, I forgot. You didn't deliver me at all. You picked me up later."

"We chose you, Willa, because we wanted you. Why, in all these years, could I never convince you of that?"

Because it isn't true, I thought, but said, "Okay, Mother, I don't feel like going into it right now. Just be assured that I've every right to go down the aisle in glistening white, should I choose to. On the other hand, I might wear a navy suit. I hear navy's going to be a very fashionable color this winter."

"Dear, as a matter of fact, I have spoken to Velma on the phone a few minutes ago, though we certainly didn't discuss what you think."

"Oh, but you told her?"

"Yes. I didn't think you'd mind. And she raised a good point."

"Velma always raises a good point . . . among other things."

"She reminded me you were my only daughter. This will be our only chance—your father's and mine—to stage a really lovely affair, and remember, you refused to come out as a debutante. After you've gone from us, we'll have nothing left to look forward to in the way of watching our children grow up and marry.

"She suggested we ought to try to persuade you and Rodney to do *us* a favor and have something a little larger than what you had intended."

"I can well imagine."

"I find I agree with her, Willa. A big wedding could be such fun—something for all of us to remember forever. I know there would be lots of work, but I could do most of it for you, subject to your approval, of course. With you working, and Velma and Maybelle and me free all day, we could help in so many ways. Oh please, Willa, let's have a grand one. It would mean so much to me."

"Would it really? I don't know. Rodney's for keeping it small. His family's not wealthy, you know. They might be uncomfortable."

"You could persuade him, dear. And there's no need for his family to worry. We would handle all the expense."

"Of course."

"Velma has promised to help all she can."

"I'll bet she has."

"Well, I know she puts you off sometimes, but remember, she has only poor Maybelle. Likely as not, she'll never get the chance to throw something spectacular for her. The poor girl is so homely, although she's just as sweet and loving as any girl I've ever seen. But Velma despairs she hasn't ever had a serious suitor."

"Velma can probably thank herself for that. But don't grieve, Mother. After all, I did manage to keep someone as fine as Rodney around for this long, so there must be hope for Maybelle."

"Yes, perhaps you're right. But there is some talk among the family—strictly confidential, you know—that she may enter foreign missionary service next year."

"Oh? Well, I can't think of anyone more suited to a life of dedication to the Church."

"What do you think of having Maybelle for your maid of honor?"

"Velma suggest that, too?"

"Not in so many words, but . . . of course, it's your decision. You might prefer having someone from Rodney's family, or another girl friend perhaps."

"There isn't anyone I know better than Maybelle. After all, if her mother is going to be running this show—don't shake your head—then Maybelle might as well have a big role, too. Besides, if she becomes a missionary, this may be her last chance to have a fling at anything so glamorous, if you can look at it that way."

"Always flippant, aren't you, dear? Still, it's kind of you to see it in that light. I'll tell Velma. By the way, do you think you could take some time off in the next couple of weeks—there's so much to do—clothes to buy, arrangements to make?"

"I've been off a week already, and I'm serious about my work, if you can believe it. I'll meet you on lunch hours every day if necessary, but I won't take any extra time."

"All right then. I'll see if Velma can go with me to town tomorrow, and we'll come by for you, go to The Fashion and to Levy's—see their autumn collection of hats. Their ad was in the paper this morning. And maybe we could stop by the Rice to see about a reception. And, oh yes, you will be married in Christ Church, won't you?"

"I haven't set foot in there for ages."

"Well, I go occasionally, and we've kept up our pledge all these years. Surely we have some right to the use of the sanctuary."

"All right. But don't count on me tomorrow. I'll have a desk piled high with work. Make it Tuesday at the earliest."

One Saturday in early October Rodney and I had our picture taken together for the *Post*. He wasn't too big on the idea at first, but Mother pulled and persuaded me through the arrangements and dress fittings, and I in turn cajoled and coaxed him through the part of the wedding affair that would include him. I was like someone riding a raft downstream. There was no time for considering what I really wanted or needed, and this was fine because the less I was forced to think about what was happening, what all this would ultimately lead to, the less I dreaded it.

After the picture, Rodney told me he had a surprise, and we drove out to the Heights. He was excited that afternoon, and I was in a good mood, too, having finished with a good part of the foolishness of wedding planning. In the weeks ahead there was only left the tying up of loose ends and the shower at Maybelle's, which I did not want but couldn't refuse.

He drove up to the curb at 1204, which had become something of an armageddon to his career in real estate. After over a year on the market, the house still defied his efforts to unload it, and lately we hadn't even discussed new ways of trying to find a buyer for it.

"Lost cause, isn't it?" I began.

"Depends on how you look at it."

"What do you mean?"

"Wait'll you see."

I think somewhere between the car and the porch, which Rodney insisted we span at a pace close to running, I had visions of a client holed up inside with his checkbook pulled out, ready to sign; yet never in my wildest dreams did I expect what Rodney had planned for me.

As we entered the spacious entrance hall he said, "Well, what does the future Mrs. Younger think of the purchase I've made? It isn't too big, of course, couple of kids from now, a dog or two, we'll have outgrown it. But it'll do for a while, won't it?"

"What in the world are you talking—?" I stopped then and looked at him closely. "You've bought this house for us."

"My wedding present to you, Willa."

"But how could we afford—you really did it? What did you use for—how perfectly insane—oh, I simply adore insanity! You crazy man!"

I was as excited as he, and we laughed like two idiots as he picked me up and twirled me around and around in the big entrance hall.

"I just knew you'd like it."

"But can we afford, I mean on your—?"

"I was able to make a good deal. The owner was tired of waiting around for it to sell, and I persuaded him that instead of giving it to another agent, he ought to make matters easy and sell it to me. He'd save money because there would be no commission involved. I've had a little money tucked away, and you know that the past couple of months have been good. We couldn't furnish it all right away, but I'm sure we could manage. Of course, we couldn't afford any help to keep it for us either, but we could do a fair job together, don't you think?"

"Do I! But it's so much more than I expected."

"Yes, and it'll be convenient to the office, but not too close to Mother, I thought of that too, and not too close to your parents, either. We'll be all on our own out here, with no one around us except new friends. Oh, there are so many potentialities, honey. I can hardly believe I did it. I know I should have asked you first, but I wanted to surprise you. You know, I've felt almost like a non-participant in all this hoopla over the wedding. I wanted to do something myself."

"It's nice, Rodney, one of the nicest surprises I've ever had."

"We can board up the undercroft."

"No, no, that won't be necessary. I've got to learn to lose my fear of a few things," I said, trying to sound more convinced of my words than I really was.

November, early December. The pressures mounted. I was trying to consider everything, to convince myself I was happy about it all, and succeeding quite well for a while. Whenever Rodney broached the subject of the wedding night, which he must have done two or three times, I managed to change the subject smoothly enough, to turn away so that he couldn't read my expression.

"Only four more weeks," he said one night. "I'll never have to go home alone again."

"Time flies."

"We're going to be so happy. I know you say you've never been happy, and I'm determined to change that. It was one reason I knew I had to buy the house—to do something really special for you that hadn't been done for somebody else before."

"You had no house then, you and Rosemarie?"

"Not quite. We rented a tiny duplex off Congress—awful place, cold in the winter and stifling in the summer."

"But it didn't matter, did it? I mean, you two were happy all the same."

"Yes, we were . . . but look, Willa. You needn't feel there's a ghost behind you all the time, or that I'm marrying you because there's no way of ever getting her back.

Believe me, that isn't so. Rosemarie was eons ago, and now that I've met you and known you, she seems even further back than ever.

"Being married to Rosemarie was like—well—a children's game. This time I'm marrying a woman, an adult. There are things about you she could never have matched. I know you'll be able to deal with whatever comes along."

"Don't credit me too much on that. I don't know . . ."

"Stop worrying. Oh yes, almost forgot. We don't have to come direct to the house after the wedding. We're going to take a little trip, but I won't say where, unless you want to know—it's your right, of course. I can't make all the decisions just because I love to pull surprises. I could tell you what I have in mind, and you can chuck the whole idea if you don't like it. I wish we could afford to take a long trip, but—"

"Surprise me."

"Good. Well then, pack your nightgown and your toothbrush."

"Yes, I—"

"Not that you'll be needing it very much." He was close to me now, not holding me, just looking into my eyes. My mouth was dry. I looked away. "You're not afraid, are you Willa? Of me?"

"Why should I be? Why in the world be afraid of you?"

"Good girl. I knew you'd look at it that way. You know I'd never hurt you for anything in the world."

"Of course. It's getting late, Rodney, and I'm tired. Let's call it a day, shall we?"

I saw Agatha Younger only once more, shortly before the wedding. She'd invited us for a dinner that turned into a showdown between her and Rodney.

"Regardless of your own personal feelings, I'm sure you both realize children deserve a Christian background," she began. "After all, how do you think I'd have overcome my grief at losing Sidney without my faith? I want you to promise me you'll raise your children in the Catholic Church."

I was too stunned to reply.

"Look, Mother, I've told you that's our business," said Rodney. "We'll make that decision when . . . and if . . . we should have children."

"But—"

"That's final, Mother."

As Agatha rose weakly and left the room I couldn't help feeling a twinge of sorrow for her. Rodney stood sternly as she passed, and after she was gone he said, "It's best to leave it at that. If I don't stop her now, she'll never give up."

I nodded, admiring his strength in front of her, yet wishing he hadn't found it necessary to insult her in her own home. It all seemed so senseless. Who cared about religion or anything else? God, what a pain to get married!

It seemed after that night time galloped at a fiercer pace than ever. I had but one more important errand. I went to Sakowitz and bought Rodney a dark gray wool winter coat, satin lined, double-breasted, elegant. It cost three times my November salary and cut into my allowance from Dad, and when I saw the silk scarf and hat that made such a terrific match, I bought them too and ordered everything delivered, the morning of the wedding, to the Heights house. Rodney was living there now, using bedroom and living room furniture given to us as a wedding present by my parents.

I also prayed for cold, clear weather on the wedding day so that he'd be disposed to wear his new coat instead of his ugly trench coat. On the card enclosed, I wrote, "It's my turn for surprises. My wedding present to you may not be as grand as yours to me, but I hope it will be just as useful. Love, Willa."

The word "love" looked queer somehow. Had I ever said outright that I loved him?

Two days later, after we'd returned home from the wedding rehearsal and dinner and kicked off our shoes, and Rodney had gone home without me for what he assumed to be the final time, I made a small, trivial decision which would wind up leading me to the truth, not only about my real parents, but about myself as well.

Chapter 6

I decided to pack my things.

For days, Mother had been after me to tell Julia which luggage I'd need, so she could be sent up into the attic to bring the bags down and clean them. Finally, sick of her nagging and a little hesitant, I guess, to do this one final, inevitable task, I said, "For God's sake, I'll get to the bags when I'm good and ready. Leave me alone, won't you?"

Mother had shrugged and shot me one of her "I give up" looks, and said no more.

Then, on the eve of the wedding, disgusted by all the phony smiling and hand shaking and thank-you-ing at the rehearsal dinner, yet determined to stick out the whole farce somehow, I lay in bed unable to sleep because I couldn't get my thoughts off the days and nights ahead, knowing in less than twenty-four hours I'd be standing somewhere in a hotel room, pretending to love being looked at naked, being touched, with no rights left to say, "Stop and leave me alone, I never want to see you again," and wondering, What have I done? Yet knowing I'd waited too long to stop what I allowed to begin . . .

I got out of bed, shivering from head to toe. At least the packing would help pass the time and get my mind off things I could scarcely stand to think about. I pulled on a robe and went up into the attic of the silent house, telling myself I could pull this off if I could just keep busy, just close my eyes when the time came and concentrate on something else. I turned on the light.

I first saw my alligator suitcase that would hold all the big things I'd be taking, and put it by the attic stair landing. All I would need, then, would be my small weekend bag, to carry toiletries and stockings. I passed by my father's heavy luggage near the front, worn from being hauled around on so many trips, then spotted my mother's a little farther back, but saw no sign of the suitcase I had in mind. I hadn't used it in a long time, and it'd probably gotten shoved back somewhere . . .

Then I noticed a pile of boxes against one wall and two handles poking out from the side midway through the stack. Must be it, I thought, and walked over to pull it out. There in my hand, instead of my weekend case, was a black carpetbag. It looked so beat up—its leather handles brittle, its bottom discolored as though it had gotten wet—I was surprised it hadn't long ago been thrown away. Yet even then something about the looks of it aroused my curiosity. I put it down on the attic floor, then pulled the heavy zipper across it and opened it wide. The soft white cambric on top looked to have been stuffed in the bag at random, and when I forced it slightly, it came out in wrinkled puffs into my hands.

Something in my memory opened up like a fan then, and I could see myself as a little girl, taking a ribbon out of my hair. My thoughts were so vivid, all awareness of present reality disappeared. The years back to my childhood sped past . . .

I am standing in front of the mirror in my room, yanking on the big taffeta bow my mother makes me wear opposite the part in my hair. I hate the bow because it makes my head look lopsided. I want to see how I look in the beautiful new hat Mother has bought. It is a grand creation of straw: wide-brimmed and banked with flowers, veiled with soft netting.

Finally, with one determined jerk, I get my bow ribbon freed, and off it comes with a snarl of hair. I walk from my room, down the hall, to my mother's room, and go to her closet. I feel safe. She is somewhere downstairs, cleaning. I pull the big vanity chair from its place in front of her dresser. The chair is so heavy, it takes all my strength to move it the short distance to the clothes closet. I open the door, push the chair well in, and climb upon the seat. But the seat is still too low. I can't reach the shelf at the top of the closet where she keeps her hats. I climb further up, balancing myself on the tufted chair back. Now I can reach the shelf. I take one quick look around, listen for sounds of her coming. Nothing.

I am confused at first because all the boxes look the same, and I can't tell which one holds the beautiful hat. Then I see, further back toward the right corner, a bag with handles. I forget about the hat and reach for the bag, intrigued by its queerness. When I pull it forward, one box is upset, and it lands on the floor beside the chair. I stop a moment, listen, then, hearing nothing, part the handles of the carpetbag and pull the heavy zipper across. I can see something white inside. I pull at it, timidly at first, then harder, and white puffs of material billow out into my hands.

Suddenly comes my mother's voice: "Willa! What in the world are you doing up there? Get down this minute!"

Her angry tone startles me and I reel around, pulling the white material in my hands and forcing the bag to follow. The bag hits my back and knocks me off balance. My mother's arms are open wide, trying to break my fall from the back of the teetering chair, but she is not quick enough. I plummet down with the chair, knocking her backward and landing so that she is pinned between the chair and the floor.

In a panic I get to my feet. She is moaning in pain. I pull with all my might to get the chair off her. Her body looks twisted, legs outstretched as though in a run, arms still widespread, her head turned to the side and pitched upward.

Over and over I am whimpering, "Mama, Mama, Mama," and she interrupts my cries to say, "Shut up crying and run for Mrs. Baxter. I'm in great pain."

Mrs. Baxter hears me screaming as I reach her porch and, flinging her dustcloth aside, runs with me all the way back to where my mother still lies, quietened yet still in that horrible posture of agony.

By this time I am in hysterics. I kneel down beside her sobbing, begging her, "Mama, Mama, I'm so sorry, please, I didn't mean to, I didn't mean to, please say it's all right, please, please, please—"

"Get away, child," says Mrs. Baxter, pulling at me. "We'll have to get her to a hospital."

"Take Willa to her room," Mother directs. And still I have my arms out, begging one word of reassurance, "Mama, Mama, Mama, please!"

Mrs. Baxter yanks me up and carries me off to my room. I kick and twist to get free but it is to no avail. She pushes me inside, slams the door, turns the key.

I fasten myself to the other side of that door, jiggling the handle with one hand, beating the door with the other, kicking the bottom with my feet. I stop at brief intervals to listen, and, hearing nothing except rumbles and movements, unfamiliar voices and the pound of hurried feet up and down the hall floor, I beat again, scream and yell, but no one seems to hear.

After a while I look through the keyhole, and see my mother going by on a stretcher just inches from me. I am transfixed by the sight of her being carted away by people I've never seen before. And then I hear her say to Dotty Baxter, walking alongside, "Willa was after that carpetbag. I'll have it thrown out of this house. I don't care if it *did* belong to her mother."

Whose mother, I wonder frantically? Then I beat and kick some more, beat and kick, beat and kick, but no one

hears. Shortly thereafter I hear no more sounds of movement. I look into the keyhole again. The hall is bare. My
mother is gone.

I lowered my head down on the folds of material, my
heart pounding away, my face bathed in its own perspiration. The memory had cut off abruptly at the sight of the
empty hall . . . it was as though nothing happened after
that. The next thing I could remember clearly was my
mother telling me I was adopted. I knew as I sat in the
attic that I must have forgotten it all even by then, or blot-
ted it out, for I'd reacted calmly to the news that I had
been "chosen," and only thought it odd that my mother, at
the end of her short explanation, had looked out the window behind me and said hurriedly, "Oh, there's your father, home. Let's not talk about this to him, shall we? He'll
be tired from working so hard. Let's not bother him about
it now, promise?"

No wonder I sensed they lied about knowing little of my
true beginnings, especially of my real mother. But my poor
adopted mother, suffering all those years of back pain because of my nosiness and thinking I was after that carpetbag when all the time I was in search of her beautiful hat.

I could have told her that, if she'd asked. But no one had
asked me anything. I'd been shut away, frightened to death
by what I'd done, then cast aside as though I didn't matter . . .

Presently I put the material back into the carpetbag,
closed it up, and carried it downstairs to my bedroom. This
time I locked the door myself. A strange sense of calm possessed me, a feeling of control I'd never had in my life. If
my adopted parents kept the carpetbag from me, then what
else, I wondered, had they kept secret and why? Why, also,
was the carpetbag not taken from the house as my mother
had commanded? Had it been retained by mistake, or intentionally?

I put the carpetbag down in the middle of my bed and
opened it again, pulling the material all the way out. It was
a cambric nightdress, with little blue cornflowers embroidered around the neck and long sleeves. I held it in front of
me across from the mirror, trying to gauge my mother's
height. She was not quite so tall as me, probably, for the
hem of the thing hit me about mid-calf.

The only other things in the bag were a pair of faded

dancing slippers with soiled, frayed ribbons attached. I pulled one over my foot: a perfect fit. Her feet, then, were like mine—very long and narrow. Oh, it was tantalizing to be so near finding what she was like. A dancer. Was she talented? Did she attend a fine school in Ohio? Was she professional? Did she give it all up only when she found I was on the way? Did she resent my keeping her from her love of the arts?

That seemed to be the lot, and what did it tell for sure? Nothing. It only opened up a whole new set of doubts and questions that probably would never be answered. I grew angry as I looked over the gown and the shoes again. Why had she rejected me, left me in some home to be picked up by the first couple who came along and liked the looks of brown-haired babies? Did she do it for the dancing, so she could go on uninterrupted in her chosen career?

And where, oh, where, was my father? How did he figure in all this? Nothing of his was in the bag. Was it possible she wasn't certain who my father was? Was he some dancing partner along the way, or musician from an orchestra she met at a theater? Could she not afford to keep me without the support of a husband, and thus deserted me in the hopes someone better able to provide for me would come along?

Was she famous now? Perhaps even been here to dance at a theater at one time or another? Could I have gone to the ballet and watched her, not knowing who she really was?

Why could I not remember anything? It was so utterly hopeless trying to piece anything together, knowing nothing. And the things in the bag only worsened it. I stuffed the gown into it. Then my hand caught inside the torn lining and felt the edge of a piece of paper. I tore into it, ripping the brittle lining six inches down.

There were four things: a musical program dated June 17, 1899, a program from an opera dated December 31, 1890 (both events held in Galveston), a single sheet of paper with a name and two addresses, and a picture. It was the picture, at first, that I stared at intently. A man and a woman, probably a wedding portrait. It was only a half-picture, each party shown to the waist, so there was no way of telling the size of either of them.

She appeared fair, kind of snobbish. This would fit: I am snobbish, and look it. The man was fair-haired also, but his face was less reserved, his smile full of a kind of inward joy. He wore a coat and a tie. She wore something light-colored with very high ruffled collar. It was impossible to date the picture, for fashion before the turn of the century always looked about the same to me, no matter what the year. And there was nothing written on the back or front. The corners were cut diagonally on all four edges, and I supposed it must have been taken from a frame before being slipped into what was now the torn pocket of the bag.

I put the photo down and looked at the piece of paper. The information was handwritten in childlike script with heavy lead pencil. Almost surely it was a youngster's work, I thought, then a new idea came to mind. I looked at both programs for the name James Randolph Byron . . . it was a small chance, but maybe . . .

Yet there was no name resembling Byron in either program, and visions of my mother coupled with a celebrity drifted from my mind. The only eye-catching name was Roman Cruz, an unusual name made more prominent by the boldness with which it was printed.

Then I thought of the shoes and picked up the opera program again. Fancier than the other, this cover was made of heavy parchment, decorated with gaily colored flowers, and printed in red filigree script, bound to its tissue-thin pages by a gold silken, tassel-hung thread. No dancers were named in the opera itself; yet, in the center between Acts there was a small notation: "Ballet Solo from 'Swan Lake,' Performed by Miss Margueretta Sterling."

Could this ballet dancer be my mother?

That would have been around ten years before my birth date in 1900. If Margueretta were a professional dancer, would it not have been strange for her to have been in Galveston again in 1899 (where I now knew I must have been conceived), saving a program from the show of a traveling band? It was possible, to be sure, but somehow did not seem probable.

My head was full of new questions, and I was more than ever confused. Again, I looked back at the sheet of paper. No doubt about it, a young boy had written it. James Randolph Byron, Number 2 Blackburn Place, Grady; and 707 Avenue L, Galveston. Well, Grady is some distance from here, but Galveston is only fifty miles away, so there was the obvious place to start, even if I were seeking someone who must have known my mother as a youngster, and might not even remember her after all these years.

I had to go, in spite of wedding plans and Rodney Younger and my father and mother and all their friends. They were of no significance in the face of what I'd found in the bag. It gave me a moment of pause, to realize how utterly detached I felt from all of them at that moment. They might have been nameless faces I'd seen in a crowd.

There was a moment of hesitation in which I considered taking the carpetbag to my adopted parents, confronting them with the proof they'd lied, then letting them tell me the truth about my past, or as much as they knew of it. It would give me no small amount of satisfaction to be able to show them up and force them to be honest with me. I started for the door.

Then a frightening thought occurred to me: what if they were keeping my mother somewhere, imprisoned in an institution? Oh, it was too horrible to believe, yet my father certainly had the means to do it, and after all, they'd lied to me from the beginning.

Even as I asked myself whether they were capable of sinister deeds, I knew I could not afford the risk. The only sure way to get at the truth was to find it for myself. They might not guess I'd found the carpetbag at first, and even if they did, it was as good a chance as any they knew nothing of the clues my mother left me in its pocket.

I sat down at the davenport and penned a note: "Dear Mother and Dad, Please forgive me, but I know now I can't go through with this wedding. Don't try to find me, for I am off in search of myself. How can I know where I want to go with my life if I have no idea where I've been? Tell Rodney I'm truly sorry. Willa."

Chapter 7

I propped the note against the bed pillow and repacked my real mother's carpetbag, just as she'd left it. Then I packed the alligator bag for myself, and waited until I was sure everyone in the house was asleep. I took a good warm suit from the closet, pulled out my heavy coat and a warm pair of walking boots. My eyes traveled over the going-away suit hanging there with Fashion tags still attached, and the chemise wedding gown hanging on the closet door like a child's angel costume for a Christmas pageant, and I thought what a waste it all was, what a mistake to think I could pull it off and play happily ever after married lady.

Shortly after midnight, I walked carefully down the stairs and left the house, surprised at how easy it was to sneak out. It was deadly cold, yet clear, and I had no choice but to walk to a corner for a cab. There was always the streetcar, probably soon to be making its way down the cable, but I always loathed streetcars for they stink and are inordinately cold in winter.

I waited ten minutes before a taxicab passed, and at twelve forty-five walked into Union Station, one of the few people around the stark, high-ceilinged hall. I bought a ticket on the GH&H, looking every few minutes over my shoulder, unable to believe it had been so easy. Then the simple possibility occurred to me that James Byron might even live right here in Houston, and as I rushed toward the telephone directory I realized that in my haste to get away, there might have been any number of solutions to the puzzle I hadn't thought of.

So many people had moved to Houston from Galveston over the years, especially after the terrible storm of 1900. Was it not possible James Byron was one? I flipped through the B's and found several Byrons, including one with the initial J, and one with R. My fingers shook as I wrote down the numbers, and thought of the glorious chance that I might come face to face with my past without ever stepping into a train car.

It did not cross my mind that anyone would resent being disturbed from sleep at one o'clock in the morning until I reached the first number, asked for James R. Byron, and was told by a sleepy-voiced woman, "Never heard of him. My name's Jenny Byron, and I ain't never been married." She slammed down the receiver in my ear.

Undaunted, I tried the other number, and was met by a similar reaction. R proved to stand for Richard, and where he came from—southern Louisiana—strangers who called on the telephone in the middle of the night were taking their lives into their own hands.

Disappointed, I told myself I should have never expected it to be that easy. I found a place to sit down, lit up a cigarette, and prepared for the long wait until eight o'clock, when the next train pulled out.

I haven't been to Galveston more than a half-dozen times in my life. I don't care for the feel of salt water and sand on my body, and after reading and hearing eyewitness accounts of that horrible storm, I never quite trusted the weather enough to enjoy an outing on the beach there.

The train pulled in at nine-fifteen, and I was able to get a cab right away. I gave the driver the address on Avenue L, and he said, "Well, miss, I can take you to Avenue L, sure 'nough, but I ain't sure about seven-oh-seven. How old is this information?"

"Over twenty years, I think."

"That explains it, then. Everything's changed here since the big storm. There may not even be a seven-oh-seven anymore. But I c'n take you on to L if you like."

"That will be fine. Just let me out anywhere you like. I can walk the rest of the way."

We drove along the geometric streets, passing palms and grand houses raised off the ground like ladies' skirts lifted to ensure not getting them muddy. I had never really noticed anything of Galveston except the beaches and main streets, and was surprised to find the town rather quaint, kind of peaceful after the hustle-bustle of Houston.

Soon we were on Broadway, a street which I did recognize, with its esplanaded center planted with tall palms and oleanders, and the two-way trolley tracks marching down. "Our finest street," said the driver with pride, "greatest houses on it. Yonder's the Moody house and further down, the Gresham res'dence. I hear tell some two hundred people found refuge in the Gresham house during the storm. He was a lawyer and a congressman, you know, just died last month. Great loss to the city, yes, sir, great loss.

"Not a whole lot left in Galveston anymore," he continued, as though he were driving a touring car full of passengers. "Place kind of died a gradual death after the storm. Oh, I mean there's a town and banks and the port and all the other, but, you know, people began movin' away right after the hurricane, shore did, and many never came back. Course, some would argue that Galveston is now greater than ever as a city, but when you drive a cab for fifteen years, you develop a kind of instinct . . ."

"Were you here during the storm?"

"No'm. My parents were, but I was visiting an aunt in Albuquerque when it blew in. Always kinda wished I'd been around to see it. Must've been a gruesome sight. Thank goodness, none of my family was hurt."

"That's good."

"Six thousand people killed, you know, worst storm ever."

"So I heard."

"Course, you'd have been too young. You grow up around here?"

"Houston. But I was far away, in Ohio, when the storm came," I said. Something occurred to me just then and I looked down at the carpetbag. Why was it water-stained only on the bottom?

"Lemme see now," said the driver, interrupting my thoughts, "Avenue L runs right down to the beach. One end is practically on the shore. Doubt if you'll ever find what you're looking for, considerin' its location and all."

"I never thought of that."

"We'll be there directly, though."

We rode the rest of the way silently. It was a lovely morning, defying the late December heading on the calendar page. Shops were opening here and there; men were walking down the street clutching their newspapers; women were hanging out wash; children were playing games. We interrupted one game of ball as we passed down Twenty-fifth Street. The little boys participating looked irritated, and I thought to myself, Just another morning for most people, calm and carefree. In the afternoon the kids would go to a theater and see a show. Fathers would return from their jobs and dinner would be on the table. Everyone would be discussing the approach of the Christmas season, with bellies still smarting a little from their overindulgence on Thanksgiving Day.

And I was apart from it, just as I had always been apart from everything, a person not doing what everyone else was doing: riding a cab instead, looking for her past, and what if she found it? Would it be what she had longed a lifetime for?

I stifled a yawn, only then realizing how tired I was. I'd slept some, in a lounge chair in the ladies' room at the Houston station, but I hadn't slept much, afraid someone would discover me there, or that I would miss the train. I'd awakened stiff in the neck and with a backache, wondering if anyone had yet noticed my absence and come looking for

me, or had they shrugged their shoulders as so many times
before, and told themselves they might have expected it?

Was Rodney even now trying on his tuxedo? Had the
coat arrived from Sakowitz? Were the florists at the church
adding white poinsettias and lilies of the valley to the pro-
fusion of red flowers already decorating the sanctuary?
Were workers at the Rice Hotel busily polishing silver and
arranging tables? Was the caterer putting sugar roses on
the five-tiered wedding cake?

I ought to have been ashamed of myself and I knew it,
but at the time I was too anxious about what was ahead to
worry about anyone else, and afraid that if I dwelled on it
too much I would lose my nerve and go back . . .

"Here's the seven hundred block. Lemme see, 742, 738,
7—"

"It's all right. I think I'll walk from here. I need to
stretch anyway, and even if there is no 707, I can knock on
a few doors and ask some questions."

"Okay, miss. I dunno what or who you're looking for,
but I wish you luck. Here, I'll get them bags for you." He
pulled each of them out, obviously puzzled by the paradox
of a genuine alligator bag standing next to a ragged carpetbag. He waited for his fare, to which I added a fifty-cent
tip, and thanked me, giving me a look that said women
would forever befuddle him.

Avenue L was like something out of a history book. Its
width wouldn't make half of Montrose Boulevard across,
and given the same amount of land on either side of the
street, there were probably three times the number of
houses, all perched together as though being thus situated
would offer better protection against high winds and water.
I remembered the pictures I had seen, taken after the
storm, of houses stacked one against the other and even
practically on top of each other, or reduced to a rubble of
loose wood, bricks and latticework, not even fully appearing until the water had finally receded. It was lucky they
had their seawall built when they did, to protect them from
an almost equal whipping by nature in 1915. Was I busy
building my own seawall now, to protect me from all the
ghosts who had hounded me for a lifetime? Would mine be
as effective as the crushed granite wall within blocks of
where I now walked?

The bags were heavy, and I was soon sorry I'd told the

driver to go, yet I couldn't have him driving me around all day as I proceeded up staircase after staircase, inquiring after James Byron. I crossed to the side of the street with the odd-numbered houses, and walked further and further down, the breeze more brisk the nearer to the beach end that I walked.

When I saw 711 my heart leapt, then there it was: 707 Avenue L, as though it had spent the past twenty years waiting for me to come. It was a pleasant, usual-looking red brick house with gray roof. There was a low red brick fence around the tiny lot on which it sat, so low one might have wondered why bother with it at all. The house was trimmed in light green, and green pots, bereft of plants, were lined along the brick rail spanning its verandah, green chairs and rockers were stationed across either side of the door, as though waiting for people to issue from the house and sit on them. (Was it a boardinghouse?)

The back part of the house extended over the driveway, forming an arch in front of the garage, and I had my first misgivings when I noticed the windows of the room above the arch were boarded up.

I left my bags against a huge oak close to the fence, and walked to the door. I rang twice, yet heard no stirring from inside, and I thought, Well, wouldn't it be just my luck James Byron isn't home, even if he does live here, even if he is still alive.

Just then the front door opened slightly, and a small Mexican woman with anxious black eyes looked out at me through the screen.

"Yes, what you want?"

"Excuse me, madam, but I'm inquiring about a James Byron. I believe he may live here, or may once have. Could you tell me—?"

"Zhames Byron? I know no Zhames Byron. You have wrong house," she said curtly, and pushed the door.

"Just a moment, please. I've come from Houston looking for him. Do you know who the former owners were? If I can just get some idea—"

"I live here five years now. My husband buy house before he die. I know no one live here before. You go away, all right?"

"Yes, all right. Thanks anyway," I told her. I could have said a lot more, but it was no use. The woman obviously understood little of what was going on around her, and was afraid of me besides. I went back down the stairs, thinking that you would never catch me living where you had to climb a dozen stairs just to get to your front door. At the fence I picked up the bags again, which now seemed heavier than before, and looked up and down Avenue L.

Should I inquire at other houses, or go somewhere and check the phone directory for a listing under James Byron, as I probably should have done first thing? There was no activity on this street, no children playing, only the sounds of distant traffic. The houses were quiet to the point of seeming uninhabited, with most of the shutters drawn. I seemed to be as far away from finding anything as I had been last night, sitting at the head table with Rodney during the rehearsal dinner, before I even knew about the carpetbag which now dug red ridges across my hand.

Then I heard a voice: a woman one house down and across the avenue was calling to me, and when I looked her way, she motioned with one hand for me to come. She was snow-headed, seated in a rocking chair on her front verandah with one hand wrapped around the end of a black wooden cane.

"You there, girl, you lookin' fer someone, are you? Maybe I know 'em. I been around for a spell."

Hope rushed up inside me again. I left the bags at her gate and walked up to her. "I couldn't hear what you was sayin' of course," she continued, "but with your grips and all, I figgered you must be a'lookin' fer somebody. That's old Janie Rodriguez lives yonder. She don't know nothin' and don't care neither. Now, who is it you was huntin'?"

"A man named James Byron. I've no idea what he looks like or how old he is, only that he probably lived here sometime shortly before 1900. Have you been here that long?"

"No, honey, not on this side of Galveston. Set down on that wicker chair, but mind your stockin's. Nobody's been on this block of L that long. I been here since '13, and that's the longest of anybody. Those who lived around here before 1900 were either killed or got away fast after the storm.

"Avenue L was completely wiped off the map, I hear tell. Every house on here was built since then, and I know ever'body who lives here now, don't'cha'see?"

Yes, I thought, and everybody's business too, no doubt. She smiled across at me, revealing a near toothless mouth. Then she paused, and wiped the saliva from around her wizened lips with a handkerchief. I was surprised to notice her nails were neatly polished and filed, and she wore a sizable diamond on her wedding ring finger.

"Yes, I was afraid that might be true. But I had two addresses for Mr. Byron—one here and one in Grady—and since I live in Houston it seemed logical to check here first."

"How'd you come to git this man's address?" she said, and narrowed her eyes. "He ain't one of them mixed up in bootleggin' is he?"

"No, nothing like that. I believe he may have known my real mother. You see, I'm adopted and I've never known who she is. Look, here's a picture of her and my father—at least I assume it's them—do you recognize either of them?"

She held the picture far away, then moved it closer. "I don't see so good anymore . . . no, never seen 'em before. You'd better go to Grady, honey. Maybe your luck will be better there."

"You're probably right. By the way, would you have a phone directory I could look at?"

"I hadn't got no phone, honey; had it taken out several years back 'cause it was too noisy, woke me up. I sleep late mornings."

"Well, thank you very much. You've been very kind."

"Oh, t'was nothing, honey. Maybe you'd stay for some coffee and cake?"

"No, thank you. I've got to be going."

"You know, I lived other side of Broadway, near the wharves, when the storm hit. Anybody ever tell you about it?"

"Oh yes, I've heard many stories. Must have been something," I said, anxious to get free of her now I knew she'd be of no help.

"Our house had water clean up to the second floor, but we wasn't hurt. My two brothers and their families stayed upstairs all night and much of the follerin' day. The rugs were ruined and some of the furniture, too, but thank you, Jesus, that was all happened to us. My oldest son worked down to Hafner's Grocery Store, and we was scared to death he wasn't gonna get home safe. But he made it, went upstairs with the rest of us."

"Yes, well I—"

"Course I seen the one in 1915, too, but that wasn't

nearly so bad. Seawall's built to withstand almost anythin' nature can throw at us."

"Yes, I saw as I came across this morning they're not done yet with the new causeway."

"You come by train, or ferry over?"

"Train."

"Well, you be careful goin' back, honey. That old railroad bridge they're usin' ain't the best in the world. I'm not traveling off this island again till the causeway is finished. Got a sister in—"

"Thanks again for the information," I interrupted, and walked swiftly down the steps toward the bags. My head was beginning to ache.

"Anytime, dear," she called. "If you're ever around here again, drop by for a spell. I just love visitors."

"Yes, I'll certainly do that," I said, wondering why anyone would want to take up with a total stranger so quickly, and whether loneliness could ever get so bad. Would it one day be thus for me, my punishment for the mess I left behind in Houston? Would I grope one day at strangers for company, chattering at people who had no interest in what I had to say?

Here lies Willa Katherine Frazier, a cold bitch . . .

It was getting near lunchtime, and my stomach was like an empty vacuum for I'd eaten little at the rehearsal dinner and had not had so much as a cup of tea this morning. I longed to put down the bags and relax somewhere with my feet propped up, have a sandwich and some hot coffee. If I walked from this point on L down to Seawall Boulevard, fronting the beach, I should be near the Hotel Galvez. They would have lunch and a place to relax for a little while, if the hotel was anything like I remembered it from when I stayed there in 1912. Maybe going there would be a waste of valuable time, but somehow I felt sure a short stay would be a welcome boost to my spirits.

It was several blocks to the end of L, and I have no idea how many more once I was walking along the Boulevard, facing the wind, holding my hat to my head with one hand and both suitcase handles in the other. My feet were so tired that each boot felt like a vise, and I resolved to find a rest room or lounge at the Galvez where I could change into a less sensible but more airy pair of pumps.

By the time I arrived at the hotel, I felt as though I'd

successfully scaled a mountain. There were few people around the great lawns that day, and those who were held hats and clothing with the same stubborn tenacity that I held mine. A trolley trundled up along the left side just as I walked up the front walk, and I cursed myself silently for being too stuck-up to ride a streetcar. The people coming out of the car looked fresh and energetic, and were calling back and forth to one another as though they were all great friends.

The Galvez is seven stories high, its long midsection flanked by a wing on each end jutting out toward the sea like welcoming arms. It was as grand as I remembered, with sweeping drives and huge palms batting in the wind, and I remembered how important I'd felt when we had stayed there in 1912, on the occasion of a business meeting held there by my father.

I went directly to the first lounge in view, and changed shoes, then with feet feeling lighter and a new sense of calmness about the whole matter of looking up James Byron, I approached the dining hall. Almost no one sat at the snowy clothed tables, and a waiter, holding a stack of menus and stationed near the door with all the formality of one expecting a banquet crowd, offered to show me a table.

I knew right off he was kind. He was a heavy man, balding, with the kind of poker face so necessary for people who must constantly put up with peevish customers. But he smiled at me, and offered to check my bags at the desk.

"No, I'm not staying, thank you. Just lunch, please."

"Very good, madam. But let me take those cases—they do look heavy. I'll keep them safely until your meal is finished."

"I'll keep this one," I said, handing him the alligator bag. I wasn't about to let the carpetbag out of my sight.

He nodded then and led me to a good table—far from the kitchen and silverware stand—in a quiet corner where one alone needn't feel self-conscious for having no one to talk with while sitting there. As soon as he handed me the menu I remembered what I'd eaten there before, which all at once seemed like the prospect of a feast to a starving man.

"Do you still have the tomato stuffed with crabmeat? It's been some time . . ."

"Indeed we do, with assorted olive and chicken finger

sandwiches. May I suggest beginning with a cup of onion soup—"

"No, just the sandwiches and coffee, please."

"Of course," he said, having written nothing down as I expected he would not. He nodded politely and suggested I await my luncheon in the sun parlor, facing the Gulf. It had occurred to me while ordering lunch that I didn't know how much money I'd brought with me. In the excitement of leaving, it hadn't crossed my mind to switch handbags from the new one I'd carried to the rehearsal dinner. I sat down in a wicker wing chair in the sun parlor, facing the window, and opened my bag. There were four ones and a five-dollar bill wadded up, and less than a dollar in change. I crammed the money back inside and closed the bag. How far would I get on ten dollars? How unutterably stupid not to have switched handbags.

Then something else crossed my mind, an envelope slipped to me during the dinner by Maybelle. I'd figured it to be some sort of well-wisher card, and stuck it absently in my purse. Maybe, just maybe . . . I pulled out the card and opened it. A fifty-dollar bill was clipped to it, and a note penned in Maybelle's roundish, uniform script followed the hackneyed "congratulations" verse:

"To Willa and Rodney, to be put toward something you'd *really* like to have, from just Maybelle. Thank you for letting me be in your wedding."

"Just" Maybelle. Was this an illustration of a newfound sense of independence from her overbearing parents? Had she saved the money on the sly, determined to outdo the garish hall mirror given us by her family and chosen, of course, by Velma?

Poor Maybelle. Was she even now washing her hair for tonight, or checking the seams in the wine velvet creation she'd made to wear?

Maybelle would be staying home tonight, a vicarious bride-not-to-be . . . Suddenly sad for her, I carefully smoothed out all the bills, and replaced them neatly inside the bag, then leaned back. I took this finding of money as a sign, as though I were doing just what I ought to by running away. Of course the money was really only half mine—and now that I'd deserted Rodney at the altar, none of it was mine and would have to be returned. However, I could worry about that later, sometime when there was nothing else to worry about . . .

The Galvez sun parlor is a bright, rectangular room. Most of the furniture, grouped around magazine tables and lined up along the deep windows for the view, is white wicker and very comfortable for enjoying the sea breeze.

Across the room there are mahogany writing tables and chairs, and big pots of ferns between the supporting pillars reaching to the high ceiling. I was alone there that day except for one old man who'd fallen asleep reading the Galveston *Daily News,* a few chairs down. How delicious, I thought, to be able to fall asleep when one wanted to, with no worries, no cares.

I crossed the room and picked up a telephone directory, almost sorry to do it for I expected disappointment even before I opened it to the beginning of the *B*'s. Byerly, Byers, Bylee, Byron. A. C., C. B., C. L., R. T. That was all. No James and no J. R. or J. Randolph. I closed it. It all seemed unreal I should be boarding a train today—if possible—for Grady, a place I'd never known of any ties with, had never seen or even passed through on other trips. What did they do in Grady? Lumbering? Mining? Was it a dead town after all this time, victimized by lack of industry coming into it, like so many others? Was it like Galveston—a little sleepy, slow-paced, easy?

I closed my eyes and let the breeze cool my face. Across the street was the famed seawall, a seventeen-foot-high bulwark, curving down to the beach. While here in 1912, my mother and I had descended the stairs dissecting it, and tread the sandy beach below. She'd kept well covered, to protect her delicate skin. I had been less inhibited, and built sand castles that rarely stood beyond one day's visit, and had to be rebuilt the following day.

So much of those days on the beach with Mother came back now. We were here three full days and two nights while Dad stayed holed up in meeting rooms at the Galvez. And when dinner was held in the evening, Mother would attend with Dad and there would be a lady to sit with me, to take me to the dining hall to eat.

Whenever we went on trips and stayed in hotels, I always wrote letters to my real mother, and mailed them at the hotel desk myself because I didn't trust my adopted mother to mail them for me. I wonder where they all went? Had the hotel clerks smiled indulgently after I'd gone, later handing the letters to Mother on the sly, thinking they were intended for her because they were addressed simply, "To Mother"?

It was at the Galvez, I believe, that I wrote my last letter. None had ever been answered, and I had attained the age of twelve: for me, the age of total cynicism.

I'd questioned Mother more extensively than ever during our trips to the beach. I suppose I'd reached the point of desperation, when I felt I must demand answers to the questions which haunted me.

Still, she was evasive, hiding her face behind the big sun hat. Yes, I came from Ohio. No, she didn't know my real parents, only that she was assured they were both dead. No, she didn't recall the name of the agency, and anyway, understood it had been burned to the ground some years later, all records housed there destroyed. No, there was no way of finding out anything. No. No. No. No . . .

"And, Willa," had said my adopted mother, "I'm tired of answering questions. Don't ask me any more."

"Excuse me, ma'am, luncheon is served."

It was the waiter, and I blinked at him, wondering for a moment where I was and what he was talking about.

As I followed him into the dining room, now beginning to fill with other luncheon guests, I noticed the hands of the clock on the wall were pointed at twelve-fifteen and remembered I was to have had lunch with my father at twelve-thirty. He'd asked me about it earlier in the week, and I'd told him I'd go with him if there was time, but after all I was probably going to be busy the day of the wedding.

"Please, Willa," he'd said, "promise me?"

"All right," I'd told him then, figuring this little show of sentimentality was probably meant to be his way of smoothing over all the years when he had had no time for me. As the waiter set the plate before me in the Galvez dining room, I thought, Well, too bad, Pop, Willa couldn't make it. You should have asked me long, long ago . . .

The lunch, which tasted even better than I had remembered from 1912, gave me a false sense of well-being as I gathered my bags once again and started out; yet it took only a fruitless inquiry at the post office (suggested by the waiter, who'd sort of taken me under his wing) to dampen my spirits all over again and convince me I was wasting my time. James Byron might even have been killed, like so many others in the 1900 storm, as suggested by one postal clerk (why had I not thought of that?). It was logical enough, six thousand people gone, and those left busy shoveling bodies out to sea in an effort to rid themselves of the stench, the danger of disease. Oh, please, please, don't let James Byron have been one of those banished from the island at the end of a shovel . . .

I boarded the train fifteen minutes before departure time at two-thirty, and in the space of time it took to travel across the bay toward the mainland, I thought seriously about dropping the matter and going home. It would have been relatively easy at this point. Mother and Dad and Rodney and everybody else would have been wondering where the hell I'd been, but perhaps they hadn't given up on me yet, canceled out all the wedding arrangements. Everyone would be so relieved I'd returned, all would be forgiven in a matter of moments. I might still be sitting in the dressing room at the church tonight, the co-ordinator from The Fashion pulling on my gown, adjusting the veil, with Mother standing by in tears (Mother always cries at weddings) and wearing her rose-colored lace dress, her wide-brimmed hat and long beige gloves with rhinestone buttons.

On the other hand, the wedding seemed less and less real as the train sped out of Galveston, and the task at hand took on more importance with each moment. If I gave up now, I might never have another chance.

The last things I remember seeing were the big supporting arches of the new causeway, just beginning to take shape, rather like the arches of a monastery of ancient times, seeming almost to sway with the motion of the water below. I fell asleep then, and slept until we pulled into Union Station, where I was already ticketed on the Santa Fe leaving at four-fifteen for Grady.

The big deserted vault that had been Union Station the night before, now teemed with people pacing briskly about, each with a special purpose by the looks of them. I bought a copy of the *Ladies' Home Journal,* a magazine I rarely read, and sat down with it, holding it close to my face lest anyone should come by who might recognize me. There was a small boy sitting next to me whose mother had given him a package of Adams California Fruit gum, no doubt to appease him into shutting up. He was busy cramming every stick of it into his greedy mouth at once, and while his chewing and staring were no bother to me as I passed the few minutes between trains; I was irritated to feel the suction of one discarded stick of gum under my shoe when I got up to leave, and, already frustrated at the necessary time wasted between trains, the wondering if anyone might see and recognize me, I turned angrily on the little wretch and said, "You little pest, you'll make me late for my train."

His mother, heretofore engrossed by some article in the *Chronicle*, slapped down her paper and gave me a stare that would cool a hot stone. I hurried to the lounge, cleaned my shoe, then literally ran to the train car, where the conductor was already seeing people up the stairs, my shoe sticking to the pavement slightly with every step. Oh hell, I thought, anyone with any sense would give it up and go home. Yet I knew, of course, that I would board the train, calmly walk to the dining car and request some ice for cleaning my shoe, and wait out the day and a half between here and Grady.

In winter the sky darkens early. On that day it first turned pink and blue, before shading into one solid drape, void of all color, and I watched its process through the train window, oddly depressed.

I had always been alone, yet never felt it quite so acutely until that moment. All ties had been severed. Should I ever want to return home and make peace with my parents, they might well choose instead to disown me. After all, they were to be credited for providing well for me, if nothing else, and this episode for them might have been the breaking point after all the years of misery they'd suffered. While I still felt I was not to be blamed for the way things happened—after all, I didn't *ask* to be adopted, did I?—I was all too aware that as things now stood I had nothing— not love, not security, not even my own bed to sleep in.

And Rodney . . . well, at least he was a devil of a lot better off for my having exited his life. He could always put the Heights house on the market again, or find someone else, someone steady and reliable like Rosemarie, and bring his happy blushing bride to see the fanlight and the undercroft. She at least would far better appreciate the house of his dreams than I had, not because I hadn't liked the house as much as he, but because she would be willing to give herself to marriage in every way, when I was not. I should miss the real estate office, though. Maybe wherever I wound up, I could find a job in another such place. Maybe, maybe if Mother was really alive, or even Father, I could start a brand-new life with one or both of them, twenty years late but willing to forgive the past and forget what I'd been cheated of.

What if, on the other hand, I did find out all about my parents, and though they were now dead the truth of them was a hateful thing to learn? How many times had I threatened Mother Frazier as a child that when I was big enough I would run away and find my real mother? It must have been as often as she clashed with me over something I was being forbidden from doing.

And there was always the small chance that what had been told me by Susan Baxter when I was ten years old was correct. Susan's family lived next door to us for nine years, before we moved to Montrose. She and I were near the same age, though she was just enough older to dangle her superior years in front of me from time to time, and we used to play together.

One day we were playing jacks out on the front porch. I had had a quarrel with Mother that morning, and was taking out all my spite by speaking horribly of her under my breath to Susan. "I hate that woman," I said. "She isn't really my mother, and when I grow up I'm going to run away and find my real mother, and live with her."

Susan had rolled her eyes and said, "You sure are stupid, Willa Frazier. Don't you know if your mother had wanted you, the Fraziers wouldn't have got you in the first place?

"Besides, she's prob'ly a prostitute. That's what my mother says."

"What's a prost—you know, that word?"

"Prostitute. Don't you *know?* Mother says it's a lady who sells herself to men for their pleasure. Mother says she prob'ly didn't have the heart to have an operation to get rid of you when she found out you were coming, so she just gave you away when you were born cause you had no place in her life."

I wasn't sure what she meant by her statement, but I could tell by her expression it was a terrible slur against my mother, and I wouldn't stand for it. I picked up all the jacks and threw them at her face, cutting one of her eyes so badly she later had to be taken to the emergency room at the hospital, and told her I'd never speak to her again, and she better get off my porch.

Of course, shortly after that, I learned exactly what Susan Baxter had been talking about, and this knowledge nagged at me no matter how much I tried to deny it. Up to that time my mother had remained untarnished as an angel in my sight, but the sheer logic of what Dotty Baxter surmised was something one had to reckon with. It might have been true. Of course it may not have been that at all, probably wasn't, and yet . . .

I had to economize on that train ride, the first time I had ever done so in my life. I didn't rent a sleeping compartment, and slept instead in my train chair, which wasn't so uncomfortable except the upholstery was a bit scratchy against my neck. I ate a candy bar for supper rather than a meal in the dining car. Food on a train is atrociously expensive, and besides, it always tastes terrible.

I slept through the night, and awoke the next morning facing a heavy, leaden sky, so different from that of the day before that it was startling to behold, as though the world had gone blank overnight. We were still a long way from Grady, and the conductor told me we had just passed through Heddings. I was unfamiliar with this area of the country, as much as with Grady itself. The train seemed always to be cresting a hill, or descending a valley, and the trees along the route hung sadly by, bereft of any foliage or personality.

This would be a long day, perhaps the longest yet, for there would be a four-hour layover in Olmada and a train change there. Other stops on the route would be few and short, and I probably wouldn't even deboard because it looked so cold outside and the steam on the inside of the chilly window brought home the fact we were moving into a different sort of climate, one less friendly.

I longed for a bowl of oatmeal and a cup of hot Postum, and decided to treat myself to that or something else—even orange juice and a sweet roll would help to fill my empty stomach—and to get some magazines to read if I could find any. At the table in the dining car I sat across from a young woman, rather pretty with auburn hair pulled into curls on top of her head, and velvety white skin. She proved to be on her way to Grady, too.

Of course at the first opportunity, I told her of my business there.

"Well, dear," she said, "I didn't think there were many reasons for anybody to go to Grady, but I must admit that's a new one on me." She stifled a yawn as though from sheer boredom, and blew a puff of smoke into the air, reminding me I was out of cigarettes. "No, I've never heard of Mr. Byron, but then he must have lived there a long time ago. I'm visiting an aunt who lives there. I'm a widow, teach school in Brenham, and she's alone too. I wrote her this fall and said I'd spend Christmas with her. The poor dear was absolutely beside herself, you know . . . wrote me back right away and begged me to come as soon as I could."

"You're young to be a widow. The war?"

"You guessed it. Seems most everyone lost something out of that pile of rubbish, if you'll excuse the reference." She was primping now, looking into a cheap jeweled compact and rearranging the hair around her face.

"Then you've never actually lived in Grady yourself?"

"Heavens, no! Have you ever seen that little hole? There simply isn't anything there. Why anyone would want to live in Grady I'll never understand. My aunt owns a good bit of land outside of town, and that's the only reason she's stayed. Poor old thing is in her dotage now . . . my uncle died twelve years ago."

"What's her name?"

"Talbeaux. Mrs. Cornel Talbeaux."

"Oh, I see. It's a nice name, but I've never heard of it."

"It's French, dear. He was full-blooded, and about the best-looking thing I've ever seen, even as an old man. Course she wasn't bad either in her day. But all of us get old, I guess, don't we? Only alternative to dying young, somebody once said."

It was nice having someone near my age to talk with, and I was just about to suggest we sit together for the rest of the trip. Then a man who looked ten or fifteen years her senior walked past and asked if she'd like to join him in the smoking car.

"Don't mind if I do," she said easily, and turned to me. "See you later, dear, and good luck."

"Yes, all right. Thanks."

It was unusual for me to be left sitting. I was generally the one who left others sitting. I could go into the smoking car if I chose to, and light up one of my own—if I could find a pack to buy—and take up with a man probably better-looking than the one who'd just picked her up, if any were available. Somehow, though, I really didn't feel like a cigarette, or the company of a stranger. I took my magazines and went back to my chair.

It was bitter cold when we pulled into the Grady depot, and the wind was like icy claws tearing at my hair and blowing my skirt. There must have been less than ten people waiting for others to arrive on trains, and inside the dimly lit building were three or four old-timers sleeping across the benches. It was too late to get anything done— even a town much larger than Grady would be dead by eleven-thirty at night—so I inquired of a sleepy ticket agent whether there was a hotel—not at all sure there was—and he directed me to the Silver Star, just a block down the street.

When I arrived there and checked in, it made no difference the room was dingy and impersonal around me. There was a gas stove lit in one corner. I pulled a rocker up in front of it, wrapped myself in my robe, and slept there. It was the warmest I'd been since leaving Houston.

Chapter 8

Morning in Grady. I awoke before seven and dressed by the stove. Even if this were a small town, there was no telling how long it would take to trace someone who lived here twenty years earlier, so time was important. I'd already been gone from Houston better than two days, and my money wouldn't last forever. If I were to find a lead on James Byron, it might call for traveling even further— maybe even to another part of the country—to locate him. I would have to sit down and evaluate everything carefully, decide how to get the money to go on, or whether to try to write him instead, and go back home.

Home? How could I return now? Had I gone on the day of the wedding it might not have been so bad, but by now the whole episode was reduced to a pile of unpaid bills on my father's desk, wasted food, wilting flowers, embarrassment in front of friends. Even if I had to take a job for a few weeks to pay my further way, I couldn't go home at this point, not with the only news being I'd given up the search, without even a triumph to cushion the blow to my parents. If I did eventually return home, I had at least to be able to say I had accomplished what I started out to do. Otherwise I should look like a little fool, on top of everything else.

I picked up the carpetbag, but left the alligator bag in the room. The sky was still heavy as I walked out of the hotel and found a cab, parked along the edge of the town square, across from the four-storied red clay county courthouse. I told the driver to take me to Number 2 Blackburn, and mentally crossed my fingers.

"You sure this the place you want, ma'am?"

"Yes. Why?"

"Well, sir, nice lookin' young lady like you and all . . . I just can't figger what you'd be interested in down there. But whatever you say." He turned around and started the cab.

I had no interest in sustaining a conversation with him, so we rode on silently three quarters of the way around the square then out a side street between old dusty buildings with pillared porches that looked uncommonly quiet for a Monday morning.

Blackburn Place lay not far from the center of town, and as we turned the corner and I saw the street sign, I understood the driver's reluctance. The whole area was a shambles, unpainted houses with sagging porches and torn window screens, and junk heaped up in yard after dirt yard. Dogs with their ribs poking out roamed around without enough energy even to wag their tails, though at one house a group of stray cats had discovered a trash can with something in it worth eating. They'd overturned the can and were rummaging through its contents greedily, howling at one another like ladies arguing over merchandise at a bargain counter. Here and there I saw a woman or an old man sitting on a porch, rocking back and forth and looking aimlessly out at the street, as though nothing in the world mattered any more and maybe never had in the first place. And I couldn't help wondering if, after all I had chosen to throw away, I wouldn't end up the same way. Alone, just as always. Here lies Willa Katherine Frazier . . .

What children I saw were ill-dressed for the blistering chill, two of them without even a pair of shoes on their feet. I hoped, oh God, how I hoped, I would not find James Byron in this Godforsaken place, for I had not counted on anything like this in catching up with my past. I put a hand on the back of the driver's seat and leaned close to his ear. "Has it always been like this?"

"Awhile, miss. Time was, this was one of the finest neighborhoods in Grady, though. You c'n tell by lookin' at these houses they ain't always looked so bad. Some of 'em are big, you know, and used to be real showplaces for the upper class."

"What happened?"

"Happened? What does happen? Progress, I guess. People began shiftin' toward the south side of town and further toward the outskirts. Then of course many moved away altogether cause there wasn't much to hold a body here. Yonder there, on the right, is the place you're looking for. Want I should wait?"

"Yes, please. I won't be long, I don't think."

He pulled up to the curb and I got out. This was one of the larger houses, two-storied with gingerbread trim, broken in places around the balcony, and rows of deep windows. I tried to conjure what it might have been like when painted properly, and with flowers planted around the large yard, windows washed to a gleam and shutters cutting a handsome contrast to the color of the frame structure. There was an old rusted Model T Ford pulled up in the yard to the right of the sidewalk, its wheels sagging as though from exhaustion of having stood for so long in one place, and a line had been strung from one end of the porch almost to the front door, for hanging clothes. Ragged underwear, dingy linens, worn-out work pants, beat around in the wind. The handle was off the screen door so that I couldn't get a grip on it. I would just have to knock extra hard, and perhaps go around to the windows if no one heard.

It wasn't long before someone did hear the knocking, and opened the door. The lady looked older than I suspect she was, with greasy hair dangling at her shoulders, pale skin, and a hopeless look which blended well with the neighborhood. She held one small child on her shoulder and carried another in her belly, and there must have been two playing behind her. She didn't seem at all pleased to find me on the other side of the door. She shifted the barefoot child from one shoulder to the other, his leg pulling at her dress along the way, disclosing her protruding navel.

"Yeah?"

"Uh—my name is Willa Frazier, and I'm looking for a party who used to live in this house long ago, named James Byron. Would you have any idea—?"

"Never heard of him," she said rudely. "Now, git outta here so's I can close this damned door. I've got enough trouble keepin' my kids from catchin' their deaths without standin' here talking to you."

With that she slammed the door in my face, and a wave of relief swept over me as I hastily walked away. If I'd found James Byron in a place like this, and he proved a shiftless, no-good character, it might bear out what Susan Baxter had told me so many years ago about my mother . . .

The driver had edged down in the seat and pulled his cap over his eyes while he waited. "Where to from here, miss?"

"I don't even know. Where would I begin to trace somebody who lived here a long time ago?"

"Good question. Post office, maybe. You check the phone book yet?"

"Last night at the hotel. Nothing."

"There's the courthouse. This here's the county seat, you know. If the person you're looking for owned the property, the deed would have been recorded there, wouldn't it? Maybe they'd tell you, I don't know. Might've saved yourself a trip by stoppin' there in the first place."

"Take me there, then. Yes, maybe that's the answer."

"Humph. Could've saved yourself the trouble," he mumbled, and we drove away.

As it turned out, I could have also saved myself the trouble of going to the courthouse. Whether the clerk who waited on me—the only one around the empty office—was telling the truth, or was lying because she was anxious to take a morning coffee break or go to the bathroom, I don't know. She would not, however, offer me any help because I had only an address, and no legal description of the property. Peering self-righteously through round, horn-rimmed glasses, she said, "Come back sometime when you've got the proper information and I'll be glad to help you," then promptly closed the glass window separating us across the counter.

I knocked on the window.

She opened it and looked out impatiently.

"If you won't help me, then will you at least direct me to the post office?"

"In the general store right across the street from the front of this building. 'Zat all?"

"Yes. Thank you for being so uncommonly kind. I'll be sure to recommend you for a gold star on your record, and a raise in pay."

I could have pursued it further, gone to a supervisor, demanding an apology and some real assistance, but something told me it was time to quit beating my head against an immovable wall and take an easy route for a change.

Pickett's General Store looked warm and friendly compared with the imposing courthouse. I walked there with renewed determination and presented myself at the Grady post office—a small window on one side of Mr. Pickett's store.

Mr. Pickett himself was busy sorting mail behind the window, whistling while he worked. I knocked on the bars. "I beg your pardon. Are you the postmaster?"

"Postmaster, telegraph messenger, store owner, and just about anything else you might be able to think of, miss. May I help you?" His eyes were lively. There was a fringe of white hair around his otherwise bald head, almost covered by the green visor he wore around it.

"I'm looking for a James Byron, who used to live at this address twenty years ago—possibly longer. Could you check on whether he has a current address in Grady? I know he isn't on Blackburn Place any longer."

He raised an eyebrow above his glasses after he looked at the paper. "No, judging by the address, and by looking at you, I would guess not. Let me see here, Byron. Wait a moment. I'll check."

He disappeared behind a curtained door, and was gone several moments. I turned and looked around the room, overflowing with all sorts of merchandise—a place where one could browse for hours and still not see everything. In the opposite corner was a black potbellied stove, which looked as though it had been planted there like a flower, its pipe growing somewhat crookedly to the ceiling. Four chairs surrounded it, gathering its warmth, two of them occupied by bearded men, their feet propped against the stove, who now turned their attention toward me.

The postmaster had returned. "No, ma'am, I don't have

a thing on him. Something about the name rings a bell, but I'll be darned if I can figure what 'tis."

The man looked genuinely concerned, and seeing this for the first time since I'd left Galveston, brought tears to my eyes. "Oh, I just don't know where to turn now, I—"

There was a shifting over by the stove. One of the bearded men spoke up, "Ain't Byron the name of that schoolteacher up north of here?"

"That's where I've heard it," said Mr. Pickett, brightening. "A Byron heads up a school that used to be the Pedagoguery. Course, folks still insist on callin' it the Pedagoguery, although they changed its name some years back and switched from an all girls' school to coeds. But he doesn't get his mail out of here. Probably gets it from up yonder in Greenwood.

"I don't know the fella's first name—do you, Zach? No? It may not be the one you're looking for, but you look kinda done in. Been lookin' for a long time?"

"All my life, it seems. I certainly would be willing to give it a try."

"It's almost certain he lives there at the school. If you could get up there . . . oh, but I just thought of somethin'. The kids are gone now, for the holidays. The place might be deserted."

"Oh, that's all I need."

"Now, don't fret. You sit down over there by the fire and I'll bring you a cup of coffee—Madge just made it, and she makes the best coffee in town—"

"No, thanks. I haven't time. But do you know if there's anyone who could take me up to the school?"

"Let's see. They've got buses come back and forth early Monday morning to pick up the day students, but course they're not running now."

"Maybe a cab could take me, although I'm short of money at this point. I've traveled almost five hundred miles to find him. Do you know how much the fare would be?"

"A good piece, I'd say, for it's a distance. Tell you what, let me see if I can get my wife, Madge, to take over the store for a couple of hours. I can take you myself. She's back there doin' her Christmas baking, but maybe I could persuade her to stay out here awhile and keep an eye on things."

"You're the kindest man I've ever met. I'd be eternally grateful to you both."

"I'll be back directly."

He disappeared behind the curtain again, and was gone a few minutes. I could hear two voices speaking back and forth to each other, and had a strong feeling Madge didn't like the idea of coming to the front of the store. Hearing them gave me an odd feeling of detachment. Here I was, everything staked on that school up there, the most important thing in the world to me, getting there. And there was poor Madge, up to her elbows in flour and spices and candied fruit, wondering how in the world she would finish her Christmas baking when her husband insisted on taking off with some girl and leaving her to mind the store.

I told myself it did not matter what Madge Pickett was thinking, or what her dilemma was, any more than it ever mattered about anyone else when I wanted something for myself. But as I stood there, looking around the store, smelling the fragrance of old leather and tobacco, of fresh coffee and spices, I lost that detached feeling, and knew I felt as sorry for Madge Pickett as I did for myself.

"It's very important I get to the school today," I told her as she came out. She was red-haired with brown eyes and an expression of suspicion on her face. "When we return, I'll help you any way I can, I promise."

"Humph. It's no bother, dearie. Any two people crazy enough to go out under a snow sky and drive that far, more power to them." Someone came into the store then, and she went across to help him as we left through the front door.

Henry Pickett drove an old Dodge Roadster that bumped and rattled every foot of the way between Grady and the school. He wasn't very tall, and sat on a cushion on the front seat in order to get a full view of the road ahead. He wore an old pair of brown leather gloves and held the wheel with arms wide apart, as one would carry a big washtub. The car was heated, much to my relief, so I didn't mind the rattling much. Besides, Mr. Pickett proved to be a good conversationalist and knew much about Grady.

"Now, that heater down on your side gets pretty hot sometimes, so you let me know if you get uncomfortable and we'll cut it off. Madge insisted we buy a heater last year, but I wish they'd find a better place to put those things than under the dash . . .

"You from these parts originally?"

"No, I've never been here before. I think James Byron might have known my real mother . . . I'm adopted, you see."

"Oh, and searchin' out your past, are you?"

"Yes."

"Well, sometimes it works out for the best, findin' a person's past, and sometimes not. Grady's a good little place to live. Not much going on, hardly any crime and very little excitement. Me and Madge raised our two boys here, but they've both married now and moved away."

"Have you lived here always?"

"Twenty-five years."

"Then you might have been here when James Byron was. Did you know any Byrons?"

"Lemme see . . . there used to be a family name of Byron, owned a second-hand furniture store downtown. I didn't know them, only that they owned the store. However, I don't know as the Byron up at the school is related to them. Likely not; people come and go a lot here, and Byron's a pretty common name, isn't it?"

"I guess so, though you couldn't tell it by the telephone directories I've looked at."

"Well, it's about forty-five minutes to the school from here, if I recall. We'll be there before noon if it don't start to snow. I sure hope we get back before it starts."

"You have lots of snow up here, then?"

"A good bit, and it's treacherous when it comes, too, three or four feet usually; makes it impossible to get around much."

I said nothing. I would have hated to get Mr. Pickett caught in the snow, but I couldn't think of turning back when I'd come this far. I looked out the window and hoped it wouldn't start until tomorrow.

"What made you think you would find this feller here?"

"Only the old address."

"Oh, and you've already been down to Blackburn Place."

"Yes."

"To look at it now, you'd never think what a pretty sight it used to be around there."

"So I've heard."

"Seems nothin' lasts forever. The good things go along with the bad, I reckon."

"Yes."

The warmth of the little car made me drowsy, and I must have fallen asleep before we were twenty minutes down the road. The next thing I knew we were pulling into a circular drive, and Henry Pickett was tapping my shoulder.

"Oh, I didn't mean to sleep. Are we here?"

"Yes'm. Don't worry, folks who aren't used to this kind of weather always get drowsy in it."

My legs now felt baked from the heat. As Henry Pickett, the soul of chivalry, got out of the car and came round to my side, I looked upon the school. It was structured much like the Hotel Galvez, with a cupola in the center from which a bare flagpole thrust up starkly, and a wing jutting out each side of the main section. Several more outbuildings were situated here and there. All of them, including the main building, looked deserted, with shades pulled down over the windows. I got out and stretched my legs.

The buildings were bathed in the silence of half-light. A shuffling sound, elusive as that of a deer crossing the snow, caused me to look quickly around. Yet there was nothing. No snow still, only the uncanny feeling of something about to happen.

"D'you think anybody's here?"

"Only one way to find out."

We mounted the steps of the main building and Henry Pickett tried the door. My heart quickened a little. It seemed so easy now, was it all to prove a big letdown, like everything else?

"Well, someone's here anyway," he said as the door yielded. "Leastwise you could pick up some information."

As we entered the foyer I felt as though I'd been transported back in time to my days at Central High. The same smell of old, well-polished wood; disinfectant from a recent floor cleaning; the musty odor of long-used textbooks. Statues were placed on pedestals here and there; Thomas Jefferson held a prominent place between the two double doorways that most certainly led to the school auditorium. Trophy cases full of the slightly tarnished fruits of labor on the sports fields lined the walls.

All of these things at Central High were gone now, for Central had burned last year. All at once I felt an aching hope the same thing should never happen here, only why should I care? And then I knew. This was James Byron's place. He was here. I knew it even as Henry Pickett announced it from the directory posted on the wall.

"James R. Byron, Administrator," he said excitedly. "Looks good, looks good. Room 104."

I think he enjoyed the taste of imminent victory himself, but stopped and said almost apologetically, "Uh—I'll wait out here. This bein' the first floor, 104 ought to be around there, down the hall or somethin'. You go on."

"I'll be back in a moment to let you know," I told him, and my voice was calm, almost confident.

Room 104 was halfway down the left wing, on the left side. The transom above the tall door was open; there was light inside. I knocked only once, softly on the milky glass, and heard a shuffle: someone flipping the pages of a book.

The man who opened the door was taller than I—his head reached the level of the painted numbers on the glass. He wore round, horn-rimmed spectacles which might have fooled anyone into thinking he was older than he was. He was neatly turned out in navy suit, his dark hair parted down the center and closely trimmed.

"Excuse me, would you be Mr. James Byron?"

"Why, yes, miss, may I help you in some way?"

Suddenly I could think of no way to empty out all the information stored up for so long. I was like a bulging cornucopia, awaiting Thanksgiving Day for someone to empty me out. Dumbfounded, I held out the carpetbag.

He looked at it in puzzlement. "Yes, are you delivering this for one of the students?"

"No, no. I'm Willa Frazier. I think you knew my mother. This was her bag."

He then narrowed his eyes behind the spectacles and looked again, closely, at the bag, as though trying to recall something.

"Look, I have some other things in my purse here—two programs, a picture, and a slip of paper with your name and two addresses on it," I said, and dug a clammy hand down into my bag.

When I pulled out the evidence, James Byron went white, then looked across at me. "Thank God, she made it after all. Is she here with you?" He glanced quickly beyond me.

"No, I've never seen her."

"Come in, come in."

I'd followed him in and waited as he fastidiously dusted

an already clean chair seat across from his desk. Then he said, "And how did you get all the way up here?" and I thought at last of Henry Pickett.

"Oh, just a minute," I said, and heaped the bag down on the floor. I ran back down to where Mr. Pickett stood inside the entrance door, patiently waiting with hands clasped behind him. He'd raised the big shade and was looking out through the glass at the sky, which seemed more than ever pregnant with snow.

"I've found him, and I'll be all right. Let me pay you something for what you've done—"

"No, sir. Glad to be able to help you out, Miss Frazier. Think you've found the secret to your past, do you?"

"At least a start. He's down the hall . . . want to meet him?"

"No, no. I'd best be on my way."

"Yes, any minute now, the snow—"

"But how will you get back?"

"I don't know right now, and it doesn't matter. I—I don't know quite how to thank you for what you've done. If it hadn't been for you I would have never found him."

"It is I, much obliged to you, for getting me out of the store for a spell. Good luck to you, miss. I hope all you find will make you happy."

I did something then that I can scarcely ever remember doing to anyone in my life. I reached up and hugged Henry Pickett. He was just a bit embarrassed at this spontaneous show of affection, and after clearing his throat and blushing slightly, smiled and opened the door. I watched him till he'd entered his car and rattled around the circular drive away from the school, and had a fleeting thought again of Madge Pickett and her Christmas baking.

When I returned, James had brought two cups of hot coffee from somewhere, and cleared a space from the mounds of paper and books on his desk, and set the carpetbag down to one side. The four paper items he had lined up in front of him, like cards in a game of solitaire, and was studying them carefully.

"There are other things . . . in the bag."

"Of course. Shall I open it? Bad shape, huh? Bottom's half rotted from water damage."

"Yes, I've been wondering where it sat, to get that way."

"Good question. She was generally careful not to get the bag wet."

He pulled out the cambric gown, and looked suddenly embarrassed. "Of course I never saw this," he said, and I couldn't suppress a smile. "The shoes," he said then, almost caressingly, and pulled them out one by one, nudging his hands down inside them. "She was always going to sew on new ribbons, but never got around to it that summer."

"Was she a professional dancer?" I asked, thinking of Margueretta Sterling.

"No, but I understand she was quite talented in any case. By the date of this opera program, I expect she may have saved it from her first taste of professional ballet. She might have eventually wound up on stage herself, except . . ." He stopped talking and looked up at me. "These things were all you found in the bag?"

"Yes. Did you expect something more?"

"Well, she did keep a diary, and with all these other mementos here it seems rather strange . . ." He dug down and felt all around inside again.

"How convenient that would have been!"

"Yes, well, so here you are, Willa. Is that what your friends call you?"

"Yes."

"It suits you. You are a little like them both, I think. They were on the tall side; she was fair and he dark, handsome. She was beautiful, you know."

"When did you last see her?"

"The summer of 1899. It was the last time for any of us, as far as I knew. I thought her dead . . . had every reason to believe she was dead."

"But what can you tell me of her? How did it happen, accident, illness?"

He sat and stared at me for a few minutes, one eyebrow raised as though he tripped across a memory yet wouldn't let it come to the surface, and I realized he was reluctant to talk about my mother. I thought of Susan Baxter's word for her . . . "Look, if we could just begin from the first time you met her. I know nothing. I was adopted by parents, who lived in Ohio in 1900, or at least that's what I've always been made to believe. They've never told me anything about my beginnings. I discovered the bag by accident several nights ago. Naturally, I had to look for my real mother."

He grimaced. "If that diary were just there. She could

have told you in her own words all about that summer. She used to record in it faithfully."

"But you could tell me if you would. Mr. Byron, I've come such a long way. If you know anything about my mother, please tell me. I've got to know the truth, whatever it is."

"But it's very hard for me to talk about . . . I was responsible, in a way, for what I assumed to be her death."

"But it's obvious she didn't die, so you needn't feel guilty about anything, unless you were trying to do her harm."

"Oh no, I wouldn't have lifted a finger to harm her . . . would have died to save her."

"Well, then——"

"But you see, she trusted me and I let her down. If I hadn't—don't you see?—she wouldn't have been lost from both of us all these years; everything would have been different. She might be with me even now."

"So you believe she may still be alive?"

"Now? Oh, I suppose it's possible, but I doubt it. I think she'd have eventually contacted me, and I know she'd never have deserted you above all. She risked her life for you, before you were born. No, she's bound to be dead."

"Still, you couldn't be sure of that."

"I've no proof, if that's what you mean."

"Then please, tell me what you know. Perhaps between the two of us we can locate her, if she's alive. I've never really believed her dead.

"Look, it will be simple. Just begin by telling me her name."

"All right, all right. Please don't misunderstand my reluctance. It's only that I——"

"Please, her name?"

"Her name was Serena Garret. She was a parson's daughter."

"And my father?"

"A traveling musician. See, here is his name in the program—Roman Cruz."

Chapter 9

An hour had passed.

James Byron had begun to unravel the tale of a summer long ago, when he'd come to Galveston on the heels of tragedy that took the lives of both his parents, and my mother had become almost like a loving sister toward him. He, in turn, had looked upon her as a goddess and her lover as a god, and even had assigned himself the role of Argus, giant of a hundred eyes, and taken on the task of directing his watchful gaze upon them, following them, sometimes, to their meeting place.

The people he'd spoken of were important to me because they were my history, the source of my beginnings . . . my grandmother Janet Garret, an invalid who sat in a chair and stared at nothing and wrote reams of poetry with a single theme that no one could understand. My mother, Serena, had seen fit to keep her picture, yet not, apparently, her poetry. Was it her way of keeping intact what she wanted to believe about Janet?

My grandfather, a shepherd of God's kingdom strayed from his flock like a wayward sheep, finding some consolation in a whisky bottle because an event which happened years earlier had eaten away at the parish in his charge as a pillworm eats at a plant. And was James correct about his keeping company with Cousin Claire? Could he have been blamed for doing so, with his life's work crumbling in his hands and his wife able to lend him nothing in the way of moral support?

And Claire herself, constantly prying into Serena's life, meddling where she had no right. Did she look upon Serena and Roman fondly, hoping to help them in some way because their love had been forbidden, or was she contriving something else for them? If so, was her housekeeper, Helga Reinschmidt, in on it too? Was Helga's trip to San Antonio that summer only a cover for something which lay ahead?

And the others . . . Professor King of the traveling band, who bore a striking resemblance to Rubin Garret; Mrs. McCambridge, who stayed with Janet and kept a proprietary eye on Serena . . .

And of course Nick Weaver, everyone's idea of a fine Christian fellow, a little self-righteous as he pored over his organ music, Serena Garret's "intended" in everyone's mind except her own.

And Porky, her boon companion and James's friend, who made me wish I'd had the experience of owning a dog. And of course Charles Becker, Claire's dead husband, about whom James had so far said so little, yet hinted so much . . .

It was almost too much to be taken in at once, all the faceless people with private motives that somehow came together like the center of a spider web by the summer's end. But how? James had a way of organized, point-by-point storytelling, that threatened to put an end to my sanity once and for all. Why couldn't he just stop and say right out what happened that day he thought she was killed? Was he taking his time, still reluctant to come to that part?

His face had clouded up as he neared the end of the tale. Then suddenly it brightened. He'd remembered a picture he owned of my mother that he'd taken himself.

"My gosh, I can't believe I just thought of it! You can even see a little of her house in it," he'd said, and darted out to his quarters in Tannery Hall to get it, leaving me so stunned at the sudden prospect of seeing my mother for the first time that all I could do was give him a gaping stare.

He'd been gone for a few minutes when, impatient suddenly at all the loose ends of the story still dangling before me, I stretched and took a stroll around the room to pass the time. Books lined almost all the wall space, floor to ceiling, and there were three full shelves of *The Literary Digest,* each volume placed in order with the next. Two filing cabinets in one corner, James's desk and leather swivel chair, and two wooden armchairs made up the rest of the simple furnishings. There were no pictures on the desk, no family articles that one always found in the principal's office at school while nervously awaiting a dressing down. There was, however, a small oil painting on one wall, which I'd only then noticed.

A young girl with light, flowing hair and small features. Something about her brown eyes was enchanting. I gazed at it, almost mesmerized by the face, which was turned not quite straight ahead, the unusual angle adding to its coyness. I was still gazing at the painting when James returned.

"She's beautiful, is she not? My mother, Ruth."

"Enchanting."

"Janet painted it in 1879, some years before her acci-dent, and Serena gave it to me when I visited Galveston twenty years later. But here's the picture you've been wait-ing for."

I took it hungrily and stared at it, trying to take it all in.

My mother leans on pointed toe in a ballerina pose, her arms upraised and arched inward, forming a frame around her head. Behind her stretches the wide verandah of her house on Avenue L. To her right two great windows yawn. A Gulf breeze, ever so slight, has blown a wisp of hair across her forehead. The expression on her young face is one of rapture.

I went on looking at it, trying to comprehend this was really my mother and I'd found her at last, and suddenly I realized tears were streaming down my cheeks. I replaced the picture on the desk and James continued, handing me a tissue as though I were a student he was consoling over some mishap. "She would have made such a lovely danc-er," he said.

"Would have?"

"Yes, within a couple of days after I shot that photo, it came to light Father Garret was frightfully in arrears about paying for her dance lessons, and she was forced to give them up. This, of course, made her even more determined to run away with Roman Cruz, once he'd promised to take her. You can imagine how pent up she must have felt . . . on the one hand, expected to marry Nick Weaver; on the other, expected to look after Janet; and worrying con-stantly over her father. Lord, it would have been enough to make me steal away on a merchant ship, I can tell you."

"Yet she, being a woman, found it more difficult to get away . . ."

"Yes, indeed, but determination always plays a big role in success. Well, to get on . . . Many mornings when I was thought to be crabbing with Tommy Driscoll, I would be following Serena at safe distance, watching to be sure she met with Roman. If one day he failed to be waiting for her, I'd be close by to comfort her.

"You see, I never felt I could trust him completely, not till the end. If you'd known the kind of mystic quality about him, you would have understood. And I was so fond of Serena, would have done anything in the world to save

her being hurt. It was the reason I gave her my addresses—in case anything should happen to her and she
have need of me.

"It never happened, of course, that he stood her up. I
know now he was as much in love with her as she with
him, yet it bothered me, this romance between them. The
mythology book never paired Apollo with Aphrodite. It
made me think he might be stringing her along for the
summer, a typical Apolline tactic. I never dreamed I could
have been correct in believing the romance wasn't to be,
but to be so wrong about the reasons. My father was right
in his conviction one can always find truth in books, but
sometimes the truth is clothed in deception."

He went to get more coffee for us.

I picked up my mother's picture again. This time she
seemed almost to come to life, as though the verandah she
posed on were instead a stage with splendid footlights.
Soon, she would move her arms and body to an étude, and
after perfect execution of the dance, would be given cheers
by the audience, and dozens of roses sent by admirers.
She'd be perspiring some, the hair around her face damp,
forming little ringlets . . . Was this what Roman promised
her, a career in front of the footlights? Did he tell her,
"Stick with me, baby; we'll go to New York together, and
I'll make you a star"?

This is what I asked James when he returned to the office.

"You're remarkably perceptive, Willa. Yes, I think he
did intend helping her get into a school that he knew of in
New York. Of course he didn't know you were on the way
till the end. She might have been frightened to tell him,
afraid he'd be put off by her clumsiness or lack of caution,
and would leave her stranded. I wish you could have
known Roman. Of course, most of my acquaintance with
him has been in retrospect. You understand, I've had years
to put these things together, to remember small items here
and there, little things said and done." He placed the coffee
between us.

"Sorry I took so long. I ran into Perkins, one of the
teachers staying on for the holidays. He couldn't decide
where to put up the tree for our little party."

"Oh, am I interrupting anything? I never thought—"

"Not at all. We plan to do our quiet celebrating on

Christmas Day. You know, this is the first year since my
tenure as administrator began, that all the students have
had a place to go for the holidays. Only people left here are
bachelor teachers—five of us—who've nowhere else to go
particularly.

"You may not appreciate that, unless you've ever gone
to boarding school. The holidays are dreadfully lonely for
the kids who have no place to go. I learned that as I was
shifted about, year after year. I went to a total of five
boarding schools before finishing, and only a couple of
times was I able to spend a holiday away from school. In
summer I was sent to camp . . ."

"But your grandfather—"

"He was ninety when Mother and Father were killed.
He died in the fall of 1900. I was truly alone after that.
Lucky some distant relatives of my father's looked after my
estate. The money from it kept me out of their hair and in
schools.

"At any rate, this year we went on a campaign to see all
the students had a place to go. Some went home with fellow students, if they had no place else to go. It gave me a
good feeling, sending them off happy."

"You take your job seriously, that's obvious. How long
have you been here?"

"Five years. Began as a history instructor. It wasn't
really what I wanted most of all, but because I was taken
away from this area before I was ready, I always hungered
to get back, under any condition."

"Do you still teach, or just supervise?"

"I have several classes a week—history, English, geogra-
phy. Depends on how our staff is running from year to
year. You know, we have both boys and girls here now,
whereas in the old days before I took over, it was a school
for girls. We've changed the name to the Tannery Institute
of Learning—you may have noticed the sign at the edge of
the grounds—in honor of the original owner. My mother
and even Claire and Betsey went here when it was the
Pedagoguery.

"Well, something else occurred to me as I poured the
coffee just now . . . Porky was poisoned toward the end of
that summer. We didn't know who'd done it then, of
course, but we soon found out. In fact, it might have been
because of Porky's death that Serena confided in me her
plans to leave Galveston with Roman Cruz.

"I was heartbroken about Porky. I wasn't a strong child at all, and after he was buried I went back to Claire's and vomited up everything in my stomach. I'd even fainted a few times in my life . . . once in Galveston, early in the summer after I was stung by a man-of-war in the Gulf, and was being carried home by Roman and Serena. They never knew, though, and I'd have been mortified if they'd guessed.

"Anyway, back to Porky, I did have some of my savings left which I kept hidden in my closet at Claire's. That, plus my earnings from the sale of crabs, came to something like twenty dollars, I think. There was a pet shop in downtown Galveston, and I went to Serena's house that night to offer to buy her another dog there.

"Serena was grateful, but turned down the idea, and that was when she told me she was running away. She gave me no details, and at the time I'm not sure she knew all of them herself. It didn't matter, though. The fact was, she was leaving, and it broke my heart. I was no good at making friends, and I'd counted so on her friendship, then to have it blown away as with the wind . . . I was worried about her, too. Even at this point, I still wasn't positive Roman could be trusted, although I realize now this was only because I loved her so, nobody would have measured up as good enough to take her away from me.

"On the morning of September 7, I stopped next door to give Serena that slip of paper you brought today, then went with Tommy Driscoll crabbing. We caught three dozen good-sized ones and had them sold within an hour.

"Serena hadn't even said *when* she was leaving. Roman had probably urged her not to take any unnecessary chances that I might spill the information to someone. I knew the departure was to be soon, because the band had to go back to New York. I figured I could find out anyway, by just keeping my eyes open. That night I went up to my room after supper and watched her house, to see if there was any sign of her sneaking out. The house was quiet. The light stayed on in her mother's room, across from my own, till sometime after ten o'clock, and then shortly after, the downstairs lights went out.

"If I put my face to the glass and moved back as far as possible toward the window facing, I could just see someone walking from the Garret house down their front walk. I watched for Serena to depart until after midnight, then, tired out and with a crick in my neck, I went to bed, know-ing I'd guessed wrong about a nighttime rendezvous. And that winds up the background of the summer."

He paused there, rose from his chair, walked over to the window, and lifted the shade. I could tell we'd come to the part that was painful to him, the part that perhaps made him wish I'd never showed up at his office door, but I couldn't let him stop now . . .

He cleared his throat and stared out the window, and folded his arms in front of him as though to shield himself from some sort of purge. His voice was low as he contin-ued . . .

"Willa, I think it only fair that I tell you . . . because of what I did that next day, your mother is certain to have suffered severe disfigurement for the rest of her life."

I caught my breath as I thought of her again, imprisoned somewhere in an institution. Before, the conjecture had seemed almost foolish, yet now . . .

Chapter 10

"It was blazingly hot that morning of September eighth, hotter than it had been all summer long. When I woke up my clothes were sticking to me and I'd soaked a big spot on my pillow with perspiration. I got up and dressed and started downstairs. I was planning to follow Serena to the beach, but Claire had something else in mind.

" 'And where are you off to this morning?' she asked.

" 'Oh, just around.'

" 'My, aren't we secretive. Well, not today. I want you to help me rearrange some boxes up in the attic, to make room for some things I'm going to move up. It won't take long.'

"Thus I was stuck, unable even to check on whether Se-rena went to the beach, and angry for having my plans foiled. We moved boxes and stacked junk in the attic until ten-thirty or so, then Claire sat down and said, 'Whew, it is stuffy up here, isn't it! Tell you what, here's a quarter. You go down to Schott's for two chocolate sodas. Hurry back, now, and we'll get to work and finish this by noon.'

"I did as she said, looking forward to the chocolate soda but still wishing I'd been able to follow Serena to the beach. I stole a glance down that way as I walked out the front gate, and even was tempted to bolt, but I couldn't see anything anyway, and didn't want to be faced with having disobeyed Claire.

"When I came back, Claire was standing at the fence, motioning for me to hurry. 'It's Serena's mother, taken ill,' she said. 'Mrs. McCambridge can't locate Rubin, so we must find Serena and get her home. Do you know what part of the beach she'd be on? Or is she there today?'

"I stood tongue-tied for a minute, knowing to tell would be to betray my only friend in the world.

" 'Well? You must know?'

" 'I'll go and get her,' I said finally.

" 'Nothing doing. We'll board the rig and go together. It'll be twice as fast. Janet is very ill, you see, and time is of the utmost . . .'

"She was walking toward the barn as she spoke to me, and I was following her numbly, my knees like jelly. Perhaps they were already gone, I thought, and if so, all the better. Except Serena would want to be with her mother if Mrs. Garret needed her. She'd never forgive me if I failed to get her in time, and the way my cousin had explained the situation, I was sure Janet Garret must be dying.

"The wind had begun to take on a kind of chill as we pulled out of the barn and headed down L—we'd had no rain the whole of August, and everything was dry as overcooked chicken. The sun had disappeared; the sky was turning sad. Claire kept repeating, 'Oh, I hope it won't rain. This time of year one never knows—oh, it mustn't rain now.'

"I thought it odd she should mind, after having tapped her barometer all month long in hopes it would show a good shower in store, and griping about the effects of baking sun on the flowers in her care at the church garden. Then I realized she probably feared a hard rain would impede our speed in returning Serena to her mother's bedside.

"I directed her to the right once we got to the beach, and the closer we came to the Seaside Pavilion, the more frightened I got at this thing I was doing. Perhaps Serena would be mad; maybe she wouldn't want to know if her mother was ill. What if I'd ruined her plans with Roman by telling where she was?

"Maybe they weren't even there. Maybe Serena had

gone off somewhere else. I was so busy worrying about betraying her that I almost forgot to tell Claire to stop in front of the Seaside Pavilion.

"It didn't matter, though. She already knew.

"She pulled up about a hundred feet from the door, and said, 'This is it, isn't it?' And I knew then poor Serena hadn't kept her secret after all.

" 'I think so,' I said.

" 'Very well, then. You run along and get her. I'll wait for you here.'

"The wind was really kicking up, whipping the flags on the building as I walked up to the door. The Seaside Pavilion was a conglomeration of turrets and battlements, and projections coming out in all directions, and flags flying everywhere—I believe I counted twenty-nine flags altogether one time. I really hoped the place would be deserted, but when I looked up at the towers, I saw the candle burning in the window of one. They must have only just lit it, as the sky was now turning dark gray.

"I didn't want to be there. I wanted to be anywhere else in the world right then, but I tried the front door, found it unlocked, and stole in. Serena had told me once that they met sometimes in the tower, but I'd never been up there. I went into a little hallway and faced a tall, spiraling stairway. I still couldn't make up my mind, knew that hesitation might keep Serena from seeing her mother before she died, but I knew too that what I was doing might forever make her look upon me as a traitor. I stood at the railing for a moment, my perspiring hand gripping it as though it were the line of a lifebuoy. Then I walked up.

"I could hear their voices inside. By this time the whole of the band was gone from the premises. The musicians hadn't come from their hotel in town that morning because the shows were over and they had only to go straight to the Union Depot. Just as I lifted my hand to knock, I thought I heard a door open somewhere downstairs, but it was a flash across my mind, nothing more. The thunder outside was rumbling like a cannon in a battle far away. I was sweating like a field hand, but resigned at last to go through with it.

" 'Yes, what is it?' It was Roman's voice, angry. A chill went through me. I couldn't take lightly the anger of Roman Cruz. There was a hesitation, a rustling, and I knew

Serena was there too. Yet I asked anyway. 'What business is it of yours?' Roman demanded.

" 'I'm sorry. Serena's mother is ill and my cousin and I have come to take her home,' I told him.

"There was muffled conversation then, and finally Serena's voice a little louder saying flatly, 'Go ahead and open it.'

"He did so, and I saw the tower room for the first time. It was a grubby little place, with a small bare bed in one corner. Serena was fully dressed, and her carpetbag and purse were in another corner on a wooden chair.

" 'I'm so sorry,' I said. 'I didn't know whether to come or not, but Claire says it's serious.'

"Serena looked at Roman as he moved to close the door. 'Mother did have one spell early in the summer, couldn't stop vomiting. We never found out what it was.'

"I began to bawl then, and while Roman leaned against the window, looking out, Serena came and knelt in front of me. 'It's all right, James, you did right. We just need a moment or two to make some rearrangements in plans.'

" 'If there can *be* any rearranging at this point,' Roman said.

"I started for the door then, so they could be alone, and heard Roman say, 'You know if you don't leave now there's no use—'

"And that's when it happened. The door swung open, almost hitting me in the face, and there stood Claire, smiling like a cat just about to get his paw on a goldfish. I shall never forget that expression.

"Roman's voice filled the room. 'What in hell?'

" 'No need to hurry,' Claire told him. 'You must forgive my little lie about Janet, Serena, but it was the only way I could figure of getting all of us here together so I could tell you a little story—this one the truth. Now, it won't take too long if the three of you will just get over there to one side, and I'll close this door so we won't be disturbed by anything . . .'

"I don't know why we obeyed her so readily, but I moved toward Serena, and she took me by the shoulder and pulled me close to her as she moved next to Roman. Roman, independent to the end, stood exactly where he had been, observing Claire with a coolness only he could pull off.

" 'Where best to begin,' she said then. 'I have a little

information for Serena, about her . . . shall we say unusual? . . . background. It's in this letter, which I found in a box I'd been storing in James's room until the day he arrived. You must all appreciate the irony in that—no telling when I'd have gotten around to going carefully through the boxes in there, if James hadn't been coming. They'd been sent from Charles's office shortly after his death three years earlier, you know.

" 'Well, to continue, and we mustn't tarry for time is important . . . the letter is from James's mother, Ruth, to my husband, Charles, and dated just one week prior to his death.

" ' "Dear Charles," she wrote, "I have wonderful news. We are expecting a child in the coming winter. I do hope this one will be a girl, to make up in some way for having missed out on Serena's growing up. Not that I don't love James more than anything in the world, but we both know the frustration of having a child we can never acknowledge as our own.

" ' "I've been so grateful for every letter you've written to me—have them all hidden together in a little cache in the attic, just as a young girl would hide her love letters—telling me of her progress, especially in dancing. I know your financial help to poor Rubin makes the lessons possible, and I only hope they can continue for as long as she wants to take them. You've been so good to our child in a million ways, while I've done nothing. And how painful it must have been all these years, knowing your own daughter was so close, yet could never be told the truth." '

"Here, Claire paused for effect, and looked across at Serena, who'd gone pale.

" ' "Of course, then, the final and ultimate cruelty—having had to give up the mayor's race because those scoundrels who opposed you somehow found out, and had the nerve to actually send someone into the sanctity of your home and threaten to expose you and our daughter—all of us. You have suffered so . . . my dearest Charles, you've no idea how this has plagued me over the years, and in as real a sense as can be, I have suffered along with you.

" ' "Of course I'm thankful more than words could express for Rubin's and Janet's great generosity in caring for Serena as their own; no matter what happened, they surely saved the day for us. Had they not intervened when they did, you and I might have done the foolhardy, selfish act we considered, and run away together, throwing all caution aside. I wanted to so much, so much. Of course I can see now the mistake in doing it. We'd have wounded poor Claire even worse than we already had, and I simply could not have borne that on my conscience. At least, Charles, you and I have been the only ones to suffer from all this . . . the only ones who ever shall suffer from our misdeeds, God willing!

" ' "I must end this now as I see Edward driving up outside. I do love Edward, you know, and he believes I love him and have never loved anyone else. He is the perfect father for his son James, and will be, I am sure, to this next child. Keep praying for a girl, won't you? Lovingly, Ruth." '

"She folded the letter and slipped it back into her pocket, then said, 'Well, James, it was just within days after Charles's death that poor little Ruth had a miscarriage, wasn't it? I wouldn't wonder, knowing the letter was either on its way or already here, and that I might have gotten hold of it. It seems a strange twist, too, that the very first thing I did upon Charles's death was to notify Ruth and Edward by wire. She thought she suffered before, what agony she must have felt knowing this letter was floating around!

" 'There now, you have the history of what's been done to me, and you know that you and Serena are half brother and sister. You might just as well enjoy it for now, because you won't have very long to do so.'

"Serena and I looked at each other, and I think a kaleidoscope of memories must have flashed across our minds within an instant, things that had happened over the summer, things that might have been if only we'd known. Roman was shifting from one foot to the other, trying, I think, to figure what Claire's plans were.

" 'You should have seen the gawky schoolgirl that arrived on the train the first of that summer in 1879,' she continued. 'For three months I worked with her, spent a fortune on new clothes for her, and coaxed her into dress fittings with the finest seamstress in town. How foolish that I never realized all I was doing was priming her for an affair with my husband, and right under my nose. Oh yes, I was sick an awful lot that summer and had to stay in bed for days on end, and leave her to Charles to entertain.

Well, I must say he did a commendable job of that! Even had her working in his office.

" 'And Janet. Weren't she and Ruth just too chummy? Janet never did like me, Serena, right from the start. She must have enjoyed immensely being a part of this bizarre trick the four of them played on me.'

" 'That isn't true,' Serena said now. 'My mother would never have intentionally hurt anyone.'

"I could tell, even as she said it, though, she was connecting it with the poems Janet had written, as I was.

" 'Janet wasn't even your mother, don't forget, and anyway, a lot you know about her,' Claire said. 'I knew her for years before you came into the world. She was cold and impossible to get close to. Thought she was very high-class, the rich girl from Virginia. Too good for me. Well, I showed her in the end.'

"Serena's voice was low as she asked, 'What do you mean?'

" 'Her accident on the stairs, of course. It wasn't that I gave her a push, exactly. However, I did prod her in the right direction once she began backing away from me that morning, and I let her fall. It served her right and Rubin, too. He'd already lied to me about their relationship, said it was meaningless because she wouldn't share his bed.

" 'Then one day she turns up pregnant with Donnie. Well, I put an end to the both of them and was never sorry. Very appropriate, too, I might add, on his christening day—the child never made it to the church! You know, they say babies who've never been baptized can't get into heaven . . . Of course, not until this summer could I really face up to my part in her accident . . . for when I read Ruth's letter I knew she'd gotten just what she deserved, so I need feel no guilt.

" 'That isn't all, either. Just this summer, who do you suppose got rid of that detestable dog of yours?'

" 'You poisoned Porky?' I said, and lunged toward her.

" 'Who else? He was around Serena too much, got in my way of tracking her activities. If he'd been around here today I'd have had to kill him in any case, and I knew getting rid of him earlier would make things easier.

" 'Then of course I had to get Helga out of the way. She was onto me, I think. She's known me for a long time, known me too well. I could ill afford to have her around.

When she comes back, all this will be over and done with, and she'll soon be getting what she deserves.'

" 'But how did you find out, or did you know, we were leaving today?' Serena asked.

" 'Ah, I think I can answer you that,' said Roman. 'Someone with keys to this place, and with information as to the plans of the band. Have you known the Professor long, Mrs. Becker?'

" 'Oh, you are a bright boy!" said Claire. 'We met at the beginning of summer, even before you and Serena met, at a dinner party at the Harringtons'. Of course it wasn't right away that I realized what an advantage he could be to me. He was just interesting to know.'

" 'And looked so much like my father,' said Serena thoughtfully.

"Claire drew in a breath. 'Shut up,' she said, and her hand went to the area of her right skirt pocket then moved away. Roman must have realized then she was carrying a gun.

"He egged her on still further about the Professor. 'So you were his friend in town for the summer . . . that's very interesting. But I'm sure you wouldn't kid yourself that King would co-operate just out of the goodness of his heart. What did you give him in exchange for information?'

" 'Oh, Serena, I can see what you find so attractive in this boy. Well, I don't suppose there's any harm in telling at this point. The Professor has been longing to retire for some time, as you might have known, and with what he's saved plus some I was able to add, he'll live quite comfortably in Miami, you can be sure . . .'

"Suddenly, it all added up for me, and I blurted out, 'Then it was you and he, all the time, not Father Garret!'

" 'Of course not,' said Serena.

" 'Keep your mouth shut,' Claire said to her. 'You irk me—trying to seem so high-minded all the time, when really you're just a duplicate of your real mother, that's all. Stayed up here all summer with this boy, and would have taken off with him for God only knows what kind of promises.'

" 'My mother may have made one mistake, but she wasn't what you imply any more than I am,' Serena said softly, and a cool, determined look spread across her face. 'Perhaps I know better than you why you're doing this.

You never loved Charles Becker, did you? You were after my father from the time they moved in next door. I've seen it in a thousand ways. You'd have run off with him, too, if he'd given you the chance, gone to the ends of the earth with him. But he wouldn't have you, would he? He never cared for you a bit, and you couldn't stand it. He may have suspected you were responsible for Mother's accident, too. That's what's really been eating at you all this time, hasn't it?'

" 'It may surprise you to learn there was a time when your father found me quite winning, Serena, although he just never had the gumption to do anything about it. And you're right about Charles too, except you don't know the whole story, and while it's none of your business I am sick to death of having him regarded as a martyr . . . a poor man unloved and driven into the arms of another woman.

" 'Did you know that I loved his brother, Damon Becker, long before anyone else, and that the only child I ever bore was his? And long after, I confessed it all to Charles, knowing he might leave me but willing to pay the consquence regardless. Did he in turn tell me of his summer with my cousin Ruth and of the conspiracy he carried on with Janet and Rubin when they found out you were on the way, at a time when I'd have been bound to forgive him, and perhaps made the first attempt at forgetting the past and making something of our lives together from there on?

" 'Indeed not. He let me live with my guilt, and would have let me believe myself the only sinner among the pious group till the day I died. If I hadn't discovered this letter from Ruth, I would have never known.'

" 'And I would be doing today the thing you've longed your whole life to do yet always were denied,' Serena answered softly.

" 'It isn't fair, why should you?' said Claire, her voice raised.

" 'Because I can't be held responsible for what was not my fault. Can't you see, you started it all by marrying Charles Becker while you loved his brother? If it hadn't been for that, none of this would have taken place. You've only yourself to blame, Claire.'

"What happened next was very quick. Claire was caught off guard by Serena's remark, for it went right to the core. She lifted her right hand as though to slap her, giving Roman the chance he'd been awaiting. He grabbed her, they both reached for her pocket at the same time, then they struggled—she was stronger than I would have believed. There was a muffled shot then, and Serena and I looked at each other, wondering for an agonizing moment who'd gotten the blow. Then Claire slumped to the floor.

"Roman's eyes traveled to the bottom of the door, and he shouted, 'Oh, God, she's set the place afire.'

"Smoke was coming in under the door. He ran up and opened it, and a wall of smoke came billowing in. Down below, you could hear the crackling noise of burning wood and see the tips of the flames. 'We'll never make it this way,' he said. 'We'll have to make a jump for it.'

"He took a chair from the corner and threw it through the window glass, then looked down. 'The sand ought to be soft enough. I think we can make it without getting hurt if we can manage to miss those damn projections and flagpoles sticking out below. I'll go first, then you, Serena, then James.

" 'Well, are you coming?'

"Serena was kneeling beside Claire, tears running down her face. She looked up at Roman, then back at me, and said simply, 'I can't do it.'

" 'What do you mean, can't? It's a safer risk than going the other way. But hurry, or none of us will make—'

" 'Roman, you and James go,' she answered softly. 'I'll try the other way.'

" 'You little fool, come on or I'll heave you out myself.'

" 'Roman . . . I think I may be carrying your child.'

"He stared at her hard for a moment, then his face relaxed and he walked over and cupped his hands around her face and kissed her cheek: a strange, gentle thing to do when time was running out. She clasped his hands and he pulled back and, looking into her face for a longer moment, released his hands and went back to the window.

"When he spoke his voice was low, husky. 'I'll get down then, go round for help. If the fire wagons are here, they'll likely be around the other side, not knowing anybody's up here.'

"Then he was gone . . . we heard a thump against the sand, a kind of deathly stillness. Serena looked away from the window. 'Would you look, James, see if he made it?'

"I walked over and looked down. Roman Cruz lay in a twisted heap upon the sand. I gulped, then looked back at her. 'No, I'm afraid not. He looks . . . come on, we'll try the stairs. It's our only hope,' I said, and she obeyed me like a little child, without blinking an eye.

"But as we reached the landing I thought of the letter. 'Just a moment, I want that letter from my mother.'

" 'Our mother,' she corrected me, and I nodded. I went to Claire's body and pulled it from her pocket, trying not to think of her as dead because I would have fainted right then and there if I'd let myself . . . I touched only the skirt and got the letter. Then we left the tower room forever. I closed the door behind me. I think it was, even then, a need I've always had to tie things up properly, to say, figuratively at least, 'Well, this is over. It is finished.'

"It looked much worse going down than it really was, I guess. The smoke was devastating, and the flames were eating up the walls all around like hungry cats. She'd started the fire in the main hall, I think, and done a thorough job of spreading it. I guess she had kerosene in the back of the rig.

"Serena hesitated at the landing and opened her mouth to speak. Then, apparently changing her mind, started down. When we were about halfway, she slumped to a kneel and said, 'James, it's the heel of my shoe, caught between the stairs.'

"I knelt down to try and free it, but after getting the skirt out of the way and finding the heel I couldn't do it, nor could I see anything much besides. Those darn boots women have only just begun to stop wearing—hers were laced up almost to the knee.

" 'It's no use, James,' she said. 'You go on out front and get help. I'll be all right for a few minutes.'

"I hesitated for a moment, afraid there wouldn't be time. But then I obeyed her, and have never stopped regretting it. I made it to a main entrance door and opened it, but as soon as the outside air hit me I passed out cold.

"Till today I'd assumed she burned to death on the stairs. The memory of her face, so trusting, has haunted a million dreams . . ."

Chapter 11

James Byron turned and looked at me then.

His forehead was wet, perspiration lined his upper lip. "I'm sorry," I said, "so sorry for you . . ."

"But, don't you see? She couldn't have got out in time without getting burned horribly. God only knows how she managed to escape at all, for soon there were people everywhere, and she would certainly have been seen."

"Look, I just won't accept that. Maybe it's because I'm seeing her here in this photo for the first time, and it's too much of a blow to think anything could have happened to mar that kind of vitality, that loveliness. But I'm convinced if she'd been left there long enough to be horribly burned, she would have died. And I'll believe that to the end, unless it's proved to me otherwise."

"Yes . . . we always want to remember the best, don't we?" he said pensively. "When my mother and father were killed, I was angered they wouldn't let me see their bodies, because I felt if I could see them I would know for sure they were gone.

"Over the years I've come to see the wisdom in being forced to remember them as they were, before the accident. It's funny, but I have Claire to thank for that. She's the one who wouldn't let me see them . . . and Serena later tried to convince me she was right. Odd, isn't it?"

He walked around and sat down again at the desk. "Perhaps you're right. Maybe there was another way of escaping, but I just couldn't be sure, you see?"

"Well, there's only one way to find out, and that's to track her down. Now, let's go on from there. You never said whether the fire wagons arrived. Did they, and put the fire out?"

"Yes, but the building burned to the ground like a wadded up piece of paper. It took less than an hour from the time Claire started the fire. You see, the Seaside Pavilion was remote, much farther down from the public beaches than anything else, because the land was cheaper down there when they built it.

"And another odd thing was that window Roman

jumped from. All the other windows in the building had
India rubber fire escape cords. Only the tower windows
were fake, so there were no fire escapes attached to them.
Had it been any other window, we could all have gone
safely down the cord."

"But you are positive my father died there, on the
beach?"

"Yes. The authorities told us he'd twisted his neck some
way in the fall. I know he must have, because I've seen
people jump further distances than that before, and survive.
It was the way he landed, perhaps trying to avoid those
projections from the building.

"I was out of my head for a couple of days, suffering
mostly from shock and inhalation of too much smoke.
When I finally awoke, in my bed at Claire's, Helga
Reinschmidt was holding my hand. It was she who'd carried me from the burning building after I'd fainted. She'd
cut her trip short after a stay in Houston, and come back
that morning. Her suspicions that my cousin was up to
something had finally got the best of her."

"Did you discuss this with her later?"

"To a degree, though I was sworn to secrecy about most
of the matter. I'll explain about that in a moment. Helga
had returned from Union Depot just as we took off in
Claire's rig toward the beach. She didn't realize then where
we were going. She took her bags into the house and
looked around, then found the door to Charles's office
ajar—Claire always kept it locked—and the desk drawer
where his gun was kept, empty. She took out on foot in the
direction we'd gone, but we were far away by that time,
and she could only guess we were somewhere along the
beach. Then, of course, she approached and saw the flames.

"About a week later, Serena's friend Marybeth Fischer
returned from abroad. Very smartly dressed she was, a
svelte, attractive girl with dark hair and eyes. I'd made up
my mind no one was going to find out about Serena and
Roman, that the least I could do was to save her good
name, so I remained tight-lipped during my visit with Marybeth.

"She'd read between the lines of Serena's letters that
summer, and right off she said, 'Serena ran away, didn't
she?' But I denied it, reminded her how much she liked the
water, and said just because . . . her body . . . didn't

wash ashore was no sign she hadn't drowned. She stared at me for a long moment, then said finally, 'All right. I can see it's no use questioning you. You're a loyal little thing, aren't you? That's good. So few people are.'

". . . And that was the substance of our conversation."

"Did you make that up all by yourself?"

"No. It was Father Garret's idea. I think he put two and two together, and figured out what had happened in the tower room with Claire. I've always had a feeling he might even have known what went on all summer between Serena and Roman, but then that's pure speculation. He could never have stood for that sort of thing openly, of course. Yet I've always wondered if he guessed the truth, and pretended—perhaps even to himself—not to know.

"Shortly after the fire that afternoon, a storm broke, a rough one—not anything to resemble the one in 1900, of course—but a bad one. Since it was Serena's habit to swim every day, and as far as everyone knew she'd gone to the beach that morning as usual, it was easy enough to pretend for everyone's sake that she'd drowned.

"I'll never forget Father Garret as he looked, leaning against the fireplace in Claire's parlor on the first day I was able to get up. He was rugged, good-looking, tall. He spread his great hands out over the mantel and looked away from me as he talked.

" 'I've spoken with Helga,' he said. 'She told me Charles's handgun is gone from his desk.'

" 'Yes, sir.'

" 'If I just speculate on some things, would you tell me whether or not I'm right? I give you my word, it would be just between the two of us. And believe me, at this point it doesn't matter what I know. You needn't cover up anything.'

" 'All right, sir.'

" 'What did Claire say up there in the Seaside Pavilion?'

" 'She told us she'd found this letter from my mother to Charles. I still have it, sir, and you can read it if you want to.'

" 'No, that won't be necessary, I don't believe. Did your mother mention Serena in her letter?'

" 'Yes, sir. She spoke of Serena as 'their' daughter—hers and Charles's.'

" 'All right, then. I can figure out the rest. Just tell me

one thing, and please tell me the truth. Did my daughter die in the fire?'

" 'Yes, sir. I tried to get help. Her shoe was caught in the stair rung—it was horrible, I—'

" 'It's all right. I just wanted to know whether she died at Claire's hand.'

" 'Not directly. Claire didn't shoot Serena, if that's what you mean.'

" 'That's what I mean. You can understand, I had to know.'

" 'Yes, sir.'

" 'You haven't talked with anyone, told anything yet?'

" 'No, sir. I've only just gotten out of bed this morning.'

" 'Good. All right. I want you to do something for me. I want you to say Serena was killed in the sea as she bathed that morning. No one need know she was near the place.'

" 'Yes, sir, if you want me to, sir.'

" 'I'm only trying to protect her memory. You see, I loved her more than anything in the world, and I don't want any vicious gossip about her final days here on earth. You can understand . . .'

" 'Of course.'

"Then he turned to me for the first time, and said, 'You're one of the finest young men I have ever met. I'm so grateful she had your friendship this summer. It must have meant the world to her.'

" 'She meant the world to me, sir. But I failed her, in the end.'

" 'No, it wasn't you who failed her at all. It was me. If anyone's to blame, I am. But we've got to keep it in our heads that it's all over now. The least we can do is protect her memory, for it will be defenseless now. Should talk get started, there would be no one around to stop it.'

" 'Yes, sir,' I told him, puzzled by his phrasing it that way. Of course I doubt he knew she was carrying you, unless he guessed that too. He did not know, as we both know now, that she risked running off by herself rather than staying in Galveston to face him or anyone else with the truth."

". . . Or to hurt him."

"Yes. That's why I can't feature her ever letting go of you. I believe she'd have gone through hell to keep you . . ."

"Anyway, the bizarre events of the whole episode were not yet over. Late that night, Father Garret climbed the stairs and went into his wife Janet's room for the final time. There he took a gun and shot her, through the heart, then turned the gun to his right temple and pulled the trigger again."

Chapter 12

James turned around in his chair and looked out the window again.

"You'd think it would've started long ago, wouldn't you?"

"What?"

"The snow. It will, you know. We'll have three- and four-foot drifts of it, at least by Christmas Day." He was talking more to himself than to me. "Winter is so silent . . . have you ever noticed? No matter how much noise people make in winter, there is still that unalterable degree of quiet all around . . ."

"James, do you think my mother tried to reach you, to let you know she was all right?"

"I don't know. Such would have been highly risky. Had she written to me in Galveston right away, anyone might have wound up with the letter. If she wrote me later here in Grady, I never received it. That's why I'm convinced—"

"You don't believe there's a chance, then?"

"No, I'm afraid not."

"I'm sorry for putting you through it all again, truly I am, yet you must be able to guess what it's like, not knowing my background, what kind of person I am or where—"

"Not at all. I'm only so thankful you came."

"What happened, then, after Father Garret committed the murder-suicide? How gruesome!"

"Yes, indeed. None of us heard the shot. Poor Mrs. McCambridge discovered his big body hunched over Janet's when she came round the next morning to stay. She kept her own house key, you see, and getting no answer to her knock, charged in and up the stairs. After she found them, she came running out of the house, screaming like a banshee. She just stood in the front yard screaming, until Helga and I ran to see what was amiss. She vowed she would never set foot on Avenue L again, and I wouldn't be surprised if she didn't stick to her word . . .

"Of course, with deaths in two families next to each other on Avenue L, the newspapers had a regular field day after that, whereas before, the fire itself had made the headlines, with only mention of my name and Claire's, and Roman's. You see, the story given them and the police was that I'd been near the Pavilion playing when the storm threatened, and my cousin had come to fetch me. Something had happened with the electrical wiring while we were in there—you know, wiring in those days left something to be desired—the fire started, and so on. I told the police I'd gone into the hall, afraid of the weather brewing, and had no idea Roman Cruz was in the tower room at the same time. It was rather limp, I'll admit, but they were willing to accept it, apparently. They still didn't connect this with Serena's death because she, supposedly, was doing her swimming down at the Fischer place, some distance further. Therefore, they failed to connect any of this with the murder-suicide."

"Poor man . . ."

"Yes. You can see how utterly hopeless his situation was. He'd pinned all prayers for a tolerable existence on Serena, and when she was gone he had nothing. I imagine somewhere along the way he must have lost his faith in God . . . perhaps partly out of guilt for what he, Mother, and Janet and Charles had pulled off on Claire. Then from what Claire said, there must have been something between Rubin and her at one time, though I don't know how far it went. The weight of his sins hung heavily on his shoulders, I guess, and everything else on top of that . . .

"It wasn't long before Helga and I left Galveston and went our separate ways. I first headed for Grady so the people 'in charge' of me could decide where I would be sent. Helga started again for San Antonio, and this time she made it.

"Claire left the house and most of her estate to Helga, you know. Before she discovered the letter to Charles from Mother, I'd been named beneficiary. Apparently she'd taken care of that right after she returned from my parents' funeral, before I got to Galveston. So then, she had to spend time through the summer having it changed again without arousing suspicion. What passed to me, after her death, was my own father's estate, then later his father's estate, both left in trust. The money off them wasn't a lifetime source, but at least it saw me through my education."

"But Helga had no wish to stick around Galveston among the ruins."

"Yes, good way of putting it. She lived until only a few years ago, remaining in San Antonio, and I never once heard from her. Then, upon her death, I received a letter from her brother Carl in San Antonio. He asked me to come down because she'd left the remainder of Claire's estate to me in her will—she'd touched almost none of it before leaving, then of course the house and all its furnishings were destroyed in the storm of 1900.

"When I went to San Antonio, Carl gave me a stack of letters she'd saved over the years, those written to her by Claire during the time she was not in service with the Beckers. There was a short letter written by Helga, addressed to me, which asked that Claire's letters be destroyed once I had read them. It was her way, I guess, of letting me know at last what information she had about what had happened—what caused—events that summer. And she also wanted to explain her loyalty to a woman who wound up so vengeful, I think. She told me in the letter that she believed herself responsible for Claire's 'bleeding spells,' as she called them, which eventually led to Claire's hysterectomy. She said she did not know how, but she must have made some mistake during the delivery of Claire's child . . . she was the midwife, you see.

"She realized Charles blamed her for hurting Claire, and she wasn't surprised that he sent her for a prolonged visit with her brother Carl at the time the Beckers moved from Grady in early 1877. Guess she didn't like being around Charles any more than he enjoyed her company. She never returned to the Beckers' until right after his death, at which time Claire wasted no time urging her to come. The source of trouble between Helga and her brother—I finally learned from him after she died—was that he resented her being in domestic service. Their family had come over from Germany some years earlier and accumulated a fair amount of wealth from business enterprises in this country. They lived in a section of San Antonio where just about all wealthy Germans lived—on King William Street in Sauerkraut Bend, on the River. There was no need for Helga to go out and work. Yet, independent almost to a fault, she insisted upon it.

"When she went back to Claire's again—after Charles's death—there must have been a nasty row between her and

Carl, and Claire knew of this. That was why she was so suspicious of Claire insisting she visit there in 1899."

"But what happened with the house after Claire's death? Did they leave it vacant? Is there any way of checking whether anything in it was salvaged before the storm, papers or anything?"

"My, you do have an inquisitive nose, Willa," he said, laughing. "No, Helga left some things up in the attic, and rented the house and furnishings through an agency. Apparently two or three families lived there at one time or another between that summer and the next—the fatal 1900."

"Do you hate Claire for what she did?"

"Hate her? Why no, not any more, though I did for a time. But I have mentioned the years I've had to think, and the years sometimes have a kind of mellowing effect on hatred. She was quite mad at the end, you see. It was so obvious, yet none of us knew. She spent most of that summer I stayed with her reliving the past, longing for Damon Becker. I think her mind shut out all the things she couldn't tolerate in herself.

"And seeing my mother and father all those months, together, loving each other, drove her to the edge."

"Yes, that and the knowledge that the one person she'd loved and trusted all her life—my mother, Ruth—had betrayed her."

"Do you think she intended to die in that fire?"

"Absolutely. You see, by doing so she'd win against fate—get vengeance on all those she hated and at the same time dictate the means of her own death."

"In the end, she didn't even get that . . . she died without knowing whether the three of you managed to escape," I said, wondering then what images might have flashed across Claire Becker's mind as she struggled over that gun.

"Yes, and without knowing about you," said James, a smile playing at the edge of his lips. Then he knitted his brow and said doubtfully, "Ohio . . . are you sure the Fraziers couldn't have gotten you from Galveston, or maybe Houston?"

"Maybe so, and only said Ohio to throw me off the track."

"Well, considering the way things happened, they probably knew as little about your background as they told you. But you seem to blame them, in a way."

"Only because they lied. It's a sure bet they knew something. They had hidden that carpetbag in our attic at home."

"But why didn't you just go to them straight off and ask?"

"It's a long story . . . goes way back. I had my reasons and I'll tell you sometime, but now I just want to get at the truth."

"Right. Maybe we can trace it right from the Seaside Pavilion. If we could only find out whom Serena sought out for help—if anyone—we could go from there."

"She must have gone to someone. Wouldn't a girl at that time have been kind of lost out on her own?"

"Yes," he said, folding his hands and looking down at the desk top.

"What about Marybeth Fischer? You said they were good friends, and apparently Marybeth had plenty of money. She might have been covering when she talked with you after it happened. Maybe she sent her away to Europe or something, till after I was born."

"I don't think so. Marybeth's family was wealthy, but I doubt she had any money at her disposal."

"If not her, then who?"

"Only one person I know of: Nick Weaver. She wouldn't have liked turning to him, but he's the only one I can figure. She had so few friends, and that many fewer she might be able to trust."

"Yes, I can understand that. But don't you think he might have told?"

"Not if she swore him to secrecy. He was quite fond of Serena in his way, and if he did decide to help her, he would have had no one to answer to. His parents lived in, somewhere . . . let me see . . .

"Ohio! Yes, that's it. At least, I think they did."

We'd both risen to our feet, and stood blinking at each other for a moment, before it registered we had no idea where Nick Weaver might be now.

I slumped down. "He might be anywhere, even dead."

"Yes . . . I have one hunch, though. Nick's greatest ambition was to be organist at Trinity Church in Galveston; he used to talk about it all the time. Supposing he made it finally, is there now, or has been there? It's worth a try."

He looked at his fob watch. "Let's see, two-thirty. He

might be giving lessons at home. We'll try there first, then if no luck, call Trinity, and even St. Christopher's, in case he's still there. If I were a betting man, though, I'd say he made it to Trinity Church, unless he died during the storm . . ."

By the looks of the sky, one might have guessed the time to be going on six o'clock. I gazed out at the winter bleakness and found myself in agreement with James about its incredible silence.

Then I picked up my mother's picture again.

How could anyone look so alive, yet be dead? Could that body, that face, be gone forever, reduced to dust somewhere under the ground? I could almost pick her up out of the photo and set her on the desk like a toy, wind her up and watch her dance. Yet, if the sunshine in this picture could be so warm and bright, and the winter but a few feet from me now so cold and forbidding, she could be gone. Summer can die. Mother can be dead . . .

James's voice grew louder as a bad phone connection worsened. "Yes, operator. Do you have a listing on a Nick Weaver, or Nicholas Weaver? No, I don't have an address for him . . ."

How many days had it been since I left Houston? Three. It would be all over now, with Rodney. What would he be doing at this moment? Working, no doubt, either in his office or out at some property.

"And, operator, if you don't find a listing, let's try the Trinity Episcopal Church, and ask for him there."

He turned toward me and winked. I felt someone had finally taken a hand in my life and would help. Someone had come along who was not at cross-purposes with me, after a lifetime of people who couldn't understand why I must know the woman in this photograph. Once I'd had a teacher who took a liking to me, for some reason, and I'd wound up pouring my heart out to her one afternoon after school, only to have her listen attentively, then look across at me sternly and say, "You are foolish, Willa. You ought to forget about this and be thankful for what you have. It's a lot more than many of us ever get."

I wondered now at the colors in the photograph of my mother. I knew she was fair, her hair light. But what of the filmy costume she wore, that hung like lengths of soft chiffon around her body?

James had his hand over the receiver now, and was whispering, "Operator finds no listing on Nick. She's trying the church, though. At least it's still there."

"Oh yes, I could have told you that. A storm survivor, raised up stone by stone with the rest of the city, during grade-raising."

He turned back. "Yes, thank you," he said, then a pause. "Yes, miss, I wonder if you could tell me whether you've ever had an organist or music director on your staff named Nick Weaver. He'd be about—

"You do? Now? Please, could you ask him to come to the phone? Yes, sorry to trouble you, but you see this is very important and . . .

"He's practicing in the sanctuary," James said to me.

A silence. An interminably long interruption in our progress, during which my hopes built and fell, built and fell, as often as the ticking of the clock on James's desk.

"Nick? Nick Weaver? This is James Byron. You won't remember me, but I lived next door to a girl you knew in Galveston long ago, Serena Garret.

"Yes, well, you will never believe who I have here. Her name is Willa Frazier and she's proven to my satisfaction she is Serena's daughter. Um-hum. She's seeking out her past, and we thought you might be able to enlighten us on what happened to Serena after she left Galveston that summer.

"No, she couldn't have been drowned. This girl has her carpetbag, you know, the one she carried her things in? She had it with her that day of the fire. Yes, I'm sure. Serena's things are still in it, and a picture of the Garrets, too.

"Yes, well, you wouldn't have any idea, would you, whom she might have gone to that day? Um-hum. Yes. Well then, I won't bother you any further. Yes, probably is at that. Yes, strange what people will try to pull off. Um-hum. Well, thanks anyway. Be seeing you."

He hung up the phone and sighed. "He claims to know nothing. Says you're a fraud, said that two or three times. Probably someone hoping to find a few dollars in all this. Few dollars, ha! Serena Garret hadn't a penny that I know of. He knows it, too. Old Hephaestus . . ."

"Who?"

"Never mind. An old joke."

"What next, then?"

"I don't know. We can try to locate Marybeth, I guess. But somehow I have a feeling he's lying. When I first told him you were here, the line might've gone dead for the silence. Then he spoke up and adamantly denied the possibility of it, even after I'd told him the proof."

"Look, maybe he doesn't know anything, and still feels she cared enough for him to have come to him if she was in trouble, so it's impossible for him to conceive anyone else might have taken her in."

"You might be right, but . . . oh well, let's give Marybeth a try. I'll get the operator back and ask for the Fischer residence, but it's a pretty long shot the Fischer place would have survived the hurricane, being right there on the beach. Maybe the family still live in Galveston, though."

He turned around again and picked up the receiver. It was my feeling that Mother would have gone to Marybeth before anyone, because they were of the same age, and she'd probably have written Marybeth about Roman. She might well have been back from Europe sooner than James had been led to believe.

He'd gotten no response on the Fischer number. "No, operator," he was saying, "I'm positive of the spelling, with a *c* after the *s*.

"Damn that storm," he said to me. "If it hadn't been for that, we might be able to do better. Fischers probably fled the island like so many others.

"Yes, operator, you have one? No, I don't know what the first name was. Let's give it a try. Ask for Marybeth Fischer, please. That'll get me what I want to know."

I could not get over the thoroughness of this man. I was sure he'd reach some information if it took all night.

"Yes, I'll talk to him. Hello, Mr. Fischer. This is James Byron in Grady. I'm looking for Marybeth—oh she is, your sister? Um-hum. Yes, well, Roy, I met your sister once, long ago. She was a friend of a friend of mine. We used to swim at your pier sometimes. Yes, Serena, that's right. I'm the boy who lived next door to her in '99 . . . yes. Look, where might I find Marybeth? I've someone here from Houston who wants very much to meet her. Oh, she does? Splendid. Could you give me her number? Oh, I see. Yes, um-hum, 119 Avenue O. And she'll be back tomorrow night? Yes. Very good. Oh, and her married name? Tracy? Yes, good. Thank you very much."

"Not till tomorrow?"

"Afraid not. But let's go down, shall we? By the time we arrive she'll be there, gone now with her husband on a business trip. You'll want to see her anyway, and so will I."

"Yes, me, but not you. Surely I can't expect you to spend your Christmas traveling to Galveston."

"But, don't you see, I have a stake in this, too, especially since I'm your uncle. I figured that out as soon as you appeared at the door."

A new feeling of warmth spread over me. Here was someone from my past, more a part of me than my adopted parents ever could be. "Shall we find out when the next train leaves from Grady, try to get transportation back to town?"

"Oh no, we'll go in my car. We're lucky that snow is holding up for us. If we hurry, we can be a good distance from here before it gets too bad." He was looking out the window now. He turned again. "You wouldn't mind going with me, would you? If we drive straight through, we'll make it by, oh, probably afternoon of Christmas Day at the latest."

"Nothing I'd like better. But the causeway leading from the mainland across Galveston Bay is out for repairs now. If you have your car, we'll have to ferry over. Only other way is on the train from Houston."

"So, we'll ferry. No problem there. Look, do you want to phone your parents before we strike out?"

"No, not yet. I'm not ready to talk with them yet."

"All right. It does seem a shame, though, right at Christmas and everything."

"Its being Christmas is the least of their worries right now . . . I'll explain on the trip down. But I've got to do this on my own, and I don't want them interfering."

"All right."

"Before we go, could you tell me what are the colors in this picture? The costume?"

"Pink. All pink, soft, almost mauve, as I remember."

"I guess the dancing shoes were once pink, too. Could we take it along?"

"Certainly. It is a treasure, isn't it? My only picture of her, the only one on that roll of film that turned out worth saving."

"I only regret I have no picture of my father."

"Hm . . . tell you what. Let's get my book on mythol-
zy down. It's up here somewhere," he said, looking

among the shelves. "At least I can show you why he reminded me of Apollo."

It didn't seem much of a substitute, but I pretended to be grateful. He was doing more for me than anyone had ever done. When he found it, and opened it to the page, a slip of brittle paper wafted like a dead leaf out onto the desk. "I didn't know this was here. Serena must have marked the place when she was reading about Apollo, then it worked itself into the margin and was forgotten."

I reached for the paper. "You know, it's funny," I said, smelling its mustiness, "it's only time really, separating me from my mother. She once touched this paper as I'm doing, and nothing is between her fingertips and mine except time. She might just have let go of it."

He looked at me kindly. "I wish we could find her alive, Willa. Sometimes I can see her in you. An expression, something in your smile, and she's almost here . . ."

"Well, here's Apollo. See the fine body contours, the muscles? Roman was like that. And if you look at the face for a moment, you can almost see him. You know, it's remarkable, but my memory of him is more like this than I realized. Notice the slight slant of the eyes."

It was hard to imagine the white statue being anything like my father, with its laurel wreath and vacant eyes. I nodded, and he closed the book and replaced it on the shelf.

"Just let me pack a bag, and we'll be off. I'll have to tell Stewart—the chemistry teacher—I'm going, and leave my presents, such as they are, with him. Need to freshen up? There's a lounge three doors down on the right. If there's anything else you need I might have it in my quarters, bachelor though they are."

"No, but we will have to stop back by the hotel and get my things."

"Very good. Now, Willa, speaking as a fond uncle, let me caution you against getting your hopes up too high. I know it's hard not to—it is for me as well, the longer we talk about it—but we may not find a thing. She may have known someone I didn't, may have gone it on her own that day."

"I was just wondering . . ."

"What?"

"Who named me Willa?"

Chapter 13

We arrived in Galveston early in the afternoon on Christmas Day.

I had had the curious feeling, as we finally left the school building, that I would not see a car in the garage, but a rig with a horse somewhere near, waiting to be harnessed and snorting the cold air from his nostrils. In the space of a few hours, the story of my mother and father and their world had become more real than the present one. I was like two people rather than one. All my history began and ended twenty years before. The Willa of then, and the Willa of now, seemed independent of each other.

The car which appeared as James pulled open two big wooden garage doors brought me back to reality with a jolt. I would have expected, I suppose, something on the order of Henry Pickett's old Dodge, to carry us rattling along between there and Galveston.

James's new black Packard, its chrome parts gleaming under the light above the garage, was, he said almost apologetically, "My only affordable luxury. I love anything well built, and this car is a sheer joy to own." He ran a gloved hand lightly along one fender. "I saved for a long time to buy it, and wouldn't give it up for any amount of money."

"It's funny, but my father—Frazier—can afford any kind of car he wants, year after year, and none of them seems to mean anything special to him except when they're giving trouble. Then he becomes boiling mad."

"Guess it's a built-in bonus of being poor. Everything you get means more."

"Yes, I'd never thought of that. But since I left home with a limited amount of cash, I have learned something about economizing. It's been kind of fun, really."

"Imagine, budgeting a lark. Oh, dear girl you haven't had it as bad as you think."

Somehow, when *he* pointed out the obvious, I didn't mind.

I am glad now we went together to Galveston, rather than my having gone alone. As the big Packard smoothly took the awful roads across the prairie, then coasted down into the hilly country before any sign of snow appeared, James first listened attentively as I poured out all my feelings about my life with the Fraziers, and my ill-fated romance with Rodney Younger, then said simply, "Yes, I see," and drove on silently for a while. Then he began remembering bits and pieces of information he'd forgotten to tell me earlier as we sat across from each other in his office.

"Did I tell you that Claire's first love—Damon Becker— was killed at sea a few months after Claire married Charles? From what I could gather by the things she told me that summer, he must have been the adventurer of the two brothers—you know, dashingly handsome, exciting, all that."

"And he never knew Claire was carrying his child. Well, at least my father died with the knowledge that I was on the way. I guess that's something. And you said Claire's infant died at about four months?"

"That's what Claire said that summer, although I didn't learn until the end that the son she was referring to wasn't Charles's."

"I wonder . . . could her lost love for Damon Becker have been part of the basis for her first attraction to Professor King? Maybe the Professor was a combination of the two men she could never have."

"That makes a lot of sense. I'd be willing to bet you hit it right on the nose."

"I wish I knew more about Charles. He must have been quite a man, my grandfather. I mean, on the surface so upstanding, and underneath a man driven by a passion for a woman he couldn't have. Wow!"

"Yes. I never knew him, of course, only saw one or two photos of him that Claire kept around. He was distinguished-looking, with good precise features, a Vandyke beard. He was a lawyer, and looked it. And apparently pretty smart. In that stack of letters Claire wrote to Helga, there was a newspaper clipping enclosed with one which had been published right after his candidacy for mayor was announced. Wish I'd kept that clipping—Helga probably wouldn't have minded—it told all about his platform. His ideas for Galveston were quite innovative for the time, and he certainly had at least the Galveston *News* pulling for him. He wanted to split up the Wharf Company monopoly, and get better services for shippers using the port. And he wanted to go to the mainland for water supply—you know, the supply on the island was already proving inadequate, although many thought if they dug enough artesian wells they'd do just fine without the help of the mainlanders.

"At least his dream on that came true—water is piped in from Alta Loma nowadays. His other dream never quite worked out."

"What was that?"

"The Wharf monopoly. The thing never has been busted—I understand they're still squabbling with the city about selling the remaining stock held by the corporation—but of course it looks as though it doesn't matter much. The race between Houston and Galveston for the number one port is all but finished, as I see it, in favor of Houston."

"Now you're talking like my father Frazier, although some argue his judgment is a bit premature. After all, the Galveston harbor is still deeper, still has a far bigger trade."

"It's petroleum—your dad's own game—that's going to make the difference. Now that they've discovered the wonder of the internal combustion engine, the demand for petroleum will never stop growing, mark my word. Houston is the obvious place for refineries because there's plenty of room."

"I guess it was purely academic, then, the question of whether Charles's winning the mayor's race so long ago would have helped."

"It was purely academic from the time that hurricane blew the island to pieces, at least to my mind. Even with the seawall, the island is too exposed to nature's whippings for anyone to be willing to chance putting big money there. Houston is much safer, yet still has access to the Gulf, and in a short while their channel will reach the depth of Galveston's. Isn't there a proposal before Congress now, for deepening it to thirty feet?"

"Yes. My father has reams of paper about it stacked around his office. And you seem to keep up with events in our part of the state pretty well."

He laughed. "Yes, even isolated schoolmasters occasionally read about goings-on in the outside world. There's little going on in the Grady area, so the *Star* and the Greenwood *Monitor* both draw heavily on news from other parts of the state, just to fill the pages."

"You know, I find myself constantly wondering what if

this and what if that. For instance, what if Charles and
Ruth—I feel I should call her Grandmother in a way, and
yet she died so young—what if they had run away when
she was expecting Serena, and he had divorced Claire,
married her. That would have changed everything."

"Yes, but it's likely Betsey—my mother's mother—
intervened. Remember, she and Claire were very close. Of
course it seems odd she would have allowed the conspiracy
to go on either . . . I guess we'll never know what her
feelings were. Maybe she didn't even know about the Garrets, was told some other family unknown to any of them
adopted Charles's and Mother's child . . ."

"Yes, and what if, things happening up to a point as they
did, my father would not have been killed, but would have
saved himself and Serena, and you. Why, you and I might
have grown up alongside each other, maybe even in New
York. Just think."

"No, I doubt they'd have ever attained custody of me.
Remember, they'd have been scorned for their sins."

"Poor James. You've grown up as lonely as I have, and
with far more reason."

"Loneliness is a state of mind, I've found. Willa, are you
sorry now you opened up this Pandora's box?"

"No, I've lived a lifetime wondering and it's time I had
some answers."

The Tracy house on Avenue O in Galveston suggested
only modest wealth. It was three-storied, with the inevitable big verandah and deep windows, the steep stairs and
lattice-covered stilts. The house was painted a kind of
murky green, with white trim, and it reminded me of the
Heights house on a smaller scale, before the application of
white paint and blue trim.

I hadn't thought much about Rodney for what seemed
weeks, though it was a matter of days, and as we sat out
front of the Tracy house while James double-checked the
address, I knew I did miss him. Poor Rodney, meeting up
with a screwball like me. What had he ever done to deserve
that?

The door was answered by a towheaded, blue-eyed boy
about ten years old. From the moment the door swung
open I felt a friendliness in the house, a Christmas atmosphere that comes only to a close family group. There were
high-spirited voices in the background, children frolickin

somewhere with their new toys. The mingled fragrances of roast turkey and mince pie and coffee wafted out at us.

"May I help you?" the boy asked in grown-up tones.

"I'm James Byron. I talked with your Uncle Roy day before yesterday. Did he tell your mother about me?"

She was coming now, a woman of forty or so whose beauty had mellowed with age, her hair, pulled back into a soft bun, beginning to streak with gray. "James, how marvelous to see you." She took his hands like a long-lost friend, then looked across as he introduced me.

"So, it's true," she said. "I never really believed she drowned, but to think there was a child into the bargain that summer. When Roy told me you'd called, I had a feeling . . . Come in, come in."

"Beautiful day for Christmas," said James.

"Yes, but the wind is so chilling off the water, just as always. That's why I wear this shawl most of the time. There's a fire in the parlor. Coffee and fruitcake?"

"Wonderful," said James. Neither of us had eaten since stopping in Sandersburg for breakfast early that morning.

"She seemed unsurprised," I said after Marybeth left the room.

"Yes, but apparently she isn't the one."

She was back in a few minutes, bearing a tray of fine, delicate china and linen cloths. "My husband has gone across town to take his parents home. They'd spent the night last night and eaten dinner with us today. He'll be back shortly."

"It's time you were told exactly what did happen the day Serena was supposed to have been killed," said James, and I leaned back in the chair and sipped coffee as he spun the tale for Marybeth . . .

"I'm looking for my mother now," I said when he was finished, suddenly weary of getting there all the time yet never arriving. "We felt that I'm evidence enough she might be alive today, and we thought you might be the one responsible for getting her to safety that day of the fire."

"Me? Of course not. I wasn't even back from Europe, didn't arrive until a week later, just as I told James when we talked."

"I simply thought you might have been trying to protect her then," said James. "It would certainly have been understandable."

"I would have. She was such a timid little thing and I was, well, shall we say I'd sowed my share of the wild oats by the time it all happened? I was thrilled to learn from her letters she had met this dashing young man . . . wish I'd saved those letters, and I could give them to you, Willa. You know, in those days little things seemed so unimportant. Anyway, I'd have done anything in my power to have been at hand to help her. I've regretted all these years I got back a week too late to save her. Of course, someone did, or she went off alone, which I doubt, because it wasn't like her."

"We've already called Nick Weaver, from Grady, and he denied knowing anything."

"Nick? Oh yes, the organ player that I loathed. He was all wrong for her, you know. She knew it too, but before that summer hadn't the courage to break away."

"Serena's courage was reborn in Willa here, who's left family and fiancé literally standing at the altar so she could trace down her past."

"But how did you get an inkling?"

"Her carpetbag. My adopted parents saved it all these years. I found it on the eve of my wedding a couple of eons ago, or so it seems."

"Oh, I see. That's good. It's always better to do as you want, then you have no regrets," she said, then took a sip of coffee and leaned back in her chair. "That was the trouble in those days. It was hard to break away. The social pressures were incredible on a young woman. She was expected to be a perfect, unblemished angel, to marry a fine man and raise her quota of children.

"Well, I eventually came round to my fine man, and had my children, but I can tell you one thing. I did it when I was good and ready, and not before. I always tried to get Serena to break out of the shackles, but she wouldn't. Then she up and did it that summer while I was gone. I was so proud of her."

I liked this person Marybeth. She had spirit. Had she had a background like mine, she would've proceeded in just the same manner as I was right now.

"Well, I hope you find her, though I doubt it seriously at this point. I believe I would have heard from her eventually. As for Nick, I can't see him helping Serena in such a clandestine situation, can you, James? I mean, he was so damned self-righteous. He would have just as soon betrayed her to Father Garret as to have taken the chance on committing a sin himself, wouldn't he?"

"Seems likely, only he was quite fond of her. Maybe he softened just a little when she was in trouble. He wasn't entirely hopeless as a person, I don't imagine."

She frowned. "Maybe not. Why don't you look him up since you're here anyway, and do a little prodding. He may know more than he lets on. It's easy enough to put someone off from several hundred miles away on the telephone. He might not find it so easy if you approach him face to face."

"You may have a point there," said James.

"Wish I could think of someone else . . . Maybe our dancing teacher, Madame D'Arcy."

"I doubt it. Serena had had to quit lessons because her father had gotten behind in paying the bills. She was terribly embarrassed, and couldn't face Madame."

"Oh, I didn't know that. How sad. No wonder she felt compelled to leave. There was really nothing left for her then, was there?"

James and I exchanged glances, both realizing Charles's financial help to the Garrets must have continued beyond his death, and only run out in the summer of 1899.

"Apparently not," said James. "Well, we'll go now and try to find Nick. We've taken up enough of your time."

"Oh, I was hoping you'd stay long enough to meet my husband, Bill, maybe have a light dinner with us—leftover turkey. We have tons of it."

"It's very kind of you," I said, "but I've waited so long, I'm anxious to get as far with this today as possible."

"Of course, dear, I understand. I admire you for striking out this way. If your mother had a latent trait of daring that only came to the surface for a short time, you've apparently inherited it, and it is a pretty good legacy to my way of thinking. I wish you luck."

"You know, her father had more than his share of daring," said James.

"Yes, I didn't know him, but he must have. Does she remind you of Serena, James?"

"Some, yes. I can see him in her too, though."

"Yes. She is Serena around the eyes a little, the height, the bone structure. Well, let me know what you learn, won't you? I'll be anxious to hear. And, by the way, we'll be moving to Houston after the first of the year. If you wind up back there, Willa, do let me know. Bill's in ware-housing—light and heavy commodities—and he's been ne-gotiating for space along the Houston ship channel. As a matter of fact, that's where we were till yesterday. As soon as the deal is set, we'll be off. There's no future here for that sort of business, if one reads the handwriting on the wall."

"So I understand," said James. "Will you regret leaving here?"

"A little. When I was younger, I found the island confin-ing, archaic, you know, all those things that cause impa-tience in youth. Now I find it peaceful, and perfect for rais-ing children. A person changes with the years . . .

"By the way, when anyone discusses our leaving, I begin to think of the horrendous job of packing, and I just re-membered something I want Willa to have . . . it'll save me from having to take it. Just a minute."

She disappeared up the stairs, and came back right away, bearing a small porcelain music box with a dancer on top.

"This is a gift meant for Serena that summer. I'd told her about it in a letter, and was going to give it to her when we returned. She was such a graceful dancer, you know, and as soon as I laid eyes on this in a shop in Italy, I knew she must have it. My daughter has begged me for it time and time again, but somehow I didn't want to part with it, even for her. Here, let's wind it up . . . there."

The "Blue Danube Waltz" began, the dancer turned round and round on tiptoe. We all stood there watching, as though expecting the toy to become my mother in the flesh, until finally it wound down and its movement was stilled.

"You must have always had hopes she lived," I said, tak-ing it from Marybeth.

"I guess I did. Always was an eternal optimist, I sup-pose," she said, and her eyes were shining with unspent tears.

"We'll let you know as soon as we learn anything," said James. "Thank you again for being so kind. You know, we tried to trace your father first, before I located your brother."

"My parents are dead. After the 1900 storm we moved up closer to Broadway, and that's where they lived out their lives."

"That beautiful beach place then, the big house, destroyed along with the rest?"

"Obliterated. The pier, bathhouse, everything. We were one of the families who took refuge at the Gresham house up on Broadway. Gresham and my father were acquainted, you know."

"I'm sorry about your house. I'd have enjoyed seeing it again."

"Well, at least it taught me a good lesson. Before that storm I thought myself quite invulnerable to bad luck. Guess everyone has to learn that error sooner or later."

"Yes, I suppose they do. Well then, good day. Merry Christmas."

As we drove away James said, "We can go by Trinity, though I doubt anyone will be around on Christmas Day. Confound it, we should have found out where he lived before I let him off the phone. Darned inefficient of me."

"I'll bet that's the only inefficient thing you ever did."

This exchange set us both giggling as we traveled the short blocks between Marybeth Tracy's house and the gothic reaches of brown brick known as Trinity Church.

There was a lone car out front, and James remarked, "If anyone is here on Christmas, by gosh, it would be Nick. I'll try the door."

As he walked up I noticed the sky beginning to change. It was taking on that leaden look like the sky in Grady, and I remembered then it had felt chillier as we left Marybeth's than when we arrived. The palm trees around the church were fluttering in the more and more insistent Gulf breeze.

James was pecking the outside of the car window. "Come on in, I just poked my head in and heard organ sounds. It's got to be Nick."

I walked with him up to the big doors, almost certain this, too, would be a dead end.

The inside of Trinity Church was dark, not at all cheerful though banked with candles and flowers of the season. Why, I wondered, were all Episcopal churches so dark? We walked up into the chancel and waited for Nick to finish his hymn playing. He looked much as I had expected, closely cropped graying hair, rimless glasses, thin lips, pale skin. He was thoroughly engrossed, and didn't realize we were around until he'd stopped to make a pencil mark on the music.

"Excuse me," said James. "Nick Weaver?"

"Oh, you startled me. Yes, may I be of some service?"

"It's me, James Byron."

"Oh."

Then he looked at me and something registered in his eyes.

"This is Willa. We'd hoped you might be free to talk with us. We're still trying to find out who might have helped Serena that day of the fire, and maybe the three of us could put our heads together and—"

"I've already told you my feelings."

"I beg your most humble pardon," I said, and pulled out the picture of the Garrets. "If I am indeed a fraud, where would I have managed to pick this up? I also have my mother's dancing shoes and some other things of hers. I can show it all to you if you wish."

He paused for some moments, then closed his hymn book. "All right, then. We'll talk, if we must. There's a diner around the corner, much more appropriate for conversations of this type than the sanctuary. I'll just get my coat."

When the steaming coffee had been set before us, James proceeded to work on Nick Weaver in his thorough manner. "I think you know something, but aren't telling. Now, why? Would you deny this girl a chance to know her real mother?"

"Your mother is dead."

He'd said it so simply, offhandedly as though it didn't matter. I felt as though someone had just dealt me a deathblow with a boxcar full of cotton balls.

James glared at Nick across the table. "Look here, do you still insist she died the day of the fire?"

"Not at all. She lived quite a time after that. I saved her, if you must know."

Chapter 14

It was stuffy in the diner. My head had begun to ache. "For God's sake, why didn't you tell us on the phone?" I asked.

"I would have been doing you no favor. Your mother was not the woman most people believed."

"I know more about my mother than you think. I'll appreciate your just telling me the truth now, and leaving your opinions out."

"She came to me, at my house while I was teaching lessons that day, driving a rig like a maniac. I saw her from the window as she pulled up, and got rid of the students through a back door, before they saw her."

James cleared his throat and asked timidly, "Was she badly burned?" and I made a tight fist and silently uttered the first honest prayer of my life.

"No. Mostly her hands, from covering her face, but nothing that wouldn't heal with time. But she looked a mess—her hair all askew, her clothes wrinkled, face dirty. I asked her what in the world had happened, but she couldn't seem to talk . . . just shook her head. First thing, I dressed the burns.

"While I was wrapping her hands, she looked up at me like a little child and said, 'It's all over, everything's ruined. You've got to help me get away from here.' She admitted she didn't deserve my help, but she said she had no one else to turn to.

"The girl was near hysteria, and I brewed her some tea to get her calmed down. Then she told me the whole sordid story of her and Roman and their little plan to run away, then of the fire in the Seaside Pavilion and how she escaped through the stage door they'd always used."

"Stage door?" James repeated.

"Yes. Their own private door, from what she said."

"But her shoe heel was caught—"

"No, it wasn't. She faked that—it was a quick decision, she told me. She realized all at once it would simplify matters all around if everyone thought her dead . . . and she could hardly have taken you with her. As soon as she was satisfied of your safety, she exited through the stage door and fled."

"I see. Then where did you take her?"

"Well, I'll tell you right quick, I came very near going for her father."

"You would," I said.

"I should have. But she cried, carried on something awful. I was really crazy about her, stupid and foolish as I was. I finally acquiesced and got both of us a connection to

Ohio, where my parents lived. I called for a replacement at the organ at the church, and left word for Father Garret my mother was ill and I had to go home immediately. I don't know whether he lived long enough to receive that message. I suppose he did. I've always felt guilty for lying to him.

"We left that night. Nobody saw us. I still harbored a notion she might marry me if I did this thing for her, and straighten up into the girl I'd known before she got fouled up . . . I don't give up on people easily, you know. I took care of her until you were born. We lived at my parents'. I wrote in a resignation to St. Christopher's and took a position up there in Cleveland at a little church.

"Nothing would do but she have her child. What she would do after that was not discussed much. I tried to get her to give you up for adoption, to sign papers before you were born, but she wouldn't hear of it, nor would she consent to marry me. She just kept saying, 'After the baby's born we can talk about it, but please now, just let me alone.'

"You can imagine my parents through all this. My mother told friends we had a boarder, and Serena lived in an upstairs room, seldom coming down as she got bigger and bigger. It was unfair enough to have pressed her on them, but it would have been unforgivable to have let anyone see her in her condition. Why, it would have set tongues wagging . . . my parents would have never lived it down."

I was not interested in what his parents thought of my mother. What kept running through my mind was all the ways she proved she'd loved me, how I was first choice in her heart, above everything. She would even degrade herself by becoming a virtual prisoner in another's home, who had no real sympathy or love for her at all . . .

"What then," James said now, "after Willa was born?"

"There was no 'after.' She died giving birth to Willa."

He'd done it again, simply, offhandedly, his statement colliding head on with my flow of thought. I stood up. "Did you give her the best care available; was everything done in her behalf? Did you have some quack come to deliver her because you were ashamed?"

Nick stared at me coldly. "Sit down, young lady, and don't make a scene. You forget, I owed her nothing. She was given every aid possible, I assure you, but she wasn strong any more. She'd grown thinner and paler from the time we left Galveston, had been ill off and on all that winter."

"Her heart was broken," said James pensively. "That's what killed her."

"Maybe so, if you can imagine anyone's heart being broken over a scoundrel like that fellow she'd taken up with. You know, I did some checking on him after I got back home. Seeing him in Galveston that summer, I was convinced I'd seen him somewhere before. Well, I couldn't get it out of my mind, though I couldn't remember where I'd seen him. I even went to one of the shows at the Seaside Pavilion, just to get a look at him again.

"Finally I had my curiosity satisfied, back in Cleveland. A friend of mine came by one night when he was in town. He'd been at that seminar in St. Louis I'd attended so long ago. We got to talking, and he brought up the subject of the Landauer scandal—it was all over the papers during that seminar.

"As soon as he mentioned it, I knew that was where I'd seen Roman Cruz. Of course, he didn't go by Roman then, and that was what threw me. He went by the name of Roland Cruz—God alone knows which name was for real. Anyway, he was a member of the symphony orchestra in St. Louis, and became involved in a love affair with the wife of the chief symphony patron—Margaret Landauer.

"Boy, when it came to light there were fireworks. Her husband divorced her, and Roman was kicked out of the symphony, and just about run out of town on a rail. Landauer—the husband—was very wealthy, a powerful man in St. Louis. I heard he told Roman Cruz in no uncertain terms to get out of St. Louis, and never come back."

"Did you tell my mother, when you found out?"

"I certainly did. Wanted to set her straight on him once and for all. But it did no good, of course. She just said she'd never held his past against him, and wasn't about to at that point, even if I was right about it being her Roman, which wasn't for sure anyway. She was impossible to reason with, the further along she got . . ."

"Go on then," said James. "You must have given Willa to a state agency in Ohio. Which one?"

"I did better than that. I'd received a letter from Trinity, offering me this job, just before the birth. It was still on my desk unanswered. I'd been mulling over it, disconsolate that I was to be kept by Serena from realizing my greatest dream. For how could I take her back there? What was I to do with them both, once the baby was born? It seemed ghastly unfair. I kept reading the letter over and over, was reading it, I think, when I heard Serena whimper with the first pains of childbirth."

"Did she suffer very much?" I asked softly.

"Of course she did. Women suffer with childbirth, don't they? Look, all was done. She just couldn't take it, that's all."

"Then?" said James.

"After she died and we buried her up there, I answered the letter to Trinity, in the affirmative. Then I wrote to a home for orphans here in Galveston, and asked them to take the child—you. They were very nice about it, and I paid transportation for them to bring you here when you were old enough to travel. Of course, I had to go along and fill my new position, else I would have lost it. Until then, a lady at the church where I played in Ohio took care of you. She was the only one up there we confided in except—"

"Except who?" I asked, with an odd instinct for what was coming.

"The Fraziers. Mr. Frazier and my father worked together at Standard. The two couples were good friends by the time Serena and I got to Ohio. In fact, my parents got the Fraziers going to the Episcopal church.

"Anyway, they wouldn't have known anything of the story, except that once when Mrs. Frazier was visiting at our house, and had gone upstairs to the bathroom, she saw Serena just making the corner on the way to her room. By that time the pregnancy was obvious. My mother told Mrs. Frazier everything."

"Everything?"

"Everything that was known. Mrs. Frazier herself was pregnant at the time, and her child was born shortly after you. Let me see, I came on down in May of 1900, and the Galveston home brought Willa down in about July, I think. They notified me they were transporting you here.

"Then in the following year, sometime in the fall of 1901, I got a letter from my mother that the Fraziers' child had died of some strange liver ailment unknown to science, and they were considering moving here so Mr. Frazier could begin his own oil business. They remembered abou' Serena and her child, and wanted to try and adopt ye when they arrived here. I sent them all the information I had, and they wrote to the home, and eventually adopted you."

"Did they name me?"

"No, your real mother named you, Willa Katherine Cruz. I don't think she ever chose a boy's name . . . some foolishness about her intuition telling her she was going to have a girl."

"I see. Did you ever come to see me?"

"No. You can understand that I wanted to put it all out of my mind."

"I was here in Galveston, then, during the 1900 storm?"

"Yes."

"Did you check on her then?" James asked.

"No, I read in the papers that the home, which was near downtown Galveston, was not destroyed, none of the kids or the staff were hurt. I remember reading they had water up to the top floor and had to move everything up to safety, and in the paper a staff member was quoted as saying, 'We got our feet wet, but, Thank God, that's about all.' "

I looked at James in sudden realization. "The bag. It must have been on the floor somewhere, that would explain the bottom deteriorating."

"Yes, of course."

"Anyway," Nick continued, "I had my own worries. Do you realize how much damage Trinity suffered? I was there from the time the weather turned bad till the thing was over. My own apartment was destroyed. We salvaged what we could at the church, but . . . Anyway, you can see that I did right by you, Willa. Certainly, I did more than could have been expected under the circumstances."

I could read the pleading in his eyes. "I'll certainly give you credit for that," I said, and thought, What you were really trying to do was to buy my mother's affections. Then, finding they weren't up for sale, you had no more regard for her. I looked across at James, and knew his thoughts followed with my own.

"Tell you what, Nick," I said. "I want to repay you for everything you did—"

"Oh no, that's not necessary at this point."

"Yes. All the money you spent on transportation, her boarding at your parents' home all those months, the food, and so forth. Would you try and figure out what would be fair? I'll contact you within a few days for your answer, and see you are paid."

"But, it's really—"

"I insist."

"Very well. There was quite a bit, if you want to know. I guess there's no reason why I shouldn't receive something in return."

"You're very deserving," I said, and he cleared his throat and took a sip of water.

"Well, from what I understand the Frazier oil interests made it possible for you to grow up in luxury, all right. You certainly had it softer than I ever did."

"That's right. I only wish they would have told me what they knew. It would have saved all of us so many years of torment if they had just told the truth."

"The truth? That your real mother was an easy woman who took up with some band player, carried on with him and got herself pregnant? Humph. Looks to me like they spared you a lot of grief."

"Yes, I suppose that's the way they looked at it," I told him, and thought then of the day I'd told Mother I planned to marry Rodney Younger. She'd inferred I might be expecting his child. I guess she always wondered if I'd inherited a bad streak from my real mother.

"Was it my adoptive parents who swore you to secrecy?"

"Actually, it was Mrs. Frazier. She was only trying to protect you. Anyone would have done the same in her place.

"Oh, by the way, something else just came to mind. You seem convinced your mother died alone and bereft, regardless of what I did for her. But she wasn't so alone, kept an admirer along the way from somewhere."

"Who?"

"I don't know. Someone kept flowers on her grave from the time she died, at least until I left there. I never found out who it was, but she did talk with various kids around the neighborhood—from her upstairs window, you know— delivery boys, kids selling things, so forth. A good many of the neighborhood boys would speak to her as they passed below, and often stop to chat. I'm sure it was one of them that put the flowers on her grave."

"What's the name of the cemetery where she's buried?"

"Cleveland Memorial, just outside of town."

"What kind of marker was put up for her?"

"Marker? Look here, now, I'm not made of money like you, Willa. I did have a little plate with her name and dates of birth and death written on it. But it was all I could afford."

"I'm not holding it against you, Nick, I just want to know. Be sure to add that expense to your statement," I said, my mind leaping ahead to the next train ride I'd be taking. I must see her grave, and must have it marked with an appropriate stone, and I must do it alone . . .

"That's all I know," Nick said now. "I'd best be getting back to the church to close up. It's getting too late to practice any more."

"By the way," said James, "Serena kept a diary that summer, yet we didn't find it in her carpetbag. Would you know—?"

"No, I never saw a diary, didn't know she kept one—not that she'd have told me about it."

"I see."

"Sorry we kept you from your work," I said. "I'll contact you within a few days about those expenses."

"Yes, I'll have something ready for you. And it's all right about the practice time. It's just that one must take the utmost care all the time to be at his best. There is always someone around only too ready to win the position of organist for himself."

"Yes, one couldn't afford to be toppled at the pinnacle of his career," James said, and I think the sarcasm managed to register with Nick. He made no reply and didn't look my way again, but pulled on his coat, set his hat acock on his head, and strolled out of the diner as though he'd just finished a cup of coffee on a regular day.

I rose from my chair. "Wait up a moment," James said. "Let's talk, all right?"

"Sure. And I'm suddenly famished. Could we order a sandwich?"

He ordered for both of us, then said, "You look different, as though you'd just had a weight lifted from your shoulders."

"In a way, that expresses my feelings just now. The puzzle is complete. I only regret Mother wasn't alive. I'd hoped against hope."

"Yes. If she had been, though, and had never tried to 'nd you or contact you, it would have proven her to be 'ss a person than you had imagined, right?"

"I suppose."

"What will you do now?"

"Heaven only knows. I've left an intolerable mess in Houston. It's going to be damned hard facing up to it."

"But you're determined to, aren't you?"

"I guess I always knew I would, sooner or later."

"You know, we always have openings at the school. You could go back with me, be a librarian, something, a clerk in the office. Nothing I'd love better than to think we could be close to each other after all these years."

I paused a moment, full of gratitude, almost wishing I could take him up on his offer . . . live in the world of isolation and simple pleasures which seemed to make him so content. Yet I knew even then it wouldn't work for me. "It's tempting, but if I can put the pieces together again, I've got a life in Houston," I said. "To go home with you would be to go on running. I can't do that forever, can I?"

"No, I guess not."

"Will you be going back right away?"

"I may meander around here for a couple of days, see a few places, call forth a few memories. I may even look up old Tommy Driscoll. Wonder if he's here."

"Let me warn you, you aren't going to find many things the same as you left them. Avenue L is a street full of houses built since the storm. Nothing of the old days exists there any longer."

"There might be something—a feeling, a mood. Are you anxious to be gone? Want to browse with me, stay the night or something, before going back?"

"No, I have no memories here. Odd, isn't it? My past surrounds me here, yet my memory is like a blank chalkboard."

"Well, then, we'll go to the station and see about getting you on a train."

As we left the diner, it was hard to tell whether the dark was falling so swiftly, or the sky was readying itself for snow. "Looks like snow, doesn't it?" said James. "Unusual for down here."

"It's been an unusual day—week."

He looked across at me then, and put an arm around my shoulder. It was the first time I had ever been touched by a member of my family, and it seemed an easy, natural gesture. We walked that way, back to the car, and when we got in I said, "You know, for the first time in my life I fee like a whole person, not two people dangling from both ends, but a whole human being."

"Human beings are forgiving creatures," he said, "or should be. You won't hold anything against the Fraziers for not telling the truth, will you? I think Nick was right on that point. Your mother meant only to spare you. Her intentions were well founded, if a little misguided."

"Yes, she, like everyone else, was a victim of her era, I guess. Poor Mother."

"And your father?"

"I believe he would have told me long ago, had she let him."

"Probably. Men are generally more flexible on that subject, except for Nick Weaver. . . ."

It is but a short drive between Trinity Church and Union Depot, and we soon pulled up near the front entrance to say our good-bys. "Here, let me write down my name and address at the school, in case you ever need me."

"As you did so long ago—for my mother?"

He laughed. "Yes, I guess so. Some things never change."

"And to play the game of 'what if' again, what if you hadn't been the efficient type you are, and hadn't thought to give my mother those addresses?"

"Then the last few days would never have happened. I'd still be tormented by guilt, and you'd be hounded by unanswered questions. . . . Here it is."

"Oh, I almost forgot. Here's your picture."

He took it from me, and gave it a long look, as though he'd have it stamped on his memory, then said, "It really should be yours, not mine, for she would have wanted you to have it."

"But it's all you have of her."

"And I'll know it's in your safekeeping in case I ever want to look at it again. Let's just say we'll share it. And by the way, be sure to send me your address when you do settle down. I'll be anxious to hear how things turn out."

"I've a feeling I'll know pretty soon, one way or another."

"I'm glad. It's a good feeling, having some idea where you're going."

When the big Packard had disappeared around the corner, I thought of James, reading his books on snowy nights, and wondered if the students and teachers would continue to be his only companions. Or, knowing now that he had not let my mother down after all, would he trust himself to a closer, more enduring relationship? I hoped he would. He had so much to give.

In the depot I went directly to the newspaper stand for a Houston *Post*. Christmas Day wouldn't be big for real estate ads, but I was suddenly curious as to whether Rodney had put the Heights house up for sale. If he had, his mind might not be open to reconciliation, in case I decided to try. . . .

It wasn't in there, and I only regretted it proved so little. He probably wouldn't run a large ad on the Heights house every day, only on Sundays. A bit edgy now without really knowing why, I folded the paper and visited the ticket agent, then went to the phone and called home.

"Dad, it's me."

"Willa, baby, where are you, where have you been?"

"Been? Twenty years into the past. But I'll explain that later. Listen, Dad, I'm in Galveston at the Union Depot. Will you please do something for me? I know I've no business asking, but—"

"Anything. You name it."

"I want you to meet me in Houston at the station, and loan me enough money to get to Ohio and back. Only a loan. I'll work for you in the office till it's all paid back, or work somewhere else, but I will pay it back. I've learned just about all I need to know about where I came from, but this is something I've got to take care of. My mother's grave is in Cleveland, and I've got to visit it. Can you understand that?"

"Yes, but wait a minute. Don't go up there. Stay where you are and let me come there. I've got to talk to you."

"No, Dad, you don't understand. I've got to visit Mother's grave, then I can come home and straighten out the mess I left—or try to. Just do this for me, please."

"No, you're making a mistake. I can't talk here because Mother's just down the hall. Trust me, will you, wait for me at the station? I'll take the next train down."

"But, Dad, I—"

"Trust me?"

"All right. But you won't try to keep me from going, will you?"

"Not if you still want to after we talk. Willa, are you crying?"

"No, Dad, almost, but not quite. It's been quite a week."

"I can imagine. Sit tight. I'll be there as soon as I can."

"Tell Mother I'm all right, won't you?"

"Yes, baby. She'll be so thankful. We've both been so worried . . ."

As I hung up the phone I thought of Dad as he must have been when the phone rang, sitting in his chair by the fire, puffing on a cigar and reading his *Wall Street Journal*. He'd be telling Mother now, having cast aside his paper and squashed his cigar in the ashtray by the phone. He would be having a hard time convincing her not to come along to Galveston with him, but I had a feeling he would succeed.

I was anxious to be bound for Ohio, and couldn't imagine what he had to tell me that couldn't wait, but then I owed him at least the courtesy of waiting for him to come and have his say. There was a train leaving Houston at eight o'clock, and if he could make that one, he'd be here in a little better than an hour and a half. In the meantime I'd sit down on one of the hard benches, in plain view of the door leading in from the tracks, and wait. . . .

"Willa, wake up!"

It was a voice, coming from somewhere far away, bothering me. I didn't want to be bothered, the sleep was so welcome, the dream of traveling through a beautiful spring countryside laden with blooming apple trees, so real . . .

"Willa, it's me, wake up."

I opened my eyes. Dad stood above in his hat and coat, and muffler, and for a moment I was a little girl again, who'd fallen asleep on the sofa, and he was waking me to send me up to bed.

"I'm so glad to see you, so glad you're all right," he said, and as he put his big arms around me I thought once more of my fears he had kept my real mother imprisoned somewhere and I hugged him hard, wishing I could make up for having been so anxious to believe him wicked.

"But you found my note, didn't you? And you guessed I'd uncovered my mother's carpetbag?"

"Yes. I'll get a taxi and we'll go somewhere out of this madhouse and have a talk. Jesus, I hate train stations, have seen my share of them, I'll tell you."

"I know a good place where we can go to talk. . . ."

The Galvez dining room under soft lights and violin music is even more welcoming than when sunlight glances off the crystal on the tables set for lunch. When we were seated I was suddenly hungry again, and ordered another tomato stuffed with crabmeat. I looked around, but saw no sign of my waiter friend from a few days ago.

Dad got to the point quickly. "I guess you know everything."

"Everything. Even your friendship with the Weavers in Cleveland. I've already spoken with Nick, earlier today."

"Okay, but one other thing. Your mother isn't buried in Cleveland any more."

Chapter 15

I stared across at him. "But how can that be? Nick said——"

"Edwynna and I met your mother, Serena, during her confinement at the Weavers. They didn't seem to want to have much to do with her; neither did your mother, really, but I liked to visit with her and got to know her fairly well.

"I don't know exactly how to describe her to you, but she was the kind of person you'd never forget: fragile little thing, tall as she was; pale and thin . . . yet there was a spirit behind her eyes that I adored, a determination never to give up. You know, it's hard to realize now, but I wasn't much older than she was at the time.

"Oh well, don't know why I keep beating around the bush. I'm afraid I fell in love with her a little. Anyone would have, if they'd known her."

"But you and Mother——"

He cleared his throat. "Edwynna was carrying Sarah at the time. Nothing happened between me and Serena, of course, God forbid. She was just so sweet, so good to talk to, so much warmer than——"

"Than Mother?"

"Your mother and I, well, maybe you've noticed a certain lack of closeness between us. It isn't that I don't love her—I do, very much—but she's a little aloof. Came from a strict background, ya know, and I think she's always been afraid to break out, really be herself. Don't know why she ever married a man like me—pushy, impatient. I didn't have a penny when we married, and not for a long time after . . ."

"And I suspect she blamed you for her accident, didn't she?"

He raised an eyebrow. "How did you know about that? You didn't remember—"

"Not until I went into the attic to pick up my honeymoon luggage and found the bag. That was when it all came back."

"I see. Well, I was going to explain all that to you tonight—in fact I planned to tell you all about it during that lunch date we were supposed to have."

"Tell me now."

"Yes . . . all right. It happened when you were about four years old—almost five. When I got home from work the ambulance was outside and they were carrying Edwynna down the walk on a stretcher.

"Dotty told me what had happened. All Edwynna said was, 'I don't ever want to see that carpetbag again. Get it out of my house.' And then I asked where you were and Dotty told me. 'You'd better let Dotty go with me to the hospital and you look after Willa. She's pretty frightened,' Edwynna said."

"She thought of me then?"

"Yes, Willa, she did. By the time I got up to your room, you'd passed out at the door. I carried you to bed and sat with you until you woke up. I couldn't tell by what you said how much it had frightened you. All you told me was, 'I fell down on Mommy, didn't I? Is she all right?' I assured you she was, although at that point I wasn't certain. Then you wanted to know why Dotty Baxter locked you in your room, and you told me how much you hated her. I tried to explain why, that she was only trying to help. That seemed to satisfy you, although you seemed a little listless. Pretty soon you fell asleep. I got Martha Stone to come over and stay with you, and I went on to the hospital to look after Edwynna.

"I thought you were all right. Then that night, you woke me up screaming. It was your right hand—the edge of it and your little finger were all swollen and bruised. First, I assumed you'd hurt it in the fall, then I realized you'd probably done it banging on the door. The paint at the bottom of the door was all chipped from being kicked on."

I stared across at him for a moment, thinking again of

the day I got sick in the undercroft in the house on Heights Boulevard, and later how my hand had ached, and how it had puzzled me.

"What is it, Willa?" said Dad.

"Nothing. Go on."

"There isn't much more. Next day I took you to the doctor to have the hand looked at, but there wasn't anything broken, and eventually it healed up fine and you forgot all about the whole thing. You must have blocked it out of your mind. I was so thankful for that. It must have been a horrible experience."

"Lord, if you'd only told me everything instead of keeping so many secrets!"

"Edwynna wouldn't let me. She was so damned afraid you'd know something about your mother. She even pulled a trick on me—told you about your being adopted and all one day when I was at work—just so I wouldn't be tempted to tell you all about your real mother."

"And maybe cause me to turn out just like her—an 'easy' woman?"

"I don't know . . . maybe," he said, looking down.

"Then it was you, wasn't it, who saved the carpetbag in the first place, without her knowing?"

"Yes. See, when we first got you, from the home in Galveston, your things were in the carpetbag along with your mother's shoes and gown. Edwynna wanted to get rid of the bag even then, but I told her that someday, when you were grown, it might do no harm for you to have something that belonged to your real mother."

"Just the gown and shoes, huh?"

"Yeah, that was all except for something else which I'll get to in a minute."

I assumed he referred to the picture, the programs, the paper, but said nothing about them because he seemed to be enjoying telling his story. "But what about after the accident—I mean, didn't she insist you get rid of the bag then?"

"Yeah. But I didn't. I told her I got rid of it, and hid it instead."

"I see. Tell me more, then, about what you knew of my real mother."

"I think I could put it best in a conversation we once had. I was rememberin' it again on the trip down. We'd gone over to the Weavers for supper one night, and Nick's father, Hal, had gone to run an errand or something. Your mother was helping Clara, his mother, in the kitchen. I went up to say hello to Serena. I always did that unless she happened to be downstairs, and she rarely was, because the Weavers didn't hold with her being there.

"I found her sitting by the open window, looking out at what was left of the sunshine. She was great big—her time would come any day.

" 'Sit down there on the edge of the bed, Mr. Frazier,' she said. She always called us Mr. and Mrs. Frazier, you understand, very proper. I remember thinking as we talked that she had a feeling she wasn't going to live through the childbirth. Don't know why I felt it, I just did.

" 'Mrs. Frazier is feeling well?' she asked.

" 'Yes, Edwynna's fine. I don't think she has long to go now.'

" 'Nor do I,' she said, then sat looking out the window for a little longer, like she was lost in her thoughts.

" 'Your child will have a good life, every chance of growing up happily,' she said finally. 'I wish I could be sure of the same for mine.'

" 'But your child will, too. Won't you and Nick marry after the baby comes? I figured you'd eventually—'

" 'Give in? No, I will never marry Nick, though I haven't told him in so many words yet. And I couldn't go back to Galveston, break my father's heart. Of course, had Roman lived, things would be very different . . .'

"She didn't know, you see, that the Garrets were both dead, nor did we, till we began the process of adoption later.

" 'Pardon me, Mr. Frazier. I don't mean to sound so maudlin today,' she said. 'I only got to thinking about the uncertainty of the future, and I—'

" 'Not at all,' I told her. I felt real sorry for her, cause there wasn't anything for her to do if she wouldn't marry Nick. She was trapped in a deplorable situation.

" 'Look, is there anyone I could contact for you, anyone you think might be of help? Anything I can do?'

" 'You're very kind, but no. I have a girl friend in Galveston who might be able to come up with some solution. Beyond her, though, there isn't anyone except a young boy I know, and he'll be having problems enough of his own just now.

" 'Perhaps you might do one thing for me, though. In the

top drawer there, in the bureau, is a diary. Would you get it out, please?'

"Gee, it seemed almost like I was invading her privacy or something. But I got it and took it over to her . . . only she wouldn't take it from me.

" 'Would you keep it, Mr. Frazier, and if anything should happen to me—no, I know it's probably silly—but, just in case, would you see my daughter gets it? I haven't written in it since the end of the summer last year, but I think there's a word or two in it that may help her some-day.

" '. . . Of course I guess it would mean a great deal more to her when she becomes a young woman.'

" 'I understand,' I told her."

"She wanted you to have me, didn't she?"

"I guess she did, though I didn't grasp that part at the time. I saw the diary got into her carpetbag after it was all over and later, after we got you, I took it out and saved it for you. Edwynna never knew about it. I have it here in my coat. I meant to give it to you and tell you about the bag on your wedding day."

He pulled it out and handed it across the table. It wasn't very large, just a small black book with brittle binding that I would open later, when I could do it alone.

"Well, where was I? Oh yes, right after she gave it to me Edwynna called me to dinner from the foot of the stairs, so we didn't have time to talk any further. As I left the room, though, Serena said over her shoulder, 'There's just one thing I want for my child, Mr. Frazier. I want her to be able to live her life as she sees fit, and to never be afraid of anything. I don't want her to have to sneak behind every-one's back for her happiness. If I can't give her anything else, I want to be sure she has at least that—a chance. And I will, somehow. The baby *is* going to be a girl, you know.'

"It was the last time I talked to her. Within a few days, she'd given birth to you and died. We went to a little grave-side service for her with the Weavers."

"Was it you, by chance, who kept flowers on her grave?"

"Yeah. Nick tell you about that? And I was the one who persuaded Edwynna to adopt you after we lost Sarah. In 1910 I went back to that cemetery in Ohio and had Se-rena's body moved to the City Cemetery in Galveston. It seemed to me she ought to be there, instead of in Ohio, and it was ten years before I had the money to do it. It was an under-the-table deal, I'll admit, and I never told anybody—certainly not Edwynna. It was just something I wanted to do for you and for her."

"So she's been here all this time, practically under my nose? Why didn't you ever tell me?"

"I couldn't risk Edwynna finding out. She wouldn't have understood."

"Tell me, how did Mother feel about the idea of adopting me?"

"Well, of course she was broken up pretty bad over losin' Sarah. She didn't cotton to the idea at first, but I persuaded her, and of course it didn't take long after we got you before she felt just like you were really hers, until—"

"Until I started being a troublemaker."

"Yeah, but that doesn't mean she never loved you, even if you did cause her concern. She just has trouble showing her love."

"Didn't she blame me, too, for the accident?"

"Absolutely not. She was as glad as I was that you were young enough to forget it."

"You know, it's funny, but I always wondered why you two adopted me. Mother didn't seem to care about me, and you spent all your time working away from home."

"I didn't work to get away from you, Willa. But a man has got to get ahead. You can understand that, surely. And I wanted you to have everything Serena couldn't give you. If she could have known for sure that we'd eventually get you, she would have expected me to provide well for you."

"Yes, I think you're right about that."

"Willa, what's bothered me from the beginning of this thing is how you could take a gown and a pair of shoes and come up with this much information."

"I had a little more help than that," I told him, smiling, "but it's too late to go into it right now. Later I'll tell you all about it, but it's too long a story to begin when I'm this exhausted."

"Yeah, I bet you are. If it weren't so late, I'd take you to the cemetery tonight, though. I know you're anxious to see your mother's grave."

"I'll stay overnight if you'll loan me some money, and go tomorrow. I want to visit her alone."

"Willa, I'm your father. You don't have to borrow from

me. Whatever I have is yours; you're the major reason I
worked as hard as I did for it."

"No, it isn't fair. I'm on my own from now on."

"All right, if that's the way you feel. But you will come
back, then?"

"Probably so. Dad, have you heard anything from Rodney?"

"Not a word. But I just know if you wanted him back,
he'd be reasonable about it. He's a fine boy."

"I don't know. I have a fondness for him that I've never
felt for anyone else, but the past few days have left my
brain muddled about everything to do with the present. I've
got to think. I thought once, earlier today, that I might go
back, try to explain to him. Now—"

"What?"

"Well, if you want the truth, the idea of marriage kind of
sickens me."

"Why?"

"Because it involves so many lies. What came about for
the past forty years was caused by a woman named Claire,
who lied from the beginning about the real meaning of
marriage, and that lie has done nothing but snowball all
along, never getting straightened out. And now, I find that
even marriage between you and Mother is something of a
lie. Somewhere, the lying has to stop."

"Look. I won't dispute that statement. But remember
that turning from Rodney if you really do love him is just
as much a lie as marrying for less than love. If you don't
make it up with him just because you want to make a point
about marriage in general, you'll only be cheating yourself.

"Whatever you decide, be sure it really is an honest decision, either way."

"It's what my mother wanted for me, isn't it?"

"Yes, it is, and what I want for you, too."

"Dad, thank you for what you did, for caring about Serena, my mother."

"I'm glad I did it, especially now. Maybe it'll convince
you once and for all that you were always loved, from
the beginning."

I didn't sleep a lot last night because I had some reading
and a lot of thinking to do.

My mother's diary is the epistle of a quiet, reserved, and
serious-minded young woman transformed almost over-

night into a starry-eyed, hopeful girl in love with a tall, mysterious stranger.

She is not terribly graphic in her diary as to the details of her love affair with Roman Cruz, and I had to read it several times to pick up the subtleties that related her true feelings for him.

What came through to me finally was her ability to let herself trust him enough to love him completely, without timidity or shame for what they did together, and, in return, his ability to make her feel not like an instrument to satisfy his desires, but a person with whom to share something beautiful and satisfying to them both.

It occurred to me after I closed the diary finally and put out the light, that Rodney Younger has given me so many more reasons for that kind of trust than Roman Cruz must have given my mother, yet I've been afraid to let myself believe in him even a fraction as much as she believed in my father.

I knew then that I'd loved Rodney Younger for a long time, yet never so much as now. . . .

There is a small brass vase at the center of the monument to my mother, and this morning I placed the small bouquet of white mums there that I'd picked up at a florist down the street from the City Cemetery.

They look nice there—a spot of gaiety in an otherwise gloomy place made even more so by the bleakness of the sky above. The monument is in simple taste—apparently purchased before my father's affinity for gaudiness came about. The epitaph begins simply enough, too: "Here lies Serena Garret, born 1880, died 1900."

But then there is something added beneath that I read over several times, unable to believe my own father had ordered it put there:

> Behold her, single in the field,
> Yon solitary Highland Lass!
> Reaping and singing by herself;
> Stop here, or gently pass!

As I knelt down beside the grave, I wondered how my father came to choose these lines from Wordsworth. Had he learned them in school years before, perhaps charged with memorizing them, and then never quite forgot them?

Or did he pore for hours over books of poetry in a library somewhere, trying to find the suitable words for describing my mother as he had known her?

Whatever the reason for his choice, I like it.

It isn't a happy poem, but then my mother wasn't happy when she died, and she was very much alone.

I stayed by her grave for a long time this morning, thinking about the cruelties of her fate. Here she lay, in the middle of the island she tried most desperately to get away from, after spending the final months of her life in the home of a family she would not have chosen to be with, her greatest joy probably brought by the pleasant visits of a man she hardly knew and the children who'd call to her from the yard below. Like Janet Garret, she was something of an invalid in the end: her spirit beleaguered; her once lithe body swollen and shapeless, confined to a small upstairs room with a view of the world outlined by the frame of a window.

I had felt somehow, before I reached her grave, that we'd carry on a kind of visit together, she and I. I thought if I brought the picture of her along, concentrated on it hard enough, I could bring her to life at least enough to imagine what she might be saying to me.

Yet the stone was cold from the winter day. Nothing moved inside me as I expected it would. If we met, it was as two strangers exchanging brief glances as they pass each other along the sidewalk.

A peculiar thought crossed my mind as I rose to leave: I went to visit my mother today, but my mother was not at home.

There was someone behind me, an old man sitting a few feet distant on a bench, his bony hands poised over the top of a cane. "Oh, miss," he said, "I notice you been here quite a while. I guess you lost someone pretty special to you."

"Yes, that's right," I told him.

"It's nice to remember the dead, honey. Now, take me, for instance . . . I hang around here because most of my friends are buried here and I like being close to them. But you're young, got your whole life ahead of you. Don't tarry here long. Life is for the living."

I nodded at him, then turned and looked down at Mother's grave. Perhaps she was speaking to me, after all.

Here lies Willa Katherine Frazier [always remained a Frazier], a cold bitch who died as she lived: alone.

I have arrived now, at 1204 Heights Boulevard.

As I feared, the For Sale sign is posted in the center of the yard, near the front walk. Yet the porch light is beaming and there are lights aglow in the downstairs windows. No need to give up hope.

I send the cabdriver away, and pause at the edge of the walk. The house has taken on a different look, somehow, and I gaze on it for some moments before going ahead, wondering what changes have taken place. Then I realize there have been no changes made to the house except in the way I see it: it looks friendly and inviting in a way it never did before.

I move slowly toward the house, thinking surely the journey from here to there has never been so long. I believe now I understand a little of what Rodney felt upon his father's death, and the old song comes back to me again:

"Hello, my baby, hello, my honey, hello, my ragtime gal." (Am I already crying, or is the cold drizzle settling on my face?)

When Rodney opens the door, all calmness leaves me.

I am talking high and fast, saying things I never meant to say until later, getting all mixed up, telling him my mother was a dancer and I have her shoes, can even wear them, and my father was a musician, and they both loved me, and I'm sorry, so sorry, and would he please talk about it and try to forgive me, and as I ramble on I realize that Rodney Younger had something to say:

"It was better, I think, that you chose to leave."

The words are like stones thrown against a wall.

"Oh, I see. Yes, if that's the way you feel, I guess . . . guess I'll go. Did I say how sorry? I did want you to know at least that much. Yes, I'll be going now. Close the door before you catch your death . . ."

I am walking away then through a blur of tears, weaving from one side of the walk to the other and thinking how utterly stupid to have sent the cab away, that I'll have to catch a trolley somewhere, but where, which way?

"Willa!"

The voice is strong, commanding. I stop.

"You didn't let me finish. Lord, will you never learn a little patience? Come inside a minute."

I turn around to see his figure on the porch, and I love the way he looks, standing there, the porch light playing on his face. I want to obey him, yet my legs are like two wooden stakes buried deep in the ground.

"All right, stay there if you'd rather. I only meant that your leaving made me realize just how little we really knew about each other, and what a big mistake we were making. It was as much my fault as yours."

"You don't think that now, we could start over, try again, take it slowly? Remember what you said long ago about life being like a stubborn automobile—"

"I don't know. It wouldn't be the same."

"No, Rodney, because I'm not the same person anymore."

"If you had only come to me that night, instead of running off by yourself. I'd have helped you all I could."

"Yes, I think now you would, but then I couldn't let myself trust you."

"And now?"

"I'm not sure, but I think I could. I've learned an awful lot about trusting this past week."

His silence at my remark speaks louder than any words, and the chill of this night has never seemed so penetrating as now.

"Well, I won't take any more of your time then . . ."

"Willa, I'd like to hear all about it if you want to tell me. I thought before that if I loved you enough, eventually you'd love me back and everything would work out. But I realized after you ran away how wrong I was . . . that I expected too much from both of us."

"Then I never really fooled you, did I?"

"No, but I did love you, even as you were then."

"Oh, but Rodney, I know who I am now and I'm not afraid any more. That's what really counts, isn't it?"

"Well, I guess it's the first step at least," he says, and the warmth of his smile melts the icy drizzle between us and calls me home.

ABOUT THE AUTHOR

Born and raised in Houston, Texas, SUZANNE MORRIS took journalism courses at the University of Houston. Later, in Tacoma, Washington, she studied creative writing with Rega McCarthy. She now lives in Houston with her husband and son where she is working on a new novel.

RELAX!
SIT DOWN
and Catch Up On Your Reading!